Gateway to Hell

Gateway to Hell

Margaret Bingley

PIATKUS

Copyright © 1991 by Margaret Bingley

First published in Great Britain in 1991 by
Judy Piatkus (Publishers) Ltd of
5 Windmill Street, London W1

*The author asserts her moral rights to be identified as
author of this work*

British Library Cataloguing in Publication Data
Margaret, Bingley
    Gateway to Hell.
    I. Title
    [F]

    ISBN 0 7499 0094 6

Phototypeset in 11/12pt Compugraphic Times by
Action Typesetting Limited, Gloucester
Printed and bound in Great Britain by
Billing & Sons Ltd, Worcester

For my stepmother, Joan, with love.

Acknowledgements

I would like to thank Maggie Noach and Jill Hughes, who were always at the other end of the phone when I needed advice, and Jo Duke who deciphered my scribbles and produced a perfect final draft.

Part 1

Prologue

The woman writhed silently on the bed as assorted pairs of hands and lips caressed her most secret places until she was afraid that she might die from the terrible, shameful pleasure that she no longer had the strength to resist.

Her eyes remained tightly closed but she could hear their voices as they whispered one to another, men and women urging each other on, and she could picture their faces only too well.

The pleasure grew; her body tensed in anticipation as she waited for the final touch that would release the wonderful, bitter-sweet ecstasy. Seconds later the shockwaves of pleasure surged over her and as her eyes flew open she screamed aloud.

She was alone.

Her body was drenched with perspiration, her heart thumping erratically in her chest but she was alone in her bed, except for her husband sleeping beside her.

She felt faint with relief, yet it was short-lived. Tonight it had been a dream but it had happened before, and she knew that it would happen again; part of her even wanted it to happen again.

She was trapped in this strange land of contrasts; of wealth and poverty, light and dark, savage paganism and civilisation. Only death could free her. Either their death or her own. Tonight, awake and afraid, she had a terrible premonition that it would be her own.

Chapter One

'*Happy birthday, dear Nicola, happy birthday to you*!'

Nicola Grainger flushed with pleasure as her friends raised their glasses in celebration of her twenty-seventh birthday.

'I hope I like being married to an older woman,' teased her husband, Howard.

'You say that every year,' she responded.

'I think there's something to be said for predictable men,' declared Andrea, a slender blonde with what Howard described as the look of an undernourished greyhound. 'David can't remember the name of his last indiscretion, let alone what he said twelve months ago.'

Howard and Nicola exchanged a rueful glance. 'More wine, Andrea,' he suggested quickly.

She shrugged. 'I might as well. Who's Melanie talking to in such an animated fashion?'

Nicola looked across the lawn to where her closest friend was standing. 'Robert, of course.'

'God! Fancy pulling out all the stops for your own husband.'

'They haven't been married long. No chance of "custom staleing" there as yet,' laughed Howard.

'Is this food ever going to be ready?' asked another friend in mock exasperation.

'Not for half an hour or so. I've had a few problems getting the barbecue going,' Howard apologised. There were a few good-natured jeers. It happened every year on Nicola's birthday, and every year Howard seemed astonished by the complexities of charcoal and lighter fuel.

4

It was another hour before they ate but no one really minded and at midnight everyone was still there, all reluctant to break up the evening.

'Happy?' Howard asked, putting an arm round Nicola's waist.

She leant forward and kissed him gently on the lips. 'Deliriously happy. I always did enjoy midnight feasts!'

Howard grinned. 'That's lucky! Seriously, I hope this lot don't intend to stay on for breakfast.'

'They'll have to get it themselves if they do,' she murmured, moving her body closer to his.

At that moment the telephone began ringing inside the house.

'Who on earth can that be?' asked Nicola in surprise. 'It's the middle of the night, for God's sake.'

'Probably old Mr Gibson down the road. Noise does carry at night and James has been a bit rowdy.'

Nicola pushed at her husband's shoulder. 'Go on in and placate him then. Tell him we're sending everyone home in the next half hour. It will give us a good excuse to get rid of them all.'

Howard disappeared into the house and Nicola stood looking around her. It was a glorious June night and the lights that Howard had fixed to the trees by the side of the path showed the garden at its most attractive. She looked at the rolling lawns and well established rose beds and thought once again how very lucky they were.

Howard's parents had helped them to buy the rambling old house on the outskirts of Guildford and although it took most of their money at the moment, she never regretted it. So many of their friends were stuck in tiny detached boxes, fighting a losing battle to move another rung up the property ladder. It was not a life she would have enjoyed and on a night like this she thought it only right to count her blessings.

Out of the corner of her eye she saw Howard emerging from the patio doors. In the yellow light from a suspended lantern his skin looked jaundiced.

'Did you manage to placate him?' she asked brightly.

Howard looked at her in confusion. 'Placate who?'

5

'Mr Gibson, of course.'

He shook his head. 'It wasn't ... Nicola, something terrible's happened.'

She felt the hairs on the back of her neck prickle and suddenly felt cold. 'What do you mean? Is it your mother? Has something happened to your mother?'

He took a few uncertain steps towards her and she saw that he was trembling. 'Howard, what is it? For heaven's sake, tell me!' Her voice had risen and everyone in the garden fell silent.

'It's Rose,' he said quietly.

Nicola's thoughts flew to the last time she'd seen her sister, standing white-faced and exhausted beside their father's grave, seemingly only kept upright by the support of her tall, dark Egyptian husband whom Nicola had never liked.

'Is she ill? Did Labib say what was the matter? Howard, tell me!'

'They're both dead,' he blurted out. 'That was someone from the British Embassy on the phone. He sent his sincere condolences,' he added stupidly.

Nicola put a hand to her throat to try and ease the sudden constriction that was threatening her breathing. 'She can't be dead. She's only twenty-nine. There must be a mistake. Ring them back. No, better still let *me* ring them back. You've got it wrong. You know how hopeless you are on the phone.'

She knew she was babbling but couldn't seem to stop herself. Howard continued to stand helplessly a few feet away from her and she felt a rush of irrational dislike towards him for telling her such a ridiculous story. She could hear someone crying in the garden and wanted to tell them not to worry, that it was a mistake, but she couldn't because of the lump in her throat, and then when Melanie and Robert took hold of her arms and tried to lead her indoors she realised that the crying was coming from her. This amused her so much that she began to laugh hysterically through her tears.

The next few minutes were a total blur until she found herself sitting in the sun lounge with her hands wrapped round a mug of strong black coffee. She could hear Howard talking to someone and several cars were starting up at the front of the house so she assumed most of their friends were leaving.

'Try and drink it,' urged Melanie, crouching at her friend's feet.

Nicola nodded obediently but the coffee tasted horrible and she felt as though she might be sick. 'Is it true?' she asked slowly. 'Is Rose really dead?'

Melanie nodded. 'It was a car accident. Everyone died.'

Nicola stared at her in disbelief. 'The children as well?'

Melanie looked confused. 'No one mentioned any children. Howard said that Rose, her husband and their chauffeur had all died. I didn't know your sister had any children,' she added gently.

'That's because she never said much about them. Howard and I wondered . . .' She let the sentence tail off. There were some things that were better kept in the family, and Rose's strange behaviour over the past six years was one of them.

All at once she began to shiver violently. She felt cold to her bones. Melanie moved to one side as Howard came back into the room and sat down beside his wife. He put his arms round her and held her tightly against him. 'I'm so sorry, darling,' he whispered, rocking her to and fro. 'I should have prepared you better, but it was such a shock that I didn't have time to think clearly.'

She rested her head against him and let his voice comfort her, trying to blot out images of mangled bodies and terror-filled final moments that kept surging through her brain like an out of control horror video.

Much later, after several cups of coffee and a lot of tears, Nicola finally began to think coherently. 'What's going to happen to the children?' she asked Howard, who was busy checking on flight times to Cairo.

'I've no idea. It was obvious this Embassy chap didn't know anything apart from the fact that Rose and Labib were dead. I presume that if we ring this number he gave me someone there will fill us in on the details.'

'Surely there must be someone in the house with the children now? Why don't we just ring there.'

'Darling, I told you what the man said. The house has been shut up and the children have gone away for a few days. I expect the number we've got is the place where they're staying.'

7

'Did he tell you who to ask for?'

'Yes, but I couldn't make the name out.'

Nicola wrapped her arms round herself and wondered if she'd ever be warm again. 'It seems dreadful that we don't know anything about the boys,' she said sadly. 'I mean, Rose could have sent us photos or something. I'm sure Melanie must have wondered why I'd never mentioned children, but since Rose virtually ignored them in her letters it didn't leave me much choice.'

'I'm sure there's something wrong with them,' said Howard. 'Let's face it, most women who'd suffered three miscarriages and two cot deaths would have shouted the birth of healthy twin boys to the entire world. She never mentioned them after the initial euphoria over the birth, and neither did Labib. Not even when they were here last year for your father's funeral.'

'It's so awful. I wonder what will happen to them now?'

'I imagine they'll go into a home or something. It really depends on precisely what's wrong with them. At the moment I think we should just find out when the funeral is and get ourselves organised for that. The rest can wait until we get there.'

Nicola nodded. She wanted to remember Rose as she'd been when they were younger, a pretty if rather quiet girl with a gift for music, but all she could picture was Rose at the funeral, her shoulders drooping and her face prematurely lined so that she looked like a woman of fifty.

'I should have talked to her more when she was here,' she said abruptly.

Howard put a hand on hers. 'You did try, Nicola. I even took Labib out to a football match to give you time together.'

Nicola nodded, remembering how she'd tried to ignite some small spark in Rose, to get even one smile out of her, but it had been hopeless. Rose, either through grief for her dead father or because of some private, deeper sorrow, had proved unreachable.

'I asked her if she had any photos of the boys,' said Nicola.

'You didn't tell me that. What did she say?'

8

'She just said no. No explanations, no apologies, just a straight no. I didn't like to press her after that.'

'Weird. Mind you, she was never the same after she met Labib.'

'That's not fair,' said Nicola.

'Come on, now! Once she fell under his spell her wits just deserted her. Even before they were married she'd become strange. It was as though she only existed through him.'

'Well, now she doesn't exist at all!' cried Nicola tearfully, and Howard felt instantly guilty.

'I'm sorry, and I didn't mean to criticise her. I was just pointing out that it wasn't your fault you drifted apart. That was the way Rose wanted it to be.'

'I hated him,' confessed Nicola. 'He took her away from us and never seemed to value her at all.'

Privately Howard had always wondered what the intelligent and intensely virile Egyptian had ever seen in Rose, who had never seemed to him to have any of Nicola's spirit or drive. He blamed his sister-in-law as much as her husband for the rift that had developed between her and her family. Her obsession with her future husband had been obvious the first time she'd brought him home from the hospital where she'd worked as a nurse, and it had increased every day they were together.

'Look, I'll ring now, shall I?' he suggested, as Nicola blew her nose and tried to stem the tears.

She glanced at the bedside clock. 'It's only five in the morning.'

'It'll be seven in Cairo. Someone's bound to be up. We'll both feel better if we can actually do something, even if it's only book our flight.'

'While you do that I think I'll have a bath. It might warm me up a bit.'

It certainly helped, but when she walked back into the bedroom some twenty minutes later Howard was sitting on the edge of the bed with a stunned expression on his face.

'Did you get through?' she asked.

'Yes, and I spoke to the man the Embassy mentioned, Sergei someone or other.'

'That's a Russian name.'

9

'Well, perhaps he is Russian, I've no idea. He spoke extremely good English whatever he is.'

'When's the funeral?'

'You're not going to believe this Nikki, but it's over.'

'Over?' Nicola stared incredulously at him.

'Over, finished, out of the way. Rose and Labib were buried two days ago.'

'Don't be silly, they only died last night.'

'According to this Sergei, the Embassy must have mislaid the message. The accident happened last Monday morning. Labib died straight away and Rose forty-eight hours later in the Anglo-American hospital on Geziro Island. The funeral was held the following day.'

'But that means Rose didn't have anyone there. It could only have been Labib's family who attended. Surely they could have told us? They must have known we'd have wanted to be there.'

Howard stood up and caught hold of her hands. 'Apparently Labib hasn't got any family. Only close friends and colleagues from the hospital attended. This Sergei didn't know anything about *us* until the Wills were read.'

Nicola felt absolutely numb. It was almost impossible to realise that not only was Rose dead, she was buried as well. There would be no opportunity to say farewell, no chance for normal grieving. She was gone and it was as though she had never really existed.

'Nicola, did you hear what I said?'

She jumped and shook her head. 'I'm sorry, I was just thinking ...'

'I said that because Rose outlived Labib by forty-eight hours, her Will takes precedence over his.'

'Well, I can't see that matters much. Rose didn't have anything of her own to leave.'

'I'm afraid she did,' said Howard quietly. 'She's left us the children.'

'You mean they're coming to live with you?' asked Melanie in disbelief as Nicola finished her story.

'Apparently that's what Rose wanted.'

'What did their father want?'

10

'Knowing Labib I imagine he'd always intended them to be brought up in Egypt, but that isn't important now. What matters is what Rose wanted.'

'But you never intended to have any children!'

Nicola sighed. 'That's what Howard keeps reminding me, and it's true, but something like this doesn't leave me with any choice. It isn't as though I don't like children − I spend my entire working life with them! The only reason I didn't want any of my own was because I see far too many who've been totally screwed up by their parents' mistakes. I didn't want the responsibility of someone else's mental health. Rose's boys are already a fact of life, and hopefully with my training I'll be well qualified to help them cope over the next few months. At least, that's what I keep telling myself.'

'What about Howard?'

'Obviously he's worried. He's busy at work, he's waiting for an overseas posting and he's always told the powers that be that he has no domestic ties. In other words, they can send him anywhere, but I've said that doesn't have to change. Children are very adaptable.'

'I should think these two will be feeling pretty insecure. How old are they?'

'Six.'

'What, both of them!' laughed Melanie.

'Yes,' said Nicola irritably. 'That's the whole point about twins, they're exactly the same age.'

'How could I know they were twins? I didn't even know you had any nephews until last night,' retorted Melanie.

'I'm sorry, I didn't mean to snap. It's all been such a shock.'

'I can't believe that the funeral's over! Surely you should have been given the chance to go.'

'It was due to some mix-up at the Embassy. Rose always said that Egyptians took days to get anything done.'

'Surely the Embassy officials are British?'

'What does it matter!' exclaimed Nicola. 'Rose has been buried and her sons are coming to live with us here. They're the facts, going over it all isn't going to change anything.'

'At least you've got plenty of room. If anything happened

11

to my sister we wouldn't have room to take on her cat let alone her children! Robert's always said this would make a lovely family house. It's exactly the kind of thing we want in a few years' time.'

'Since you're the one who's so anxious to have a large family, I hope you'll be on hand to help me when the boys arrive,' said Nicola.

'Of course I will, but you're the child psychologist. I don't imagine you'll need a lot of help.'

Nicola rubbed her hands over her eyes. They felt heavy and gritty and what she really wanted to do was close them, preferably for a week. 'I'm only used to the theory. I don't expect it to be quite as easy in practice.'

'When are they arriving?' asked Melanie.

'I gather there's quite a lot of red tape to be sorted out. According to this Sergei guy they won't be free to leave for a few weeks, which gives me a little time to get the house more child-orientated. I thought the sun lounge would make a good playroom for them. There's plenty of cupboard space for toys and ...'

'What sort of things do they like?' Melanie interrupted.

'I've no idea. War games, sport, teenage mutant turtles ... all that I suppose.'

Melanie glanced at her watch. 'I'll have to go soon. I'm due to give a facial and manicure to one of my least favourite clients at two. I only popped in to see if there was anything I could do.'

'Just be there!' said Nicola fervently. 'I shall need you on the end of the phone for the next few weeks.'

'It's more likely to be the answerphone but I'll do what I can. By the way, why didn't you ever talk about them?'

'I didn't think you'd be interested. I mean, they were always very remote even to me. I've never seen them, you know.'

'I know, but even so ...'

'Don't worry, you'll doubtless be hearing plenty about them from now on.'

'What about dinner on Friday? Are you and Howard still coming?'

'I should think so. I'll let you know tonight.'

12

'That'll be fine.' Melanie stood awkwardly in the kitchen doorway for a moment. 'I'm really sorry about Rose, and Robert is as well. It seems so dreadful, right on top of losing both your parents last year too.'

Nicola felt the tears filling her eyes and blinked hard. 'Thanks, I'm afraid I can't really ...'

'It's OK. I just wanted you to know that we understand what you're going through. How about coffee Wednesday morning? Or will you be at work?'

'No, I've cancelled my appointments this week. I didn't think I'd be able to concentrate too well.'

'Very wise. See you on Wednesday then. Come at ten-thirty. That will give us time for a chat before Andrea and the others arrive. After that it's all sex and roving husbands.'

Once she was alone, grief and despair swept over Nicola again and laying her head on the table she wept, both for Rose and for the six-year-old boys she'd left behind.

'We don't have to do this, you know,' said Howard for the sixth time that evening.

'Of course we do,' said Nicola firmly, carrying their coffee cups through into the lounge. 'It's what Rose wanted.'

'I can't imagine why. She didn't want us to have anything to do with them while she was alive. I can't even remember their names, can you?'

'I looked it up on the birth announcement card.'

'Which just shows how out of touch we were! What are their names then?'

Nicola pulled a face. 'Torquil and Tarquin.'

'Good God! Hardly the sort of names to enable them to fit discreetly into a prep school in Guildford.'

'When Rose and Labib chose the names they weren't anticipating them living in Guildford.'

'I suppose it's better than Mohammed. Nikki, be reasonable about this. We've always agreed that we didn't want children, that they'd only get in the way. You've been adamant from the time we got engaged that you didn't want any. You've argued against them so convincingly that the prospect of taking on someone else's six-year-olds with accompanying neuroses scares me to death.'

13

'They're not just someone else's, they're *Rose's* children – my own nephews.'

'It's going to be a ghastly upheaval for them and for us. I don't suppose they know any more about us than we do about them. They've lived all their lives in an entirely different culture. Labib seemed to think that women were a distinctly inferior species who existed solely for his benefit. I can't imagine you're going to like that kind of thing under your own roof. Let's face it, you and Labib used to argue all the time when he was working over here.'

'They're not Labib, they're just two little boys who need a home.'

'That sounds very touching, but what kind of a home do they need? We still don't know why Rose never talked about them do we? No photos have been airmailed to us. They could be deaf, blind and dumb for all we know.'

'Don't be stupid.'

'They could, Nicola. No one has ever told us anything about them. That's the truth, the bottom line if you like. We are blithely taking on a lifetime's responsibility for two children about whom nothing is known. I find that a very frightening prospect and I just think we should consider it all a little more carefully before we jump in with both feet.'

'There's nothing more to think about. I might have failed Rose in lots of other ways, but I won't fail her here. She wouldn't have left us the care of the boys if she hadn't thought they'd fit in with us. She was their mother. Their welfare would have come first with her.'

'Labib came first with her! First, second, third and last. Her whole world revolved round him, and even those ghastly miscarriages and infant deaths were only seen as a tragedy because she was failing to give him sons. Your mother told us that much.'

'Do you love me?' asked Nicola abruptly.

'Of course I do. It's because I love you that I'm worried.'

'I have to do this,' she explained softly. 'Maybe it is stupid, but I feel that I didn't try hard enough to find out what was the matter with Rose. When her letters tailed off, when she kept refusing to come and see us, they way she looked at

14

Daddy's funeral ... I never really made enough effort to find out what was wrong and now I'll never know. But I can make it up to her through the children. I need to do this and I need your support more than I've ever needed it before. Please, Howard, say you understand and that you'll back me up all the way?'

'I don't really understand,' he said slowly, 'but if it's what you really want then of course I'll back you up. I'm just not sure what kind of a stepfather I'll be.'

'They'll only need love,' she promised him. 'That shouldn't be too difficult, surely?'

Howard shrugged. 'That rather depends on what kind of children they are.'

'At six, children are pretty much alike the world over. I don't suppose these two will be very different from your brother's boys, and you seem to enjoy playing football with them whenever you get the chance!'

From then on, Howard ceased trying to change Nicola's mind and together they fitted the second bedroom out with bunk beds and bought some games and books to make the room more welcoming, but in the back of his mind he was constantly worried by the secrecy that had surrounded the boy's first six years. When the Saturday morning of their arrival finally dawned he drove Nicola to the airport with a sense of deep foreboding and the distinct fear that their life together would never be as good again.

Chapter Two

'I do wish it had been a nicer day for them,' complained Nicola as they dashed from the car to the airport through pouring rain. 'Do they have much rain in Egypt?'

'Not in the middle of summer. Let's go and check that their flight hasn't been delayed.'

Nicola sat down on the nearest seat and bit nervously at her lower lip. She was only too well aware of the confusion and fear that Rose's children must be experiencing and wished she felt more in control of her own emotions, but her dry mouth and churning stomach told their own story. She so desperately wanted to give a good first impression, to make the boys feel that she was someone they would be able to trust, but it was proving impossible to behave naturally, and if there was one thing all children were good at it was spotting a fraud, as she knew only too well from her work.

'Delayed an hour!' announced Howard, sitting down next to her.

'An hour! I don't think my nerves can stand it.'

'I can't imagine why you're so nervous. We're only about to embark on an entirely different way of life,' he said dryly.

'Stop it! I don't need reminding. I do hope they're all right.'

'It's a routine flight not an expedition up the Amazon. Of course they'll be all right.'

'I didn't mean that.'

'I know. I'm worried too,' he admitted.

They both lapsed into silence, their thoughts drifting once again to the secrecy that had surrounded the first six years of

16

the children's lives. When the flight was finally called they looked at each other in a moment of blind panic.

'They can't be that bad,' murmured Howard unconvincingly as they watched the first passengers streaming through the gate. 'After all, they've been allowed on a general flight.'

'Perhaps they travelled in the luggage hold,' suggested Nicola mournfully and they both laughed. At that moment a man in his early thirties detached himself from the general throng and began to walk purposefully towards them with a small boy holding each of his hands.

Nicola stopped laughing and stared at him. He was amazingly handsome. About six feet tall, he had a mane of dark brown hair streaked liberally with grey while his face, dominated by startlingly high cheekbones and deep-set dark eyes, had all the arrogant awareness of its own beauty that could occasionally be seen on the faces of famous heart-throbs. She just had time to register the full mouth with a hint of petulance at the corners when he caught her eye and smiled at her, displaying incredibly white teeth.

Nicola wrenched her eyes away from this god-like creature who was attracting the attention of every woman in the vicinity and looked down at the children. They were very much their father's sons with olive complexions and liquid brown eyes but where his hair had been straight, they both had curls falling over their ears and across their forehead. They were small for their age, obviously frightened and − much to Nicola's relief − physically perfect.

Temporarily struck dumb by an unusual feeling of self-consciousness, Nicola was relieved when Howard extended a hand to the man. 'You must be Sergei. I'm Howard Grainger. We spoke on the phone once or twice.'

The teeth flashed again, but the smile wasn't quite as wide as it had been for Nicola. 'That's right. I'm sorry we're late. Our flight was delayed at Cairo.'

Nicola crouched down to put herself on a level with the children and smiled into their anxious faces. 'Hello, boys. I'm your Aunty Nicola and this is your Uncle Howard.'

They stared at her, their eyes bright but watchful.

17

'You're absolutely identical, aren't you! How will I know which one of you's which?'

They moved closer together and linked hands.

'Let me guess,' she continued, anxious to make sure that they could speak. 'Are you Torquil?' She put a hand lightly on one boy's shoulder.

For a moment his eyes went blank but then, to her great relief, he nodded. 'Sometimes,' he agreed politely.

Nicola blinked. 'Sometimes?'

'*Sometimes I'm me,*' he explained.

'*And sometimes I'm him*!' concluded his twin.

Then, the explanation over, they both smiled at her, turned towards each other and nodded with satisfaction.

Nicola gave a small laugh. 'I think you're trying to confuse me! Well, I'll probably have to put a badge on each of you until I get to know you better. Is that what they do at your school?'

They seemed puzzled by her question and turned towards Sergei, their small hands tugging at his trouser leg. He was in the middle of talking to Howard but broke off at once to give them his full attention. Then they conversed in rapid French that left Nicola totally in the dark until Sergei finally propelled them towards her.

'They're very nervous,' he said quietly, his voice pleasantly deep and reassuring. 'I think it best if I leave now. The longer I stay, the harder it will get for them.'

Nicola was mesmerised by his beauty. His skin was flawless and she had a ridiculous but urgent desire to reach out and touch his face. For a moment their eyes met and held, and his pupils darkened and dilated. She actually felt herself begin to sway towards him before a muffled sob broke the spell and she looked down to where the twins were wiping tears from each other's cheeks as they struggled with their distress.

Howard, who'd dismissed Sergei as an effeminate foreigner, was deeply touched by the children's plight and couldn't understand why Nicola wasn't down on her knees comforting them. 'Don't cry,'he said kindly. 'We've bought you some nice toys and they're all waiting for you at our house. Once you get used to the strangeness, I'm sure you'll be very happy with us.' He put a hand on each of their heads.

18

They both wriggled away, their expressions affronted.

'We don't like . . .'

'. . . being touched,' they announced, each of them taking half of the sentence. At that moment their expressions were cold, but almost immediately they began crying again, knuckling at their eyes and whimpering softly.

'You'll see Sergei again,' promised Nicola as she finally turned her attention back to the boys. 'I'm sure he'll come and see you when you've settled in.'

She glanced up questioningly. Sergei nodded, and almost imperceptibly the corners of his mouth lifted, as though he and Nicola shared a private joke.

Howard caught the end of what he considered to be a self-satisfied smirk and briskly shook the man's hand. 'Well, thanks very much for delivering them to us safely. It's bound to take time but I'm sure they'll soon be feeling much more cheerful.'

Sergei nodded to himself, his eyes following a leggy brunette who was walking by on impossibly high heels.

He half-turned towards her and at once the twins were galvanised into action. They hurled themselves at him and clung on to his legs like small monkeys.

'Don't go! We don't want . . .'

'. . . you to go.'

'*We want to go back home*!' they finished in unison.

They were crying loudly now and people were looking at them and shaking their heads sadly as they realised they were witnessing an emotional parting.

Sergei lost all interest in the brunette and lifted the boys up, one in each arm. 'I'll be back soon,' he promised. Nicola nodded her agreement from Howard's side. 'Once you're settled in and being good, your aunt will let me know and I'll come back so that you can show me your new home. Is that all right?'

They looked intently at him, glanced at each other for a final check and then nodded, releasing their grip on his arms and sliding slowly back to the ground. They were all so obviously at ease with each other that Nicola felt cruel separating the three of them, but Howard was fidgeting restlessly beside her and it had to be done.

19

She grasped each of the boys firmly by a hand and smiled at Sergei. 'Don't worry, we'll take very good care of them,' she assured him.

'I can tell. I think they're very lucky children,' he said quietly.

Nicola flushed and glanced uneasily at Howard. 'Have a safe flight back,' she added brightly.

'I wish you luck,' he said ambiguously, turned on his heel and promptly disappeared into the crowd.

'Right, let's go and find the car,' said Howard with relief. 'What kind of car do you boys like?'

They shrugged, turning their heads to try and see where Sergei had gone.

'Do either of you want to use the loo before we go?' asked Nicola.

They gave the matter a moment's consideration.

'I don't think ...'

'... we do.'

Nicola laughed. 'Don't either of you ever speak whole sentences?'

They didn't seem to hear her and Howard shook his head. 'Just let them alone,' he muttered. 'At least they're comparatively normal. It looks as though we were worrying for nothing.'

'Yes. It's strange that Rose never mentioned Sergei.'

'If her children didn't merit a mention I can't imagine why that smug popinjay should have been newsworthy.'

Nicola raised her eyebrows. 'I thought he was rather dishy, and the only reason she might have mentioned him was because he's obviously close to the children and so presumably was close to the whole family. Don't the boys look like Labib?' she added as they left the shelter of the airport lounge and faced the heavy rain again.

'Not really. He had a much heavier face.'

'I meant colouring and things. Where did we leave the car?'

Howard tried to remember and couldn't. For a moment he stood, trying to picture the cars next to it, but every time he tried to concentrate the ridiculous and incongruous image of a camel kept coming into his mind. It was so startling and

20

disturbing that he finally gave up thinking and began to walk very quickly indeed up and down the lines of cars.

Nicola followed more slowly behind, the boys on either side of her, their eyes gleaming with what could very easily have been amusement.

Both children were absolutely silent on the journey home. Nicola was afraid that Howard's annoyance at the delay in finding his car had affected them but they didn't seem upset, simply withdrawn. When the car finally stopped in the front drive they crowded together in a corner of the back seat, their arms wrapped tightly round each other.

'This is your new home,' she said gently. 'Don't you want to come and have a look at it?'

They shook their heads, their eyes enormous.

'Well I need some food,' announced Howard. 'What's for lunch, Nikki?'

'I wasn't too sure what the boys would like. There's plenty of cheese, and I could make a green salad.'

'Sounds great. You take them in while I bring the cases.'

Nicola was impressed by Howard's matter-of-fact approach. She knew that she should be the one helping the boys relax but the meeting at the airport had been so different from anything she'd imagined that she'd been thrown off balance. Sergei had disturbed her more in ten minutes than any other man before, and she was both ashamed and annoyed. Mesmerised by him, she hadn't taken nearly enough notice of the children, and that was unforgivable. She felt that she ought to apologise aloud to Rose.

'Mummy!' shouted one of the twins. She twisted round in her seat in surprise but they were both staring blankly at her.

'Did either of you say anything?' she asked softly.

They shook their heads.

'Come on!' called Howard. 'You're not planning to spend the rest of the day in the car are you?'

'Sorry! Come on, boys, let's go.'

They sighed heavily, linked arms and began to clamber awkwardly out of the back seat.

'Let go of each other for a moment!' laughed Nicola as

21

they struggled to squeeze out of the passenger doorway, but they simply pressed closer together until finally they fell out on to the gravel drive and then pushed themselves to their feet, looking around the front garden questioningly.

'Why is it so dark?' asked one of the twins.

'It isn't really dark.'

'Where's the sun?' queried the other.

'Hidden behind the clouds. With any luck it might come out this afternoon.'

'It's all dull!' they muttered as they marched past her and in at the front door, then they stopped in the small passageway, confused by the number of doors leading off.

Nicola pushed open the one to the kitchen. 'In here. This is where we eat our breakfast and snacks. The dining room's through the hatch there.'

'Where did ...'

'... the other side go?' they asked.

Nicola realised they meant the other doors from the front passageway. 'The one opposite leads straight into the garage and the one in front of you takes you into the sun lounge. At least it used to be the sun lounge. We've converted it into a playroom now.'

'Who plays there?' asked one of the twins.

'It's for you two to use! Look, I shall have to know which one of you I'm talking to. Tell me how I can tell the difference.'

'It doesn't really matter.'

'We can be whichever one you like.'

Nicola shook her head. 'That's not right. You must know your own names.'

'We share them!' they chorused, sliding open the hatch into the dining room.

'I'm quite sure you don't, and until I know who's who I don't think I can get you any lunch.'

She'd meant it to come out lightly but knew that she'd ended up sounding irritated, which she was. They seemed so slippery and elusive; she needed something concrete to grasp so that they became individuals in her mind.

'All right, I'm Tarquin,' said one of the boys. 'Look,

22

my socks are blue,' and he pulled up the leg of his cotton trousers.

'And I'm Torquil, my socks are green,' said the other, extending a leg for her to view them.

'Well, that's a relief, although it might be more useful if it was something a little more visible that distinguished you! Do you always wear blue socks, Tarquin?'

'No, but I do today.'

'It would help me if you always wore something blue, and Torquil could have say a green handkerchief. What do you think?'

'Well, whichever one of us has the blue socks will be Tarquin for that day,' promised Torquil.

Nicola decided to let the subject drop before she lost her patience. 'Would you like to see your room before lunch?' she asked cheerfully.

'Not really,' responded Tarquin, pulling pieces of fluff off his blue socks. 'Do you have any pets?'

Torquil's head turned quickly towards the window above the sink. Nicola followed his gaze and saw that Lily, their tortoiseshell cat, was cleaning herself on the window ledge outside.

'As you can see we've got a cat, but you mustn't tease her or she might scratch.'

'Why would we tease her?' asked Tarqin.

'Well, children sometimes do tease animals, even if they don't mean to be unkind. They think it's a kind of fun, but cats don't have the same sense of humour as children!'

'Where's the lunch then?' demanded Howard, coming back from putting the children's cases in their room.

'It won't be long. I was just trying to sort out which twin was which.'

Howard glanced at the boys who both shrugged their shoulders at him.

'Seems reasonable. Come on then, which one are you?' He reached out a hand towards the nearest boy, but he promptly took two steps backwards and his nostrils flared. Howard was disturbed. 'What's the matter? I'm not going to hurt you.'

'We don't like . . .'

'. . . to be touched.'

23

'*We've already told you that*!'

'Hey, steady on! There's no need to get aggressive about it. Look, I promise not to touch, OK?' He put his hands in his pockets. 'Now, are you Torquil or Tarquin?'

Suddenly the boy's eyes clouded and he glanced to his twin for help. 'I can't remember!' he wailed and burst into tears.

As his twin ran to his side to comfort him, Nicola took several deep breaths and tried to keep her tone even. 'I think we'd better just guess who's who for today, until you both settle down. What do you say, Howard?'

He stared at her in astonishment. 'I say that I'd prefer to find out here and now which one of them's which.'

'Very tactful!' she muttered out of the corner of her mouth as both the boys began to sob. 'Find them a can of Coke each, will you? Come on, boys, don't get so upset. This is pretty strange for all of us right now but things will settle down, I promise.'

Placated by the Coke they settled themselves on chairs by the pine-topped table and sniffed and snuffled their way through the drink, only the occasional trembling of their bottom lips indicating that the tears were still perilously close at hand.

They then picked their way through the meal, nibbling at some of the cheese and taking three tomatoes each while ignoring the green salad. Then they both took a yoghurt but after their first mouthful they turned to each other in astonishment, their faces wrinkling in distaste as they quickly pushed the cartons away from them.

'Obviously not followers of the great cult of Sainsbury's,' commented Howard with a grin.

'I've got some Greek yoghurt. Perhaps they'd prefer that?'

'I think they'd be better off looking round the rest of the house. I don't suppose they're all that hungry.'

Nicola wasn't very hungry either and it was with some relief that she led them out of the room, shepherding them in front of her like an infant teacher.

Howard watched them leave and then sank back gratefully into his chair. His relief at their apparent normality at the airport was rapidly evaporating. He didn't think they were playing tricks on Nicola, in fact he didn't think they seemed the kind of children who'd ever play tricks. He suspected that they were suffering from some genuine identity crisis, and it disturbed him.

When Nicola eventually returned she looked exhausted. 'Well, I think they've seen all there is to see. They seemed to like the garden, although I think they expected something bigger, and the bunk beds are a great success. Apart from that you could safely say that they were decidedly unimpressed by the whole set up.'

'Unimpressed?'

'They're apparently used to a lot of cooks and bottlewashers. The concept of looking after themselves, without the assistance of personal servants, had obviously never entered their heads. I'm afraid they're going to need a lot of help with things like washing and dressing for a few days. They actually held out their feet for me to take off their shoes!'

'They seem to be having even more trouble with the concept of individual identities.'

Nicola frowned. 'I'm not sure that's a genuine problem. I don't think it can be really. I mean, they're six years old! They must have come across social situations where they had to function separately.'

'Unless they've never been outside their home environment.'

'Why do you say that?'

'I thought it might explain Rose's silence. If they've always had some kind of identity problem ...'

'I'm quite sure that Sergei would have told us if there was a problem like that. They're tired, nervous and confused, that's all. It's probably some form of self-protection. We can't hurt them if they don't exist, that kind of thing.'

Howard pulled a face. 'You're the expert but they seem genuinely confused to me.'

Nicola's shoulders slumped. 'All this nervous tension's worn me out. They've only been here three hours and I'm exhausted.'

Howard stood up and stretched. 'I think I'll go and wash the car now the rain's stopped. If you need me just shout.'

25

'OK. Howard?'

'What?'

She smiled at him. 'Don't forget I love you.'

'I'll remind you later tonight!'

Nicola couldn't wait for the evening. At least once the boys were in bed she wouldn't be worrying about their emotional well-being all the time. She was starting to feel considerable sympathy for parents who found the responsibility of children too much to cope with.

'I need a good child psychologist,' she told herself, and smiled ruefully. She still wasn't too worried, knowing that most problems resolve themselves in time.

'That's the first day safely negotiated,' said Howard as he climbed gratefully into bed.

'I wish I'd known they didn't eat pork. Did you know?'

'I remembered once they said. Don't worry about it. They ate the vegetables, they won't starve in one day. The sherry trifle went down a treat. Presumably alcohol's acceptable in low doses!'

'Perhaps I ought to make another one in the morning? With Melanie and Robert coming to tea it might be a good idea anyway and ...'

Howard put a finger to her lips. 'Let's not talk about them now. I can think of more interesting things to do than discuss the merits of sherry trifle.'

Nicola wriggled as he slipped her nightdress from her shoulders and began to stroke her breasts. 'Don't do that, Howard. I'm tired.'

'Come on, you'll enjoy it once we get started. You always do.'

'I wish you wouldn't tell me how I'll feel! I won't enjoy it and I'd rather not have an argument about it either.'

'This isn't an argument, it's called gentle persuasion.'

He moved closer to her and ran his tongue round the inside of her ear. Nicola sighed and lay quite still. After a few moments he abandoned her ear and moved one hand beneath the hem of her nightdress, his fingers moving lightly up the inside of her legs. Nicole put her knees together and started to turn away from him.

26

'Come on, Nikki, this isn't like you.'

'I'm sorry but I'm too tired and tense and I won't enjoy it. Perhaps tomorow?' She despised herself for bargaining but didn't want him to become resentful and blame the children.

'I want to make love to you now, not tomorrow.'

It was suddenly too much trouble to keep arguing. Nicola sat up in bed and peeled off her nightdress.

'Right, there you are. I'm ready. Do you intend to keep your pyjamas on all the time?'

Howard glared at her, sat on his side of the bed and slipped off his pyjama trousers. Nicola glanced quickly at him and was grateful to see that he was already erect. With any luck it would be over in ten minutes, she thought optimistically. Pushing back the duvet she patted the empty space next to her.

'Come on then.'

'I don't think I want to do it any more. I've never been one for individual sports.'

'Meaning?'

'That it won't be much fun if you don't participate. Let's just forget it, shall we?'

Nicola shrugged. 'I wish you'd make up your mind. Sometimes I wonder how you've managed to get on at work. Indecision should have been your middle name.'

'You really can be a bitch sometimes,' he said softly.

Nicola blushed. 'I didn't mean it. It's only that ...'

'Spare me the "When are you going to put up the kitchen shelves?" and "Isn't it time you did something about that summerhouse?" routine, will you? I know it off by heart. I'm going to get a drink.'

They rarely argued and Nicola desperately wanted to make the peace between them. 'Howard, I'm sorry. I'm finding this more of a strain than I expected and I honestly haven't got any energy left tonight.'

'I said forget it.'

He crossed the room, opened the bedroom door and found himself face to face with the twins.

'What the hell are you two doing there?' he asked furiously.

They stared up at him, two identical pairs of eyes boring into his.

'Our Daddy's much ...'

'... bigger than you.'

Howard remembered with acute embarrassment that he'd been facing the door when he'd taken off his trousers. If the boys had been looking through the keyhole they would have seen everything.

'It's rude to snoop,' he said shortly.

They peered round him into the bedroom where Nicola was propped up on one elbow trying to hear what was happening. When they saw her they joined hands and ducked under Howard's restraining arm.

'I couldn't sleep,' they cried in unison. 'I kept having bad dreams.'

'What, both of you?' asked Nicola, swinging her legs out of bed. For a moment that checked them and they stopped in their tracks, a frown creasing their foreheads.

'Perhaps they only have one dream between them,' said Howard crossly as he left the room in search of the increasingly desirable whisky.

The twins were crying now and Nicola put an arm round each of them. Although they stiffened under her touch they didn't draw away and she felt a rush of affection for them.

'It was only a dream. I'll take you back to bed and leave the light on for the rest of the night. Do you think that would help?'

'A night light?' asked one of the twins. 'Why? We like the night. It's our favourite time.'

'In that case I'll just tuck you up and give you a drink.'

'I'm Torquil,' said one of the twins. 'Why is Uncle Howard so small?'

'He isn't small. He's six foot tall!'

Torquil smiled. 'I meant his ...'

'Why's your hair red?' interrupted Tarquin. 'Do you dye it? Ayeesha dyes hers with henna.'

'Who's Ayeesha?' asked Nicola with interest.

'Just a friend of Daddy's.'

'And a friend of Sergei's,' Torquil pointed out.

'The answer is no, I don't dye my hair. This is its natural colour. Do you like it?'

They shook their heads. 'Not really, it's ...'

28

'. . . too bright and frizzy.'

'Ayeesha's got long straight hair and she's beautiful!'

Nicola, who'd always had more than her share of male admirers, wasn't too upset by their verdict, but she resolved to ask Sergei about Ayeesha when she saw him. If she'd been a friend of her sister's then she'd like to talk to her.

One of the twins laid his head on her lap and turned to look up at her. 'She wasn't,' he said flatly.

Nicola felt a shiver run down her spine. She waited for a moment, hoping he'd clarify the statement, but instead he put his left thumb in his mouth and closed his eyes.

'Wasn't what?' she asked slowly.

His long eyelashes fluttered and he gave a small, sleepy sigh of contentment. She turned to the other twin, but he had curled himself up on the bed, right thumb in mouth, and looked equally sleepy.

Howard walked back into the room, tumbler in hand. 'What's the plan then? Do we retreat to their room?'

'Don't be silly. We'll just carry them back to bed.'

'Did you hear what they said to me?' he asked incredulously when he and Nicola were back in their own room.

'Yes, they said it to me as well. They're quite right, of course.'

Howard looked quizically at her. 'How would you know?'

'Come on, Howard! Labib had shoulders like a barn door. He was much bigger built than you.'

'Is that what they meant?'

'What else could it have been?'

Howard thought for a moment. 'I suppose you're right. It just didn't seem that way to me at the time. I suppose I felt a bit exposed, if you'll excuse the pun!'

Nicola laughed and then curled herself round his back as she got ready to sleep. She didn't really believe that was what the twins had meant either, but she had no intention of letting Howard know. At times like this, maximum discretion was called for to keep the household running peacefully. She thought she might mention it to Melanie though. It would certainly amuse her.

29

Chapter Three

'How dreadful! Poor old Howard!' spluttered Melanie. 'He must have felt terrible!'

Nicola glanced towards the lounge where Robert and Howard were testing some new speakers for the hi-fi. 'I tried to convince him they'd meant his general build but I'm not sure he believed me. It must have been the last straw because he claims he didn't sleep all night.'

'But how would they know?' queried Melanie. 'I mean, even if your brother-in-law was hung like a stallion how would the children know?'

'I expect they'd seen him in the bath or something.'

'I suppose so. Still, pretty embarrassing all round. They're lovely looking boys, aren't they?'

'Not as gorgeous as the hunk who brought them over.'

'Really? Tell me more.' Melanie's eyes sparkled.

'He was only the most attractive man I've ever seen in my life! God, he was out of this world.'

'Truly?'

'Truly, Mel. I felt like some schoolgirl in the presence of her idol. He was just ... I can't begin to explain. You'll see him when he comes over.'

'You mean he's coming here?' Doesn't Howard mind?'

Nicola laughed. 'He's coming to see the boys, not me! Actually, I think Howard thought he was a bit effeminate.'

Melanie groaned. 'Don't tell me he's one of those delicately pretty men!'

'No! I told you, he's a hunk. About six feet tall, collar-length dark hair and the most incredible cheekbones. And his mouth! Yum, yum!'

'Tea nearly ready?' asked Howard from the doorway.

'Not yet, it's only half-past four.'

'I thought I heard you yum-yumming in here.'

Both the women burst out laughing.

'I'm glad someone's feeling cheerful,' he continued, plugging in the kettle. 'These new speakers are useless. By the way, the kettle doesn't boil unless you plug it in.'

'He sounds unusually snappy for Howard,' remarked Melanie when he'd gone.

'The boys have come as rather a shock to his nervous system.'

Melanie helped herself to a chocolate digestive discuit from the tin. 'Have you heard any details about the accident?'

'Not really. Rose and Labib were being driven into Cairo. Apparently there's a fairly steep slope at the end of their road and the car's brakes seized up. They ran straight into the rush hour traffic and never stood a chance.'

'How horrible! Sometimes when we're driving along the motorway I try to imagine what it would be like to see a car cross the central reservation and hurtle towards us. I've always thought those last seconds must be horrendous.'

'You are weird,' said Nicola, sorting out the tea cups and pouring more sugar into the bowl. 'I can't think why you put yourself through that sort of thing.'

'It's a kind of good-luck talisman. I suppose I subconsciously think that if I bring it out in the open then it won't happen. I never used to do it. Only since I've been married.'

'You must have been much happier single!'

Melanie grinned. 'Of course I wasn't. Robert's the most fantastic thing that's ever happened to me, only ...'

'Only what?'

'I can't believe that it's going to last. He could have married anyone he chose and ...'

'And he chose you,' Nicola pointed out for at least the twentieth time. 'He's lucky too, remember. You're a super cook, a really good beautician and a very supportive wife. Not all men are that fortunate.'

'I do try, but yesterday, Mrs Gillespie made me late and I

31

didn't have time to cook anything before Robert got home. He didn't seem to mind, we went out for a Chinese, but I felt really guilty.'

'You don't have to be perfect, Mel,' said Nicola gently. 'Just because your parents' marriage failed it doesn't mean yours will. Now stop worrying about death on the motorway and uncooked dinners and tell me what I should do about a school for the twins.'

They were discussing the merits of two nearby prep schools when the boys came in to the room. Dressed in red cotton shorts and yellow T-shirts they gave off an impression of energy that almost made the air hum.

'Hello,' said Melanie, using her special children's voice. 'And how do you like your new home?'

'Not really . . . '

'. . . very much.'

'*We want to go back to our own home again.*'

'I suppose it all seems very strange to you now, but soon you'll make lots of friends and then you'll be happy again.' Melanie's voice rose brightly at the end of the sentence, like a story teller on Jackanory.

'That's a really . . . '

'. . . horrible dress.'

'*You look ugly in it.*'

Shocked, Melanie drew away. Nicola couldn't believe her ears.

'That's very rude!' she said firmly. They both looked at her, eyes blank. 'I want you to say sorry at once. I'm quite sure you weren't allowed to talk like that to any of your mummy's friends.'

'Mummy didn't have any friends,' said one of the twins with a chilling lack of emotion.

Nicola glanced at his blue socks. 'That's probably because you frightened them all away, Tarquin. Now say sorry at once.'

'I won't. I'm not sorry, am I?' And he turned to his twin.

'No, not at all sorry,' confirmed Torquil.

'It doesn't matter,' muttered Melanie, crimson with embarrassment.

'It most certainly does! If you don't apologise then I'm afraid we won't be able to have that game of cricket on the lawn after tea.'

The boys' eyes narrowed and they tightened their mouths, shaking their heads firmly from side to side.

'Right, that's it then. No cricket. Now go to your room and play until tea's ready.'

For a moment she thought they were going to defy her but then they turned and went off obediently. She spread her hands apologetically. 'I'm really sorry, Mel. I can't think what got into them. They must have been trying to show off.'

Melanie glanced down at the lilac and cream Laura Ashley dress. 'I wouldn't have minded so much if this hadn't been one of my favourite frocks!'

Privately Nicola had always thought that Melanie needed brighter clothes that were fitted rather than the long, loose designs she favoured but she would never have said anything for fear of threatening her friend's already low self-esteem. Not that the boys could have realised how much damage their words would have done she thought, it was just very bad luck that they'd decided to be rude to someone as vulnerable as Melanie.

'Don't mention this to Robert,' begged Melanie as they took in the tea things. 'He might agree with them!'

'Of course he wouldn't, but I won't say anything. Howard would be livid and I can do without any additional aggravation.'

Tea and a walk on the Downs passed off without any trouble and by the time Melanie and Robert left, Howard's good spirits had been restored.

He put an arm round Nicola's shoulders. 'How about a drink?'

'Not yet. I've got to bath the boys and put them to bed. I'll have one when I'm finished.'

'You can have another when you've finished!'

'No, honestly, I don't want one now. I've got a bit of a headache.'

His face fell. 'I can't believe this!'

She shrugged his arm off. 'Don't worry, I won't let it spoil

33

your evening's entertainment. Just don't make me have a drink yet, OK?'

'*My* evening's entertainment? You mean *you* don't enjoy it?'

Tarquin's face peered round the door. 'I need a bath. I'm dirty.'

'You can both have a bath in a minute. Just wait in the playroom.'

'Where's the bath lady?'

'I'm the bath lady. Don't worry, I give a mean bath!'

Torquil joined his brother. 'You can't bath me,' he said firmly. 'You're not special.'

'Either you bath yourselves or I bath you. There isn't anyone else. Please go into the playroom and wait.'

'Nicola, do you think you're making enough allowances for the boys?' asked Howard diffidently. 'Far be it from me to criticise an expert but they only arrived yesterday and you've spent most of the afternoon glaring at them and telling them to go into another room. I should think Robert and Mel must have been a bit surprised.'

'If you must know, they were rude to Melanie and I let it get to me.'

'What did they say?'

'They said she looked ugly in the dress she was wearing.'

Howard laughed. 'At least they've got good fashion sense. She always looks dreadful in those long frocks of hers.'

'I know it doesn't seem much, but Melanie's very insecure.'

'I imagine the twins are pretty insecure right now.'

Nicola nodded. 'You're right. I shouldn't have made such a big thing of it. It was only that they seemed to have honed in on her weakness and I didn't like it.'

'They only met her today. How would they know anything about her numerous neuroses.'

'Melanie isn't neurotic, she just needs a lot of reassurance.'

'Fine. I'm not going to argue about Melanie, of all things!'

'Well, what did you want to argue about next then?' she snapped, and then they both stared at each other in astonishment.

'Why do we keep quarrelling?' asked Howard. 'We never

34

used to.'

'I don't know. I suppose it's just pressure. We're on edge with the boys and take it out on each other. It's absolutely normal.'

'Well, I don't want it to be normal any more,' he said firmly.

Nicola went up on her toes and kissed him. 'It won't,' she promised. 'From now on I'll count to ten before I say anything.'

'I'll believe that when I see it! Look, why don't I help you bath the boys?' Nicola felt a sudden, irrational wave of anger so great that it almost took her breath away. 'We'll take one each. A job shared is a job halved, yes?'

She nodded, quite unable to speak because of the fury that seemed to be blocking her throat. Quickly she turned away and began to sort through the cupboard under the sink for soap that she didn't need just to give herself time to calm down. The ridiculous thing was that she'd wanted Howard to help her, had even imagined the pair of them playing cheerfully with the boys in the bathroom, and yet the moment he'd spoken something else had taken her over, some extraordinary feeling that he was intruding on something private, invading an area of her life that didn't concern him.

'What are you looking for?' he asked at last.

'Some soap. It's all right, here it is!'

He kissed the back of her neck. 'Love you,' he whispered.

'Love you too,' she responded mechanically, and wondered why she was suddenly beginning to query if that was really true.

Unused to the paraphernalia of bath time, it took ages to assemble the requisite numbers of towels, sponges, flannels and soaps but at last it was all ready. Torquil and Tarquin stood at the side of the bath like small mannequins, waiting for the adults to undress them.

'You shouldn't be here,' said Torquil as Howard peeled off his T-shirt.'

'Why not?'

'It's women's work, not men's.'

'I wish I lived in Egypt. It sounds as though it's a good place to be a man.'

35

'We don't want you here,' added Tarquin, watching as Nicola peeled off his blue socks.

'Have you got any clean blue socks for tomorrow?' asked Nicola, tugging down the red shorts.

'I don't need blue ones tomorrow. I'm green tomorrow. It's his turn to be Tarquin. I've been Tarquin all day and I'm fed up with him.'

'Look, guys, this isn't a game,' said Nicola firmly. 'You were both christened or whatever, weren't you? I mean, you were given names when you were babies.'

'Of course we were,' said Torquil, pulling away from Howard's helping hands and miraculously removing his own underpants. 'We were given four names to share between us until we're grown up. This water's too hot.'

'It's only tepid. I didn't think you'd want a cold bath. What do you mean about being grown up? Don't you keep the same names all your life in Egypt?'

This seemed to amuse both the boys who sat down in the water together and giggled behind their hands.

'They're just winding you up,' said Howard. 'Hey, what's that mark you've got on your chest?' He pointed to a discoloured patch below one of the boy's collarbones.

'It's only a burn.'

'I've got one too,' said his twin, moving his arms to reveal an identical mark.

'How did you both get burned in the same place?' asked Nicola in amazement. They frowned at each other and then began splashing the water around. 'Didn't it hurt?' she persisted.

'We were only babies ...'

'... at the time.'

'Yes, but ...'

'Leave it,' said Howard with a grin. 'They're having a good time. They're actually laughing, let's not spoil it for them.'

'I only wanted to know,' said Nicola meekly, privately resolving to question the boys more closely at a later date.

Either the bath or the strangeness of it all seemed to have caught up with the twins because they went straight off to sleep and didn't stir when Nicola checked on them before she and Howard went to bed.

36

'I quite enjoyed today,' Howard confessed as he reached for her.

'Good. I'm grateful they're six years old. Imagine taking on two babies!'

'It doesn't bear thinking about. Two women now ... that's quite a different prospect!' He laughed as his hands reached for Nicola's breasts. She tried hard to respond normally, to behave as she usually did, but it was very difficult when her body refused to show any interest at all in Howard's attentions. If he noticed her deception he didn't say anything but she felt guilty at her lack of enthusiasm. She felt even more guilty at the end because as Howard moved in and out of her with increasing speed, an image of Sergei Cheparukhin suddenly flashed into her mind and her body responded instantly.

As Nicola cried out with excitement the twins slept soundly in one of their twin beds, hands linked, and in a small, dark room on the outskirts of Cairo a man and woman nodded to each other in silent satisfaction.

Once Howard returned to work on the Monday, Nicola knew that it was up to her to make the twins' numerous adjustments as easy as possible. They complained constantly about the weather, finding the lack of bright sunshine depressing, and both showed a distinct aversion to getting wet in the rain.

'When will it be summer?' they asked her. She explained that this was July, the middle of an English summer, and their faces fell as they retreated to their room, muttering to each other.

In the house they played reasonably well on their own but on trips into Guildford they became uncontrollable, running wildly through the shops snatching at books and toys as they went.

On one particularly difficult afternoon, when they'd swopped most of the shampoos and bubble baths around in the Body Shop, Nicola — angry and embarrassed by their behaviour — slapped them both on the legs.

'I've had enough!' she told them furiously. 'If you don't learn to behave better than this you won't ever come out with me again.'

37

Far from looking upset or penitent the twins went bright red in the face and began to scream. They screamed and screamed until they had no breath left, and all the time they yelled they rolled around the shop floor, kicking out at anyone who approached.

'I didn't know what to do,' Nicola confessed to Howard that evening. 'Everyone was staring in stunned silence. I'm sure I saw Andrea in the doorway. Heaven knows what she thought.'

'I'm beginning to think they've never had any discipline in their lives,' said Howard despondently. 'Whenever I tell them not to do something their faces go totally blank. I'm rather surprised. I'd have thought Labib was heavily into discipline. He certainly seemed to keep Rose in her place!'

'I don't think that's very funny.'

'It wasn't meant to be. Didn't you ever get the impression that she was afraid of him?'

Nicola shrugged. 'Not really. I know she ran around after him before they got married, but that was because she enjoyed it. Later on I didn't see enough of her to judge.'

'We both saw them at your father's funeral. She was like a pathetic puppy cringing around him all the time.'

'She wasn't well.'

Howard snorted. 'That's what Labib said. She didn't look ill to me.'

'She looked old.'

'Probably worn out taking the twins shopping! Do the boys mention their parents much?'

'They sometimes mention Labib, but never Rose. I don't want to bring the subject up, it's better to let them come round to it in their own time. And talking of emotional trauma, I'll have to get back to work next week. I've had a word with Martin and he suggests that I see my patients here until school starts in September.'

'If you think the boys will stay out of the way, I suppose that's all right. Have you made an appointment for us to see the heads of Rushton's and St Hugh's?'

Nicola shook her head. 'I couldn't get hold of the head of St Hugh's but Mr Leslie — he's the deputy head of Rushton's — can see us Tuesday week at 11 a.m.'

Howard took out his diary. 'No good to me, I'm afraid, I'm doing the annual reviews of my staff that week. You'll have to go on your own.'

'It must be wonderful to be so important you can never be spared,' said Nicola sharply.

'That's not fair, Nikki, and you know it.'

'Do I?'

'I didn't ask to have the boys here. We've always known that children wouldn't fit in to the lives we lead, that was partly why we decided not to have any.'

'A pity we didn't tell Rose. She might have chosen someone else to bring up her children, someone who didn't have a husband married to BP.'

'She'd certainly have done better with someone who wasn't a trained child psychologist. You seem to be making an absolute pig's ear of this whole situation.'

They glared at each other and Howard refilled his wine glass. 'I'm going over some figures for a meeting tomorrow. Do you want me to speak to the twins about the scene today?'

Nicola shook her head. 'No thanks, I've got to handle it myself. I'm sorry I started on at you. I'm just so confused. I didn't have the faintest idea of the amount of work needed to bring up children.'

Howard bent down and kissed her forehead. 'I know. It's certainly different round here now. I just wish there was more of your sister in them. A little quiet subservience wouldn't go down amiss!'

'It was sex, you know,' said Nicola as he started to walk away.

'What was sex?'

'Rose used to say that they had the most incredible sex life. She seemed to think that there wasn't another man in the world like Labib.'

'Pity she didn't look better on it then. The things you women discuss! I hope you never mentioned our sex life?'

'Only in a general way, and she didn't talk about it much. Just once, after he and I had been arguing for nearly an hour and I said I didn't know how she could stand being married to such a narrow-minded chauvinist.'

'We'd better not send the twins to a mixed school then. I'm not up to coping with irate mothers just yet.'

Nicola laughed and began to clear the dishes from the table. While she was stacking them in the dishwasher the twins, already dressed in their pyjamas, came into the kitchen.

'We thought we ought ...'

'... to say sorry.'

Nicola sat back on her heels and looked carefully at them. 'Are you really sorry?'

They nodded.

'And you won't do it again?'

They shook their heads.

'Then we'll forget it. I'm glad you're here. I wanted to talk to you about school. Let's go in the playroom and sit down together.'

She took each of them by the hand, aware as usual of a very slight resistance when her fingers first closed on theirs.

'Now, as you know, all children have to go to school,' she said cheerfully, sitting between them on the sofa. 'There are two nice little prep schools only ten minutes' walk from here and next week I'm going to see a teacher from one of them to talk about you two. I wondered how far you'd got with reading and spelling and numbers? If I bring you some paper and pencils, would you show me what you can do?'

They looked a little nervous and one of them pulled on her sleeve. 'I'm Torquil today. Torquil isn't very good at writing and things.'

Nicola tried not to smile. 'Never mind, that's what school's for. How about Tarquin?' She turned to the other twin. 'Are you good at writing?'

He looked thoughtful. 'I think Tarquin's quite good at sums.'

'Good for Tarquin. I'll get the paper.'

She settled them down by the small glass-topped table and watched with interest as Torquil grasped the pencil in his left hand while Tarquin used his right. They both bent over until their noses nearly touched the paper and busied themselves industriously.

She left them alone for nearly half an hour, expecting every minute to be called back, but when she finally returned they were still scribbling.

'Here are Tarquin's sums,' said the boy proudly.

'You should say, "Here are my sums",' Nicola corrected him.

He looked quite cross. 'Aren't you going to look?'

'Sorry. Yes, of course I am.' Her eyes went down the pages and once again she had to hide a smile. 'These look very impressive, but they're not sums, are they?'

'Yes they are! They're formulae.'

'Really? I doubt if prep schools round here are quite up to formulae. Shall I give you some adds and see how you get on with those?'

'What are adds?'

Torquil looked up from his work. 'They're finger sums. Two add two, five add one, all those things.'

Tarquin scowled. 'I've forgotten all my finger sums.'

Nicola suspected that he'd never learnt them, and wondered where he'd learnt to make up such impressive-looking formulae. Anxious not to humiliate Tarquin, she turned back to Torquil. 'What have you done then?'

'Drawing. Torquil's only any good at drawing today.'

She took the pages off him and her sympathetic smile disappeared immediately. The top drawing was quite horrible. Heavy dark lines and disembodied eyes gave off an unmistakable impression of barely suppressed anger.

'What is it?' she asked quietly, thumbing through the other pages and finding that all the drawings were similar.

'Bits of bodies and things. That's an axe in the corner. A really sharp axe.'

'Can either of you write your name?' she asked, quickly putting the drawings face down on the sofa.

'Which one am I?' asked Torquil.

'You're Torquil,' she said patiently.

'I can spell that!' he said cheerfully, and promptly picked up the pencil in his right hand.

Nicola wondered if he'd used the left hand by mistake the first time and turned to Tarquin. 'How about you?'

'I'll try.' He transferred his pencil from his right hand to his left and began to write.

41

It was then, as they both bent their heads obediently to the task, that Nicola finally let the thought that had been at the back of her mind for the past two days, surface: There was definitely something not right about them. It wasn't just that they were twins, or confused by the upheaval in their lives; they weren't as confused as she was. They both knew exactly what they were doing and were probably behaving exactly as they'd always behaved. They didn't understand their separate identities and they automatically polarised their behaviour. If one was right-handed then the other used the left. If one did sums the other did art. And it was all done automatically, without the need for consultation. Even their split sentences weren't planned, they spoke with one voice.

'Wasn't the work . . .'

'. . . any good?'

She looked down at their anxious faces as they stood hand-in-hand in front of her. 'It was fine, you both tried very hard. How long have you been going to school at home?' As she spoke she glanced at the illegible scribbles that were meant to be their names.

'We didn't go to school,' admitted Tarquin.

'We always had teachers at home,' explained his twin.

'Didn't your daddy want you to go to school?'

'School's for ordinary children. We've been learning special things.'

'Perhaps I ought to find out a little bit more about these special things before I choose you a school.'

Tarquin nodded. 'We think you should. We might not like ordinary school.'

'Shall I ask Sergei?'

They beamed at each other. 'Yes, that's a good idea!'

'Fine, I will. Now, I think it's your bedtime. What did you do about friends if you didn't go to school?'

They looked highly indignant. 'We don't need friends. We've got ourselves.'

'I think you need friends quite badly,' she told them gently. 'When you grow up you won't be able to do everything together will you?'

Torquil kicked the hall skirting board. 'You sound just like Mummy!' he said petulantly. 'She didn't understand either.'

42

'You mean Mummy wanted you to go to school?'

'Mummy wanted us locked up!' said Tarquin. 'Wasn't that a bad thing for a mummy to want?'

Nicola was so shocked she didn't know what to say.

'Our Daddy said he'd rather lock *her* up!' laughed Torquil, giving the skirting board one final kick and then setting off up the stairs. 'He said she'd have to live in a straight jacket and be fed down a tube. That always made her cry and then she used to leave us alone.'

'She didn't like being tied up,' Tarquin explained as he followed his twin up to bed.

Nicola's legs were trembling and she sat on the bottom step and closed her eyes. She'd been waiting for the boys to mention Rose but what they'd said was so horrible that she now wished they'd continued their silence. Eventually, telling herself that it was probably just a dramatised version of an ordinary family argument, she began to feel better and decided not to mention any of it to Howard.

As soon as breakfast was over the next morning, she searched through Howard's desk until she found Sergei Cheparukhin's telephone number. It took her nearly half an hour to get through but when he finally came on the line his voice was as clear as if he was in the next room. She found she was gripping the telephone far too tightly with excitement.

'Are the boys all right?' he asked at once.

'They're doing very well,' she assured him. 'Homesick for the sun but coping manfully.'

'They're bright children, they'll manage.'

'Actually, that's a very encouraging thing to hear,' she said with a laugh. 'I'm trying to find them a school and they say they've always been taught at home until now. Is that right?'

'Labib felt that they might get bored in a large class of mixed ability. He wanted them to be stretched from the beginning.'

'Well, it doesn't seem to have worked. Neither of them could write their names last night and I just wondered ...'

'Of course they can write their names.' He sounded personally insulted, as thought she'd accused *him* of stupidity.

43

'They like to play tricks on people. I can assure you their reading and writing is well advanced for their age.'

'The thing is, Sergei, not only couldn't they spell their names, they seem to have great difficulty in deciding which twin is which. I mean, they take it in turns to be Torquil! I don't know how to handle it because the confusion seems quite genuine to me.'

There was a long silence. 'Hello?' she said anxiously. 'Are you still there?'

It sounded as though he was talking to someone in the background for a few minutes and when he came back on his voice was reassuring. 'Let me speak to them,' he suggested. 'I'm sure I can sort it out for you.'

'But if there is a genuine problem I'd like to know. I am a trained psychologist.'

'I didn't know that.' He was obviously surprised.

'Well, it's true, and so I'm quite capable of helping them through any identity problem they may have. I just need to know how long the problem's been there and ...'

'There is no problem.'

She could tell that he was becoming annoyed. 'I'm afraid there is,' she repeated firmly.

'Put them on the line, please.' It was a request that sounded like an order and she obeyed him instantly, surprised at her own docility.

The twins huddled round the receiver, jabbering away in rapid French. Nicola had taken their impeccable English for granted. Now she realised that they were bi-lingual and was very impressed. After several minutes they held the phone out to her and ran off again, lookng extremely cheerful.

'What did you talk about?' she asked with interest.

'I explained to them that they were worrying you. They were very sorry. You shouldn't have any more problems. As for this school, I don't suppose it matters too much. They'll be able to cope with the lessons wherever you send them.'

'Fine, then I'll use my own judgement.'

'I'm sure that will be excellent, Nicola.' His voice seemed to caress her name and she felt a shiver of excitement.

'When are you coming to see them?' she asked as casually as she could manage.

'After they've started school. I don't want to come too soon. It might negate all your good work.'

'Perhaps in October then? That's when the schools here have half-term.'

'I'll just look in my diary.'

Again she thought that he was consulting with someone. 'Early October's rather difficult,' he said regretfully.

'It will probably be the last week of the month.'

'In that case I'll pencil it in. You're doing a wonderful job. They're very happy with you.'

She found that hard to believe but decided to accept the compliment. 'It's very kind of them to say that. They're not very keen on my cooking as yet!'

'Don't worry, they don't need much food. How's your husband coping?'

'He's still a little shell-shocked but at least he's got someone to play football with during the winter months!'

'I have to go now,' he said abruptly. 'I think about you a lot, all three of you, and look forward to this half-term.'

Before she even had time to say goodbye he'd broken the connection and she stood with the receiver to her ear listening stupidly to the humming of the dead line.

Suddenly the two boys came running up to her. 'I'm Tarquin!' said one. 'I'm going to be Tarquin *all the time.*'

'And I'm Torquil,' said the other, slightly less enthusiastically.

'Are you both quite sure about that?' she asked teasingly.

'Of course we are,' said Tarquin. 'Sergei told us, and he knows everything.'

She felt uneasy. 'He only told you to use your proper names, didn't he? I mean, he didn't decide which one of you was which! Your mummy and daddy decided that when you were born.'

'Mummy didn't decide anything,' said Torquil contemptuously.

'She didn't have any brain!' laughed Tarquin.

'That's very unkind,' said Nicola sharply. 'Rose was my sister and I don't like hearing you saying such horried things about her. Perhaps she was a quiet person but she most certainly wasn't stupid. She was a very good nurse once. That's how she met you father.'

'We know that,' Torquil sounded bored.

'Good, then perhaps you'll stop calling her names.'

They nodded obediently, opened the fridge and began searching for tins of Coke.

'I know something else about Mummy,' said Tarquin, holding out a tin for Nicola to open.'

'What's that?'

'Well, when the car crashed her head got chopped off.'

Nicola nearly dropped the can. 'That's a dreadful thing to say!'

'It's true,' said Torquil casually. 'The word's decapitated,' he added helpfully.

'Go away,' said Nicola in a low voice. 'Go outside or go up to your room but get away from me right now!'

They went without a backward glance, taking their unopened cans of Coke with them.

On the 4th September they began their first term at St Hugh's Preparatory School where the discipline, as far as Nicola had been able to ascertain, was strict and the academic standards high. She was extremely glad to see them go.

Chapter Four

'You know very well that I can't come to the gym,' said Nicola wearily.

'How come we never go anywhere these days?' retorted Howard. 'I don't think we've been out of this house since the boys arrived.'

'How do you think I do the shopping? By tele-ordering?'

He picked up some of the celery she was chopping for a salad and popped it in his mouth. 'This is leathery. When I said we hadn't been out of the house, I didn't mean it literally. I do know that you make hasty forays into the town for provisions. I was talking about social outings, remember? Evenings at the health club; dinner at Mel and Robert's; drinks at the Queen Victoria. Surely most parents don't cut themselves off entirely from the rest of the world?'

Nicola sat down on a kitchen chair and ran her fingers through her auburn hair. 'No, they don't, but at the moment it's difficult. I honestly don't feel that I can ask anyone to sit with the boys yet. Their temper tantrums frighten us — think how much worse they'd be for an outsider.'

'I don't understand why the school isn't doing them more good. We're paying them enough. Doesn't their curriculum include discipline?'

'If you're not happy with their schooling, you go and speak to the headmaster. After my last visit I don't care if I never go there again,' responded Nicola.

'All he said was that he felt the boys needed professional help. What's so wrong with that? You're a professional. It shows touching faith in your colleagues.'

'I think that's what annoyed me. Dammit, he knew I was an expert and sat there telling me that I couldn't recognise a troubled child even when it was living under my own roof. It was humiliating.'

Howard looked at Nicola's weary face, at the fine lines at the corners of her eyes and the dark circles beneath them, and cursed both Rose and Labib for leaving them their children.

'OK, I'll go to the gym alone, but we are going to Melanie's dinner party on Friday night, aren't we?'

'Providing that Robert agrees we can let the boys go to sleep in their spare room we are. Melanie hasn't raised it with him yet.'

'She's leaving it a bit late.'

'That's because he hasn't been too happy lately. Trouble at work, I gather. Blame it on the Russians. The prospect of eternal peace hasn't done much for the sale of munitions.'

'Will you be all right on your own?' he asked hesitantly.

'I'm not alone. I've got the boys, remember! Anyway, I'm desperately behind with my notes. I've got about three tapes to transcribe before next week. Once they're in bed I'll probably catch up on some of that.'

Howard stood behind her and bent down to wrap his arms round her shoulders. 'Keep smiling, things are bound to improve. We probably had unrealistically high expectations. Rose and Labib kept them so isolated there are bound to be teething problems.'

'I know, it's only in the evenings I get low. When I first get up and my energy level's high I feel quite optimistic! If you see Andrea at the club tell her I can't make the theatre trip next week will you?'

'Sure. Hello, boys, done your homework?'

Since starting school the boys had taken to wearing a letter of the alphabet pinned on their jerseys. A for Tarquin and O for Torquil. According to the badge it was Tarquin who spoke first.

'We can't do it because . . .'

'. . . it's just too easy-peasy!'

'You get off to the gym,' said Nicola briskly. 'I'll go

48

and look at their work. Don't be late back. I need an early night.'

She kissed Howard on the cheek and followed the boys into the playroom where their exercise books lay on the floor.

'I thought I told you both to work on the table? You'll ruin your books if you leave them lying around. Torquil, show me what you're meant to be doing.'

He held his book out at arm's length. 'Sums, they're in the back.'

'Why the back?'

'I felt like using the back.'

'You're meant to start at the front of exercise books. You haven't done any of these!'

'Why do you have to start at the front of a book?' demanded Tarquin.

'Because that's what the front's for!'

'Why?'

'I don't know!'

'It's a silly rule. All rules are silly. Haven't they ever heard of the science of chaos?'

Nicola laughed. 'The science of chaos? Of course they haven't. You've made it up.'

Torquil frowned. 'I haven't. It's real. Sergei told me about it.'

'Well, I think he was making it up. Have you done any of your sums?'

'No, and I'm not going to. You can't make me.'

Nicola gripped him tightly by the shoulders. 'Don't under-estimate me, Torquil. I'm getting tired of the way you two play up over homework and before long there won't be any sweets, crisps or coke for either of you until the sums and spellings are done.'

'We don't ...'

'... really care.'

Sweets are bad for our teeth!'

'Fine, then I'll stop buying them.'

Torquil threw his exercise book across the room. 'Stupid old sums!'

Nicola was suddenly reminded of one of her patients earlier in the week, a ten-year-old boy who'd been consistently abused by adults as he was shuffled from one home to another while his unmarried mother flitted from man to man in her search for love. That boy had thrown things defiantly round her room, taking the attack into the enemy camp before she too had a chance to hurt him. She looked at Torquil thoughtfully.

'What are you afraid of?' she asked gently.

Both boys looked at her in surprise.

'No one's going to hurt you, you know. We know it's a strange and difficult time and we want to help you.'

Tarquin's bottom lip began to quiver. 'We want to see Sergei.'

'He's our friend,' explained Torquil. 'Our only friend,' he added sadly.

A picture of Sergei flashed into Nicola's mind, but to her embarrassment he was stripped to the waist and there was a woman lying beneath him on an enormous circular bed. He had his hands on her breasts and his movements were slow and erotic.

'Is he your friend too?' asked one of the boys.

Nicola snapped back to reality, feeling herself blushing. 'Yes ... well, no. I don't really know him, do I?'

'When can we see him?' persisted Tarquin.

Still shaken by her vision, Nicola had a job to think straight. 'At half-term,' she said at last. 'He's coming to see you at the end of the month. You must have some good work to show him by then or he might be disappointed.'

'Do you think he's handsome?' asked Tarquin with a small smile.

'I hadn't really thought about it.'

'Ladies do think he's handsome. Ayeesha likes him a lot.'

Nicola couldn't restrain her curiosity. 'And does he like Ayeesha?'

'He likes all the ladies.'

'Except Mummy,' said Torquil quickly. 'He didn't like her.'

'How can you possibly know that?'

They looked at each other and grinned. 'He told us.'

'I'm quite sure he didn't. Now, are you going to do this work or not?'

They suddenly seemed to lose interest in the argument. 'All right,' conceded Torquil and picking up their books they settled down to work.

Feeling hot and flustered, Nicola went into the lounge and took out her tapes, but she couldn't concentrate. No matter how hard she tried to work she kept seeing incredibly erotic images of Sergei as he continued caressing the faceless woman of her imagination.

'This has got to stop!' she said aloud as the visions became even more graphic, and she picked up the telephone to call Melanie.

It was over half an hour later when she finally replaced the receiver and although she waited nervously for a while, her mind remained clear. Blaming the whole thing on exhaustion and the fact that she and Howard had scarcely had any time or energy for lovemaking during the past three weeks, she decided not to dwell on it any more, and allowed herself one final cup of strong coffee before putting the boys to bed.

'Everything all right?' asked Howard when he came in.

'Fine. Homework's done and they're both asleep.'

'What bliss! Let's have an early night then.'

Nicola, aroused by her visions of Sergei, agreed enthusiastically, but to her intense disappointment it was all over far too quickly and almost before she'd had time to start enjoying herself, Howard was turning over to sleep.

'What about me?' she complained.

'Sorry,' Howard was already drifting off to sleep. 'I just lost control.'

'Brilliant!' she muttered and picked up some of her case notes.

'I might be back late tonight,' said Howard the next morning as he tried to gulp his over-hot coffee on his way to catch the 7.15. 'The department meeting doesn't begin until four so God knows when it'll end.'

Nicola was scrambling eggs for the boys. 'Fine. I'll leave your meal on one side and you can put it in the microwave.'

'Where will you be?'

'I'm taking the twins swimming, remember?'

'On your own?'

'No, Melanie's coming too. We arranged it last night. She wants me to help her learn to swim and this seemed like a good opportunity. Oh, yes, and I forgot to tell you that Robert says the boys can use their spare room so the dinner party's on for Friday. Andrea and Graham will be there, and Debbie and Brett.'

'Who the hell's Brett?'

'Her latest admirer, six foot three of Australian manhood, so you'd better smarten yourself up or I might lose my heart to another!'

'After last night's performance I'm not surprised. I'll make it up to you tonight,' he whispered as he bent to kiss her goodbye.

'Make what up?' demanded Torquil suspiciously.

'Pity you two weren't born a few hundred years ago. The Spanish Inquisition could have used you both.'

'What was the Spanish Inquisition?'

'Like the KGB,' explained Tarquin to his twin.

'Close, I suppose!' See you all tonight. Try not to frighten the other boys, twins.'

'He really is a jerk,' said Torquil as the front door slammed behind Howard.

'A weedy jerk!' agreed Tarquin.

'That's quite enough of that,' said Nicola, putting their scrambled eggs in front of them. 'If it weren't for Howard, you two wouldn't be here now.'

Neither of them looked as though that would have been any hardship and not for the first time, Nicola wondered where they thought they would have gone if she and Howard hadn't offered them a home. She decided that when she had more time she'd try and get them to tell her.

'What about my kiss?' she reminded them when she dropped them off outside the school gates.

'Do we . . .'

'. . . have to?'

She looked around at other mothers being hugged and kissed by their children. 'I suppose not, but it makes me feel good inside.'

52

'It makes me want to puke,' said Torquil, and was out of the car and running before she had time to answer.

'Me too,' said Tarquin politely. 'Goodbye.'

He followed his twin more slowly through the gates, and as Nicola drove away she had the impression of children drawing away from the two of them, making a path through which they could pass without making any physical contact. Only as the boys passed did they come together again in the usual jungle of playground rough and tumble.

It proved a difficult day. In the morning she had to pass on her suspicions of physical and mental abuse on a seven-year-old girl, and all the afternoon was taken up by a fourteen-year-old boy who'd developed sudden and acute school phobia. Despite a careful and sympathetic session she still had no idea of the cause by the end of the appointment, and disappointment weighed on her mind on the drive home.

'Why so glum?' asked Melanie when she arrived just before seven, swimming costume and towel clutched tightly under her arm.

'Only work. A swim will do me good. Ready, boys?'

They came clattering down the stairs, dressed in identical red and blue tracksuits but with their badges prominently displayed.

'We're good at swimming,' announced Torquil.

'Lucky you. I can't swim at all,' admitted Melanie.

They narrowed their eyes and stared at her. *'Not at all?'*

'Not one single stroke. Nicola's going to teach me.'

'Is she good at swimming then?' asked Torquil.

'I'm good at teaching it,' said Nicola, pushing them out of the front door.

'People who can, do.'

'People who can't, teach!'

'It might surprise you to learn that I've heard that before. Now get in the car.'

They leapt into the back seat and began a loud discussion about the other children in their class. Nicola heard several scathing references to wimps and weeds but ignored it all. She knew that twins often had initial problems making friends at

53

school. In time they'd develop more separate identities and be more receptive to other children.

'You're quiet,' she said to Melanie as they drew up outside the swimming pool.

'I'm nervous. Does all this belong to BP?'

'Yep, it's one of the few perks of the job. It takes a bit of time to get here but it's worth it because it's always so empty. I hate local pools where small boys keep jumping in on top of you.'

Nicola took the boys into the women's changing room with them. They were if anything small for six and she didn't like the idea of them alone in the men's room. They changed within minutes and dashed off in the direction of the arrows, not even waiting for her permission.

'I wish I was that keen!' said Melanie.

'You'll be fine. It's very shallow this end.'

Much to Nicola's relief the twins didn't need any assistance at all as they swam up and down the pool using a powerful crawl and then practised their diving technique from the lower of the two boards. It was fortunate because Melanie needed all the help Nicola could give her.

Her teeth chattered with fright every time she took hold of the side rail, and her body was rigid with tension. When she eventually took her legs off the bottom and let them float out behind her as she gripped the rail like a drowning woman, Nicola felt a small surge of triumph.

By the end of an hour Melanie was actually smiling and even dipped her head under water. 'I think I'm going to like this!' she exclaimed as she surfaced, water dripping from her face and hair. 'I've always wanted to learn but . . .' Suddenly she stopped talking and stared over Nicola's shoulder, her eyes bulging with fear.

Nicola quickly turned to see what was happening, her scalp prickling, but there was nothing there at all. The twins were still at the deep end, wrestling playfully with each other like seal pups.

'What is it?' asked Nicola, turning back to her friend. Melanie had now turned chalk-white and was making whimpering sounds in the back of her throat. She pointed a trembling finger behind Nicola again, and then began to fight for air as the tendons of her neck stood out like whipcords.

'There's nothing there, Mel! Are you ill? For heaven's sake, what's the matter?'

Nicola was beginning to panic. Melanie seemed to be having some kind of fit as her arms started to jerk in splashing motions on the surface of the water and she continued to gibber unintelligibly.

'Stop it!' shouted Nicola, badly frightened herself now, and almost without thinking she swung a hand and slapped her friend round the face.

The slap echoed round the almost deserted pool and the twins stopped their playing, pulling themselves out of the water and sitting on the edge, looking down towards the two women.

Melanie's eyes closed for a moment, and when she opened them again they were no longer filled with terror. Instead they looked puzzled and she looked around her in confusion.

'What happened?'

'I've no idea. One minute you were telling me how happy you were and the next you were scared witless.'

'But I saw ... Where is it? Where's it gone?'

'Where's what gone?'

'The ...' She shivered. 'I'm going in. I'm frozen.'

Nicola followed her out of the water. 'What did you see, Mel?'

'Forget it. I just freaked out or something. Put it down to nervous tension, all right?'

'Melanie, I've never seen anyone so scared. What happened? Was it something I did?'

'Of course not. You were wonderful. A really super teacher.'

Melanie's sentences were coming out jerkily, and she was shivering from head to toe as she pulled on her overlong skirt and brushed cotton top. 'I've always been scared of water. Now I know why!'

'But nothing happened, Melanie. I was there and you were doing really well.'

'Was I? Well, that's nice to know because I most certainly won't be coming again.'

55

'This is ridiculous.'

Melanie suddenly sat down on the wet bench and looked up at her friend. 'That's right, it's ridiculous, and I've made a fool of myself so can we not keep on about it? I'd rather like to draw a veil over the whole thing.'

'At least tell me what you thought you saw.'

Melanie glanced uneasily around her, and dropped her voice. 'You'll think I'm mad, Nikki.'

'Of course I won't!'

Her friend took a deep breath. 'All right then, I thought I saw this huge octopus — you know, like something out of a Jules Verne novel? It was about ten feet high and had huge tentacles that were reaching out for me. It was a disgusting grey colour with things hanging all over it, sort of dead things and seaweed, stuff like that.'

Nicola felt her mouth drop open and she stared at her friend in disbelief. 'You thought you saw that here? In the BP pool?'

'Yes,' muttered Melanie.

'But, Mel, that's ...'

There was the sound of wet feet on the tiles and then the boys came crashing through the plastic curtain and into the cubicle.

'You left us!' said one of them accusingly.

'We could have been gobbled up,' said the other.

'By what?' asked Nicola with a weak smile, grateful for the diversion.

They shrugged and waited for her to peel off their trunks. 'By anything really,' said Tarquin, pulling on his tracksuit top.

'A sea monster, a shark, an octopus or something,' continued Torquil.

With a sound that was suspiciously like a sob, Melanie pushed her way past the boys and out of the changing room. Nicole frowned. 'Why an octopus?'

'Because they're big ...'

'... and yukky.'

'*And they eat little boys*!'

Their expressions were totally guileless and they scuffled and giggled their way outside and then raced off to buy

56

themselves some chocolate while Nicola, utterly confused, went in search of Melanie and then sat next to her in silence until the boys joined them.

No one spoke during the drive home.

'A wonderful meal, Melanie,' said Howard with satisfaction. 'It's nice to remember that there was life before the microwave.'

'If you kept reasonable hours we wouldn't need a microwave,' responded Nicola, less than pleased by his comment.

'Now then,' said Robert lightly. 'How about a game of backgammon?'

The women groaned as the men began to disappear into the study, leaving them alone.

'How are the boys?' asked Andrea, ignoring her coffee and refilling her wine glass.

'They're fine.'

'Really? Aren't they rather a handful?'

'Well, they're not easy, but then six-year-old twins aren't meant to be easy!'

'They're gorgeous to look at, just like their father as I remember.'

'I didn't know Labib had made such an impression on you,' said Nicola in surprise.

'Well, he did. I suppose what struck me most sharply was the air of suppressed energy about him. He positively fizzed with it, even at the funeral. Most inappropriate, but then it wasn't his father.'

'No, it was mine and Rose's.'

Andrea smiled her irritating smile. 'Quite, and Rose most certainly didn't fizz. She didn't even splutter.'

'It was a very difficult time for us,' protested Nicola indignantly.

'He was old. We all have to go some time.'

'He was only sixty! Anyway, there was more to it than that.'

'Really? Do tell.'

'It doesn't matter, just family problems,' said Nicola flatly. She didn't like to think about that time herself. It had been such a shock. First her father's death, and then that terrible discovery . . .

'They didn't come back when your mother died, did they?' persisted Andrea.

'No, well, it was only a few weeks later and under the circumstances . . .'

'Suicide's just too horrible to think about,' declared Andrea with a mock shudder. 'Imagine missing your husband so much you killed yourself. I can understand a woman doing it when her husband retired but not when he died!'

Nicola realised that Andrea was already the worse for drink and turned away. 'I'll just check on the boys,' she said to Melanie. Her friend, who'd been unusually quiet all the evening, nodded.

They were both asleep in the same bed, lying flat on their backs with the covers pushed off to reveal their clasped hands. It was the way they always slept and no amount of persuasion could keep them in separate beds. Nicola pulled the cover up again and looked carefully at their faces in the light from the streetlamp outside.

She searched and searched for some resemblance to Rose, but Andrea had been right – there was none. Their skin tone and colouring were all Labib's, and their firm chins and generous mouths were also his. 'What did you think of them, Rose?' whispered Nicola softly. 'I wish I knew.'

'Don't you get enough of them at home?' hissed Howard from the doorway.

She turned round guiltily. 'Sorry, but Andrea was off on one of her bitchy tirades and I used them as an excuse to get away.' She tiptoed from the room and joined him on the landing.

'What was she on about this time?'

'Daddy's death and everything that followed.'

'I don't know why you stay friendly with her. She's such a bitch, and David's not much better.'

'The boy's will be all right with us, won't they?' she asked anxiously.

'Of course they will. You're wonderful with them.'

'I try,' she said as they went to join the others. 'I really do try, but I never get anything back. If they'd just be a little more demonstrative, show some spark of affection, it would make everything much easier.'

'I'll show you some affection when we get home,' promised Howard and she squeezed his hand.

But once they were back in their own home and had re-settled the boys, their lovemaking proved even more unsatisfactory than the previous time, leaving Nicola frustrated and Howard humiliated.

'I can't understand it!' he complained. 'I'm not some inexperienced eighteen year old. What's happening to me?'

'It doesn't matter,' she said mechanically. 'Worrying about it will only make it worse.'

'How can I help worrying about it? Sometimes I think those boys have put a jinx on us.'

'Go to sleep,' she said quietly, grateful that he didn't know about her dreams. These were becoming more and more explicitly erotic with every night that passed, so much so that tonight she found herself anxious to fall asleep, hoping that at least in her dreams she might find some satisfaction.

Chapter Five

'Don't forget it's the twins' open evening tomorrow night,' said Nicola as Howard sat reading the evening paper.

He glanced at his watch to check the date. 'I forgot all about that. If I'm late back you'd better go without me.'

'I don't believe this! We've been talking about the open evening for the past week and now you claim it slipped your mind. Honestly, Howard, there are times when you drive me mad.'

'Hard as this may be for you to grasp, the chance of a posting to Belgium ranks a little higher on my list of priorities than looking at school books.'

'I can't think why you're bothering to put yourself forward. We can't possibly uproot Torquil and Tarquin again this early.'

With a sigh, Howard lowered his paper. 'If you remember, at the time the job was first discussed Rose and Labib were still alive and the twins unknown and unseen nephews, a cause for idle speculation and nothing more.'

'Well, they're here now so why don't you explain that you're no longer available?'

Howard rarely got angry but he was beginning to find it hard to control his temper now. 'Because I *am* still available,' he explained shortly. 'I'm not putting my entire career on hold because of the boys. This could be a big step forward for me, and if I get it then they'll have to adjust.'

'For someone who always sees everyone's point of view you choose the most extraordinary times to dig your heels in. Here we are, bombarded by phone calls and letters from the school, all telling us that the twins are anti-social and disturbed, and you decide to try and uproot them again.'

'I'm thinking of us for once.'

Nicola shook her head. 'No you're not, you're thinking of yourself.'

'But you wanted to move to Belgium. Ever since Sue and Kelvin went there you've been anxious to try a few years there.'

'That was before the twins. It's different now.'

'It most certainly is!' said Howard with feeling. 'I notice that Lily stays away most of the time these days.'

'That's because the boys liked to play with her and she isn't used to it. She'll come round.'

'Let's hope the school's as obliging. Now is there anything else you want to complain about or can I get back to the paper?'

Nicola felt her heart sink. 'I don't mean to keep complaining, it's just that sometimes I could do with a bit more support from you. I'm dreading this open evening as it is. I really do need you there with me. Teachers always seem to take more notice of men.'

'I'll do my best.'

'Howard, do you think they're improving at all?'

'No, they seem exactly the same to me. Self-centred and with tempers that make McEnroe look like a saint.'

'That's made me feel much better!'

'I don't see any point in lying about it.'

Nicola felt like bursting into tears. 'Oh, go back to your paper. Honestly, sometimes I feel like a single parent.'

'I can't imagine why. You aren't really a parent at all. That's half the trouble. If they were my sons I'm sure I'd feel differently about them. As it is they don't even seem to come from the same planet as us, and although I assume Rose really did give birth to them there's no visible sign of her contribution to their makeup. They're all Labib, aloof and faintly superior.'

Nicola knew that he was telling the truth, but she was determined to turn them all into a happy family unit eventually.

*

61

'And you're Mrs ...?'

'Grainger,' said Nicola, glancing round the room, her eyes searching the walls for something from the twins.

The young woman teacher frowned. 'Grainger? I'm not sure ...'

'The Rachid twins.'

'Oh, the twins.' Her expression hardened. 'Yes, well, of course we are having difficulties with the twins. Have you seen the headmaster yet?'

'No. My husband hopes to be here later and we thought we'd see him together.'

The young woman nodded. 'That's probably a good idea. I'm Miss Johnson and I teach them Art and English. At least, I *try* to teach them Art and English. They seem to have very fixed ideas about how to do things and my words usually go in one ear and out the other. Discipline certainly isn't their strong suit.'

Nicola felt herself flushing. 'It's been very difficult. As you probably know, both their parents were killed, and although they're my nephews I'd never even met them until they arrived here to live. It wasn't until I got down to choosing a school that I discovered they'd only been used to tutors, and obviously the tutors gave them quite a lot of personal freedom. I haven't liked to be too hard on them because of the obvious difficulties in adjusting to a different country — well a completely different way of life really.'

'But they aren't trying to adjust, are they?'

'I thought they'd done quite well,' Nicola said defensively.

'They run riot here, I'm afraid. Tearing up and down the classroom, pushing the other children if they get in their way, chattering to each other all through lessons — it's been very difficult. In fact, I've had several complaints from parents this very evening.'

'I don't know what you expect me to do about it,' said Nicola helplessly. 'I mean, you're their teacher.'

'We aren't allowed to use any form of physical punishment.' Nicola was shocked to see from Miss Johnson's expression that she would personally have liked to use physical force on the twins.

62

'Violence really isn't the answer to anything,' she said levelly.

'We've tried everything else.'

'I see.'

'Their headmaster will doubtless confirm this.'

'Yes, I'm sure he will. Don't they ever do any work? I've looked around but I can't see anything of theirs on display.'

Miss Johnson flushed. 'We couldn't possibly display any of their work. It's all with the headmaster.'

'But are they keeping up?'

'Goodness me, yes. They're probably a long way ahead of the other children in terms of ability. Their drawings are well co-ordinated and their use of language quite exceptional.'

'I suppose that's something,' said Nicola, smiling with relief.

Miss Johnson looked doubtful, and Nicola quickly stood up to end the interview. There seemed no point in continuing it when the headmaster had all their work and so she left the classroom. To her intense relief, Howard was just coming in through the front door as she approached the office.

'The train was delayed,' he said breathlessly, running his fingers through his hair in an attempt to tidy it. 'I haven't been home at all. Do I look presentable?'

'You look fine. Put your glasses on, they make you look quite intimidating.'

'Do I need to look intimidating?'

'From what I've heard so far, yes!'

Mr Watson had been headmaster of St Hugh's for ten years and was proud of his record. The school had become a recognised feed for several of the major public schools and discipline was known to be of an exceptionally high standard, which was why he was determined to do something about the Rachid twins.

He greeted Howard and Nicola with a frosty smile and then began sorting through the various notes of complaint, some from members of staff, and others from parents.

'We seem to have rather a problem with your boys,' he said in a grave voice.

63

'In what way?' asked Howard, his expression one of apparent surprise.

'In all ways. Their work is, to say the least, undisciplined and their behaviour totally unacceptable.'

'Perhaps you wouldn't mind being more specific,' said Howard politely.

Mr Watson pushed some paper across the desk. 'Take a look at this. It's their art work. Really, most disturbing indeed.'

Howard glanced through the pictures and handed them on to Nicola. 'A bit peculiar, I grant you, but well drawn.'

'It isn't what they were asked to do. Miss Johnson said ...'

His voice droned on in the background as Nicola went carefully through the pictures. They all depicted some kind of murder or killing. There were severed limbs partially hidden by rocks and trees, decapitated heads littered a sandy beach and deformed figures lurked in every landscape. That was bad enough, but to make it worse every picture also contained one larger, main figure. It was sometimes a man and sometimes a woman, but whatever the gender the sexual organs were enormous, totally out of proportion and in exceptional detail.

The drawings were vivid, sophisticated and undoubtedly the work of very disturbed minds. Nicola was suddenly fearful, wondering what had happened to them to make them so sexually precocious.

She looked at the headmaster, who was still talking to Howard. 'This is sick,' she said abruptly. He stopped in mid-sentence and stared at her. 'You should have told us earlier,' she continued angrily. 'They need help. Surely you know that? This is a classic sign of a child in trouble.'

For a moment he had the grace to look ashamed. 'Normally, yes, I'd agree with you, Mrs Grainger. But the boys aren't worried by what they draw. They seem to imagine it's normal. Just as they fail to understand that all their essays shouldn't contain bloodshed. Even when writing about "My Favourite Toy" they both managed to insert a violent scene.'

'The same scene?' she asked sharply.

'No, not the same. One of them had a toy guillotine chop off a child's finger and the other had a child suck a lead model and die choking on its own vomit. Quite different in their own way.'

'We don't get this from them at home,' said Howard. Nicola was impressed by his calmness and the way he made it sound as though the school was to blame when all she wanted to do was make her escape at the first possible moment.

'That's probably because they exhaust themselves here. Unfortunately, these last few days they've carried their obsession over into other areas. We've had three or four complaints about them touching some of their classmates.'

'Touching?' Howard was genuinely amazed this time. 'They don't like being touched themselves.'

'I mean, sexual touching. Comparisons, that kind of thing.'

'You mean "you show me yours, I'll show you mine"? Well, that's always gone on at school.'

'Not here,' said Mr Watson indignantly. 'This school has an excellent reputation and I'm afraid the twins don't appear able to fit in. I must therefore regretfully ask you to remove them from school at the end of term.'

'But they've only just got here,' said Nicola incredulously. 'Surely you could wait until they've had some help? It's obvious they need therapy and counselling. There's something very wrong and we'll do all we can to put it right, but moving them at Christmas will be very traumatic.'

'I'm sorry but I have the other pupils to consider. Tarquin and Torquil frighten their classmates. I've had parents ringing up with tales of terrible nightmares and floods of tears on school mornings.'

'You're blaming the twins for other children's nightmares?' asked Howard incredulously.

'All the parents say that their children's dreams concern the twins, that they call out the boys' names. We can't ignore what we're told.'

'But what are they doing? Are they bullying the other children? Is that the problem?'

Mr Watson shook his head. 'We've seen no sign of bullying.'

'Then what are you saying they do?'

'I don't know!' The headmaster sounded both baffled and angry. 'I've absolutely no idea what's happening but I can see for myself that many of their classmates are becoming anxious and tearful. The twins will have to go.'

'Right,' said Howard briskly, standing up. 'I don't think there's any need to discuss this further. The boys have obviously presented you with a problem that you and your staff are not sufficiently qualified to deal with. It's plain that it's in the interest of the twins that they be moved. Nothing you've said has given me any confidence at all in the way you've handled this problem. If anything, you seem to have made it a great deal worse.'

'If you feel like that about it then perhaps you'd like to remove them at the end of the week? Then they needn't return after half-term.'

Howard looked at Nicola, who nodded. 'I think that's probably a good idea. I suppose you've no suggestion as to a more suitable school for them.'

'Not within the normal framework of education, no.'

When they got to the door, Howard turned back to the headmaster. 'Never mind, look on the positive side. A few weeks with the twins has probably toughened up those of their classmates who are destined for the harsh reality of Eton in a few years.'

Nicola couldn't suppress a smile, but once they were safely outside both she and Howard looked at each other in despair.

'What's wrong with them?' asked Howard in bewilderment. 'How could they draw those disgusting pictures?'

'I don't know. They're very disturbed, that's obvious. What I can't make out is what's at the bottom of this. Did it begin when Rose and Labib died, or does it go back further? I suspect the latter.'

'They're only six for God's sake! How could they know about all that?'

'Howard, you'd be amazed at what children today pick up. If they watch a lot of television then . . .'

'They've been living in Egypt, Nikki! There's no airing of sexual problems on their TV. They've grown up surrounded by servants and tutors. How could they possibly have learnt all this?'

'I suppose it rather depends on what the servants and tutors were teaching them,' she said quietly.

'But Rose and Labib were there!'

'I know. I'm as puzzled as you are, but what we have to do now is try to help them. I can easily get them an appointment with Tanya, she's a wonderful psychologist, kids adore her.'

'Don't you think it might be better to wait until this Sergei chap's been over? After all, he must know them as well as anyone.'

'If you think I'm showing him these drawings you can think again!'

'Come on, Nikki. You're dealing with this kind of thing all the time at work.'

'That's different; I'm not involved.'

'I'll show him if you won't.'

'I'll see how it goes. He'll be here in a few days. I should find a chance some time, but if I still lack the courage I'll let you take over.'

'What are we going to say to the boys?' asked Howard when they arrived home.

'I'll say we don't think St Hugh's suits them and we're going to have a look at some other schools before term begins again. We don't have to say the headmaster threw them out. That wouldn't be at all helpful.'

'Suppose they're upset?'

'I don't think they will be,' said Nicola. 'They haven't settled there, and they haven't made any friends. As long as they're together they're fine for the moment. At least they're still young.'

'Not young enough!' muttered Howard, the memory of the pictures still fresh in his mind.

He was right, thought Nicola, following him into the kitchen. Somewhere along the line their childhood had been taken from them, and now Rose's silence about her children began to take on a much more sinister significance.

As Nicola had suspected, the twins seemed totally unaffected by the news that they were going to change schools. They

67

were only interested in one thing: the arrival of Sergei Cheparukhin.

'He will still come, won't he?' asked Tarquin anxiously.

'We haven't got to wait for half term at another school?' enquired Torquil.

'*We couldn't bear that*!' they finished in unison.

'Don't worry,' soothed Nicola. 'He'll be here next Monday.'

'Let's hope he can shed some light on their artwork,' said Howard. 'I don't want to get them into Rushton's only to find myself hauled up before the head again.'

'Neither do I,' agreed Nicola with feeling.

Howard glanced out of the lounge window. 'Where are the boys?'

'Out cat hunting. We haven't seen Lily for days. They offered to try and find her.'

'In the garden?'

'They're going to try all the gardens in the road. They seem to imagine she's caught in a trap. I tried to explain there aren't any traps in suburban gardens but they didn't believe me.'

'I wish I was a cat. I'd like to disappear for days at a time too.'

'You do, only you call it going to the office. What plane's this Russian coming on?'

'He should arrive at Gatwick at ten-thirty Monday morning. He said he'll get a taxi here. I pointed out that would cost a fortune but he wasn't bothered. He'll be with you in time for lunch. And talking of lunch, we're invited to my mother's on Sunday for roast beef and all the trimmings.'

Nicola groaned. 'How can I keep the twins under control there? There isn't enough room for us all.'

'Mother says it will be cosy! She's asked Chris and Benjamin as well.'

Nicola liked Howard's brothers, but singly. On their own they were amusing and good company. Together they competed for attention, each trying to outdo the other with witty stories and tales from the two colleges where they worked as lecturers.

68

'Is she mad?' asked Nicola incredulously. 'She's seen the boys rushing around here. There won't be room for them to move if your brothers join us.'

'What does it matter?' asked Howard easily. 'You know how my mother enjoys a family get-together. If it makes her happy, where's the harm in it?'

'Fine. I hope you're going to keep the twins amused because I'm not! It's difficult enough here with large rooms and a big garden. The idea of coping with them in a two up two down town house makes me feel ill.'

'The trouble with you is that you worry about things too much in advance. Talk about crossing bridges!'

'I wouldn't worry so much if I didn't have to do it for both of us.'

'I'm not going to end up having a coronary in my early forties. Worrying is time-consuming and unproductive.'

'You sound like a fortune cookie. Worrying comes with parenting, it's part of the job.'

'When I'm a parent I'll start, all right?'

Nicola made an exclamation of annoyance. 'I wish you wouldn't say things like that. To all intents and purposes you are a parent now.'

'I'm sorry, Nikki, but I can't agree with you. I'm responsible for the boys, guardian of their moral and physical welfare if you like, but not their father. Labib was their father, and he's got a lot to answer for!'

'But I'm their aunt. That's a blood relationship whether you like it or not.'

'I'm not saying you're not a relative, I'm talking about me. Although I'm surprised you're so anxious to claim any ties!'

Nicola gave up. 'You'd better ring your mother and confirm then.'

'No need. I've already accepted for us.'

Before Nicola could make any protest there was a tap on the window and they looked up to see the twins standing outside on the patio, cradling Lily in their arms.

'She must be hurt!' exclaimed Nicola, dashing into the playroom and out through the french windows. 'Where did you find her, boys?'

'At the side of the road,' said Tarquin. 'She's quite stiff. I think she got run over.'

Nicola's eyes filled with tears. 'Poor Lily, she never did have any road sense. Why don't we bury her in the garden?'

'You're crying!' said Tarquin in surprise.

'I'm upset. We've had Lily ever since we got married. That's over six years. I'll miss her.'

'Does that mean your marriage will end now?' asked Torquil with interest.

'Of course not! But it marks the end of a special time for me.'

'If you want her to curl up in a box, you'll have to break her neck,' said Tarquin. 'Shall I do it for you?'

'No!' shouted Nicola, feeling quite sick. 'Howard will find a big box and we'll dig a deep hole so that other animals can't dig her up. Then we'll put her in the ground, say a few words and cover her up. Will you help me?'

They nodded, still fascinated by the cat's rigidity. 'Will she flop again later?' demanded Tarquin.

'I suppose so. Howard, come out here a moment, would you?'

'She'll rot later,' said Torquil. 'The fur will start to smell and she'll fill up with gases and then ...'

'Shut up, you horrible ghoul!' said Howard sharply, cuffing Torquil gently round the ear. 'Can't you see you're upsetting Nikki?'

Torquil promptly dropped the dead cat and jumped away from Howard. 'You hit me!' he said furiously. 'How dare you hit me? No one's allowed to do that, no one at all. I'll tell my father and you'll be punished.'

Howard looked into the angry little face and was taken aback by the expression of fierce hatred. 'You're not in Egypt now, you know,' he said gently.

'That doesn't matter. You still can't hit me! Don't you know anything?'

'Do stop shouting,' pleaded Nicola. 'If you want to quarrel, go and do it somewhere else. I've got a headache as it is.'

'But he hit me!' continued Torquil, apparently unable to come to terms with the insult. 'My father will . . . '

'Your father's dead,' said Howard abruptly. 'You live in my house now, and you live by my rules. You were deliberately upsetting Nicola, that's why I slapped you. Now, shall we forget all about it and get on with burying poor old Lily?'

'Bury your stupid cat yourself!' shouted Torquil. 'I'm glad it's dead, and I wish we could bury you with it, so there!'

He turned and ran off, but surprisingly Tarquin remained behind. He'd already picked up the dead cat from where his twin had dropped it and now he started whispering to it as he softly stroked its furry back. Howard was quite touched.

'I'll go and get a box,' he said quickly, but it took longer than he expected and he was surprised to find Tarquin still talking to the cat when he returned. 'She can't hear you, you know,' he pointed out as he took Lily's body and put it inside the supermarket carton.

'Her Ka can still hear.'

'Her car?'

'Ka, that's spelt *ka* and it means spirit.'

'Is that so? I had no idea. Where do you want her put, Nicola?'

They settled for a spot under the farthest apple tree and when it was all over, Nicola put a daffodil bulb in the newly-turned earth. 'There, when that comes up in the spring we'll all remember Lily. Now, how about a cup of tea?'

'Will you get another cat?' asked Tarquin, who was becoming restless without his twin.

'I don't know.'

'A dog would be nice.'

'No dogs,' said Howard firmly. 'We've got enough to do around here without adding a dog.'

'Torquil and Tarquin like dogs.'

'*You're* Tarquin, aren't you?' queried Howard, watching Nicola hurry ahead of them into the house.

'No, not today. I'm Torquil today. Look, I've got a different badge on. See, it's an O.

'But you had an A on a moment ago. I saw it when you were bending over the ground.'

The small boy smiled a rare smile, put a hand in the pocket of his jeans, and slowly brought out another badge. 'I swopped just now!'

'You mustn't do that, it's confusing for everyone. Besides,' he added with an attempt at jocularity, 'if you've got both the badges, your poor brother can't be anyone!'

'We've got two badges each, stupid! And, anyway, he's me and I'm him. Your silly name badges don't mean anything. It's like putting a marmalade label on plum jam — it's still plum jam in the jar!'

Howard looked into the sharp, intelligent eyes and was touched by a flicker of fear. 'That's true, but you both have names, don't you? We're not trying to change that. We just want to get those names right.'

'I'm going in,' said the boy. 'I don't want to talk to you any more.'

Howard caught hold of his arm. 'Wait! We have to sort this thing out.'

'No we don't. We know who we are, but you won't listen! You're always trying to change everything round and we don't like that. Wait until Sergei comes. He'll stop you doing it.'

Howard let go of the boy and rubbed wearily at his eyes. 'I certainly hope he can put one or two things straight for us. Go on then, go and join your twin.'

'Your cat belongs to us now!' shouted the boy as he ran off. 'She's all ours, we've got her ka.'

'Much good may it do you,' muttered Howard. He'd found the entire conversation more than a little unnerving.

That night, when they went to bed, Howard tried to make love to Nicola again, but once more it ended almost before it had begun and left them both rather embarrassed with each other.

'Look, I honestly don't know what's the matter,' he said awkwardly.

'Neither do I,' said Nicola in a strained voice.

'Perhaps if we try again a bit later on?'

She shook her head. 'No thanks, once is more than enough at the moment. Honestly, I'd rather we didn't do it at all while this is happening.'

72

'That'll only make things worse! Perhaps I'd better go and see the doctor.'

'He'll probably suggest you think of other things, like all the shelves that need putting up, and the walls that need painting. Isn't that supposed to slow men down?'

'You're not being very helpful, Nikki.'

'I'm sorry but I don't feel very helpful. I really needed you tonight. It's been a horrible day and . . .'

'I know, I know. I'm sure it's got something to do with having the boys along the landing.'

'Surely that ought to make you impotent, not premature?'

'I'm so sorry, in that case I'll try to become impotent! I suppose it would cure the present problem, but it seems a little bit drastic.'

'I wasn't suggesting you should become impotent.'

'Well, that's what it sounded like.'

'Go to sleep, Howard. We're at your mother's tomorrow. I'll need all my strength for that.'

Howard turned his back on her and lay staring wide-eyed at the curtains as they moved gently across the surface of the open window. It made him think of summer, and gradually memories began to lull him to sleep. Then, at the last moment, just as he began to topple over the edge into sleep, a terrible ear-splitting yowling broke the silence of the night.

Howard jerked awake, his heart racing madly in his chest. Beside him, Nicola lay frozen with fright. 'What was it?' she whispered.

'It sounded a bit like a cat.'

'A cat?' She jumped out of bed and ran to the window, pulling back the curtain to stare out. 'Howard, there's something under the apple tree, right where we buried Lily. You don't think it's a fox trying to dig her up, do you?'

He groaned. 'Surely foxes don't yowl?'

'You'll have to go down and look,' she said tearfully. 'I can't bear to think of her being dragged off and eaten by a fox.'

'How can you possibly see what's going on?'

'It's a full moon tonight, there's loads of light.'

Howard thought that was typical of his luck as he pulled

73

on a dressing gown and pushed his feet into his slippers. 'OK. I'll go and check. You stay here.'

At the end of the landing he put his head quietly round the door of the twins' room. To his surprise they were sitting cross-legged on the end of one of the beds. Their eyes were shut and it looked almost as though they were praying.

'What's going on?' he demanded.

Their eyes snapped open and they turned their heads towards the door.

'What the hell are you doing?' he asked edgily. 'It's gone oneo'clock.'

'We heard ...'

'... a horrible noise.'

'We were ...

'... dreadfully frightened.'

They wrapped their arms round each other and shivered in mock terror.

'It was only a cat!' said Howard firmly, but they ignored that.

'We think ...'

'... it was Lily.

Howard's unease increased. He tried to push it away. 'Lily's dead. Dead cats don't scream in the night. I'm going to make sure it wasn't a fox trying to dig her up, and when I come back I want you two back under the covers.'

They didn't answer and he gripped the torch that he'd brought with him even more tightly as he fumbled with the bolts on the back door and crept out into the garden.

It looked most peculiar at night, the branches of the trees silhouetted against the sky like the outstretched arms of a skeleton. 'Pull yourself together,' he muttered under his breath. 'This is your own garden in Guildford, not a graveyard in Salem.'

As he approached Lily's grave he saw that some of the turned earth had been spread over the edge of the grass, and when he swung the torch directly on the freshly dug grave he realised that he was too late. The daffodil bulb lay on its side, the mud had been thrown everywhere and the cardboard box was open and empty.

He bent down and peered in. There were no teeth marks

on the lid of the box, just dozens of tiny scratches on the inside of it. He frowned, wondering how any animal could have scratched the inside of the box but not the outside. It made no sense at all, but whatever the explanation it was clear that Lily had gone.

'Dam!' he muttered furiously, wondering how on earth he was going to tell Nicola. 'Damn and blast the stupid cat!' Not that he was really angry at the cat, but he couldn't think who else to swear at. He'd been so sure that he'd dug deep enough too.

As he walked back down the garden path the soft mud squelched under the soles of his slippers and he had to take them off and wipe them on the metal grid by the patio doors. That done he picked them up and carried them, walking up the stairs in bare feet.

There was no sound from the boys' room and he could just make out the shape of their two heads close together on one pillow. Relieved that he didn't have to tell them anything, he continued along to the bedroom, and pushed open the door.

He fully expected Nicola to be standing at the open window, but amazingly she was fast asleep in bed. He could hear her even breathing as he crossed the room. As silently as possible he took off the dressing gown, pulled back the corner of the duvet − and found himself staring into the glassy eyes of a mud-covered Lily.

His scream shattered the silence of the house. Nicola gave a cry of alarm and shot upright. 'What is it? What's the matter?'

He couldn't speak. His teeth were chattering and he couldn't tear his gaze away from the stiff body of the cat. As he stared a tiny grub wriggled out of the corner of her mouth and dropped on to the cotton sheet beneath. With an inarticulate cry he wrenched the duvet further back.

'Get out!' he shouted at Nicola. 'Get out of the bed!'

She obeyed immediately, backing away towards the door with fear. 'What is it? What have you found?'

He put his hand to his mouth, trying to stop his teeth from chattering together. 'It's horrible,' he muttered, 'Just horrible.'

75

'What is?' Nicola was beginning to lose patience. Her throat was tight, her stomach churning, and all Howard could do was keep repeating that something was horrible. She decided to look for herself and walked round to his side of the bed.

'Don't!' He tried to push her away. 'Don't look, Nikki. It's too horrible. I'll deal with it. Just give me a moment.'

She caught hold of his outstretched hand and gripped it tightly. 'Tell me what it is!'

He shook his head.

Nicola let go of his hand and edged in front of him. For a moment she didn't speak and Howard braced himself for a scream, but when she turned to face him she didn't even look upset, instead there was a curious expression on her face.

'There's nothing there,' she said in a low voice. 'I can't see anything at all. You must have had a dream.'

Coming on top of everything else it was too much, and Howard lost his temper. 'Are you blind? Can't you recognise your own cat when you see it?'

'Do you mean Lily?' she asked nervously.

'How many cats do we have? Of course I mean Lily.'

'But Lily's dead.'

'I can see that. What I want to know is how a fox could carry her up to our bed without your hearing anything!'

He was still shaking all over and Nicola kept her voice low and reassuring. 'There's nothing there, Howard. Lily's buried in the garden. You've had a bad dream.'

'Don't talk to me as though I'm half-witted! Lily is *not* buried in the garden. If you remember I went out to check on her, and when I got there I could see that she'd been dug up. I'm amazed you didn't stay awake long enough to find out what had happened. You made enough fuss before I went.'

'Howard, you didn't go into the garden. It must have all been part of the dream.'

He pushed her roughly out of the way. 'Are you telling me that there isn't a dead cat in our bed? That . . .' He stopped. Nicola was right. The bed was empty, the sheet unmarked.

'But I saw it!' he shouted, his hand checking the bottom sheet. 'I even saw a grub crawl out of her mouth!'

76

'Howard, stop it!' Nicola was close to tears. 'That's a horrible thing to say.'

'It's what I saw, woman.'

'None of it happened,' she repeated more firmly.

'But I went outside. I took the torch and ... The boys saw me. They'll confirm it.'

'I'm not waking the boys to confirm a nightmare.'

He walked across the room and picked up his slippers. 'There, look at these.'

'What about them?'

'There's mud on the bottoms.'

'I can't see any.'

'That's because I wiped them thoroughly, but there *was* mud. I felt it squelching.'

'Well, if you did go, you must have been sleepwalking because I certainly didn't know anything about it. Now come back to bed.'

'Aren't you worried about the cat?'

'She's dead. What is there to worry about?'

'Didn't you hear what I said?' he shouted angrily. 'Something's dug her up.'

'Only in your dream.'

Howard went to the window and stared out at the garden. 'You'll be able to see from here. Come on, come and look.'

Nicola was becoming frightened, but in order to calm him down she obeyed. 'I can't see anything, Howard. It's pitch black out there,' she said nervously.

'The moon will be out in a minute. It must have gone behind a cloud.'

'There isn't any moon tonight. Howard, please come to bed. It's two o'clock in the morning.'

'There was a full moon and I saw Lily's empty box. Come along, we'll go out there together. Perhaps that will convince you.'

'This is ridiculous!' protested Nicola as she pulled on a robe and some old trainers. 'I don't want to go out and look. There's nothing I can do if she has gone. I just want to sleep.'

But Howard ignored her, half-dragging her through the

house, past the sleeping boys, down the stairs, out through the patio doors and across the damp grass. 'Right, see for yourself,' he instructed, shining the torch on the ground, but the mud was undisturbed, and the daffodil bulb still safely in the ground.

He didn't know what to say. Wordlessly he let Nicola lead him back indoors, then sat by the kitchen table as she made him a cup of tea, putting in plenty of sugar. 'It doesn't matter,' she said at last. 'Lots of people have vivid nightmares. Perhaps it was the cheese you had for supper.'

He didn't answer because there was no point. No point in reminding her that he usually had cheese for supper, and no point in telling her that he still didn't believe it was a nightmare. He didn't know what had happened, or how, but he thought he knew why. It was revenge, and the perpetrators of the revenge were upstairs asleep at that very moment. He wouldn't tell anyone of course, because they'd say he was mad; but he knew that he wasn't. He was absolutely sane. But there was something wrong with the twins. Something dark and horrible, and he knew that he must find out what it was and learn to protect himself and Nicola from it.

'Better?' she asked with a smile.

He looked into her anxious and loving eyes and was dreadfully afraid for her. 'I'm fine,' he said after a moment's hesitation. 'Like you say, it must have been the cheese.'

Hand in hand they went up the stairs to bed again, and in the small single bed Labib's young sons wrapped their arms round each other, made small sounds of contentment and dreamt their own, special dreams.

Chapter Six

They all woke late the next morning, and in the general rush
to get ready to go to Howard's parents for lunch there was
no time for Nicola to talk about the events of the night, but
Howard's pallor and dark circles beneath his eyes told their
own story.

More worried than she liked to admit, Nicola didn't feel
in the least ready for coping with the twins all day but for
once their behaviour was impeccable. They ate all their food,
remembered to say please and thank you, and let Howard's
brothers take them to the nearby park for a game of football
while their father escaped thankfully to his golf club. Nicola
wasn't sorry. She liked her father-in-law but sensed that he
was finding it difficult to take to the twins.

'Aren't you playing, dear?' asked Howard's mother.

'I've twisted my knee,' Howard lied.

'What a shame.' She turned to Nicola who was getting
cold standing watching the others rush around. 'You must
be so proud of them, Nikki darling. They're such beautiful
boys.'

'Do you think so?'

'Of course, and polite with it. Not like Julia's grandchildren. They're absolutely undisciplined. She says that
visits from them leave her exhausted for a week. I suppose
your brother-in-law was a strict disciplinarian.'

'I don't think so. They aren't usually this well-behaved.'

'I'm sure they are! At least you've got something to remind
you of your sister. It must be a comfort.'

Nicola shrugged. 'I can't see anything of Rose in them.

They're all Labib. Faces, gestures, attitude . . . it's Labib they resemble. Rose was so gentle, and so anxious to please. I find it difficult to believe the boys belong to her at all.' She bit her lip, surprised to find she was on the verge of tears.

Howard, who'd been listening to the conversation, moved away. He was exhausted by the shocks of the night and felt quite unable to join in any paean of praise concerning the boys.

He watched his eldest brother Benjamin come off the worse from a very physical tackle with one of the twins and shouted out some encouragement. 'Don't give up, Ben! Chase after it, you lazy devil!'

Benjamin looked over and laughed. 'They're too rough for me. Want a go?'

'No thanks, damaged knee!'

'Very wise. Christ, that hurt!' Ben spun round to find that one of the twins had run up behind him and kicked him on the achilles tendon. 'What did you do that for?' he demanded.

'Sorry, I thought I saw the ball.'

'The ball's up the other end!' said Ben crossly.

'It was a mistake, keep your hair on.'

Ben, who was beginning to suffer from a receding hairline, felt very put out indeed and limped across to join his brother. 'I don't know which one that was but he's got a mean kick on him.'

'Wasn't he wearing a badge?'

'Yes, two in fact.'

'In that case I've no idea.'

Ben rubbed at his leg. 'It's quite eerie the way they're so alike, isn't it?'

'Pretty spooky. Ben, I've got a chance of a posting in Belgium.'

'That's wonderful! I bet Nikki's thrilled.'

'Well, not really. She doesn't want to uproot the boys again.'

'They'll be all right, won't they? They seem quite self-confident.'

'I suppose so. Only, I think we might be safer here, where we know people and have got relatives around us.'

'Safer? What the hell do you mean, safer?' asked Ben in concern.

Howard turned his head towards him. 'Did I say safer? I meant better off. We can get help with babysitting and things over here. There we'd have to start from scratch, and good friends aren't made that easily.'

'You'd be mad not to go. It's what you've always wanted.'

'I'll think about it a bit longer. Don't mention it to Mother.'

'Don't mention what to Mother?' asked Nicola, coming across to join them.

'The move to Belgium. Shall we go back now? I'm cold.'

'I hope Howard isn't coming down with anything,' said his mother anxiously when they said their goodbyes. 'I've never seen him looking so peaky.'

'He's having trouble sleeping,' explained Nicola.

'Are you going to give Nana a kiss?' asked Howard's mother eagerly. Nicola looked at their shuttered faces and waited for the refusal.

'Of course ...'

'... we will.'

'We like kissing Nana!'

'So sweet!' enthused the older woman as the boys climbed into the car. 'I adore it when they share their words like that. I could just hug them to death.'

'Me too,' muttered Howard under his breath, and then the car was pulling away and the visit was over without any disasters occurring.

'You were very good today,' said Nicola when she tucked them into bed. 'It was a pleasure taking you out.'

'Sergei comes tomorrow,' said Tarquin, struggling to take off a sock.

'That's right. Is that why you were good?'

'Yep. He'll be surprised that I can dress myself.'

'There's more to dressing than socks and pants!'

'Well, I can dress myself a little bit.'

'I suppose, between you, you could just about dress a whole person!' she laughed. They looked at her in some confusion. 'Well, you do the top bits, don't you, Torquil? The shirt and jumper. And Tarquin does the underclothes — that makes one person dressed.'

'*Yes, me*!' they chorused.

'All right, we're not starting that again. Now close your eyes and off to sleep with you. Tomorrow will be an exciting day.'

'Are you excited?' asked Tarquin, fixing her with a penetrating stare.

'I'm happy for you both.'

'Aren't you a bit fizzy inside?'

She was, but she had no intention of admitting it. 'Of course not. I'm far too old to fizz! God bless.'

They both blinked and put a hand to their chest.

'What's the matter?'

'Nothing,' said Torquil quickly. 'We had a burp stuck. 'Night 'night.'

Nicola frowned and turned off their light, wondering why they'd both made the same movement at exactly the same second.

'Shall we have an early night?' she suggested to Howard after she'd laid the breakfast table for the morning.

'I thought you didn't want to start sex any more?'

'I meant to sleep! We hardly had any sleep last night, I'm exhausted.'

'I'm all right.'

'You don't look it. Your mother was quite worried about you.'

'When isn't she worrying over one or other of us?'

'Howard, that's not fair. She's a good mother, and I'm very fond of her.'

'Her judgement's not too hot. She seemed to think the twins were angels from heaven.'

'She's just proud to have grandchildren to show off to her friend Julia.'

'Knowing how prejudiced she is I'm surprised she's willing to call them grandchildren. After all, they're foreign.'

'She probably thinks they're better than nothing!'

'I suppose you're looking forward to seeing your handsome Russian again,' he said acidly as they were climbing into bed.

'Of course I am. I want him to help us with the boys.'

'Just make sure that's all he helps you with,' said Howard irritably.

Nicola knew why he was worried and tried to ease his fear. 'Don't be silly. What chance will I have of misbehaving with the boys around?'

'I notice you don't say you wouldn't like to if you had the chance.'

'Oh, for goodness' sake, stop being so childish! Goodnight, Howard.'

She was soon asleep, and despite his anxiety Howard too was quickly in the land of dreams, and this time the night passed peacefully, so that by morning he felt almost human again.

'I'll try and be home early,' he promised as he left the house after breakfast. 'Hold dinner for me if you can.'

'What time do you call early?' asked Nicola.

'Six-thirty to seven, OK?'

'Fine. Have we got any decent wine?'

Howard grinned. 'He's worth a good wine, is he? There's a decent white Bordeaux in the cellar. That should be good enough.'

Nicola watched him drive off and then began whisking round the house, hastily straightening cushions and putting away toys, papers and magazines. It wasn't a job that she liked, and but for Sergei's visit she probably wouldn't have bothered this morning.

When the downstairs rooms were straight she took the hoover and polish up to the guest room and began cleaning that. The sound of the vacuum cleaner woke the boys who came in sleepily.

'Is he here yet?' asked Tarquin, glancing round the room as though expecting to find him lurking in one of the corners.

'I told you, not until lunch-time. Mind out of the way, I want to hoover there.'

'Why are you doing housework? Where's your servant?'

'You know I don't have any servants!'

'Not even to get things right for Sergei?' asked Tarquin in surprise.

83

'Not for anyone. If you get out the clothes you want, I'll help you get dressed as soon as I've finished.'

'The clothes I want to wear . . .'

'. . . are in the dirty clothes basket.'

Nicola sighed and switched off the cleaner. 'What clothes are they?'

'My tracksuit,' they said together.

'They'll be going in the washing machine this morning. If I tumble them dry you can have them before Sergei arrives.'

'Why don't you . . .'

'. . . use a laundry?'

'Laundries are expensive and lose your clothes. Anyway, with a washing machine and tumble dryer I don't think I should need a laundry.'

'Mummy always . . .'

'. . . used a laundry.'

'I'm sure it was a great help to her. Now mind out or I'll never get done. Do you think Sergei would like some flowers in his bedroom? And don't split your answer between you, please.'

Torquil shook his head. 'I don't think he'll want flowers. He isn't a lady.'

'OK. No flowers by request.'

She switched the cleaner back on and after a moment the twins left. When she'd finished and joined them in the bedroom, they were sitting on the edge of one of the beds arguing over their badges.

'I don't want it!' shouted one angrily. 'I had it yesterday *and* the day before that. I want the other one now.'

His twin snatched a badge out of his hand and clutched it tightly. 'It's mine. Sergei said it was mine. He *told* you that on the phone. We've got to do what he said.'

Nicola walked briskly into the room. 'I'm relieved to hear you intend to do what someone says. Now stop being silly and put your badges on the bed. I'll pin them on once you're dressed. Come along, take off your pyjama jackets.'

She dressed them quickly, then picked up the badges and put one in each hand. 'Right, now which one of you is Tarquin?'

'Me!' They both shouted.

'If you don't tell me the truth, neither of you will be allowed to stay up for dinner tonight.'

They looked anxiously at each other, put their heads together, whispered urgently and then turned back to her.

'I'm Tarquin,' said one of them, reaching out for his badge.

Nicola felt uneasy about this charade they continued to play out so frequently. 'You really are Tarquin, are you?' she asked, watching him closely. 'This isn't a trick?'

He looked very irritated. 'I've just said I am!'

'But is it true?'

He pursed his lips and made a soft growling sound deep in his throat. Torquil leant towards her. 'He doesn't mind being Tarquin really, but when you nag it makes us quite cross.'

'I get quite cross when you two start being so stupid. Never mind, if he says he's Tarquin then he gets the A. Why should it matter to me if it doesn't matter to you?'

She was astonished when they both started to clap. 'You understand?' said Torquil delightedly. 'Now we won't have to ask Sergei to tell you. That's nice!'

They were so obviously thrilled that she wished she deserved their praise. 'I think you two should be part of an exam for child psychologists!' she exclaimed as they jumped up and down in front of her. 'Not many would qualify though. Now, can you keep yourselves busy for the rest of the morning? Your bedroom's a disgrace.'

'Of course we can,' smiled Tarquin. 'Will Sergei bring the sun with him?' he added hopefully.

'I doubt it. Off you go then. I've left the cereal on the table and the milk's in the jug in the fridge. Don't take too much, the milkman hasn't been yet.'

It was nearly twelve o'clock before the house was straight enough to satisfy Nicola. Once she was sure the boys were all right, she decided to ring Melanie.

'Mel? It's me, Nikki. Listen, the gorgeous Russian arrives any minute and Howard and I wondered if you and Robert would like to come over to dinner on Saturday evening. It will just be Sergei and you two, but we thought it would be nice for him to meet some of our closest friends; to reassure him the twins are mixing with nice people!'

85

'Well . . .' Melanie sounded doubtful.

'The boys will be in bed,' promised Nicola.

'In that case, we'd love to come. It's not that the twins are badly behaved or anything, but they make me feel unseasy. Just being around them sets me on edge. Ever since our trip to the pool I've felt funny when they're near.'

'They weren't near us in the swimming pool, Mel!'

'I know I'm being stupid but it's how I feel. Perhaps I'm going mad,' she suggested lightly. 'Can you get Alzheimer's disease at twenty-four?'

'I've no idea. It's more likely to be all that chocolate you eat.'

'I've cut down!' protested Melanie. 'Robert read that scientists fed chocolate to laboratory rats four times a day and after six months they . . .'

'Mel, scientists can make rats do anything they like in laboratories. Let's face it, they probably had more chocolate in those few weeks than any human being has ever consumed in a lifetime.'

'But they went mad and started attacking each other.'

'If you turn on Robert, let me know. I'll come and applaud!'

Melanie giggled. 'I do stand up to him sometimes, you know, but he works so hard that I don't like to add to his stress.'

'Tell me the old, old story. So you will come on Saturday?'

'Try and stop me! I hope he's as terrific as you claim.'

'So do I. Since I've only seen him the once I could be in for quite a disappointment. God, that's a car. I'll have to go. See you Saturday, if not before.'

'He's here!' shouted the twins, running to the front door and tugging on the iron ring. 'Open up, door. Sergei's here!'

'I feel we should have trumpeters lining the drive,' laughed Nicola, opening the door for them.

'He won't mind,' Tarquin assured her. 'He knows he isn't so important over here.'

'I *am* relieved. Steady on, you'll hurt yourselves on the gravel.' But they didn't hear and raced away.

Nicola stayed by the front door and felt a lump fill her throat as they reached Sergei and he bent to pick them up, settling one in the crook of each arm and kissing the tops of their heads as they made small sounds of excitement.

Then he looked up the drive to where Nicola was waiting. Her first thought was that Melanie wouldn't be disappointed. He was, if anything, even more attractive than she'd remembered and as their eyes met she felt a sharp tugging sensation in her solar plexus.

For what seemed an eternity he kept his eyes locked with hers, then his long lashes swept down as he blinked and broke the spell. Released, Nicola moved towards him and held out a hand.

'It's lovely to see you again. The twins are beside themselves with excitement. How was the flight?'

'Quite boring as usual.' His fingers tightened on hers and her whole arm began to tingle. 'This is a very nice house,' he remarked, glancing up at the creeper-covered walls. 'It's extremely picturesque.'

'We're fond of it. Neither of us is keen on modern houses. They haven't any soul.'

'Come and see our playroom,' said Tarquin. 'It's a super place, we've got our toys in there.'

It was the first time either of the boys had expressed any opinion on their room and Nicola was delighted that they liked it.

'We've got a good bedroom too,' added Torquil. 'It's only little but the beds are neat!'

'Actually it's quite large,' Nicola assured him.

Sergei looked thoughtfully at her. 'Don't worry, I didn't think they were in a boxroom.'

'Well, no but ...'

'They're very lucky to have such a nice home.' His mouth smiled while his eyes searched hers as though looking for a message, and not about the house.

She had never been so affected by the physical presence of any man before, and deliberately moved to the other side of the room, trying to put distance between them. 'I'm sure the boys have loads to tell you,' she said brightly. 'Perhaps you'd like some soup and rolls and then they can take you to their playroom and ...'

'I'm not hungry, thank you.'

She bit her lip. 'In that case, perhaps you'd like to see your room? Just follow me, it's ...'

He moved forward and put a hand on her shoulder. The skin beneath her jumper began to burn and she turned her head sharply towards him. 'The boys can show me,' he said easily.

Nicola continued to face him, fascinated by his silken skin that made such a constrast with the five o'clock shadow round his jaw line. His mouth was unusually full, definitely the mouth of a sensualist, and almost buried in the right-hand corner there was a tiny dimple that she suddenly had an urgent desire to kiss.

Very slowly he lifted his left hand and laid a finger on her lips as he whispered a word she'd never heard before. She waited, watching the pupils of his eyes dilate and darken as she swayed towards him.

'Come on!' shouted one of the boys. 'Come and see your room.'

The spell was broken. Sergei lifted his head and looked over to the boys. 'I'm just coming.'

With the eye contact gone, Nicola realised that she'd been holding her breath and released it with a soft gasp, then waited as the room spun crazily. Sergei gave her a small nod of approval, smiled briefly and then went after the boys.

Once she was alone she sat down on a chair and tried to pull herself together. 'This is quite ridiculous,' she muttered fiercely. 'Just because he's young and handsome it is no reason to behave like a lovesick teenager.' She tried to conjure up a picture of Howard, but Howard's features refused to be summoned.

Deciding that keeping busy was the answer she resolutely turned her attention to warming the soup that Sergei didn't even want, but all the time she was listening out for his voice and her stomach continued jumping and lurching in a most peculiar fashion, as though it thought she was on a big dipper at a funfair rather than standing in her own kitchen.

She was the only one who ate any lunch, sitting alone at the kitchen table while Tarquin and Torquil chattered non-stop to Sergei in the playroom. She could hear them, but none of the words meant anything as they conversed all the time in rapid Arabic.

Occasionally during the afternoon she went in to ask them if they wanted drinks or biscuits, and every time the twins glared at her as though she were an intruder while Sergei's eyes travelled over her approvingly. Although he said little and smiled not at all she knew that she wasn't mistaken. He found her as attractive as she found him.

Howard arrived home at five past six, earlier than at any time since the twins' arrival. He and the Russian greeted each other coolly, Howard with the reserved politeness that was the hallmark of most Englishmen.

While he dispensed pre-dinner drinks and the men discussed the situation in the Middle East, Nicola supervised the boys as they changed into smart navy trousers and blue and white striped shirts that they'd bought with them from Egypt.

'You two look very handsome,' she complimented them. 'You'll break a few hearts when you're older.'

'Like Sergei?' asked Torquil, glancing at her out of the corner of his eye.

'Yes, in a way.'

After that she had a quick shower and then rifled through her wardrobe trying to decide what to wear. Finally settling on a pair of black velvet culottes and a pale lilac blouse, she stood in front of the mirror and tried to study herself dispassionately.

It was her hair that was her one claim to glory. Thick, wavy and a glorious shade of deep auburn it always attracted attention, and she was fortunate because her cream complexion was unblemished by freckles, the curse of so many women with red hair.

She studied her face thoughtfully. Her eyes were all right — brown with tawny flecks, they were at their best when she was vivacious, shining with warmth and intelligence. In repose they were just brown eyes. As for her mouth, that had never pleased her. Her top lip was too small, and her teeth although white enough were uneven. Rose's teeth had been perfect, like two rows of pearls, and that had always seemed unfair to Nicola when they were young.

'Never mind, you'll do,' she told her reflection, and bent closer to outline the bottom of her eyes with a green pencil. Then she put on plenty of mascara for emphasis and sprayed herself with a bottle of Venice perfume that Howard had brought back for her from Italy.

'What's going on in here? Are you having a facelift or something?' enquired Howard from the doorway.

Nicola spun round. 'Have I been a long time? Sorry. I had to change the boys first.'

'They've been down for ages. I'm absolutely starving.'

'I won't be a minute.'

'He's here for the boys,' Howard reminded her. 'There's no need to dress to kill.'

'I'm not. I've had this blouse for ages.'

'I don't remember seeing the culottes before.'

'Well, no, they are new. At least, I've had them some time but there hasn't been an occasion to wear them.'

'We do have people to dinner quite regularly. How come the Russian deserves the culottes?'

Nicola felt a rush of irritation. 'Do go away, Howard. Does it matter that much what I wear?'

'Not as much to me as it does to you, by the look of it.'

When she went into the lounge a few minutes later, Sergei jumped up from the settee and waited for her to sit down.

'It's all right, I've got to dish up in a minute,' she said with a smile. 'Howard, do you think I could have a dry sherry?'

'You look most attractive,' said Sergei, giving her an appreciative glance. 'I was told that English women have no dress sense. It's obviously not true.'

Howard snorted and handed her a glass of sherry. 'Nicola spends a fortune on clothes. If she couldn't manage to find something suitable for a quiet meal at home it would be astounding.'

'How ungallant,' said the Russian, glancing disdainfully at Howard.

'That's me, an ungallant Englishman. What's for dinner then? Borscht?'

90

'Steak casseroled in red wine, jacket potatoes and a green salad.'

Howard turned to Sergei. 'Since the boys arrived we have green salad with everything.' Sergei didn't respond. 'Don't they like anything else?'

'As far as I'm aware they eat almost everything.'

'Well, not here.'

The twins were playing with toy cars on the carpet. 'That's because the vegetables are all mushy,' explained Tarquin. 'We like them crisp.'

'I'm afraid it's Howard who likes watery vegetables,' said Nicola gleefully. 'Years of his mother's cooking had that effect on all her children. They probably think that's what they're like in the shop!'

Sergei drank steadily through the meal, consuming more than his share of the two bottles of white Bordeaux before moving on to brandy without any apparent effect.

Howard, who'd given up trying to match him early on but had still drunk more than usual, watched in some irritation.

'I suppose you can't drink at home,' he was saying as Nicola returned from putting the boys to bed.

'Why do you say that?'

'I understood alcohol was banned in Muslim countries.'

'Egypt isn't quite as strict as other places. Alcohol is readily available.'

'Labib never drank.'

Sergei raised his eyebrows. 'He drank in his own home. It was his wife who was teetotal.'

Nicola poured herself some Cointreau on ice and settled into an armchair. 'Really? But Rose used to enjoy a drink. When we were young we used to spend hours in this super wine bar and once she drank ...'

'I think she was afraid of losing control of herself,' he explained. 'She had a very tight personality.'

Howard laughed. 'Tight usually means drunk, or half-cut.'

'Tight means tight,' said the Russian flatly. 'A tightly enclosed person, not at all relaxed and outgoing. She was not like her sister in this respect.' He smiled intimately at Nicola who smiled back at him.

91

'Nicola certainly isn't teetotal,' agreed Howard. 'If she was cast away on a desert island she'd need a few crates of dry white wine to sustain her.'

Nicola leant forward in the chair. 'Sergei, would you say Rose was happy in Egypt?'

His fingers stroked the stem of his glass. Nicola watched the movement and tried to imagine what it would feel like to have him caress her in the same way.

'I think so,' he said slowly. 'As far as I could tell, but I didn't know her very well. It was Labib I was close to.'

'And the children,' said Nicola.

'The children too, of course.'

'Are you a doctor?' asked Howard.

'No, not at all. I'm a scientist. My work lies in the field of research.'

'Medical research?'

Sergei frowned, as though he found Howard's questions intrusive. 'In a way,' he conceded.

'Well, if it wasn't medical I don't see how it could have had anything to do with Labib.'

'Howard!' exclaimed Nicola. 'You sound as though you're cross-examining Sergei.'

'Just interested. We know next to nothing about what went on in Cairo,' he explained to the Russian. 'It's only natural we're curious. It helps to understand the boys.'

Sergei nodded. 'Of course.'

'So how come you're close to the boys?'

'I lived in their home. I was Labib's guest. He made me one of the family.'

'When did you move to Egypt?' asked Howard, reluctantly passing the brandy back to their visitor.

'It was early in 1987. Things were changing at home. Mikhail Gorbachev had altered the way of things and money for my kind of work became short. Grants were withdrawn, funding ceased. I was fortunate enough to meet Labib at a medical convention in Cairo and we got along well together. He invited me to join his team and I accepted.'

'But he was a surgeon. How could you fit into a medical team?'

Sergei's lips lifted into a smile that was suspiciously like

92

a sneer. 'He was far more than a surgeon. He was a man of great vision. He had just started an innovative research project with his own money and my particular abilities were useful to him. Naturally I wasn't required to cut up any bodies, alive or dead!'

He laughed quietly to himself, but Howard remained resolutely unamused.

'Why didn't the boys go to a proper school?' he asked abruptly.

'Howard, we've got plenty of time to talk about this another day,' said Nicola reprovingly. 'Poor Sergei must be exhausted.'

He rose gracefully to his feet and looked down at her, a tall handsome man who was turning her world upside down. 'I am a little tired. If you would excuse me now? In the morning I shall be fully refreshed. We must talk more then.'

'I'm at work in the morning,' Howard pointed out.

'I think I know the problems with the boys rather better than you,' said Nicola quietly. 'I'll talk to Sergei about the school.'

'Are you sure you wouldn't like to take the brandy up with you?' Howard enquired sarcastically.

Nicola glanced at him in amazement. It was totally out of character for him to be so rude to anyone, let alone a man who was a guest in their own home. Fortunately Sergei didn't appear to notice he was being insulted.

'Thank you, no. I'm sure I'll fall asleep straight away. Goodnight, Nicola, and my thanks again for a delicious meal and a most hospitable welcome.'

'He made it sound as though you flung yourself on him the moment he arrived,' commented Howard as they loaded the glasses into the dishwasher. 'I suppose you didn't?'

'Of course not. You were really rude to him just now. It was unforgivable.'

'I'm afraid I don't like him.'

'You made that very clear.'

'No clearer than you made your admiration. You hardly took your eyes off him all the evening. That probably made him pretty uncomfortable. He must be years younger than you.'

'Of course he isn't! Honestly, Howard, you do say some stupid things sometimes.'

'How do you know? Have you asked him?'

'No I haven't. I'm going up to bed.'

'You could always look in on him, check there wasn't anything he needed.'

'If I go in to him, I'm more likely to go for something I need!' she said sharply.

Howard went very white and stared at her. 'That is a very unpleasant remark indeed, Nicola.'

'Not as unpleasant as what you've been suggesting.'

'It's a greal deal more unpleasant than anything I'm ever likely to say.'

She looked objectively at him and found herself wondering why she'd ever chosen to marry him. Compared to Sergei Cheparukhin he was so ordinary. He kept his mid-brown hair short, his face was over-long and angular but without any suggestion of high cheekbones, and his eyes were too small.

'What are you looking at me like that for?' he asked uneasily.

Nicola realised that he wasn't just ordinary, he was actually unattractive. She mentally put his glasses on him and then discarded them — the bookish image was no more appealing. She also noticed that his hairline was receding very slightly, not much yet, but no doubt in time he'd be as bald as his father. Compared with Sergei's thick mop of hair he was already thin on top. Certainly she had no desire to run her fingers through Howard's hair.

'What is it? Have I grown a third eye or something?'

'You haven't grown anything,' she said with some asperity. 'All you've done is shed some hair.'

'Shed what?'

Suddenly she just wanted to get away from him. 'Do take that stupid expression off your face,' she said irritably. 'And hurry up with the dishwasher. I want to get to sleep.'

At least she would have Sergei to herself the next day, she thought gratefully as she took off her clothes. Perhaps they could go out somewhere with the boys if the weather was fine. It would be easier to talk outside the house. She didn't want

94

to end up sounding as though she were quizzing him too.

'We'll go to the animal park,' she said aloud, and then stood in front of the mirror again, but this time totally nude.

She was quite pleased with what she saw. At least her breasts were good, full and with no hint of a sag. Her waist was acceptable as well, slender enough to let her wear her dresses belted, but she wasn't quite so keen on her hips. They were a little too rounded, and when she viewed herself from the side there was the suggestion of a sag round the cheeks of her bottom.

She turned face on again and ran her hands down her body, watching her nipples harden in the cool air. The touch of lips on her shoulder made her jump. She hadn't heard Howard come in, hadn't even seen him in the mirror ... The full implication of this hit her like a blow. She spun round and gazed at an empty room. So much for the power of suggestion, she thought shakily, but then she heard a sigh and felt the touch of gentle warm air on the nape of her neck. Soft lips nuzzled at the individual vertebrae of her spine, working their way slowly towards her waist. Her flesh leapt as her head jerked backwards in response. It was gentle and sensuous, sending the blood coursing through her and she felt a throbbing right at the core of her as her own breath quickened.

'You'll catch pneumonia standing there with the window open,' said Howard curtly, shutting the door with a bang. 'I thought you were tired.'

The sensations vanished, leaving Nicola trembling, confused, and suddenly cold. 'Did you have to make me jump like that?' she demanded irritably.

'I hardly tiptoed along the landing. You were miles away, busy admiring yourself in the mirror. Why not get the handsome Russian to come and have a look? I'm sure he'd appreciate it. He's probably done quite a bit of research among young Egyptian women. You could show him a bit of English pallor to contrast with those dusky maidens.'

'For God's sake shut up about Sergei, will you!' she snapped,then pulled on her nightdress and drew the duvet up over her head. Howard wasn't just ugly, he was a bore as well

95

she told herself furiously, and it was only much later, when she was about to fall asleep, that she felt ashamed of herself because she knew that really Howard was nice-looking, clever and witty, and that until she set eyes on the Russian she'd never felt any discontent with him at all.

'He's as disruptive in his own way as the twins,' she thought sleepily, but unfortunately by morning the thought had slipped away from her and she was once again caught up in Sergei Cheparukhin's calculated net of seduction.

Chapter Seven

'At least it isn't raining,' said Nicola cheerfully as the twins pulled on their anoraks and gloves.

'It's very cold,' complained Tarquin. 'At home it's never cold like this. It's always bright and hot. When can we go home again?'

'This is your home now,' Nicola reminded him, glancing at Sergei for support but he was looking out of the kitchen window, his thoughts miles away.

'It isn't!' exclaimed Torquil. 'We're just staying here until things get better.'

Sergei turned away from the window and held out his hands. 'Come on, boys. Let's go for our walk.'

Nicola was relieved that they caught hold of his hands so willingly. When going out with her or Howard they always hung back from physical contact. 'Haven't you brought a jacket?' she asked the Russian. 'It's bound to be chilly on the Downs. The wind's cool today.'

'I won't be cold.'

It wasn't long before the children ran on ahead of them, chasing each other boisterously and shouting as they went.

'They look well,' commented Sergei. 'Has it been a difficult time for them?'

Nicola sighed. 'Yes, but it's been even more difficult for us.'

He put his hands in the pockets of his jeans and slowed his pace to hers. 'In what way?'

'In lots of ways. I suppose the worst thing has been trying

to cope with their continuing inability to grasp the importance of separate identities.'

'Didn't that improve after I talked to them on the phone?'

'For a time, but they were still only pretending to be two different people. Did you notice their badges, the A and the O?'

'Yes.'

'Well, they were to help the school work out which was which. A for Tarquin, O for Torquil, but although it seemed a good idea I found out that they swapped the badges around. In the mornings they took it in turns to be Tarquin and Torquil!'

He stared ahead to where the twins were wrestling on the edge of the path. 'If you were six years old and an identical twin, don't you think you might enjoy swapping identities now and again? Just for fun?'

'I don't think they are doing it for fun. I think they're doing it because they genuinely don't know which one of them's which.'

The path began to climb sharply and Sergei put out a hand to help her. As soon as she put her hand in his, her heart did a somersault and ended up in her throat where it threatened to choke her. His fingers squeezed hers slightly and he glanced sideways at her, assessing her reaction.

'I'm all right, thanks!' she said breathlessly. 'I've done this walk masses of times and Howard never helps me!'

'As you like.' He gave a small smile.

'Well, do they?' she persisted, the skin on the palm of her hand burning where he'd touched it.

'Do they what?'

'Know who they are?'

'They don't think it matters very much. When Labib was alive he didn't force the issue. He understood that together they feel more complete, more able to cope with the world. When they're a little older they'll separate of their own accord. For the moment it's probably kinder to let them be.'

'But they aren't one person, they're two, and the more they refuse to face this, the more confused they'll become. A strong sense of identity is very important to a child. Believe me, I know this from experience.'

Sergei raised his eyebrows and his forehead creased, giving him a prematurely aged look. 'Of course, I forgot, you're an expert.' He made it sound trivial and amusing, as though she'd just reminded him that she was a Bingo caller. His tone annoyed her.

'Yes, I am, and a good one too. I think I'm more qualified to judge their mental health than you are.'

'Naturally, but Labib was their father.'

'Labib was a very headstrong man who always thought he was right.'

Sergei smiled. 'Such indignation! Whenever he spoke about you he was highly complimentary. He found you stimulating company.'

'We couldn't stay in the same room for five minutes without arguing; if that's stimulating company then he was right.'

Nicola stopped to look about her, still annoyed that she didn't seem to be making any progress with the Russian, and even more annoyed with herself for being so ridiculously aware of his physical presence all the time.

'If it worries you so much then use their second names at home. They'll respond to them well enough. But only at home.'

She looked at him in surprise. 'What are their second names.'

'Alpha and Omega.'

Nicola looked ahead to where the boys were shooting each other with pieces of wood. 'Alpha and Omega?' She felt uncomfortable, as though she was failing to understand something very important.

'That's right. That's probably why they accepted the badges quite happily, but they don't associate the letters with their first names.'

'Why did Labib and Rose give them such peculiar names?'

Sergei shrugged. 'Perhaps because Labib knew there wouldn't be any more children. They're both the beginning and the end.'

Nicola shivered. 'I think it's weird, and it doesn't help

99

either. All right, so they know who they are, but Alpha and Omega are all part of a whole, aren't they? As you say, the beginning and the end, neither is complete without the other.'

'You're making it more complicated than it is.'

'Perhaps,' she said doubtfully.

He put an arm round her shoulders. 'You worry about things too much. The boys are fine. Their lives are already mapped out for them, it really doesn't matter too much what you do. They'll survive anyway.'

His arm felt extremely strong and protective but at the same time something in her withdrew from the sense of power that flowed through him. It made her feel too helpless and she began to walk ahead of him. 'I take it you believe in destiny?' she asked with a laugh.

'Certainly I believe that our death is predestined; it's within us from the moment we're born and there's nothing we can do to change it.'

'How depressing! What's the point in eating all the right foods and avoiding smoking then?'

'There's no point at all. If you were meant to die of lung cancer then you would smoke. If you're meant to die of heart disease, die you will, whatever you eat. No one talks more nonsense than the medical profession. Look back over the years and see how they contradict themselves from generation to generation, and meantime nothing changes. People continue to die of the same diseases, regardless of what the medical profession says.'

'I don't think that's true. We know a lot more now, and we're beginning to learn to take more responsibility for our own health.'

'The only difference that makes is that when someone becomes terminally ill they've got the added burden of guilt.'

Nicola felt irritated. 'You're wrong, but I'm not going to spend the morning arguing about it with you.'

He caught up with her and turned her towards him. 'I didn't mean to annoy you. We all have different beliefs, that's all I meant to say.'

'You depressed me,' she admitted. 'Suddenly everything

100

seemed pointless. It was as though you were trying to take away hope.'

He reached out and touched her gently on the cheek. 'You're beautiful, Nicola, really beautiful. I hope Howard appreciates you.'

'Of course he does!' She smiled brightly. 'He appreciates me despite my faults.'

'And what are they?'

'I'm inclined to be bossy, and when I'm over-tired I get extremely unreasonable and expect everyone to do what I want before I've even had time to tell them. There! Now you know.'

'I don't think you're happy,' he said quietly. 'I could make you happy.'

'Don't be silly,' she said briskly, her legs turning to jelly as she sternly reminded herself that she was a happily married woman.

'I could make you happy in ways you've never even imagined,' he told her, his eyes locked on to hers.

'If you really want to make me happy then perhaps you can explain why the boys produce such disturbed drawings in art lessons.'

For a moment he looked angry, and she thought he was going to walk away without answering but then his face regained its more customary tranquil expression. 'What do you mean?'

Nicola told him.

By the time she'd finished there was a fine drizzle and she thought that Sergei, who was only wearing a short-sleeved shirt, must be frozen but he seemed oblivious to the weather.

'Why are you so worried?' he asked thoughtfully.

'Because they're obviously very disturbed. They must have either seen or experienced things that they shouldn't have done, and it's worrying them. They ...'

'Do you mean sexual experiences? Is that what's bothering you?'

She saw that he was smiling and felt extremely annoyed. 'Yes, that's what's bothering me, as it ought to bother you.'

'You're quite wrong, Nicola, it isn't sexual at all. They're

101

only copying drawings that they've seen at exhibitions and on the walls of tombs.'

'I didn't see any scarab beetles or pharoes, just these deformed creatures mutilating bodies all over the place.'

'You sound so disapproving! Not every country's history can be depicted with nothing more troubling than an arrow through a king's eye! These are pagan gods the twins are drawing. You must make allowances for warmer blood flowing through Egyptian veins!' He laughed deep in his throat.

'Are you sure that's what the drawings were?'

'I'll show you. Alpha! Omega! Come here a moment.'

At the sound of the names the twins stopped in their tracks and began to run back to them. Nicola watched closely when they stood in front of Sergei.

'In your art lessons, what did you draw?' he asked casually.

'Set.' They answered with one voice, standing almost proudly in front of Sergei, their heads held high.

'Sex!' exclaimed a horrified Nicola.

'Set, an Egyptian god,' said Sergei scathingly.

'Did you explain what was happening in the pictures to anyone?'

They shook their heads.

'We thought . . .'

'. . . everyone knew about Set.'

'I'm afraid not. It upset your teachers.'

'They were . . .'

'. . . very silly teachers.'

He nodded agreement and signalled for them to run ahead again.

'Well, how was I meant to know?' asked Nicola defensively.

'Do all psychologists jump to such sick conclusions quite that quickly?' he asked.

Nicola flushed. 'You can't be too careful these days. Terrible things happen to children now. Incest, rape, black magic . . . there's no end to the atrocities adults inflict on them.'

When he didn't reply she looked up at him and found him

staring off into the distance, just as he had in the kitchen earlier that morning.

'You asked the question but you aren't listening to the answer, are you?' she demanded accusingly.

Slowly he turned back to her, blinking once or twice to clear his mind. 'Yes, I was listening. You were talking about black magic.'

'Not just black magic!'

'No, about all the dreadful things your imagination had conjured up after seeing the drawings.'

'Is this Set well known? I've never heard of him.'

'I think we should turn back. The rain's getting heavier and the boys might catch cold.'

'I should think you're more likely to catch cold.'

He called to the twins and then began to retrace his steps. 'Set is the Egyptian god of the night. He had a brother named Osiris, a good and wise ruler, whom he hated. In the end Set murdered Osiris and cut his body up into millions of pieces that he scattered all over the land. Where the pieces fell the earth became fertile.'

'That's horrible! I hope this Set was punished?'

Sergei smiled. 'Not straight away, perhaps because this didn't take place in England! In the end he was killed by the son of Osiris' widow and condemned to the perpetual darkness of the tomb, with no chance of eternal life.'

'He sounds perfectly horrible to me. Why don't the boys draw a more attractive god?'

'Why do children prefer the Joker to Batman? Evil's always more attractive, don't you think?' he asked lightly.

'Perhaps in comic strip heroes but not generally – at least, I hope not. So what you're saying is that there wasn't anything to worry about. That they could have stayed on at the school?'

'The school sounds quite dreadful. I'm sure they're relieved to be free of it, but the drawings themselves are harmless. They're part of their cultural history.'

Nicola gave a small sigh. 'I feel a bit stupid now,' she confessed.

'It was an understandable mistake. The boys disturb you, and you put two and two together and made five.'

'They disturbed the other children too,' she pointed out. 'The headmaster said he'd had a lot of complaints from parents.'

'Perhaps they need a school where more allowance is made for creative intelligence and imagination.'

'Yes, but . . .'

Sergei grabbed hold of her hand and began to pull her down the side of the hill. 'No more talking! Let's run, this rain's not very pleasant now.'

They raced together hand-in-hand, Nicola a little frightened of tripping as he pulled her along far more quickly than she would normally have run. When the path led out on to St Jude's Road she expected him to release her, but he didn't. Instead he continued running until they reached the house, and it was only in the shelter of the front porch that he finally let her go.

Breathless and exhilarated she put her key in the front door but before she could open it, Sergei had pulled her fiercely against him and in an instant he was kissing her forcefully, his mouth hard against her rain-covered lips and she didn't even try to resist him. Instead she felt her entire body mould itself against him and his hands gripped the side of her face as the kiss went on and on, melting her bones until he suddenly released her so that she half-fell against him.

She put up a shaking hand to touch her lips. They felt swollen and bruised. Her breathing was quick and shallow and she felt dazed, like someone waking too quickly from a deep sleep.

Sergei reached across her and turned the key, pushing the front door open with a foot. 'In you go, boys,' he instructed, and Nicola tried to compose herself as the twins pushed past them and ran indoors.

'Did they see?' she whispered anxiously.

'They saw nothing,' he assured her, pushing her ahead of him through the door. 'And even if they did, they wouldn't talk.'

Nicola walked straight through the house and into the lounge, then collapsed on to the sofa and waited for her heart to stop racing. She could hear the boys up in their bedroom, making shooting noises as they played with their action figures.

Sergei followed her into the room and stood in front of her. His clothes were saturated. Water dripped from the bottom of his jeans and off the ends of his long hair. He was breathing quickly too, and when Nicola looked up at him she could see desire written all over his face. He reached down for her and despite herself she took his hands and let him pull her to her feet.

For a moment she thought he was going to speak, but then his arms went round her and he began kissing her again, only this time his tongue found its way past her lips and flicked delicately round the inside of her top lip before thrusting into her mouth as he pressed his hips against hers.

She could feel his erection against her thigh and found that the images this conjured up took away almost all her self-control so that she began rubbing against him, making small noises in her throat. His hands moved up inside her kagoul and under her jersey, and within seconds he'd pushed her bra up and his hands were grasping her breasts, the thumbs making tiny circles round her nipples while all the time he continued to kiss her almost savagely. Then he moved his left leg between hers so that she could press her public bone against his thigh.

Nicola had never felt such desperate desire for anyone. Frantically she began to undo the buttons on his shirt, then her hands moved lower, trying to slip down the front of his jeans but he stopped her, imprisoning her hand with one of his own while the other continued to tease her breasts. Then his mouth relinquished hers and almost before she realised it, he was breathing lightly into her ear, and then his tongue was there, rough against the smoothness of her inner ear. She jerked, her hips ground against his leg again and then her body shook as she was swept by a climax that forced a startled cry from her. Shocked, she felt the dampness between her legs and then Sergei moved away from her and she staggered and would have fallen if he hadn't reached out to steady her.

She had never felt so embarrassed in her entire life. She was blushing with shame, as hot and confused as if she were a teenager caught necking in the back of a car, and her body was still trembling as she forced herself to look the Russian full in the face.

He was studying her with grave consideration, almost assessing her reaction, and she couldn't help contrasting his cool detachment with her own confusion. But then he smiled at her, and there was warmth in his eyes and his hands touched her lightly on each side of her waist and he moved close to her once again.

'I'm not sorry,' he said huskily. 'I've been wanting to do that ever since I first saw you at the airport.'

'Look, I'm not in the habit of . . . I honestly don't know what came over me. I've never kissed anyone like that since I got married. I just . . .'

'Not even Howard?'

Her confusion deepened. 'Yes, well − no, not really, but that wasn't what I meant.'

'If I were your husband I'd kiss you like that all the time.'

'Well, you're not my husband.' She was reminding herself as much as him.

'You wanted it too.'

Nicola nodded. 'Yes, I did, but that's not the point.'

'I think it is. I think we're meant for one another.'

'And I think we need a cup of coffee. I can't imagine why the boys didn't come down. Normally they're constantly asking for drinks and biscuits.'

'We were fortunate,' said Sergei with a shrug.

'I suppose so.' She couldn't stop herself from putting a hand on his arm. 'Sergei, it mustn't happen again. Howard trusts me. He . . .'

'I don't want to talk about Howard. I want to talk about you.'

Nicola shook her head. 'There's nothing to say. It's the boys we must talk about. After all, that's why you're here.'

'I came for you,' said Sergei softly. 'Haven't you been waiting for me?'

'Certainly not!'

'Or dreaming about me?'

She blushed, remembering her dreams.

'You're wasted here, only half alive in this horrible, damp

country. You can't imagine what your life could be like.'

'Life in Egypt didn't seem to suit Rose,' said Nicola briskly, grateful that her heartbeat had finally steadied down. 'Now, let's have that coffee.'

'You know I'm right.'

'You sound very confident of yourself. The boys told me you were something of a ladykiller.'

For the first time, genuine annoyance crossed his handsome face. 'That's nonsense. I've had very little time for women in my life so far. Nicola, wait!' He reached out and caught hold of her wrist, pulling her back towards him, and she looked at his full, sensual mouth, remembered how it had felt pressed to hers and began to lift her face up to his.

Just at that moment the front doorbell rang.

'Don't answer it,' said Sergei urgently.

'I've got to answer it. If I don't the boys will come to see where I am.'

'No they won't!'

She pulled away from him, and then realising that she was still in her wet kagoul began peeling it off as she walked towards the door.

'Hi!' said Melanie brightly. 'I got back early from the facial this morning and thought I'd come and make sure your visitor got here safely.'

Nicola ran a hand through her hair and hoped that she didn't look as warm as she felt. 'Yep, he's here.'

Melanie lowered her voice. 'Don't I get to see him? After all you said, I'm keen to judge for myself!'

'He's not that special,' said Nicola casually.

'Come on, you're just trying to keep him for yourself!'

Nicola stood to one side, forcing herself to smile. 'Okay, come in and see for yourself. I was just going to make us a coffee. Would you like one?'

Although Sergei had followed her into the kitchen there was no sign of him there now, and Nicola thought she could hear him upstairs with the boys.

'Howard went to work then?' asked Melanie.

'Why shouldn't he?'

'I thought he might be afraid of leaving you alone with the handsome Russian.'

'Don't be ridiculous!' Nicola felt her face going scarlet and saw Melanie's eyes widen.

'You're blushing! Nicola, what's going on?'

'Very little could go on with the twins around.'

'True, but in your head it could be different!'

'We want a drink!' shouted the boys, rushing into the room. Nicola was extremely glad to see them.

'Fruit juice or coffee?'

'Fruit juice, please.'

Melanie looked at the twins a little nervously. 'I hear you're going to a new school next week.'

'Does your husband ...'

'... like your clothes?' they asked.

Now it was Melanie's turn to blush. 'Yes, why?'

'Because we ...'

'... certainly don't!'

They laughed softly to themselves, putting their heads close together and nudging each other with their elbows.

'I see you've changed,' said Nicola briskly, catching sight of Sergei in the doorway. He'd discarded his wet jeans and shirt and changed into a pair of grey slacks and a startlingly white open-necked shirt with the sleeves rolled up to the elbows. For the first time she realised that he was quite pale compared with the twins, and although his hair and eyes were dark his complexion was that of a much fairer person.

He'd towelled his hair off and combed it straight back but already, one lock had flopped forward over his left eye, the grey streaks contrasting with the apparent boyishness of the rest of his appearance.

Melanie seemed quite stunned by him. She was openly staring, and there was a delicate pink flush along her cheekbones as Nicola introduced her.

Sergei smiled politely, but there was no warmth in his eyes, and no suggestion of that special intimacy that Nicola had noticed between them right from their first meeting. She was relieved, wanting despite herself to believe that she was special to him.

'Acutally the reason I came across,' explained Melanie, 'was because I remembered Howard saying how he'd have liked Sergei to have a chance to look at Rushton's school

108

and I thought that if you were able to look round this week I could always babysit while the three of you were there.'

'We don't need a babysitter!' they chorused, their dignity offended.

'Well, perhaps I should say childminder, is that better?'

They wrinkled their noses and didn't bother to answer her. 'What do you think?' she continued.

Nicola glanced at Sergei who ran his tongue along his top lip as he considered the question. She had to look away, afraid her face would betray her. 'It might be helpful,' he conceded, running his fingers through his hair in an attempt to get it out of his eyes.

From under lowered lids, Melanie watched him and decided that handsome as he undoubtedly was she didn't like him, and neither did she like the unsettling effect he had on her stomach, which was lurching around in a most unpleasant manner. She knew that Robert wouldn't like him either. He was too foreign, too aware of the effect he produced.

'It's kind of you to offer,' said Nicola. 'If Howard can get us an appointment, I'll let you know. You are both coming to dinner Saturday night still?'

'Of course. Shall we bring the wine?'

'No, Howard's already chosen some. You know what he's like about wine.'

Melanie finished her coffee and stood up. 'Right, I'll get back. Two full facials and a massage this afternoon. I shall need to take on some help if this continues.'

'What does she do?' asked Sergei after Melanie had left.

'She's a beautician. She goes round the area giving facials, manicures, pedicures, that kind of thing.'

'A beautician? She should begin her work at home!'

'There's nothing wrong with Melanie's appearance, but she chooses to go for the understated look. It's only because she suffers from a basic lack of confidence. She had a very unfortunate childhood and ...'

'She's just how I expected English women to look,' said Sergei dismissively. 'A faded rose, like your sister who was so aptly named.'

'Rose wasn't at all faded before she married Labib. If you'd known her before you'd have been shocked by the way she changed. When she came to our father's funeral last year I hardly recognised her!'

'Yes, of course. I remember Labib telling me about the funeral.'

Nicola looked sharply at him. 'What exactly did he tell you?'

'That the death was unexpected, and caused problems within the family.'

She felt a tightness in her chest. 'Did he tell you what kind of problems?'

'No, I assumed they were financial.' The tightness receded. 'Were they?'

'Not exactly. Look, I have to do some shopping this afternoon. I thought you might like to take the boys out somewhere, and then this evening, when Howard's home, perhaps you could tell us exactly what kind of tutors the boys had and perhaps fill us in a little more on their upbringing?'

'Is your husband a good lover?' he asked quietly.

Nicola stared at him. 'You shouldn't ask that kind of question! It's far too personal.'

'Obviously he isn't. If he were, you would have said as much.'

'Sergei, don't do this. My relationship with Howard has nothing to do with you. You're only here for a few days.'

'I want you,' he said flatly. 'I want you to belong to me. I want to take you back to Egypt and set up home with you. That's why I need to know about Howard.'

She tried to laugh. 'You're being utterly ridiculous, and it isn't flattering because I can only think you must imagine I'm incredibly stupid. You caught me at a bad time, today. Things are a bit strained with Howard right now and ...'

He interrupted her. 'Your friend didn't like me.'

'Melanie? I'm sure she did, but she's very shy.'

'I'm tired. I'm going to rest on my bed. When you go shopping I'll take the boys out if that's what you want, but we'll be here when you get back. What time does Howard get home?'

'About six, but I might not be home much before then. I ought to call in on Andrea and ...'

He was out of the kitchen before she'd finished talking and

110

she knew that she wouldn't call in on Andrea, that she'd hurry through her shopping and back home because he'd be waiting for her. She had the frightening thought that no matter what she did or didn't do they were eventually going to become lovers, either because that was what he wanted and he was used to getting his own way, or — and this disturbed her more — because what he'd said that morning was true, and it was all part of her destiny, inevitable from the moment she was born.

Normally, when she had plenty of time, Nicola enjoyed going round Sainsburys but today every delay was irritating. Even her own brain seemed to conspire against her, refusing to make a decision on the simplest of choices. After she'd stood gazing helplessly at the assorted cheeses for several minutes she simply pointed at the two nearest her and asked for a pound of each. She was relieved to find that one of them was a farmhouse cheddar. Howard might have found it surprising if she'd gone home with nothing but soft cheese.

It was the same at the fish counter. The different names kept going round and round in her head as she stared at the fish and the fish stared back. Their glassy eyes reminded her of Lily just before they buried her, and that in turn reminded her of Howard's nightmare. By the time she'd remembered all that, she no longer wanted fish.

'Pull yourself together,' she muttered as she picked up a dozen assorted yoghurts. 'You're not a lovesick teenager, you're a wife and foster mother. Concentrate on what you're doing.' But it was no good, she was still rushing in her mind, trying to get home so that she could have some time with Sergei before Howard returned.

And yet, if she was honest, she knew that Sergei's approach was not the kind that would normally appeal to her. She had never been attracted by the cave-man, look-and-pounce approach that he represented. She'd despised Rose for succumbing to just that kind of attraction in Labib. But this time it was different. Mentally she might be aware of his failings; physically she was helpless.

The shopping took twice as long as usual to pack into boxes, and then Nicola had to take a suit of Howard's to the cleaners in the middle of town, which meant a considerable walk from

111

the car park. As she rushed, so the minutes ticked by, and it was four-thirty before she finally deposited the shopping on the kitchen table. That left at the most an hour and a half, she reasoned, probably less because she would have to shower and change before he got home.

'I'm back!' she called, puting her head out into the hall.

The twins came running down the stairs. They were wearing new jerseys, bright yellow with a blue face in the middle of the chest.

'They're nice. Did Sergei buy them for you?'

'Yes, he thought they . . . '

'. . . were nice and bright.'

'So they are. Let me look at the face. Good heavens, its tongue's sticking out!'

They both grinned. 'Yes, Sergei said that he'd like one too.'

'I'm sure he would. In fact, I could have done with one at the shops. The woman in front of me in the queue took hours to pay. I could have screamed.'

Torquil peered into the boxes. 'Did you buy any humus?'

'Yes, it's in the smallest box. What did you do apart from get a jumper each?'

'We talked about lots of things. All our friends in Cairo, what the servants have been doing, that kind of thing. Were you in a hurry to get home because of Sergei?'

Nicola gave a strained laugh. 'Of course not. I just didn't want to leave you alone for too long.'

'I think you were hurrying back for Sergei. Tarquin thinks so too.'

'There are some chocolate biscuits in there somewhere. You can have a couple each if you like.'

'A bribe!' they shouted in glee, and began rummaging in the boxes.

She felt a brief desire to shake them but suppressed the idea, knowing she was only annoyed because they were right. She was beginning to realise that it had been stupid to rush because with the twins there she and Sergei wouldn't be alone at all.

Sergei strolled in from the passage. 'I didn't hear the car.'

'Where were you? I could have done with some help unloading.'

112

'I was in the back garden. It's larger than I imagined. Haven't you boys got anything to do?'

'Oh yes, very ...'

'... important things!'

They grabbed at the packet of chocolate biscuits, glanced quickly at Nicola to see if she was going to protest and then made off up the stairs with it. Alone in the kitchen with Sergei she suddenly felt breathless.

'It is quite large. We've been approached by a couple of builders wanting to buy the piece at the bottom, but although we could certainly use the money I think it would spoil everything. We're nice and secluded at the moment and ...'

'Why were you gone so long?' he demanded, moving purposefully towards her.

'I'm sorry, everything seemed to take twice the time it usually does.'

He put his hands on her shoulders and dug his fingers into her. 'Did you keep me waiting on purpose?'

'Of course not. I couldn't think straight.'

'Don't worry about thinking now. Let your instincts take over,' he whispered. Then he was kissing her again, and it was even better than the first time. When he finally released her she was light-headed with pleasure.

Dazed she took a few steps away from him, aware that she was no longer in control of herself and that if he suggested taking her on the kitchen floor she would probably agree. But he didn't. All he did was study her for a moment and then with a nod of satisfaction he went to the sink and poured himself a glass of water.

Nicola felt at a considerable disadvantage. 'Haven't you anything to say?' she asked shakily.

'Yes, but there isn't time. Your husband will be here in a minute.'

'Howard? Of course he won't. He's never home before six.'

'Perhaps he doesn't trust me,' he said blandly.

Nicola stared at him. 'Don't you feel guilty?'

'You're the one who's betraying his trust, not me.'

'What a rotten thing to say!'

'It's only the truth.'

113

'Well, thank you for reminding me.' She was furious.

'You don't like facing the truth, do you? And yet you spend all your working life searching for it in disturbed children. I find that fascinating.'

'Good. I'm glad it isn't just my body that fascinates you,' she snapped.

She went to walk past him to the fridge but he caught hold of her arm. 'Don't be silly, your quarrel isn't with me. It's with your husband. He's the one who can't satisfy you. I could open up a whole new world for you. A world of unimaginable delights, new sensations, experiences beyond belief. You wouldn't believe the things I can show you, but you have to want it. It has to be your decision.'

'I don't know what you're talking about,' she said tightly. 'Let go of my arm. If Howard really is coming home early then ...'

Just then she heard car wheels on the gravel drive, and when she turned to the window and saw her husband's car outside she felt cold all over, staring at the Russian in disbelief. 'How did you know?'

'I've got bionic hearing!'

'Don't make a joke of it. How did you know he was nearly home?'

'You wouldn't believe me if I told you,' he said contemptuously, and the corners of his mouth turned down in what was unpleasantly close to a sneer as he walked out of the room, leaving her to greet Howard on her own.

'This is a surprise,' she exclaimed as he walked in, hoping that her voice didn't betray her agitation.

'The meeting was cancelled. I decided to get the early train. Been shopping?'

'Yes, Sergei took the boys out while I went to Sainsburys.'

'I thought we could eat out tonight.'

'What about the boys?'

Howard's face fell. 'I forgot them! Never mind. How about a takeaway?'

'I was going to do sweet and sour chicken with rice.'

'Fine, I suppose I can wait a couple of hours.'

'We're normally the ones waiting for you,' she pointed out.

Howard threw his raincoat over the back of a chair. 'Where is everyone?'

'The boys are upstairs. Sergei's probably with them.'

'How's he been today?' Howard was watching her closely.

'Fine.' She tried to sound casual, although her voice seemed to her to be shaking. 'We went for a walk this morning, and cleared up the problem with the art while we were out.'

'Really? In what way?'

'I'll tell you later. Sergei also made a useful suggestion about getting the boys to answer to their names, and generally explained a few other things about them. Then we split up for the afternoon. I thought we three adults could talk in more detail during the evening.'

'Is he good company?'

Nicola shrugged. 'The boys seem to think so. They've behaved beautifully. Which reminds me, Melanie said she'd look after them for a couple of hours if we wanted to take Sergei to look over Rushton's school one evening.'

'I've booked an appointment for tomorrow, seven o'clock. I hadn't intended taking him, but I suppose we could.'

'He might be able to tell if the school would suit them. We don't want to make another mistake, do we?'

'No, it's too damned expensive. Did you ask Sergei about the trust fund mentioned in the will?'

'I thought I'd leave the money side of things to you.'

Howard put an arm round her shoulders. To her dismay she felt herself tense. She had an overwhelming urge to shake him off. 'Are you all right?' he asked solicitously. 'You look a bit uptight.'

'Really? I expect it's just because I've been rushing round town. I could do with a sherry though.'

He released her and opened the cupboard door. 'Fine, I'll get us some glasses. He hasn't been a nuisance, has he?'

She bent her head over the sink to hide her confusion. 'Who, Sergei?'

'Who else?'

'No, he's been very helpful. It was nice to have a break from the boys.'

'That's all right then. It's funny, I've felt really on edge all

115

day. I kept thinking about you stuck on your own with him here. I realised that we don't really know a damned thing about him, and I suddenly had the terrible thought that he could be some kind of psychopath; that I'd come home to find you hacked to pieces.'

'Hacked to pieces?'

'I know it sounds stupid but that's what I kept thinking. God knows why.'

Nicola remembered the story of Set. 'Must be telepathy. I heard a gruesome little fable myself. I'll tell you about it when we're in bed.'

But by the time they went to bed, Nicola was far too tired to talk about an Egyptian fable, and Howard — exhausted by the extensive discussion about the boys' childhood — had forgotten all about it. Not that it would have interested him. He was a very practical man.

'We really do appreciate this, Melanie,' said Nicola, pulling on a three-quarter length woollen jacket.

'That's all right. I don't suppose the boys will be any trouble.' Although Melanie smiled she seemed a little anxious and Nicola looked to Howard to reassure her.

'I wouldn't bank on that,' he said, ignoring his wife's expression of dismay. 'They're usually nothing but trouble.'

'They're watching a video,' said Nicola quickly. 'They've got their own TV in their room. I've told them they can stay up 'til we get back so you probably won't even see them.'

Sergei was listening to the exchange with apparent amusement. He'd changed into a grey pinstriped suit for the visit, and with a pale blue shirt and navy monogrammed tie looked breathtakingly handsome.

Nicola, who'd hardly dared look at him since Melanie arrived, was aware of everything about him, from the unusual, spicy tang of his cologne to the expensive dark leather of his shoes. She'd spent the entire day avoiding being alone with him, and yet now — in front of Howard and Melanie — she felt as though she was being drawn helplessly towards him like a pin to a magnet. And she wanted him. She wanted him more than she'd ever wanted anything in her life.

116

'Nicola, are you ready?'

'Sorry, I was miles away,' she confessed.

'You certainly were. I've asked you three times! Come on, let's go. We'll take our car, Sergei. You can leave yours here.'

At the front door, Nicola turned back to Melanie who was still looking anxious. 'They've been really good today, Mel. You won't have any trouble,' she promised.

'I'm not bothered, honestly. I've got a book, and some knitting that I should have finished weeks ago. It's nice to have a quiet couple of hours. When Robert's around I always feel I ought to be an interesting companion!'

'Come on!' called Howard irritably. Nicola left.

Melanie was alone.

Everywhere was deathly quiet. Normally there were plenty of creaks and groans in the house but not tonight realised Melanie as she settled down in the lounge. She was also surprised that she couldn't hear the twins' television, but assumed their room was too far away.

After a moment she picked up her knitting and tried to concentrate on that, but she was quite ridiculously nervous, and her fingers fumbled with the wool making her drop stitches.

'Bother!' She began to search for the pattern, unable to remember exactly where she was, but before she could find her place she heard feet on the stairs and turned defensively to the open doorway.

One of the twins was standing there. She didn't know which one because he didn't have his badge on.

'Hello.' She tried to smile, knowing her fear was ridiculous.

'Hello.' He didn't smile back.

'Everything all right up there?'

'The video's gone wrong.'

Melanie groaned inwardly. She knew nothing about mechanical things.

'It doesn't matter. I think it's just the batteries in the remote control,' he assured her.

Melanie didn't realise she'd voiced her lack of mechanical skill aloud. 'Do you want me to come and look?' she asked.

117

He nodded and held out a hand. 'Yes, we do.'

'Let me put my knitting down. Will it be safe there?'

'Of course it will. The cat's dead, didn't you know?'

'Lily's dead?' She was shocked. Nicola had doted on the cat.

'She was run over. We buried her carefully in the garden. I don't suppose she's been dug up yet because we put her a long way down.'

'That's good,' she said faintly.

She was quite touched when he took hold of her hand. Nicola often said how much the boys avoided physical contact, but this one was actively instigating it. His fingers were warm and they gripped hers tightly.

Their bedroom door was closed but as soon as they arrived the other twin opened it, and then stretched out his right hand towards her. 'Do come in,' he said politely. 'Let me take your hand.'

'I'm very honoured by all this attention!' she said lightly.

With a twin on each side of her she walked to the foot of their beds and then when they sat, she sat too, her hands still imprisoned in theirs.

'What's wrong then?' she asked, just a little too brightly.

They turned their dark eyes on her. 'What's the matter?'

'Are you afraid?'

She shook her head. 'No, of course not. Why should I be afraid?'

'You're all trembly and ...'

'... your hands are sweating.'

'Well, perhaps you'd better let go of me then,' she sugested, but if anything they gripped her hands more tightly. 'I thought there was something wrong with your video?'

'There is, watch!' said one twin.

'Watch very carefully!' urged the other.

Melanie wished that she'd never come upstairs. They were terrifying her, and yet they were really behaving very well. She realised that she was being silly, but still wondered why she'd let them get her up here.

'I can't see anything!' she protested. 'The screen's quite blank.'

'Wait!' they whispered.

Almost at once, the bedroom light went out, and Melanie gave a little squeak of surprise. The room was in pitch darkness, even the street lamps outside had been extinguished. Her heart began to thump in her chest and she tried to pull her hands free.

'I'm afraid the video won't work at all now, we seem to have a power cut,' she explained.

'Sit . . .'

'. . . down.'

They tugged at her hands, holding her fast.

'*Just watch the screen!*'

'I don't want to,' said Melanie, sounding like a frightened three year old.

'Concentrate!' instructed one of the twins, and she felt a sharp pain in her head. Automatically she turned towards the television and to her astonishment the screen began to glow. She looked carefully at it. The pain in her head was subsiding but she felt rather peculiar, as though someone had filled her skull with cotton wool.

The screen light expanded and then, after one or two flashes of colour, figures began to appear. She frowned. There was something familiar about the people. She wondered if she'd seen the film at the cinema some time.

There was a man standing beside a bed. He was wearing a smart suit and there was something familiar about the way he stood.

Slowly he took off the jacket and put it across the back of a nearby chair, then he stepped out of his trousers, folded them neatly and began to take off his tie.

'What kind of film is this?' she asked. The twins didn't reply.

A movement on the bed caught her eye. She hadn't noticed the woman lying there before, but she couldn't imagine how she'd missed her since she didn't have a stitch of clothing on and was displaying her undoubted charms for the whole world to see.

The man had taken off all his clothes now and climbed onto the bed to join the woman, but Melanie wished she could see his face. She was certain she knew him.

As he lowered himself next to the woman he glanced briefly

119

over his shoulder and smiled at the camera, finally giving her a clear, unmistakable view of his face. It wasn't a well-known actor at all. It was Robert. Her own husband, Robert.

'No!' She heard her own cry of protest, but couldn't take her eyes off the screen as Robert proceeded to make totally uninhibited love to the woman who gasped and panted beneath him, apparently driven to a frenzy of lust by all he was doing. Neither of them spoke at all until the woman was on her knees, taking Robert into her mouth with obvious pleasure, doing the one thing that Melanie had never yet been able to bring herself to do, and then as Robert threw back his head with pleasure he actually spoke her name. 'Charlotte!' he groaned and his body jerked.

Melanie screamed. The screen flickered and went blank. The lights came back on. Her hands were released. Everything was normal again.

She sat on the bed, sick and shaking. She'd just been faced with her most secret fear and she didn't know what to do. She whimpered softly.

'I don't think . . . '

'. . . he does like the way you dress!'

At the sound of their voices she stared across the room to where the twins were standing side by side together. Still shaking, she got to her feet. 'Where did you get that?' she demanded.

'From the video shop,' said one.

'Don't tell lies. I want to know how you got hold of that.'

The other boy ran to the recorder and took out the tape. He thrust it into her hand. 'Look, it says Baker's Videos on it. See!'

She did see. She also saw the title. '*Winnie the Pooh and the Honey Tree.*'

'That isn't what we saw!' She was beginning to feel angry as well as frightened.

'It's what *we* saw.'

'What did *you* see?'

'Filth!' she shouted. 'I saw pornographic filth! It was disgusting. How can any normal woman be expected to behave like that? What kind of girl is she anyway? Call

120

herself a secretary? She's no better than a prostitute.'

The twins backed away from her, towards the landing.

'I think I heard . . .'

'. . . Nicola and Howard.'

Before she could say anything more they'd turned and run, dashing down the stairs at top speed, shouting for Nicola as they went.

Melanie bent down and put the tape back into the machine, pressing Play as she did so. Immediately the screen was filled with bright, colourful pictures of Pooh Bear and Tigger. She pressed her knuckles to her mouth to keep back the sobs. If that was on the tape, then how had she seen what she had? How had the twins managed it?

She didn't know the answer, but she knew that she was never going to have anything to do with them again. They were evil, there was no other word for it. What she'd seen was disgusting and depraved and it was their fault.

When she reached the top of the stairs she saw that Sergei Cheparukhin was at the bottom, staring up at her. She went hesitantly down, suddenly more frightened of him than she was of the twins. He kept his luminous dark eyes on her every step of the way, but when she reached the last stair he leant across, resting his arm on the bottom of the banister and blocking her path.

'You look pale,' he said in a tone of mock solicitude.

'Excuse me, please.' She tried to get past but his free hand caught hold of her wrist, the fingers burning her skin.

'Stay away from here,' he said quietly. 'Nicola doesn't need you any more.'

Melanie stared at him. 'What do you want?' she asked in bewilderment. 'Why have you come here?'

He smirked. 'Did you enjoy the video?'

'No,' she said furiously. 'It was disgusting. Those children should be locked up. There's something wrong with them.'

'All they did was make you face your own fears. If anyone's disgusting, it's you!'

She remembered the swimming pool and the tentacled monster that she'd seen. 'Get out of the way,' she repeated firmly. 'I have to speak to Nicola.'

'If you tell Nicola, I shall come to visit you in your dreams,'

121

he warned softly. 'By the time I've finished with you, all you'll want to do is kill yourself. Do you understand?'

'I . . .'

'You see, I know you better than you know yourself. Better than you'd ever wish to know yourself.' His voice dropped, became caressing. 'Look! Let me show you.'

Melanie had a sudden mental image of herself crawling naked along the ground, reaching out her hands, begging for something that she knew she needed without knowing its name.

Sergei put out a hand and delicately traced the line of her jaw. She was frozen with fear. 'You want to be punished, don't you? You know that's what you deserve. And you like it. Remember?'

All at once the protective screen that had kept the memories at bay was torn aside. She could see herself as she'd been when she was younger. Could feel the touch of hands that she'd forgotten, and heard Sergei's voice saying the very things that the other man had said so many years ago.

'Robert deserves better than this,' whispered Sergei. 'You should have told him. Your whole marriage is based on lies. Suppose he knew what you used to do? How would you explain that? He thinks you're shy, but you're not really shy at all, Melanie. You're just ashamed, rightfully ashamed. Perhaps someone should tell Robert? Tell him everything?'

His fingers stopped caressing her face and as his hand dropped to his side she was finally released. '*Let me alone*!' she screamed and almost fell off the last step, running like a mad woman through the kitchen, past an astounded Nicola and Howard, and out through the front door into the welcoming darkness of the night.

Nicola and Howard stared at one another. Sergei gave a small smile and felt the satisfaction of a job well done, while up in their room, Torquil and Tarquin sat watching the tale of "Winnie the Pooh and the Honeypot".

Chapter Eight

'What did Robert actually say?' demanded Nicola for the third time.

Howard rubbed his hands wearily over his face. 'He said that Melanie had arrived home very upset, gone straight into the bedroom and locked the door against him.'

'Didn't he try to find out what was wrong?'

'I've no idea. He obviously didn't want to talk to me about it, for which I can hardly blame him. If your wife goes over to her best friend's for an hour's childminding you hardly expect her to arrive home a gibbering wreck.'

Nicola clenched her fists. 'It's so frustrating not knowing what happened.'

'The boys did say she'd had a telephone call.'

'What kind of telephone call drives you mad?'

Howard shrugged. 'I've no idea. Perhaps it was obscene.'

'Melanie isn't twelve years old. An obscene call's unpleasant, not something that drives you barking mad.'

'You'll just have to go round in the morning and talk to her yourself,' said Howard. 'Look, it's gone twelve and I have to catch the 7.10 in the morning. Do you think we could try and get some sleep now?'

'You can if you like. I couldn't possibly sleep yet. I just wish she'd said something. I feel dreadful letting her go like that, but it happened so quickly. We'd only just walked in the door.'

Howard switched out his bedside light. 'Perhaps Sergei made a pass at her!'

'I don't know how you can make jokes. Melanie looked

123

petrified. Something awful must have happened. I'm sure the twins know more than they're saying.'

'Low as my opinion of the twins is, I find it hard to believe they were responsible for tonight's mysterious happenings. They said Melanie had a strange turn when you went swimming. Is that true?'

'Yes, she did. I'd forgotten. It was really weird. She'd been doing so well, then all at once she got a terrified look on her face and rushed out of the pool.'

'There you are then. She's obviously going a bit peculiar. Probably the strain of trying to make ugly old women look like beautiful young ones!'

'No,' said Nicola thoughtfully. 'I think there's a lot more to it than that. It could be that she's going through some kind of emotional crisis which has brought suppressed fears to the surface, or ...'

'Goodnight, Dr Freud.'

Within minutes, Howard was asleep, but Nicola was wide awake and full of energy. Taking care not to wake him she went downstairs to the kitchen and made herself a mug of tea. Before she'd had time to drink any of it, she was joined by Sergei.

He was wearing a pair of striped pjyama trousers but no jacket and she was surprised to see that his chest was smooth and hairless. She picked up her mug. 'Would you like some?'

He shook his head. 'I'd prefer strong coffee. Couldn't you sleep?'

'No, I keep thinking about Melanie. She didn't say anything to you, did she?'

'I only saw her for a few seconds. She came rushing down the stairs and straight past me like a bat out of hell. I thought she must have seen a spider.'

'It would have had to be a pretty big one to make her scream like she did! How much sugar in your coffee?'

'Three spoonsful. Is Howard asleep?'

'Yes.'

Nicola half-expected him to make some attempt to kiss her but his expression was abstracted. 'I liked the school,' he said unexpectedly.

124

'Did you? I'm not sure the discipline's good enough. It's a pity we had the commotion with Melanie, I was hoping to hear what Howard thought.'

'The boys should go there,' said Sergei firmly. 'It will suit their particular abilities.'

'For causing mayhem, you mean?'

He smiled. 'That and other things. Some of the artwork was excellent.'

'I didn't see any sexually deformed Egyptian gods on display.'

'Next time I'm over here we'll find an exhibition of Egyptian art. Then perhaps you won't be so disturbed by what the twins draw.'

'Next time? When are you going back?'

'On Sunday.'

'Oh no!' Nicola stopped, dismayed to realise how much the thought depressed her.

'I won't be gone for long,' he assured her. 'Just a few weeks.'

'That's all right. It was only that I hadn't really thought about you leaving yet.'

'I'll miss you,' he said gently.

'Well, it's probably a good thing.'

'Of course it isn't. We should be together all the time, and we will be before too long.'

'Look, I really think I ought to explain that I'm very happy with Howard,' said Nicola awkwardly. 'I know I haven't behaved very well, but there's no question of us splitting up or anything like that. We've got a good marriage most of the time. Since the boys came it's had a few difficulties but nothing major. I still love him.'

'I don't believe you,' said Sergei in an amused tone. 'You're used to him, and you probably like him, but you certainly don't love him. He seems more like your brother than your husband.'

'He isn't a bit like a brother!'

'No? When did he last make love to you?'

Nicola moved uncomfortably in her chair. 'I think that's private.'

'Not recently then!'

125

'Sex isn't everything.'

'When it's good it's nearly everything!'

She stood up. 'I think I'd better go back to bed. Why don't you take the boys off for a game of football or something tomorrow?'

Sergei stayed sitting in the chair, looking up at her with obvious amusement. 'Off you go then, back to Howard. Does he snore?'

'No!'

When she drew level with him, he was on his feet in one smooth catlike movement and he placed his hands on her shoulders, moving his thumbs lightly against the base of her throat. He put his lips against the soft skin there and breathed gently against her, his tongue licking her flesh with tiny, catlike movements. She shivered, putting her head back and exposing more of her throat. Almost imperceptibly the pressure of his thumbs increased to the point where it was nearly uncomfortable and then she felt his teeth grazing her skin.

'I want you,' he whispered. 'Let me make love to you. Let me show you what it can be like.'

His voice was like a drug making her relax, and when his hands moved she swayed against him until he put one arm round her waist and began to untie her robe with his free hand, while all the time his tongue and teeth were wandering over her sensitive flesh. Carefully he lowered her on to a chair and his mouth left her for a moment as he struggled with the knot in her sash.

Freed from the sensations he'd been arousing, she suddenly came to her senses and pushed at his chest. 'Get off, Sergei! This is ridiculous. Let me go. I want to get back to bed.'

When she struck out at him he lost his balance and took two quick steps away from her, allowing her to get to her feet again.

'This has to stop,' she said breathlessly. 'I know it's as much my fault as yours but please leave me alone. I love my husband.'

His face twisted with rage and she was appalled by the hatred that flared in his eyes. He lifted a hand as though to strike her and she flinched, putting up an arm to protect herself. The movement seemed to bring him to his senses because the rage died away at once and he moved to one side.

'If that's really what you want,' he said politely, making room for her to pass.

'It is. Goodnight, Sergei.'

He didn't answer but all the way upstairs she felt as though he was watching her, his eyes burning into her back. Even outside her bedroom door she could still feel the force of his anger, yet when she turned and looked behind her there was no sign of him.

Nicola knew that she'd done the right thing. Much as she was drawn physically to the Russian, she was beginning to realise that he was not quite what she'd imagined at first. He was colder than she'd anticipated, remote to the point of rudeness with most people, and with no sign of lightness or humour in his character.

Just the same, lying awake next to Howard, her body still aroused by Sergei's touch, she couldn't help regretting what she'd said. It had been right and necessary, but common sense and logic were poor weapons against physical attraction and she knew that if she were going to keep him at bay then she must avoid being alone with him at any time.

The next morning Sergei slept late. He was still in bed when Nicola left the twins playing with some space Lego while she went to see Melanie. At first she thought her friend wasn't going to answer the door, but eventually she did, slipping the chain on first and peering out anxiously.

Nicola was shocked by her pale face and sunken eyes. 'Mel, I had to come over. Whatever happened last night?'

Melanie's eyes flickered, her gaze darting suspiciously along the street.

'Let me in, Melanie. It's a bit cold out here.'

She shook her head.

'Please, Mel! Look, was it something the twins did? They deny it, but I know you and they don't always hit it off. If they did anything then I should know about it.'

'Go away,' hissed Melanie. 'I don't want any more to do with you.'

127

'This is ridiculous! Surely I'm entitled to know what upset you? You were in my house at the time. I feel responsible.'

'Leave me alone.'

'Mel, you're my closest friend. If you can't talk to me about this, then who can you talk to?'

Melanie's eyes widened and she swallowed nervously. 'I can't talk to anyone. I never have, and I'm not going to start now. What makes you think you've got the right to pry into my private life?'

Nicola looked over her shoulder, feeling stupid arguing through a crack in the front door. 'I'm not prying! For heaven's sake, I told you about my family problems when Daddy died. Can't you talk to me about this?'

'I didn't ask to hear your family problems, you volunteered them, and there's nothing like that scandal in my family, I'm pleased to say. Nothing at all. We were perfectly normal. I had a wonderful childhood, it was perfect, absolutely perfect, and anyone who tells you differently is a liar. Do you hear me? A liar!' She was shouting harshly and Nicola took a step back in shock.

'There's no need to scream at me, Mel! I can hear you perfectly well. Has Robert called the doctor for you?'

Her friend's eyes stopped darting around and fixed themselves on Nicola. 'Why should I need a doctor?' she asked fiercely.

'Well, you seem a little disturbed. I thought ...'

'I don't need a doctor. I don't need anyone at all. I'm never coming out of this house again, and you're never coming in it. Is that clear? Is it?'

'Yes, it's quite clear. Look, you go back to bed. I'm sorry I disturbed you. I'll ring this evening to see how you are. Okay?'

'Ring all you like, I shan't answer.'

Nicola continued to back down the path. 'It's all right,' she said soothingly. 'I'll ring when Robert's back. He can tell me. You get some rest.'

When she got to the gate she looked back and saw that the door was already shut and she thought that she could hear the sounds of bolts being shot as well.

Deeply shaken, she spent most of the morning lost in

128

thought, wondering what could possibly have happened to Melanie to cause such a mental collapse.

Sergei and the boys went off at eleven and at two o'clock Nicola decided to ring Andrea and see if she'd phone Melanie for her.

'I'll ring if you like,' said Andrea in a bored tone, 'but I can't really see the point. She's obviously gone round the twist.'

'Melanie's the last person to behave like this! She's always so careful and controlled. You know how anxious she is to please everyone.'

'It's probably the strain of ministering to that stuffed shirt of a husband of hers. Not that he's any better than he should be. Hey, perhaps that's it. Perhaps he rang her up and told her about his affair. That would explain it all.'

Nicola frowned. 'What affair?'

'Any affair!'

'Do you know Robert's been having an affair?'

Andrea laughed. 'Of course not, but I wouldn't be surprised. David saw him with this gorgeous girl in a pub in the City one lunch time. He said Robert was very careful not to catch his eye.'

'I hardly think Robert would ring Melanie when she was here to tell her about an affair.'

'Then I've no idea, unless the girl called her, of course.'

'How would the girl know Melanie was here?'

Andrea giggled. 'Why do you keep putting obstacles in the way of my explanations? Look, when do I get to see this hunk you've got staying with you?'

Nicola sighed, wishing she'd never told anyone that Sergei was attractive. 'He goes back on Sunday so you probably won't see him at all.'

'We're free tonight!'

'I tell you what, if you promise to try and talk to Melanie this afternoon, then you and David can come round for a drink this evening. Fair?'

'We'll be there,' promised Andrea. 'I'll tell you how I get on when I see you.'

'Andrea and David for drinks?' groaned Howard. 'God,

wasn't last night enough for you? What do we do if Andrea goes into hysterics on us?'

'Well, that isn't very likely, is it? I'm going up to change. Your dinner's in the microwave.'

'They're here!' called the twins just before eight o'clock, running down the stairs and through the kitchen to open the door.

Andrea was wearing a bright red suit with a tight skirt that ended above the knee and a long boxed jacket that finished below her hips. With her blonde hair piled up on top of her head and immaculate make-up she looked quite stunning.

The twins stared at her and she stared back at them. 'You look nice,' said Torquil, following her into the lounge. 'I like bright clothes.'

'So do I. Which one are you?'

'I'm Tarquin.' His twin dug his elbow into his side. 'No I'm not! Sorry, I'm Torquil.'

'Aren't they weird!' laughed Andrea, turning to her husband. David, who wasn't at ease with any children, let alone these two, nodded.

'Who's the lady ...'

'... crying in your office?' the twins asked him.

David's face tightened and his mouth opened slightly as the boys stared at him. 'What office?' he asked.

'The one where you ...'

'... do all your work.'

'Shouldn't you be in bed?' he demanded.

At that moment, Howard joined them. 'Sorry I'm late. I've only just finished eating. The train was delayed. Off to bed, boys.'

'David was on time,' said Andrea. 'Don't you two normally catch the same train?'

'I caught an earlier one today,' explained David quickly.

'And it got you back here at exactly your normal time? How amazing! A whisky and water for me, Howard. Where's Nicola?'

'Either putting on her face or helping the Russian put on his!'

'I can't wait to see him,' confessed Andrea. 'I wore red in his honour. Red is still allowed in Russia, isn't it? There are

130

so many taboos there now I wasn't absolutely certain. Is it Lenin or Stalin who's in fashion at the moment?'

'I thought it was religion. Anyway, he doesn't live in Russia any more.'

'Not to worry, I'll talk to him about his work. That always makes men feel good. What does he do?'

'Wander around looking handsome, pausing occasionally to run his long, artistic fingers through his equally long and artistic hair!'

Andrea laughed. 'I see. Not your favourite person?'

'Not my favourite person. He's good with the twins though.'

'Who's good with the twins?' asked Nicola, appearing with Sergei and smiling at Andrea and David.

'Our Russian friend here,' explained Howard.

'That's certainly true. Sergei, this is Andrea Fletcher and her husband David. David's something brilliant in adertising and Andrea does a lot of charity work and keeps track of local gossip. Isn't that right?'

'I certainly got plenty from Melanie this afternoon! It's lovely to meet you, Sergei. Nicola's told us *so* much about you.'

His hand held Andrea's just a moment too long and he looked deep into her eyes. 'What kind of charity work?' he asked politely.

'Oh, nothing gruesome or tiring. I just work in a charity shop a couple of mornings a week and sit on one or two committees. I'm a good organiser.'

David studied the Russian with interest and shook hands briskly. 'An interesting time to be a Russian,' he commented.

'I was actually born in Georgia, in the town of Merkhuli.'

'That's still Russia, isn't it?' said Nicola, opening a bottle of wine.

'No, it's Georgia.'

'Rather like being Welsh or Scottish,' explained Howard.

'I suppose you drink vodka!' teased Andrea.

Sergei's eyes moved down to her legs which were crossed and on prominent display. Andrea smiled at him, aware of his interest and pleased by it.

131

'He usually drinks brandy, by the bottle!' exclaimed Howard.

'And what exactly do you do?' asked David, who hadn't taken his eyes off the Russian.

Sergei reluctantly stopped looking at Andrea's legs and turned his attention to her husband. 'I work in medical research. That's how I know the twins. I'm employed by the same hospital in Cairo that employed their father.'

'What kind of medical research?'

'The secret kind,' said Sergei flatly.

Nicola gave a smothered laugh and David flushed. 'I was only being polite,' he said irritably.

'Were you educated in Russia?' asked Andrea, recrossing her legs and watching with satisfaction when his eyes moved back to her.

'Of course. I went to school in Moscow.'

'Georgian education not good enough?' asked David sarcastically, still annoyed by the snub.

'I was selected for special education. In those days you had no choice about such things. It was an honour to be chosen.'

'So you were one of those who flourished under the old system. It must have been a shock when Gorbachev came along.'

'Not really. The change had been necessary for some time. Many of us had anticipated that the old order would change.'

'I don't understand Russian politics,' said Andrea, managing to make it sound an achievement.

'Is that why you wear such short skirts, to distract from your lack of mental abilities?' asked Sergei rudely.

Andrea was thrown into confusion, and didn't know what to say or do. She quickly uncrossed her legs, stretched them out in front of her, changed her mind, tucked them away beneath the chair and stared at Sergei in bewilderment.

'That's right!' said David with obvious pleasure. 'Andrea believes that looks are everything. It certainly helps socially but it makes for bloody boring conversation at home.'

'You chose to marry her,' said Sergei, leaving him at a loss for words as well.

132

Nicola glanced at Howard who was listening in astonishment. 'More whisky anyone?' he said quickly.

Sergei looked about him. 'I'm sorry, have I said something
wrong?'

'No, of course not,' said Nicola with a smile.

'I understood that the English liked nothing more than a
good discussion. You're a country that sets great store by
freedom of speech.'

'Obviously tact wasn't on the curriculum in Moscow,'
muttered Howard as he refilled David's glass.

'No, it's all right. He was quite correct,' said David,
recovering himself. 'So, how do you like Egypt?'

'It's very different,' said Sergei slowly. 'The people are
more volatile than Russians, but warmer too.'

David moved his chair nearer and they continued to talk
quietly to each other, virtually excluding everyone else.

Nicola turned to Andrea. 'Tell me about Melanie,' she
said eagerly. 'Did you get to talk to her?'

Andrea had been staring wistfully at the Russian but she
managed to tear her attention away.

'Yes, I spoke to her. Mind you, I didn't get any sense out
of her. She was really quite rude to me.'

'Rude?'

'Well, she made it clear that she didn't intend to tell me
anything because it was tantamount to telling her problems
to a town crier! I assured her I could keep a secret if I was
asked but that didn't cut any ice. She just kept telling me
to leave her alone.'

'Did you ask her what happened here?'

'Yes, but she claims she just suffered a sudden panic attack
and had to get some air.'

'She needs a psychiatrist,' said Howard. 'It's Robert I feel
sorry for.'

'Melanie doesn't have panic attacks, does she?'

'Not to my knowledge. Nicola, do you think I could have
some more ice in this?'

The two women went out into the kitchen. 'I didn't really
need ice,' confessed Andrea. 'I only wanted to tell you that
you were right. He's absolutely divine, isn't he! God, what
wouldn't I give for a chance to try him out!'

133

Nicola stared at her. 'Andrea, he was terribly rude to you just now. I was so embarrassed, I didn't know how I was going to apologise to you!'

'Rude? Oh, you mean about my legs and my brains. He was only trying to be humorous. Russians are notoriously heavy-handed over humour. I'll bet he isn't heavy-handed in any other way though. With those cheekbones and eyes he must have women throwing themselves at him all the time.'

'He hasn't mentioned it!'

'If he were staying with me I wouldn't be able to keep my hands off him. Although David probably wouldn't let him stay with me! Howard's very trusting.'

'He knows me well enough not to worry,' said Nicola, hoping a thunderbolt wouldn't strike her dead on the spot.

'Perhaps he made a pass at Melanie?' exclaimed Andrea. 'You know how devoted she is to Robert. That would have been enough to make her scream!'

'He'd only just walked in the door,' said Nicola stiffly.

'It was a joke, darling! You shouldn't worry about Melanie so much. She's always been a bit strange. All those long skirts, and refusing to discuss anything interesting.'

'Not everyone's obsessed with sex!'

'That's their loss. Let's go back. I'm going to feast my eyes on him for as long as possible. Trust David to monopolise the most attractive man to come my way in years.'

It was gone midnight before David and Andrea left, and David was again talking to Sergei about Russian politics. Andrea finally lost patience and got into the car on her own, turning on the ignition.

Howard had stayed indoors to collect the glasses and Nicola said goodnight to David as she passed him and Sergei at the gate. When she was inside she looked out of the kitchen window and saw that he and Sergei were still in close conversation. In fact, they were so close that it looked as though they were touching and she moved nearer to the glass trying to get a better look, but her breath misted up the window.

She rubbed at it, and as it cleared she thought that she saw David put a hand on Sergei's arm, as though to make a point, and Sergei then lifted a hand and touched David on the side of his face, much as he'd sometimes touched Nicola when kissing her.

'I'm going mad,' she muttered, turning away from the glass. 'I'll end up like Melanie if I'm not careful.'

'What was that?' asked Howard.

'Nothing, just talking to myself. Howard, let's get up to bed. I'm tired.'

'Sergei isn't in yet.'

'He'll lock the front door. We don't have to wait for him.'

'If you're sure.'

Once in bed, Nicola turned to her husband. 'Let's make love, Howard. It's been ages.'

'Nikki, I'm tired. It's late already.'

'Please, Howard.' She ran her hands over his chest and began to kiss him. He began to respond, reluctantly at first and then with increasing enthusiasm, but despite everything he was totally unable to get an erection and finally turned away from Nicola in frustration.

'It doesn't matter,' she whispered. 'We've had a lot to drink and you did say you were tired.'

Howard didn't answer at first but after a few moments he turned back to face her. 'I don't want Sergei staying here again.'

She was startled, wondering if she'd somehow aroused his suspicion. 'Why not?'

'I don't know. I just don't like him. I know the children love him and obviously he'll have to come and see them again, but he can stay in a hotel or something. I don't want him in my house.'

'Go to sleep,' said Nicola quietly. 'We'll talk about it tomorrow.'

But the next day they didn't talk about it, because when they woke in the morning it was to the news that, during the night, Melanie had killed herself.

Howard was the first to hear. The phone went just as he was eating his breakfast and Andrea, almost unintelligible because of her sobs, asked him to tell Nicola.

'How did she do it?' he asked, horrified at the thought of gentle Melanie involved in violence.

Andrea caught her breath in a sob. 'Robert wouldn't say, but the milkman told David there was blood everywhere.'

'How would the milkman know?' said Howard scornfully. 'I don't imagine Robert asked him in for a look round.'

'Well, that's what he said. I suppose she cut her wrists. It's all so horrible. But why? She had everything to live for.'

'I'll tell Nikki, she's bound to call you back later,' said Howard abruptly. He replaced the receiver and sat at the table, his appetite gone. It was some time before he could find the courage to go upstairs and tell Nicola.

All Nicola could think was that it was her fault. Something had happened the night Melanie babysat, something so dreadful that she'd cut herself off from everyone and then taken her own life. She knew that if it hadn't been for the babysitting, her friend would still be alive. The knowledge frightened her.

Howard stayed at home until ten, but then had to leave for a meeting. 'Why don't you ring my mother? I'm sure she'd be happy to come and keep you company,' he suggested.

'I don't want her here.'

'I thought you liked my mother?'

'I do. That's why she can't come.'

Howard frowned. 'You're not making much sense, darling. Look, I simply have to go. Are you sure you'll be all right with the boys?'

Nicola nodded. 'Sergei will take care of them.'

'Yes, well ...'

'I hope you're not expecting me to tell him he can't stay here any more?' asked Nicola.

'No, of course not. Not yet! But eventually one of us will have to say it.'

'I'm not up to discussing Sergei again this morning, Howard.'

'Well, if you're sure you're OK?'

'Just go, will you!' she snapped.

No sooner had he obeyed than the twins appeared in front of her. Her eyes were heavy from crying and she had a thick headeache that made her feel slightly sick.

'Are you all right?' asked Tarquin, putting his head on one side and staring at her.

'I'm upset.'

'Because that lady died?'

'Melanie was my closest friend.'

'Did you cry when our mummy died?' asked Torquil putting a hand absent-mindedly on her knee.

'Yes, of course. She was my sister and I loved her very much.'

'You shouldn't cry. Death's just ...'

'... a continuation,' explained Tarquin.

'I hope you're right.'

'If she was a good lady she'll pass the test,' said Torquil earnestly.

'What test?'

'The judgement test, of course. Was she good?'

'Yes, very good. Melanie was always kind to everyone.' Nicola's voice broke and she started crying again.

'That's all right then, isn't it?' said Tarquin, his tone making it clear that he felt she should stop crying.

'Did she really kill herself?' asked Torquil, his eyes huge in his face.

Nicola wiped the back of her hand over her eyes. 'I don't think it's necessary for you to have all the details. Where's Sergei?'

'On the telephone.'

Nicola glanced across the room. 'No, he isn't. The phone's there.'

'He's gone out to phone, it's more private outside.'

'Who's he ringing?'

Torquil glanced at his twin. 'I really don't think it's necessary for you to have all the details!'

'That isn't very clever, Tarquin,' said Nicola wearily.

'I'm Torquil. Can't you see my badge?'

'Look, I'm not functioning too well today. I'd appreciate some peace.'

They fidgeted around the kitchen, moving cups and plates and opening the fridge to look for food.

'Find something useful to do.'

'When will she have a funeral?' asked Torquil.

'I don't know. Early next week, I suppose.'

'If she was going to be made into a mummy they'd have to pull her brain out through her nose and put it in a jar. Did you know that?'

Nicola's stomach heaved.

'Then they'd cut her stomach open and pull out all the insides and cover up the big ugly cut with a magic eye made of wax.'

Bile rose in her throat.

'Of course you need special instruments ...'

'... and stuff to disguise the smell.'

Nicola ran to the sink and retched violently. The twins linked hands and stood close behind her, watching with interest. When her stomach finally settled, she splashed some cold water on her face, took two deep breaths and turned back to the boys.

'That was a really horrible thing to say.'

They stared at her, eyes unblinking.

'Did you hear me?'

They moved closer together. *'It was the truth.'*

'That's beside the point.'

Tarquin's lips curved in a smile. 'Mummy was all right,' he said happily. 'Her head was so smashed in that her brain was spread over the road. They didn't have to do anything with that.'

Nicola had a terrible vision of her sister's head lying in the middle of the road with blood and brains spilling out, and without thinking she caught hold of Tarquin by the shoulder, turned him round and slapped him hard on his bottom.

Torquil drew in his breath and pulled his brother away. 'You shouldn't have done that!' he shouted furiously. 'You're not allowed to hit me.'

'Us!' cried Nicola, equally furious. 'There are two of you, remember!'

Tarquin, red-faced and trembling, glared at her. 'You shouldn't have smacked me. It isn't allowed.'

'If you don't like being smacked then behave like human beings.'

The boys lifted their heads and their nostrils flared as they stared at her, their eyes gleaming like black coals.

Their chests began to rise and fall slowly and the sound of heavy breathing began to fill the room. The noise was astonishing. Each inhalation was rasping and the exhalation began softly but grew louder until it sounded as though there was a large, injured animal dying in the room. Their eyelids drooped, their mouths opened and their bodies looked boneless as the terrible, laboured breathing continued to increase.

'Stop it!' said Nicola, panicking at the sight and the noise emitting from their mouths.

Suddenly there was a flash of silver in the air in front of her and she gasped as she felt an electric shock run through her. Before she had time to recover, the washing machine suddenly started up, water rushing in to fill the empty drum. Startled, she turned her head to look at it and at that moment there was a whirring sound from the other side of the kitchen as the blades of her food processor began to turn, cutting at the empty air.

'What's going on?' Frightened she turned to the boys, but they seemed to be in a trance and their breathing was becoming more and more laboured until it sounded like a ghastly death rattle.

Nicola ran to the washing machine and turned off the switch, but the machine kept running, the water splashing against the door as the level rose almost to the top. Startled she realised that the start button wasn't even on. She then had to dash across the room as the electric carving knife began to spin on the work top.

'Stop it!' she yelled at the boys. 'Whatever it is you're doing, just stop!'

In reply the tumble dryer started up and the electric kettle suddenly began belching out steam, over-riding the automatic cut-out.

Nicola heard herself sobbing as she ran from one appliance to the other trying vainly to restore some order. Abruptly the kitchen cupboard door flew open and she stared in disbelief as the vacuum cleaner began moving crazily out over the kitchen floor despite the fact that the cord and plug were still wrapped round the upright handle.

The noise was incredible. Machines clunked and clicked,

139

gadgets whirred and spun, steam hissed from the kettle, and over it all the dreadful, tortured sound of heavy breathing continued relentlessly.

Tears streamed down Nicola's face and she fell to her knees. 'Please, stop it! I'm sorry I hit you. I'm sorry! I'm sorry! Just make it all stop!' But the twins didn't hear her. Their heads had fallen on to their chests and veins bulged in their foreheads as their bodies were wracked by the strain of breathing.

Nicola began to crawl towards the doorway and into the hall, where the power switch was located, but she could only move very slowly because of the random flashes of electricity filling the air. When she at last neared the door it began to open on its own and she stared up fearfully, wondering what would appear in front of her.

To her overwhelming relief it was Sergei. 'What the hell's going on in here?' he asked in astonishment, reaching down towards her.

She grabbed hold of his hands. 'Help me, please! Everything's gone mad. All the machinery's working on its own and the twins are ... No!' She screamed as a bright blue light filled the room and a fierce shock ran down her spine. Her body jerked helplessly and she bit her tongue, tasting her own warm blood.

'Alpha! Omega! Enough!' shouted Sergei, lifting Nicola up in his arms and crossing the room. When he reached the boys he put her carefully on the floor and placed a hand beneath each of the boy's chins, so that he could look directly at them.

'*Wa'if*! *Bass*!' he ordered.

Their eyes opened. They stared at him and their breathing began to quieten.

'*Marra tanya. Lissa bardu*!' he whispered, and instantly the room became silent.

He turned his attention back to Nicola, bending down and putting his arms round her as she leant against him, still crying weakly. 'Ssh!' he soothed, rocking her gently. 'It's all over now.'

'I only slapped him,' she said weakly. 'They were saying terrible things and I ...'

He pressed his lips against her hair. 'Don't worry, you're quite safe.'

Nicola put her arms round him and felt his heart beating against his ribs. 'How did they do it?' she whispered fearfully, but he didn't answer. Instead he continued to soothe her until the trembling stopped and she was able to stand on her own again.

She looked about her, expecting to find the kitchen in chaos yet it all looked perfectly normal. 'Where's the vacuum cleaner?' she asked Sergei.

'Don't tell me you want to start cleaning the house now.'

'Of course not, but it was in the middle of the room. It came out on its own, when everything else was going mad. Did you put it back?'

He looked puzzled. 'I haven't touched anything.'

'What about the washing machine? Is it still full of water?'

'I'm afraid I don't know much about electrical appliances. Should it be full of water?'

'Not when it's empty of clothes. That's what was making such a terrible noise. Well, that and the tumble dryer and everything else electrical in the room. What did you say to stop it?'

He looked concerned. 'All I heard was the noise the boys were making.'

'Well, yes, I know that was awful, but it wouldn't have been so bad on its own. I was petrified. I thought those electrical flashes were going to kill me.'

'What electrical flashes?'

'Sergei, you saw them! One hit me just as you came in. Look, I bit my tongue.'

'All I did was stop the boys screaming. There wasn't anything else happening. The only other noise was you yelling at them!'

'Sergei, either I'm going mad or you are! Every single appliance in this room started up by itself just now. Why did you think I was so frightened?'

'What I saw was two very angry six year olds throwing a big temper tantrum, and that's what I stopped. Nothing else was happening.'

She grabbed hold of his arm. 'Don't do this to me! I know you saw it. You looked as horrified as I felt when you stepped into the room.'

He shook his head in apparent puzzlement. 'I'm sorry, believe me I'd like to help you, but all I saw was the twins in a fit of rage. Labib used to handle them at times like that and I tried to say the same kind of things to calm them down.'

'No, that isn't true! You're lying. Why? Is it because you're trying to protect them? Is that why you're really here? Is there something wrong with them? Something that people mustn't know? Perhaps that's why Rose never talked about them.'

'You had a bad shock this morning,' he said gently. 'I think you should go upstairs and lie down. I'll keep the boys out of your way.'

She was shaking with indignation. 'Yes, I did have a shock, and that was quickly followed by another one when the boys decided to take over my kitchen.'

'I'm sorry about your friend,' he said softly.

Suddenly it was all too much for Nicola and she swayed on her feet. Immediately, Sergei's arm went round her and he guided her into the lounge. 'Sit there. I'm surprised Howard left you alone today.'

'He had a business meeting. Besides, I'm not alone. I've got you.'

There was a moment's silence.

'That's right,' he agreed. 'You've got me.'

She was shocked to realise that she wanted him to kiss her.

'Why did you go out to use a telephone?' she asked abruptly.

'It was a private call. I didn't want the boys to overhear me.'

'I thought perhaps you didn't want me to overhear.'

He raised his eyebrows. 'Why should I want to keep any secrets from you?'

'I don't know.'

'I'm going back to Egypt tomorrow. There's a problem in the laboratory, they need me there.'

'The boys will miss you,' she said calmly.

'Will you miss me too?'

'Goodness, I don't know. At first, I suppose. I've got used to having you around.'

'I'll be back before Christmas.'

Nicola remembered what Howard had said. 'Well, if it's in December it won't be very convenient for us,' she said awkwardly. 'Howard has to go to Brussels for a couple of weeks and he wouldn't want to leave us alone here. It wouldn't look right.'

'You mean he doesn't trust us?'

'It isn't that, but people might talk.'

'He doesn't like me, does he?' asked Sergei.

'Howard takes time to get to know people. He's quite shy really.'

'It isn't important. I don't like him either.'

'Sergei!' She was shocked.

'What's the matter? Why should I like him? He isn't my husband. It would be far more shocking if you didn't like him.'

Nicola's head was beginning to throb. 'Well, I do like him, so that doesn't apply. I think I will go and lie down now, I definitely feel wobbly. You'd better take the boys out to lunch. You could always go to McDonald's, they love that.'

'Where does your hospitable husband suggest I stay in December?' he asked coldly.

'He thought a hotel or guest house. There are plenty nearby.'

'That's what I'll do then. You should try and sleep. You look exhausted.'

Nicola nodded. 'Sergei?'

'He turned quickly. 'Yes?'

'I didn't imagine anything this morning. It happened, and you and I both know it happened. Tell the twins that if it happens again they'll find themselves sitting opposite an exorcist before they have time to blink.'

'An exorcist?'

'Or a spiritualist, or anyone else who deals with the paranormal. Somehow I don't think they'd want that to happen.'

'I wouldn't want it to happen either,' he said softly. 'In fact, I'd go to a great deal of trouble to make sure that it didn't.'

Nicola felt cold. 'Why?' she whispered. 'What's special about them?'

He hesitated. 'I can't explain now. Perhaps in December. I will see you then, won't I?'

'Yes, of course! It's only that Howard would rather you weren't here at night.'

'Poor Howard!'

Nicola looked at him and was convinced that he knew exactly why Howard didn't want him in his house at night. 'It isn't you, is it?' she asked in confusion. 'You're not to blame? You can't be!'

He went into the kitchen and came back with a mug of coffee that tasted strangely bitter. 'Sleep now,' he murmured as she gave him back the empty mug. 'You'll feel better after you've slept.'

As though in a daze she got up from the sofa and went upstairs where she collapsed on to the bed and slept for several hours. When she woke she couldn't remember very much about the scene in the kitchen, or what had happened after it. All she could remember was that Melanie was dead, and she lay there for another half hour, sobbing for the loss of her closest friend.

Chapter Nine

Nicola wanted to take the boys to Heathrow airport on the Saturday afternoon, so that the three of them could see Sergei off, but he vetoed the idea immediately.

'The boys will get upset. I'd rather say goodbye to them here.'

Nicola was disappointed. It would have given her an opportunity to say her farewell in private too. As it was she had Howard hovering at her elbow.

'I'll be back soon,' Sergei promised the twins who were quiet and pale.

'Before Christmas?' asked Torquil.

'Yes, before Christmas — that's providing Howard and Nicola don't mind?'

Nicola glanced at Howard, still hoping that he might change his mind and let Sergei stay with them again.

'Let us know the exact date and Nicola can book you in to the Shirleycroft. It's very near Rushton's. You'll be able to pick the boys up after school for us!' he said lightly.

Sergei stared at him. 'You mean, I can't stay here?' The twins began to grizzle, looking reproachfully at their uncle.

'I'm going to be abroad for a few weeks about then. I don't think it will be a good time to have you here. If it's a question of money ...'

Sergei flushed. 'Of course it isn't money.'

'No problem then.' Howard held out his right hand. 'Have a good flight home.'

Sergei ignored the outstretched hand and turned to Nicola. 'Thank you for your generous hospitality,' he said warmly.

145

'You've made me feel one of the family and I'm grateful.'

Nicola's smile was restrained. She felt uncomfortable under Howard's gaze. 'It's been nice for the boys, for all of us, to have you here.'

'Until December then?'

She nodded. 'Until December.'

Torquil and Tarquin began to cry and Sergei took hold of their hands. 'Come out to the car with me. I've got something for both of you.'

Nicola and Howard stayed indoors, watching through the window as he and the twins walked down the drive.

'I can't say I'm sorry to see the back of him,' said Howard with feeling. 'Perhaps now everything will get back to normal.'

'I can't even remember what normal is any more.'

'Normal is when your life revolved around me rather than Sergei!'

She gave an exclamation of annoyance. 'That's ridiculous. The only person who was obsessed with Sergei was you; and I can't help wondering who you'll blame tonight when eveything goes wrong.'

'Thank you for your faith in me, it's most heartening,' said Howard wryly.

The twins came slowly back into the house. 'What have you got?' asked Nicola. They looked at each other and closed their right hands protectively over their presents. 'Let me see,' she coaxed.

'It's just . . .'

'. . . a good luck charm.'

'I think I could do with one of those!' laughed Howard.

The twins glared at him and loosened their fingers, holding out the charms towards Nicola. They were tiny gold figures and she picked one up to study it more closely. Only an inch tall it showed a man with the head of a ferocious-looking wolf.

'What's that?'

'It's Wepwawet,' explained Torquil.

'The God of Death,' clarified his twin.

'Yuck! Why not have something a bit more attractive, say the God of Life?'

They looked mildly amused. 'Wepwawet belongs in Abydos, that's our special place.'

'Is that where you lived in Cairo?'

Her ignorance seemed to amuse them. 'We lived in Heliopolis! Don't you know anything? Abydos is where you go to die!'

'Well, it doesn't sound very nice, but they're certainly lovely figures, although it seems an odd choice for a good luck charm.'

Torquil snatched his charm back from her and put it in the pocket of his jeans. 'You're stupid. Why don't you know more about our country? Aren't you interested?'

'Well, it's never seemed very important to me before. People in Guildford don't go in for gods and godesses much. Apart from the great god money of course!'

They sighed and turned away from her and Nicola felt a pang of guilt. 'Perhaps you'd better teach me yourselves,' she suggested. 'How about that?'

'You're always busy . . .'

'. . . with your work.'

'That isn't true!' Nicola exclaimed when they'd gone. 'I haven't done any work at all during half-term and when they're at school I try to keep my casenotes out of the way until they're in bed.'

Howard shrugged. 'Don't take any notice. They're only trying to wind you up. If you ask me it's a good job they've left Egypt. All this talk of death and destruction can't be good for children.'

'I don't know, they seem totally out of place here. Still, perhaps they'll fit in better at Rushton's. I certainly hope so.'

That night they went to bed early, and much to his relief Howard found that he was able to make love to Nicola perfectly satisfactorily, at least from his point of view. Her responses though were rather muted.

'All right?' he enquired as they settled down to sleep.

'Fine.'

'I told you it would be all right once he'd gone!'

'That's just silly, Howard. How could Sergei possibly have affected you?'

147

'They say sex is largely in the mind. Perhaps I couldn't get him out of the way!'

'That's your fault, not his.'

'It wasn't anyone's fault, it just happened. Fortunately it justifies my insistence on a hotel for him next time.'

'Since you won't even be here, I fail to see how you're going to benefit,' she said irritably, wishing that she'd enjoyed the sex more.

Howard put his arms round her. 'Let's not argue again.'

She tried to relax but his arms seemed unusually heavy and his touch irritated her. Finally she turned away, wishing that she didn't keep seeing disconcerting images of Sergei in the bed with her instead of Howard.

Monday was the day of Melanie's funeral. It was also the first day at Rushton school for the twins. As Howard had taken the morning off for the service he was able to take the boys, and saw them safely in to the office where a kind-looking middle-aged lady gave them each a book to look at while waiting for the Head to arrive.

'Don't worry, they'll be fine,' she assured Howard.

'I'm more worried about you!' he said with a smile.

The secretary smiled back but the twins lifted their heads and stared thoughtfully at him.

'Just a joke, boys!'

'Goodbye,' they said quietly. Howard's smile faded and he left.

The local church was packed with mourners. Nicola held Howard's hand tightly during the service and her composure finally broke when they were paying their respects to Robert after the service.

He looked dreadful. With an ashen face and sunken eyes he'd aged ten years in a few days and when he held out his hand to Howard, it trembled.

'I don't know what to say,' confessed Howard awkwardly. 'We're both so very sorry.'

Robert nodded, unable to speak.

'If there's anything we can do,' said Nicola helplessly. 'Anything at all.'

His head continued to nod and Nicola was reminded of

148

the figure of a tiny Chinese mandarin that her mother had owned. When you touched its head it began to nod, and then continued nodding for several minutes.

Nicola leant forward and kissed Robert on the cheek. 'I'll miss her,' she said tearfully. 'It won't be the same any more.'

Robert swallowed hard. 'I don't know what I'm going to do,' he muttered.

When they were in the car, Howard glanced back to the church gate. 'Who was that attractive blonde woman in the grey suit?'

Nicola had noticed her as well. 'I've no idea. Probably one of Mel's clients.'

'It was Robert she was watching.'

'Really? Well, I've no idea. You know, I can't believe I'm never going to see Melanie again.'

'I'm getting rather tired of death,' said Howard. 'First your parents, then Rose and Labib, and now Melanie. It's almost as though there's some kind of curse on people we know.'

'That's ridiculous,' said Nicola swiftly, but she shivered despite herself.

For the next few weeks life progressed relatively calmly. The twins were happier at Rushton's than they had been at St Hugh's and when Nicola plucked up the courage to speak to their form teacher she seemed very pleased with their academic progress, although she admitted that socially they had remained separate from their peers. Nicola didn't mind. As long as they weren't causing trouble she was content.

At the beginning of December, on the night before Howard left for Brussels, Sergei telephoned from Cairo.

'I can fly over on Thursday,' he told Nicola. She felt a treacherous surge of excitement. 'I was wondering if Howard had changed his mind about where I should stay?'

'I'll ask him,' said Nicola and Howard took the telephone from her.

'As I thought, I'll be away,' he said briskly. 'We'll book you in to the Shirleycroft from Thursday night. I've checked, it's very homely.'

149

'Did he mind?' asked Nicola anxiously when he came off the phone.

'Yes, I think he did but that's just too bad. Torquil! Tarquin! Sergei's coming over on Thursday.'

'We know that!'

'You do? How come?'

They went rather pink and shuffled their feet. 'Well, we sort of knew,' said Torquil. 'Sergei told us he'd be back before Christmas.'

'And we *hoped* it would be this week,' said Tarquin.

'Will he be here for our birthday?' asked Torquil.

'When's your birthday?' asked Nicola in surprise.

'On the twelfth.'

'I had no idea! I suppose I've got it in my birthday book but I haven't looked at that lately. It's lucky you mentioned it. Do you want a party?' Howard groaned.

'Will Sergei still be here?' repeated Torquil.

'God knows,' said Howard. 'If it's anything like his last visit he probably will.'

'And is he staying here?'

Howard shook his head. 'No, he'll be at a hotel right opposite the school.'

'That's not ...'

'... very kind.'

'Well, it's the way it's going to be. You'd better start thinking about what presents you'd like.'

When they went to bed that night Nicola was still trying to decide if she should let the boys have a party.

'They never go to any themselves, so I don't see the need,' said Howard, who was tired and wanted to get off to sleep.

'I just thought it might help them integrate better. I know it's a kind of bribery but so what? We could have a theme party — Ninja turtles or something.'

'The mothers will love that. Sitting up all hours trying to sew some kind of turtle suit!'

'You only need headbands and imagination. Yes, I think that's what I'll do. They can have a turtle party.'

'Perhaps Sergei would like to dress up as well?'

'You know, I feel bad about not having him here to stay.'

150

'Well, I don't, said Howard firmly. 'I feel very good indeed. Now, could I be allowed to sleep?'

He was asleep within minutes, but almost immediately the dreams began. At first they were just generally confused as he dashed through airport terminals missing planes and losing his luggage but then the scene changed and he found himself sitting at his desk at work, only the room was empty of all other furniture and Torquil and Tarquin were standing opposite him.

Even in the dream he knew this was wrong and tried to get them to leave. 'Go home,' he told them firmly. 'You don't belong here.'

They were less childlike in his dream, their expressions more mature than in reality. He found them decidedly unappealing.

'We've been sent ...'

'... to punish you.'

The abrupt announcement panicked him out of all proportion and he began to sweat, drops of perspiration forming on his forehead and under his arms. 'Children don't punish adults,' he said briskly. 'Home you go.'

They moved nearer to his desk.

'We're not really children.'

'We're not really real!'

The room began to shrink and Howard's fear increased. 'Of course you're real,' he blustered, but they smiled and shook their heads.

He was very hot in the dream and looked to see if his windows were open, but to his amazement they'd been replaced with metal shutters festooned with padlocks. 'I need air!' he shouted. 'Give me back my windows.'

One of the twins leant across the desk towards him. 'You won't need air much longer,' he assured him. 'You'll soon be dead.'

'It's you, isn't it?' shouted Howard wildly. 'You're the ones killing everyone. Labib, Rose, Melanie, you killed them all!'

He stood up, rested his hands on the desk top and tried to take a calming breath, but his lungs seemed reluctant to function and his chest felt tight.

151

'Look at that!' said one of the twins admiringly. 'You've got two beautiful hands!' As he spoke, his twin's arm flashed through the air, a sharp pain shot up Howard's arm and he watched blood spurt into the air as the metal cleaver severed his hand at the wrist. The hand crawled forward a few inches leaving a trail of blood and tissue behind it, then came to a stop and began to shrivel.

'That's better!' exclaimed the boys, and promptly severed the other hand as well. The pain was indescribable, and Howard sank back into his chair, his eyes hypnotised by the two bleeding stumps at the end of his arms. Almost immediately his chair began to spin and as he was whirled around in a circle, blood from his arms sprayed into the air and spattered against the white walls.

'Now for the ears!' shouted the twins.

Howard screamed and tried to kick them away but they leapt on to his lap and began to saw away at both sides of his head.

'Please, stop!' he cried. His voice sounded strange, as though his lungs had water in them. The pain in his head was so intense that it made him cry, but to his horror his tears were made of blood that dripped down his cheeks and fell with a splashing sound on to his trousers, slowly turning them a dull shade of rust.

'Got them!' the boys cried in triumph, and they jumped off his knees and ran round the room each brandishing an ear aloft as Howard sat in helpless agony with blood flowing down over his face and chest.

'Now for his head!' they cried eagerly, and each produced a huge scimitar-like blade and advanced towards him.

'Be brave now.'

'It's nearly over.'

'*You don't need a head anyway, you never think*!'

'Why?' asked Howard, still weeping tears of blood, but the question came out as an unintelligible gargling sound as he tasted blood in his mouth. It didn't matter. The twins had understood him.

'Because of the hotel!' said one fiercely.

'You kept him away from us,' explained the other. 'That was a bad thing to do.'

152

'*A very bad thing indeed*!'

The scimitars swung back, their eyes glowed with excitement and Howard's scream of terror finally broke through the nightmare. His eyes opened as he sat bolt upright in bed.

'No!' he screamed again, still confused and certain that he could feel the blood dripping down his face.

'What is it? What's the matter?' Nicola came awake with a start and snapped on the bedside lamp.

Howard took his hands away from his face and then screamed again as he saw that they were covered in blood. 'Help me!' he yelled. 'They've cut off my ears! It wasn't a dream. Oh God, someone help me!'

Nicola jumped out of bed and ran round to his side where he was trying to scramble out. 'It's all right, Howard. You're having a nosebleed that's all. Here, let me pinch the bridge of your nose.'

'But there's blood everywhere. My pyjama jacket's soaked! It's my ears, look, see for yourself. Oh, God, what will I do?'

Nicola stared at him in disbelief as he began to sob, his tears mingling with the blood from his nose and getting smeared all over his face by his hands.

'Howard, it was a dream. Mind, you're getting your hands covered in blood. Tip you head back, quickly.'

'My hands!' He sat forward and put his hands palms uppermost on his knees. 'They're all right! It *was* a dream then. God, what a relief!'

'Lean back!' said Nicola again. 'It's very bad. Perhaps I should call a doctor.'

Howard had never known such relief. 'It's all right, it's nothing,' he said quickly. And compared with the nightmare it was nothing, nothing at all. Gradually the bleeding stopped, but Nicola made him stay perfectly still with his fingers pinching the bridge of his nose while she fetched him clean pyjamas and a fresh pillowcase.

'Whatever did you think had happened?' she asked quietly when his colour began to return.

Howard shivered. 'I'd rather not think about it just yet. It was terrible. I've never ... It's beyond words, Nikki.'

153

Now that it was over he felt very cold and his teeth began to chatter. 'You'd better get under the duvet,' she said. 'How about a mug of hot, sweet tea?'

'No, I'll be all right now.'

'You're not worried about this trip to Brussels, are you?'

He almost laughed in her face. 'Brussels? This hasn't got anything to do with Brussels! This is that damned Russian's fault.'

'Really, Howard! I think you're getting paranoid about Sergei. How can he have given you a nightmare and a nosebleed?'

'I don't know, but I'm quite certain that he did. He's angry because I won't let him stay here and this is his way of getting revenge.'

'You should listen to yourself,' said Nicola, putting the blood-stained pyjama jacket into the linen basket. 'I presume it's shock addling your brains but you really should get a hold of yourself. Sergei Cheparukhin may not be your idea of the perfect guest but he is only a medical researcher, and an ordinary human being.'

'It's his fault,' Howard repeated obstinately.

There was a tap at the door. Nicola opened it and found the twins standing outside.

'We thought we heard ...'

'... lots of shouting.'

'*We were frightened.*'

They peered round her and looked intently at Howard who was lying propped up on one elbow.

'Howard had a nightmare, that's all.'

'There's blood on his face,' said Torquil with interest.

'He had a bit of a nosebleed.'

Tarquin's eyes widened. 'A nightmare *and* a nosebleed?'

'That's very unlucky,' said Torquil.

His twin nodded. 'Very unlucky indeed!'

Howard glared at them. 'Bugger off, the pair of you. You've done enough for one night.'

They flinched and moved closer to each other.

Nicola's concern for Howard was rapidly vanishing anyway, and this was the last straw. 'Really, Howard!

154

I'm sorry, boys, he's had a nasty shock. You run off back to bed. He'll be all right now.'

She closed the door on them and turned back to the bed. 'How could you speak to them like that? They were worried about you.'

'They came to gloat. I could see it in their eyes. They were smiling!'

'They were not smiling. Honestly, Howard, I don't know what's happening to you. Perhaps the trip to Brussels will do you good. Something certainly needs to.'

Howard looked at her set expression and knew that if he wasn't careful he was going to alienate himself from her. 'Nikki, I'm sorry, but there is something strange going on. Don't you think there's something strange about the boys? And Sergei?'

'No, I don't.'

'Don't they ever make you feel odd? Don't you ever find yourself thinking strange thoughts when they're around?'

Nicola hesitated. 'What kind of thoughts?'

'I don't know, all kinds. Camels! The day they arrived here I found myself looking for a camel instead of a car.'

Nicola sighed. 'All I know is that since they arrived you've been having some difficulty in letting them into our life. That's understandable, but it's your problem, not theirs.'

'If you could forget Sergi's chocolate-box good looks for a few minutes and think about him dispassionately you might realise that one or two aspects of his character are distinctly odd. I mean, where does he really come from? What do we know about his family or friends? Nothing, that's what! Nothing at all. And what is this work he does in Egypt? It seems peculiar to me that he can fly back and forth to England whenever he likes. After all, we're meant to be the boys' guardians, not him. We'd never heard of im before your sister died, and yet now he seems to be *the* authority on the twins. How come? Surely their tutors or nurses should know more about them than him?'

'I can't imagine what all this has to do with your nightmare,' said Nicola coldly.

'When I get back from Brussels I'm going to ask him a few more penetrating questions,' said Howard firmly.

155

'I'm surprised you dare if he's in such control of your dreams.'

He didn't want to, but thought that if he could find out more about the Russian it might help him to keep his marriage intact. He sensed that Sergei was determined to stay near the boys, and Howard knew that he'd be willing to give them up and let Sergei take them back to Egypt if it was the only way he could preserve his marriage.

The boys meant nothing to him, but Nicola meant everything; if the Russian thought that he could have her as well then he was very much mistaken.

On the Thursday morning the boys were up and dressed by seven o'clock. It was the first time they'd dressed themselves without any help and Nicola was delighted.

'Well done! Perhaps Sergei should come and see you more often.'

'Is he ...'

'... here yet?'

She laughed. 'It's not even breakfast time.'

They sighed and ran to the kitchen window. 'This is a funny house,' said Torquil, peering out at the damp morning. 'Why does your kitchen look out over the front garden?'

'Because the front door's really the back door. It's just that as the back door's the first one people come to, they think it's the front, and after a while we decided that if everyone was going to get it wrong we might as well have a decent door put there and use it as a front entrance.'

'At home we've got an enormous front door and porch, but a tiny back door that leads out to a courtyard. You'd have to be very stupid indeed to get our doors muddled up,' said Torquil.

'Do you miss your home a lot?' asked Nicola quietly.

Tarquin nodded. 'Yes, we do. We miss it every second of every hour of every day. It's horrible here, always cold and wet; and the people are horrid too. There's no colour to anything. Everything's drab, even clothes. We can't wait to go back.'

Nicola felt sad for them. 'Perhaps we could take you back for a holiday in the summer. Would you like that?'

They shook their heads. 'No, we want to live there. We can wait.'

'But you won't be able to live there until you're grown up. Howard and I can't just pick up sticks and emigrate. He has his work to do.'

'I guess we'll have to leave him behind then,' said Tarquin casually. 'Where's the Shirleycroft Hotel?'

'Opposite your school.'

'Will we see him arrive from our classroom?'

'I doubt it, but he'll be there to meet you when school ends and you can bring him back for dinner tonight.'

'Is he *allowed* to eat his dinner here?' asked Torquil sarcastically.

'Yes. Now, have you given me all your party acceptance slips?'

They nodded, gulped down their hot oat cereal and then stood by the kitchen door. 'We're ready to go now.'

'It's only half-past seven, you can't go to school yet!'

Tarquin scowled. 'We want the day to get started.'

Nicola put out a hand and smoothed some hair back from his forehead. He let her do it but she could see the effort it cost him not to move away. 'It will pass,' she promised. 'Even Christmas Eve passes eventually.'

'What's Christmas Eve?'

'The day before Christmas Day. You know, when Father Christmas comes.'

Torquil laughed. 'Father Christmas doesn't come to Moslems!'

'But surely you used to get presents? I know Howard and I always sent you something.'

'We've never had . . .'

'. . . Father Christmas visit us.'

'I didn't know you were brought up as Moslems. Rose told me your father no longer practised his religion.'

'Perhaps he didn't. Perhaps . . .'

'. . . we were brought up as something completely different.'

They both watched her intently, but Nicola had a difficult patient arriving at nine and didn't have time for theological discussions. 'Perhaps you were,' she agreed. 'Now, off and

157

clean your teeth. I want to get my notes sorted out, so stay out of my way for ten minutes, there's good lads.' They went without argument, and she realised how much easier they were to look after when they knew that Sergei would soon be with them.

It was twelve-thirty before she'd finished with her nine o'clock patient and she felt exhausted. Making herself a corned beef sandwich she took it into the lounge to watch the news, but no sooner had she taken a bite than the telephone rang.

'Yes?' she asked wearily.

'Nicola, it's me, Sergei.'

Immediately she felt less tired. 'You're here! That's splendid, the boys will be delighted.'

'And you? Are you delighted too?'

'They certainly behave better when you're here.'

'That wasn't quite what I meant. Unhappily, I've got a slight problem. Just before I arrived the wife of the man who runs this hotel was rushed into hospital. This has left him without a cook or a laundry maid. In fact, he doesn't seem to know how he's going to cope. He isn't taking any new guests for the time being, but of course I'm already here.'

'Well, the meals aren't any problem. You can eat with us.'

'I'll tell him that.'

'I suppose if he really wants to close down for a few days you could always sleep here too, it's only that . . .'

'No, really, I'm sure he won't close completely. Howard wouldn't be at all pleased if he learnt that I'd slept with you.'

Nicola felt her pulse quicken but she didn't respond.

'What time do Torquil and Tarquin come out of school?'

'Three-fifteen. Shall I meet you at the gates?'

'It doesn't matter. I can manage on my own. Until this afternoon then.'

'Yes,' she said quietly. 'Until this afternoon.'

She'd never known three hours to pass as slowly. She kept checking that her watch hadn't stopped, and turning on the television in search of distraction, only to turn it off again as she found herself listening to yet more people discussing their alcohol-related or sexual problems.

In the end she found herself, like Torquil earlier in the day, standing by the kitchen window staring hopefully down the drive. She heard the car just before it appeared and went to the front door, then stood in the doorway watching as the twins tumbled out of the back seat.

They ran to her, their faces glowing with excitement.

'He's here! He's really here.'

'He was waiting at the gates, just like you said.'

Nicola bent down and kissed them both on the forehead. 'Did it seem a long day?'

Torquil nodded. 'Yes, it jolly well did. But we knew . . .'

'. . . it would be worth the wait,' completed Tarquin.

'We're going to show him our turtle T-shirts,' said Torquil, and they ran indoors, leaving her to greet Sergei on her own.

He had stopped a few feet away and stood looking towards her, his long hair damp from the steady drizzle that was falling. He was paler than she'd remembered and the streaks of grey were more prominent in his black hair but if anything the attraction that he held for her had only increased during his absence and she felt a physical ache in her solar plexus as she waited for him to move towards her.

He seemed reluctant to take the last few steps but finally he took his hands out of the pockets of his dark coat and walked purposefully across the gravel, swiftly grasping her hands in his.

'I've missed you,' he said quietly. 'I've been away too long.'

She knew that she ought to say something light and amusing about the children, but she didn't feel either light or amusing. She was almost consumed by a physical desire for him that made speech impossible.

He moved closer and she felt the dampness of his coat. 'Did you miss me at all?'

Nicola nodded, then closed her eyes as he ran the fingers of one hand tenderly down her jawline. 'I'm here now. That's all that matters,' he whispered. She trembled violently. 'Don't be afraid. It will be wonderful. You have no idea how wonderful I can make it.'

But even as she stood there in the drizzle, her body

physically spellbound by his presence and desperate for further physical contact, a part of her mind stood back and told her to run. To get away from him now, before anything had happened, before he had the opportunity to show her the wonderful world he promised. And the same part of her mind kept repeating Howard's name over and over, as though it were a mantra offering protection against the Russian invader. But then he bent his head, brushing her mouth with his cold lips, and as icy fire darted through her veins the still small voice of reason was extinguished.

'Come on!' shouted one of the twins irritably. 'We've got our T-shirts out. You'll be all wet if you don't come in.'

Sergei lifted his head but kept one hand gently in the small of Nicola's back as he propelled her into the house ahead of him and each finger felt as though it were scorching her flesh beneath her jersey, leaving a burning fingerprint behind when the hand was removed. Lightheaded, she sat down on the sofa and watched Sergei walk off with the boys.

She had no idea how long they were gone, but the twins looked amazed to find her sitting in the same place when they returned.

'We thought you'd have some cake ready for us,' complained Torquil.

She lifted her head, trying to concentrate on what he was saying. 'Sorry?'

'Can we have a cake?' repeated Tarquin.

'Yes, of course. And I'll put the kettle on, I was just ...'

'Sergei says the lady who runs his hotel's dead. Can he stay here now?'

'Dead?' Shocked she looked directly into Sergei's eyes, seeking an explanation there.

'I didn't have time to tell you. She died at three o'clock.'

'But that's terrible. Had she been ill a long time?'

'I've no idea. Her husband's very shocked. He's closed the hotel.'

Nicola was rapidly coming out of her state of confusion. 'Why didn't you tell me that straight away?'

'I had other things I wanted to say first.'

She blushed and spilt some of the boiling water on to the work top. 'Damn!'

'Let me,' he said quickly, and took the kettle from her unsteady hands. 'You shouldn't let it upset you. After all, you didn't know her. People die all the time. They're dying in their thousands every second of the day.'

'Yes, but fortunately I don't have to know about them. This is different.'

'I wondered if you could recommend another hotel?'

Her mouth felt dry. 'Not really, that was the only one Howard bothered to check out.'

'Perhaps you have a guide I could look through?'

There was an inevitability about it all that took the responsibility away from Nicola. She felt that even if he did go somewhere else he was going to end up standing in her kitchen once again, still waiting for the words that he wanted to hear and she wanted to speak.

'You might as well stay here.' She was proud of the fact that she managed to make her voice quite off-hand. 'The spare bed's made up.'

'I'll fetch my case in from the car when I've had my coffee. After all, we don't have to tell Howard.'

'He's due back Saturday morning; he'll see for himself then.'

'He might be delayed.'

'I doubt it. The boys have a party in the afternoon, he won't miss that.'

'Business can ruin the best-laid plans. We'll have to wait and see.'

'It doesn't matter,' she said levelly. 'He'll understand.'

Sergei smiled.

Howard rang at eight o'clock on the Saturday morning.

'Nicola, I hate to do this to you but I'm not going to make it back today,' he apologised over a crackling line .

'What! Howard, you can't do this to me. I've had twelve acceptances for this party — that makes fourteen children with the twins. You promised faithfully you'd be here.'

'It's a last minute thing. I thought it was all cleared up last night, but now it seems I was wrong and we've got to have further discussions. I can't leave, it would cost me my job.'

'I can't believe this!' she protested, remembering Sergei's comments the day he arrived. 'You've never had to stay on an extra day before.'

'I can't help it, Nikki. You'll just have to say happy birthday to the twins for me. They won't mind. They've got Sergei there, haven't they?'

'Yes.'

'Well, don't sound so miserable about it! At least he can lend a hand at the party.'

'I don't want him to help with the party,' she said fiercely. 'I need *you* here, Howard. It's really important that you get here.'

'That's not true and you know it. You can manage perfectly well without me. Better, probably. I'm sure sexy Sergei will be much better than me at party games!'

Nicola closed her eyes, frighteningly close to tears. 'Howard, I want you here. Please, try and come home.'

'What's the matter? There's nothing wrong, is there?'

Tell him, shouted a voice in her head. Tell him that you're afraid you won't be able to resist the Russian. Tell him you're not yourself any more.

She lowered her voice. 'It's difficult to explain over the phone.'

'You'll have to speak up, this line's dreadful.'

She gripped the receiver more tightly. 'I want you back here,' she whispered. 'I need you.'

'I'm sorry, I can't hear a word. There's the most awful interference on the line. Look, I'll be back tomorrow lunchtime at the latest. Sergei's booked into the Shirleycroft all right, has he?'

She leant against the kitchen wall and realised that Sergei was standing in the doorway opposite, watching her. 'Yes,' she said dully. 'He booked in to the Shirleycroft as soon as he got here.'

'Fine. See you soon. I'll think of you during the afternoon. Love you.'

She wanted to say that she loved him too but the words wouldn't come and she replaced the receiver without another word.

'Some kind of problem?' Sergei asked.

162

'Howard's been delayed. He won't be back until tomorrow.'

'That's very unlucky for Howard,' said Sergei in an amused voice.

'But no surprise to you?'

'These things happen. Don't worry, I can do anything Howard was going to do.'

'I'm sure you can.'

He put his hands on her shoulders. 'Don't fight it, Nicola. There's no point.'

She pulled away from him, grateful that he couldn't see her body's instant response to his touch. 'I have to get on. There's a lot to do before three o'clock. I don't suppose you're any good at making sandwiches are you?'

'I'm good at anything I put my mind to.'

'Then put it to work on egg and mayonnaise sandwiches. The boys will get you a loaf and the low fat spread. Just keep going until the eggs run out.'

Upstairs in her bedroom she studied her bright eyes and glowing complexion in the dressing table mirror. There was no doubt that she was looking her best at the moment and she knew that this was partly due to Sergei's presence, yet even now she was afraid of moving forward, of committing physical adultery. It was one thing to kiss and enjoy being desired, but quite another to give herself over to another man entirely.

'Why couldn't you get here, Howard?' she demanded of the mirror. 'You've never trusted Sergei, how come you're willing to leave me alone with him today?'

Even as she asked, she knew the answer. Howard hadn't had any choice. What Sergei wanted, Sergei got. And right now he wanted her.

'But why?' she asked, studying her face in the dressing table mirror. As she looked her reflection gradually began to change. Her hair lost its auburn shine and became a mousy brown, her eyes dimmed to a washed out blue and there were small lines between her eyebrows. Puzzled she turned to check herself in the long mirror in the wardrobe door, but she looked exactly the same as usual there.

'Must be the light,' she said aloud. But it wasn't. Her

163

reflection in this mirror was still changing, and now the face looking back at her wasn't her own at all. It belonged to Rose. She was looking at her dead sister's face.

'Rose?' She put out a tentative hand and touched the cool glass. 'Rose, what is it? Tell me, please.'

Roses expression grew anguished and her pale lips moved soundlessly. Although frightened, Nicola knew that she had to hear the words, had to understand her sister's message. She moved so close to the looking glass that her breath clouded the surface and she wiped it clear with a tissue.

Again Rose's lips moved, but more slowly this time, so that Nicola could almost make out the word.

'Well? Are you saying that you're well? Is that it?'

Two tears rolled down Rose's cheeks and this time there was a whisper of sound in the room.

'Hell? You're in hell? But, Rose, why? What's happened to you?'

The pale lips moved again, and the faded blue eyes were filled with urgency. 'I can't hear!' shouted Nicola in despair. 'It's no good. I can't hear what you're saying.'

Once more the words whispered around her, almost teasing her as she strained to make sense of them.

'Make way for hell? Is that it? Rose, am I right?'

Rose's expression said she was wrong, but now the image was fading and as the mirror cleared Nicola found herself once again looking at her own reflection. Stunned, she sat staring blankly into space, remembering her sister's anguished face.

The sound of laughter outside brought her to her senses. Blinking and rubbing at her eyes she looked out into the back garden where the twins were wobbling around the lawn on their new bikes. Sergei was with them but he seemed to sense her presence and glanced up at the house.

For a moment she was tempted to duck back out of sight but then he waved and smiled at her and she realised how ridiculous she was being. She had no reason to hide, and so she waved back.

Playing with the children in the garden he looked far less threatening. He was still handsome, of course, but with the glass between them she was no longer aware of that extraordinary sexual magnetism that she found so overwhelming.

'So much for the egg sandwiches!' she said aloud, but she didn't really mind. At least it made the Russian seem more human, and after her experience with the mirror she needed normality.

At three o'clock the twins positioned themselves by the kitchen window so that they could look out for the first arrivals.

At three-thirty, Sergei joined them in their vigil.

At three forty-five the twins left the window, went into the lounge and put on a Ninja turtle video.

At four o'clock Nicola finally accepted that something had gone wrong. She looked at the party food on the dining-room table, at the carefully wrapped packages of sweets and balloons for the visitors to take home and at the bulky parcel for passing round the circle and wondered if she'd put the wrong date on the invitations.

'Give me a name,' she said to the boys. 'Any name.'

'Bernard.'

'What's his surname?'

The twins sighed and stopped the video tape. 'Whose surname?' demanded Tarquin.

'Bernard's, of course.'

'Bernard who?'

She felt like screaming at them. 'The Bernard you've asked to the party.'

'We don't know any Bernard. You said . . .'

'. . . give me a name, so we did.'

'I want the name of one of your guests so that I can find out why no one's arrived yet,' she said slowly.

'They haven't come . . .'

'. . . because they don't like us.'

'That's nonsense. Their mothers accepted. You brought the acceptance slips home.'

'Yes, but the children didn't want to come. They kept whispering about it at school.'

'Why don't they like you?' she asked softly.

The twins pursed their lips and looked thoughtful.

'Perhaps it's because . . .'

'. . . we get into their minds.'

'I don't suppose it really matters why they don't like the twins,' said Sergei abruptly. 'The point is, they aren't coming.'

'But all this food!' wailed Nicola. 'And the games and everything. It's such a waste. I don't know how their parents can be so rude.'

'Perhaps they're all ill,' said Torquil unconvincingly.

'Or all pretending to be ill,' put in his twin.

'I think it's terrible! You must be so upset,' said Nicola, suddenly aware that the boys had been unusually excited and now it was all for nothing.

'We don't mind,' they said together.

She looked at Sergei. 'What do you think we should do? Take them out somewhere for tea?'

'I think it would be a good idea to open a bottle of wine and make a start on the tea ourselves. There's no point in wasting it all.'

'You can't open a bottle of wine at four o'clock in the afternoon!'

'Is there a law against it?'

'No, but it's just silly. Wine doesn't go with egg sandwiches.'

'Then we'll leave the egg sandwiches to the boys.'

Nicola gave in. The desolated atmosphere of the empty, party-decorated rooms had brought home to her as nothing else could have done the fact that the twins had been no more successful at integrating into Rushton's than St Hugh's. Despite all her efforts they were just as much outsiders now as when they'd arrived, and the problem could no longer be ignored. She was going to have to do something about it, but despite all her training she had no idea what that would be.

Sergei gave her a glass. 'Here, I hope you like a sparkling white Italian!'

'I could do with a sparkling anything at this moment.'

He touched his glass to hers. 'To the boys' seventh birthday.'

She smiled. 'Happy birthday, boys!'

But as she and Sergei drank their wine the boys slipped

quietly away to the dining room. They ate some of the food and then began to clear the table, tidying up everything they could find. They moved swiftly and silently, aware that Sergei would want no distractions from them at this vital moment in the plan.

Eventually, after what seemed an interminably long time to them, they heard footsteps on the stairs and when they tiptoed into the lounge and saw two empty wine bottles on the glass-topped table they looked at each other and smiled in satisfaction.

Chapter Ten

Nicola felt as though she were floating on air. The wine had been potent and she had scarcely been aware of what was happening until she found herself in the bedroom with Sergei behind her, both standing in front of the wardrobe mirror. He put his arms round her waist, and she looked at their reflection.

Her hair was tousled, her cheeks flushed, and she seemed to glow with good health. By contrast Sergei looked pale and reserved, but his dark eyes burnt in their deep sockets and his apparent self-containment only excited her more, because she knew how much he wanted her. She realised that he too was watching them in the mirror, and laughed.

'What's so amusing?' he asked, his hands sliding up towards her breasts.

'You are. You look so solemn. Has anyone ever told you that your face is shaped like a triangle?'

'No.'

'Well, it is, and you've got eyes like a cat.'

'You talk too much.'

'I know. It's because I've had too much to drink. Howard says it always makes me gabble.'

'Perhaps Howard doesn't know how to keep you quiet.'

Her laughter died in her throat. 'And you do?'

He nodded. 'Yes, I rather think I do.'

She turned away from the mirror and faced him. 'I don't usually do this sort of thing. I've never once been unfaithful to Howard, never.'

'I know.' He was already undressing her. Zips and buttons

seemed to fall open at the slightest touch of his fingers. There was no fumbling or tugging, his movements were smooth and deft.

'I think you've done this before,' commented Nicola, her head spinning as he laid her back on the bed.

'I'm certainly not a virgin!'

The air felt cool on her flesh and she shivered, reaching for the duvet. Sergei put out a restraining hand. 'Leave it. I'll keep you warm.'

She watched as he stripped off his own clothes, folding them neatly on the chair before lying down beside her.

Nicola wanted to put out a hand to him but shyness stopped her. She was beginning to wish she'd had a little more wine. Here in the cool bedroom the effects were suddenly wearing off too quickly.

Sergei propped himself up on one elbow and looked down at her, his gaze travelling from her head to her toes.

'Don't look at me like that,' she protested. 'I know I'm overweight, and it all settles round my hips. It's horrible.'

'You're perfect, absolutely perfect.' He put out a hand and trailed his fingers down the inside of her arm. 'Do all redheads have such creamy skin?'

'I don't know, I've been been to bed with one!'

He bent down and she thought that he was going to kiss her but instead he began to lick at the delicate skin beneath her ears, his tongue surprisingly cold. She shivered. Sex with Howard was comforting and safe; she was used to his touch and knew what to expect. This was different.

Sergei breathed gently in her ear then thrust his tongue into the opening, and she found herself twisting towards him as her body began to respond. Encouraged by the movement his hands started to move over her, one of them imprisoning her left breast. His grip was harsh yet he managed to move his individual fingers delicately in tiny circles, brushing as though by accident against the stiffening nipple.

Only now did he begin to kiss her, his mouth totally enveloping hers as though he were trying to take her over completely. She attempted to turn her head away but immediately one of his hands caught hold of her face, imprisoning it, and within seconds she felt his other hand between her legs. At first his touch was as harsh as his kisses, but once his fingers touched her inner moistness the pressure changed until it was so light that it was unbearable and she tried to push herself against him, afraid that it wouldn't be enough.

'Keep still,' he whispered, and she felt the roughness of his stubble scraping against her cheek. She liked the sensation, and he seemed to know intuitively that it excited her because he moved himself so that he could do the same against the tender flesh of her breasts. Her breath caught in her throat and she heard herself moan softly.

The whole pattern of his lovemaking was built on contrasts. Contrasts of touch, of pressure and lightness; contrasts of sensations, the roughness of his stubble and the liquid smoothness of his tongue; and contrasts of kisses, harshly demanding one moment, tender and teasing the next. Nicola's body responded like a violin to the touch of a master player.

Before his recent problems, Nicola had always considered Howard a good unselfish lover but Sergei seemed absolutely disinterested in his own satisfaction and not until she was totally exhausted, her body limp after repeated orgasms, did he finally cover her body with his and enter her. For several minutes he moved slowly and smoothly within her, until she could feel the sensations building once again towards another peak. She opened her eyes and found him staring down at her with a look of intense concentration.

'Yes,' she whispered. 'Now, please.'

For the first time since he'd begun to make love to her, his lips curved upwards in a smile and he grasped her hips, lifting them off the bed so that he could move more freely, and suddenly the movements changed and now it felt as though he were assaulting her, so violent were his thrusts. She whimpered a small protest until she realised that the pleasure was greater than the discomfort, and then the whimper changed to a gasp until with a muffled scream she was shaken by a climax so intense that for a fleeting second she lost all sense of time and place and was aware only of the ecstasy flooding her body.

She twisted in an uncontrollable spasm, her hips rising with a life of their own, and at that moment Sergei finally gave one final, brutal thrust and threw back his head in his own silent moment of pleasure. But not ecstasy. It took other things for Sergei to achieve total ecstasy, things that he knew he would teach her in the future because she had proved even more responsive than he had dared to hope. He knew a moment's satisfaction at the thought that Labib had chosen the wrong sister as his wife.

Nicola lay silently with her eyes closed. Her body was drenched with sweat and she felt limp and boneless. All she wanted to do was sleep and she turned her head to see if Sergei's eyes were closed. She was disconcerted to find that he wasn't even lying beside her. Instead he was dressing swiftly.

'What's the hurry?' she asked in bewilderment.

'The twins will think they've been abandoned.'

Nicola sat up, and immediately remembered all the wine she'd drunk as her head spun and pain jabbed behind one eye. 'I forgot all about them! God, suppose they say something to Howard?'

'What could they say? They don't know anything. They're probably watching television. Time doesn't mean anything to children.'

'What is the time?'

'Eight o'clock.'

'It can't be!'

He shrugged. 'See for yourself.'

She felt hurt by his brisk detachment. 'That's ridiculous. We must have been up here for hours.'

'If a job's worth doing, it's worth doing properly. Isn't that what they say?'

'I don't think I particularly care to be referred to as a job.'

He looked puzzled. 'What's the matter?'

'Nothing. Where are my clothes? I'd better dress too.'

'You're angry with me. Why?'

She didn't want to sound childish and say he wasn't making enough fuss of her. 'I'm not, I'm angry with myself. I don't know how I'm going to face Howard.'

'Tell him the truth.'

171

Nicola stared blankly at Sergei. 'Are you mad? He'd walk straight out of the house and that would be the end of our marriage.'

'Good.'

'Is that what you want to do?' she asked incredulously. 'Was all this just some game to you? An attempt to destroy my marriage?'

He stepped forward and caught hold of her shoulders. 'No, it wasn't a game. I want you for myself. I want to be able to make love to you like that whenever I like. I want you to belong to me, not Howard. And you will, one day.'

'Let go of me! I don't happen to *belong* to Howard, I'm his wife, which is an entirely different thing. And if my marriage did end, I wouldn't belong to you either. I don't know what it's like where you come from but here women do have an identity of their own.'

He sat on the edge of the bed, reached out a hand and began to caress her nipples lightly again. 'Of course you don't belong to Howard, he isn't strong enough to own any woman.'

'And you are, I suppose?'

Sergei nodded. 'Yes, I am.'

'That isn't strength, that's just chauvinistic crap.'

He raised his eyebrows and looked faintly amused so that when the pain shot through her right breast she didn't connect it with him for a moment. Instead she gasped, her eyes suddenly clouded.

'What is it?'

'A pain, I . . .'

She looked down and saw his fingers resting on her breast. 'That hurt!' she exclaimed in fury.

'It was meant to hurt. I don't like being insulted.'

'Get away from me. I want to get dressed.'

Almost lazily his hand wandered across to her other breast but this time she was prepared and pushed at it. 'I mean it, Sergei. Let me go.'

This time he laughed, and again a shaft of pure pain lanced through her so that she cried out. She was frightened now. This wasn't something that she understood and she struggled to sit up, but he casually pushed her back and then began to

172

kiss her. He kissed her softly, caressingly, his tongue lingering in the soft corners of her mouth; gentle exquisite kisses that turned her to liquid, and after a few minutes the pain from her nipples and the excitement from his kisses mingled into one and when he entered her again she wasn't surprised, because it all seemed part of a pattern that she now accepted would lead to absolute and total fulfilment for her.

This time her climax was fierce, and her cry was nearly one of pain as her weary body spasmed helplessly again and again. Sergei looked down at her exhausted face with the long lashes lying against her cheeks and gave a nod of satisfaction as he withdrew. His own pleasure could wait. The opportunity to teach her a lesson had been too good to miss and now he was satisfied that he had nothing to fear from Howard's return.

'I'll go down and get the boys ready for bed,' he whispered. 'You rest for a while.' She nodded wearily and listened as he finished dressing and let himself out of the bedroom.

As soon as he'd gone she opened her eyes and sat up, looking down at her body and seeing the tiny marks on her breasts that would undoubtedly turn to bruises, bruises that Howard must never see.

She was disgusted with herself. Disgusted by her betrayal of Howard but even more disgusted over her betrayal of herself. She knew that the sex the second time couldn't be called lovemaking, that it was a parody of the kind of lovemaking she and Howard enjoyed, and yet she'd loved it. That final moment, the fusion of the pain and the pleasure, had been incredible, and she'd even relished Sergei's domination of her mind and body. But only then. Now, alone and totally sober, she didn't relish it at all.

Slowly she got out of bed and went into the bathroom where she filled the tub with water as hot as she could bear and then lay in it, submerged up to her neck, hoping that hot water would wash her clean.

Later, her skin red and uncomfortable, she slipped into a jade green track suit, put trainers on her feet and brushed her hair vigorously until she felt up to facing the world again.

'We're going to sleep now!' called Tarquin, meeting her on the landing. He was clutching a teddy bear hot water

173

bottle to his chest and looked at her with disconcertingly knowing eyes.

Nicola nodded. 'I'm really sorry about your party. I'll speak to some of the mothers tomorrow, find out what went wrong.'

'It doesn't matter. We don't like parties much.'

Nicola crouched down to his level. 'Do you like *any* of the children?'

He frowned. 'Well, not really, but we wouldn't, would we?'

'Why not?'

'Because we're different. That's why we didn't go to school at home.'

'Wouldn't you like to be the same as them sometimes?'

It was obvious the thought had never occurred to him before and he gave it a moment's consideration. 'It would be pretty boring I should think.'

'Why boring? What can you do that's so exciting?'

'Anything we like really. It all starts up here.' He tapped the side of his head.

'You mean you play imaginary games?'

Tarquin, whom Nicola had thought for some time was the most amiable of the two, gave her a rare smile. 'No, that's not what I mean! You know really, you just don't want to believe it.'

'Tarquin, I don't know anything. I've had several years of training so that I can help children but I can't seem to help you at all. I need you to tell me what I should do.'

'To help us?'

She nodded.

'Nothing at all; we don't need any help. We're happy. Are you happy?'

'Well, I suppose so. I hadn't really given it much thought.'

'You look happy now.'

She blushed to the roots of her hair and straightened up. 'That's because I've had a nice rest and slept off the wine that I shouldn't have drunk! Where's Torquil?'

'I'm Torquil.'

'No, you're not. I can see your badge. Besides, I'm

174

beginning to realise there's a difference between the two of you. You're certainly Tarquin.'

'I'm not, honestly I'm not. I'm Torquil but it's my day to be nice.'

'Well, are you Alpha or Omega?'

His face darkened and he screwed up his nose. 'Now you've spoilt it all! I'm Omega.'

'All the time?'

'Yes, all the time. I don't choose to be Omega, I *have* to be.'

'Why?'

'Because that's what I am. I'm Omega, the end.'

'The end?'

'Yes, you know, Alpha and Omega the beginning and the end. I'm the end.'

'The end of what?'

'Everything, I suppose. The entire world. Yes, I'm probably the end of the entire world!' Now he laughed aloud but Nicola didn't respond because there was something about his laughter that she didn't like.

'You're certainly the end at nine o'clock at night! Off to bed with you, and your twin too. Where is he?'

'Asleep. He's worn out with practising.'

Nicola frowned. 'What's he been practising?'

'Just things. 'Night 'night.'

She checked in their bedroom to make sure that Torquil had told the truth and saw that his twin was indeed fast asleep. Then she went hesitantly downstairs, wondering what on earth she and Sergei were going to talk about for the rest of the evening.

'I thought I'd go out for a drink,' said Sergei the moment she appeared, which removed the worry immediately.

'Good idea. Where will you go?'

'Somewhere near. Where would you sugest?'

'There's the Old Oak. That's only about a fifteen-minute walk away. Sergei, about tonight.'

'What about it?'

'It can't happen again. When Howard gets back I think we ought to try and find you somewhere else to stay. If you were around I'd give myself away.'

175

He frowned. 'You mean you're intending to carry on as usual with Howard?'

'Yes.'

'I think you may find that more difficult than you imagine.'

'I know it won't be easy but it's what I want to do.'

'Are you sure?' He took two steps towards her.

'Don't touch me, Sergei. We both know what will happen if you do, but that doesn't mean I should abandon my marriage. It's just lust. It can happen to anyone but too many people mistake it for love. I'm not going to make that mistake.'

She expected him to say something more, to make a fuss or protest that he did love her, but he didn't do anything. He simply stood and looked at her and his steady appraisal unnerved her.

'I can do it, Sergei. I can put tonight behind me, but I need your help.'

'You won't get it.'

'Then I need your absence.'

He nodded. 'I'll move out tomorrow.'

Nicola was astounded. 'Tomorrow? Where will you go?'

'I've no idea, but I can tell that you're serious so I think I should go. It wouldn't be easy for me to watch you with Howard either, although you don't seem to have given that any thought.'

She hadn't, because she didn't believe that Sergei was emotionally committed to her. Now she began to wonder if she was wrong.

'I'll ask at the pub tonight. They might know somewhere,' he continued.

Perversely she was beginning to wish that he'd made more effort to change her mind. 'You do understand why, don't you?' she asked.

'Yes. It's your final attempt to save your marriage. Howard's entitled to that much from you.'

'I *will* save my marriage.'

He slung his coat over his shoulder and turned back to her. 'Your marriage is over, Nicola. There's nothing left to save.'

176

She waited until he'd gone and then put her head in her hands. He was absolutely wrong, her marriage wasn't over, but unless she managed to put tonight totally out of her mind and concentrate on Howard then it would end, and in order to do that she must cut Sergei right out of her life. Unfortunately the twins still needed him.

On a sudden impulse she decided to invite Howard's parents to Sunday tea. That would please Howard, subtly exclude Sergei, and help her slot back into her proper position in the family unit. The late invitation was accepted with delight and at last Nicola felt able to attempt a night's sleep.

In fact she fell asleep so quickly that she never heard Sergei come home, or knew that he spent over an hour in with the twins, talking quietly and earnestly to them as they sat cross-legged like miniature buddhas and absorbed all he said.

Howard stared at Nicola in disbelief. 'You've invited my parents to tea today? What on earth made you do that? All I want is some peace and quiet.'

'I thought you'd be pleased. You're always saying we don't have them here often enough.'

'I've just been working flat our for five days in Brussels. If you wanted to make a gesture why choose this weekend of all weekends?'

'I thought it would be nice for us.'

'Meaning who? The twins? They aren't that keen on them. Sergei? He's never even met them. You? Hardly! So who exactly does that leave?'

'I thought a family day would be pleasant. I'm very sorry if it doesn't suit you, but you can ring and cancel yourself because I only rang at nine last night and they'll think we're quite mad.'

'What time do they arrive?'

'About three.'

Howard looked at his watch. 'Great, that gives me exactly four hours to recuperate. Do you think you could spare me for a short nap, or have you arranged for me to take the boys to football?'

177

Nicola sighed. 'There's no need to make a big drama out of it. OK, so you're tired; I'm often tired but it doesn't stop me doing things. All you have to do is be pleasant when they arrive. I'm not asking you to make the sandwiches or bake a traditional fruit cake, you know.'

'I happen to think it's bloody inconsiderate. Where's the Russian?'

'Sergei's in the back garden with the twins. They're still getting the hang of their new bikes.'

'I forgot to ask how the party went.'

Nicola grimaced. 'Not too well actually. No one turned up.'

'No one?'

'Not a single child. Obviously the twins are no more popular now than they were at St Hugh's.'

'But didn't they all accept originally?'

'Yes, or at least their parents accepted for them. They must all have ducked out at the last moment.'

'Without even a telephone call? That's incredible. It's a good job I wasn't here. I'd have rung round a few of them. Politeness doesn't cost anything.'

'We'll have to have a word with their teacher,' said Nicola reluctantly.

'Yes, well, I thought ...'

'You're back then?' said Sergei laconically from the doorway.

Howard turned his head. 'Observant of you.'

'The party was a real fiasco. It's lucky I was here. Nicola was very upset.'

She turned away and busied herself at the sink.

'How's the Shirleycroft?' asked Howard politely.

'I've moved to the Royal Oak. The landlady at the Shirleycroft's been taken ill.'

'Well, it's good to see you again.' Howard didn't sound in the least convincing. 'Are the boys around?'

'In the garden.'

'I'll go and have a word with them.'

Alone together, Nicola and Sergei exchanged a brief glance. 'How did you sleep last night?' asked Sergei.

'Very well indeed.'

'I'm not surprised!'

She coloured and shook her head. 'Please don't say anything about yesterday.'

'I want to. I enjoyed making love to you. You were so responsive.'

'Be quiet!' she whispered furiously. 'Howard's only in the next room.'

'I suppose he'll want you tonight,' he said moodily.

'He is my husband.'

'I'll be thinking of you both.'

'Why will you be thinking of us both?' asked Howard, suddenly appearing in the doorway that lead into the front passage.

'I was talking about Christmas time in Egypt.'

'Really? I didn't think Christmas was celebrated out there.'

'Your sister-in-law used to celebrate it. It was the only thing she ever put her foot down about. Not the religious aspect, but the festivities.'

'How about in Russia?' asked Howard.

'No, we didn't celebrate it in Russia. I was always too busy anyway.'

'Even as a child?' smiled Howard.

'Especially as a child.'

'How sad. You sound like something out of a particularly depressing Dickens novel. Have you read any Dickens?'

Sergei shook his head. 'No, I couldn't get past Noddy.'

Howard flushed. 'Right, I'll go and unpack. Since my parents are coming I suppose I'd better make an effort to liven myself up. I'll take a shower. That might help.'

As soon as he'd gone upstairs Sergei crossed the room and put a hand beneath Nicola's chin. 'Where's it all gone?' he asked quietly.

'All what?'

'All that sparkle. Last night your eyes were glowing. Now they're quite dull. That's what he does to you. He takes all the sparkle away.'

'Of course he doesn't! Do you think you could find something to do elsewhere? I'm rather busy at the moment.'

His fingers closed round her elbow. 'You can't go back,

179

Nicola. It won't work, not now. You need me as much as I need you.'

'Excuse me, I want to get to the fridge.'

The fingers tightened so that she winced with pain. 'You'll find out I'm right. What went on between us yesterday was special. You won't feel like that with anyone else. And there's more — I can teach you to enjoy things you don't even know exist.'

She looked up at him angrily. 'Has it occured to you that I might not want to learn about these things? That there could be aspects of last night that I didn't find particularly attractive?'

He shook his head. 'You enjoyed it all. Remember, I was there. I saw you.'

'Let go of me, damn you!' The pressure of his fingers relaxed and she rubbed at her arm.

'Have it your own way then. But when you're finally ready to face the truth, let me know. I'll be waiting for you.'

'It will be a long wait.'

'I can be very patient over important things.'

'That's fortunate. Hello, boys. What can I do for you?'

'We can just about . . .'

'. . . ride the bikes now.'

Nicola smiled. 'Wonderful!'

'Would you like . . .'

'. . . to come and see?'

'I certainly would. Do you still wobble?'

'Just a little,' said Torquil. 'But we're almost steady most of the time.'

Nicola laughed. 'Do you know, I'm quite relieved when they find something difficult,' she confessed to Sergei as they went out into the garden. 'It makes them just a little bit more normal.'

The two adults stood on the path and watched as the twins rode tentatively round the edge of the lawn.

'They'll ruin the grass,' said Sergei.

'It doesn't matter. It's not a good lawn, too full of couch grass and dandelions. Besides, it will have the rest of winter to recover.'

'What do you think?' called Tarquin.

180

'You're doing very well.'

'We're going to try something else now. Keep watching.'

They got off their bikes and dragged a plank of wood across the lawn, resting one end on the top of a wooden crate they'd moved out earlier. 'Be careful,' cautioned Nicola.

The twins glanced at her with a strange expression in their eyes and then got back on their bikes. Torquil was the first to go. He pedalled as fast as he could straight over the lawn and up the plank, then shot off into the air, spun the bike round, landed back on the plank and coasted down to where the adults were waiting.

Nicola couldn't think of anything to say. She was still trying to work out exactly what he'd done, and how he'd had the strength to turn the bike in the air.

'My turn!' called Tarquin. He drove at an equally breakneck speed up the plank but stopped dead at the end, jerked the handlebars back so that he was balanced on his rear wheel only, spun it round in a circle several times and then came back down on two wheels with his hands clasped over his head in triumph.

Sergei looked down at the path and concentrated all his attention on a tiny beetle making its way through the moss. Nicola looked at the two boys and they looked back at her.

'You should join a circus,' she said at last.

They smiled.

'When did you really learn to ride bikes?'

'Only yesterday, but we found ...'

'... it wasn't at all difficult.'

'Have you tried flying without using an aeroplane?' she asked sarcastically.

Tarquin grinned. 'You're cross, aren't you?'

'No, but I think you've both been telling me fibs. I think you've had bikes before and we probably made a mistake in getting them as your presents. Is that what you're trying to point out with this demonstration?'

They shook their heads.

'There's no point in this kind of fib.'

'It wasn't a fib!' said Torquil angrily. 'We've never had bikes before.'

181

Tarquin nodded. 'He's right, but we wanted to give you a surprise. What's wrong with that? Grown-ups are meant to like surprises.'

Torquil's eyes fastened on Nicola's. 'Mummy was always getting surprises from Daddy. He used to say, "Another little surprise for you tonight, Rosie," and she used to start crying.'

The hairs on the back of Nicola's neck prickled. 'Crying?'

'With excitement!'

'She was quite a crying sort of person,' confirmed Tarquin. 'Did she cry a lot when you were children?'

'No, she didn't.'

Sergei touched Nicola on the arm. 'I think Howard's trying to attract your attention.'

She looked back at the house and saw him waving at her from the lounge window. 'His parents must have arrived early. Put the bikes away boys. It's a damp day and they'll get rusty if you leave them out.'

'We don't have days like this at home,' muttered Torquil as he pushed his bike past Nicola. 'Why don't you come away with us? It's much nicer in Egypt. You'd like it there.'

'I probably would but Howard's work is here.'

'He doesn't have to come. He's a nerd!'

'That's very rude!' exclaimed Nicola, but the boys had gone on ahead and she could see her mother-in-law waiting in the playroom so she had to let the remark pass.

'Aren't the boys looking well!' exclaimed Howard's mother, hugging their tense bodies tightly and planting kisses on their twisting faces. 'You're so lovely I could eat you both up!' The boys smothered giggles while Sergei stood watching, his face expressionless.

'This is Sergei Cheparukhin,' said Howard. 'He's over from Egypt for a few days to visit the boys.'

'Not an Egyptian name, is it?' asked Howard's father.

'He's Russian, Dad.'

Sergei shook his head impatiently. 'I'm from Georgia.'

'Where's that then?' asked Howard's mother. 'I thought Georgia was part of Russia.'

'It's part of the USSR,' said Sergei politely. 'That isn't the same thing.'

'I suppose you're all anxious to come over here now and escape from the results of all that communism? Russians are strange creatures. One minute they believe one thing, then they get told their belief was wrong and they immediately throw themselves whole-heartedly into an entirely different way of thinking. Talk about sheep!'

Sergei's lip curled and Nicola quickly rushed into the conversation. 'I don't think that's quite fair, Father-in-law! Besides, it's very rude to talk politics when you've got a guest'

'I don't mind,' said Sergei. 'Bigotry fascinates me.'

Howard's father went bright red. 'Bigotry? I'm not a bigot, I was stating a simple fact. For centuries the Russian people have had to change their thinking at the drop of a hat. It isn't your fault, it's just the way of the world. You wait, in another fifty years Gorbachev's name will be mud.'

'It's mud now in the food queues. He's not a popular man in Georgia.'

Howard's father frowned. 'Obviously there are problems, but he's a wonderful man. I mean, who'd have thought a few years ago that you'd all be free?'

'Free to starve? Stalin was born in Georgia. Now, there was a man to admire.'

'Really? You don't even live there any more so I can't think why you're getting so heated about it,' retorted the older man.

The twins' heads turned from right to left as they followed the conversation. They moved slowly until they were on each side of Sergei, then gripped his hands in theirs.

'Let's not argue,' said Nicola cheerfully. 'Why don't you boys show Grandma and Grandpa your birthday presents?'

After that, conversation turned to more general topics although Sergei had little more to say for himself. The twins behaved well but Nicola thought they seemed very excited and their eyes continually darted to Howard's father throughout the meal.

After they'd eaten, Howard asked his father to go outside and look at the Saab for him. 'It just isn't ticking over right. I've been to the garage but they say there's nothing wrong.'

183

'What petrol are you using?'

'Unleaded, it's been adapted.'

'Probably better to mix in the occasional gallon of ordinary four-star. Still, I'll take a look.'

'Do you know anything about cars, Mr Cheparukhin?' asked Howard's mother.

'Not a thing. I'm not mechanically minded.'

'He's a scientist,' explained Nicola.

'That must be interesting.'

'Riveting,' he agreed laconically, then strolled to the kitchen window and looked out to where the other two men were standing round the car, while the twins hovered nearby.

It was cold outside and Howard's father hadn't put on his coat. He decided not to linger there too long. It wasn't just the cold wind, he felt uneasy as well. The darkness seemed more intense than usual, and although the trees were motionless he could hear a sound like the rustling of the wind.

'I'll turn the engine over a couple of times,' called Howard from inside the car. 'It has to warm up a bit before you can hear it.' His father nodded and pushed his hands into his pockets, then jumped as something brushed against his arm.

'There's a cat stuck up the tree, Grandpa,' said one of the twins.

Mark Grainger had not taken to the twins at all. Normally he liked children but there was something about the boys that bothered him. Nevertheless, there was a touching appeal in the way the boy was gazing up at him and he'd also called him Grandpa for the first time.

'Which tree's that, lad?'

'The horsechestnut at the end of the drive. We can hear it miaouing.'

'Cats can take care of themselves.'

'It might be a kitten. Would you just have a look for us? We could ring the RSPCA if it is stuck.'

Howard put his head out of the car window. 'Dad, are you listening?'

'Just a moment. I'm going to look at a cat for the boys.'

184

Howard frowned. 'Cat? What cat's that?'

At the end of the drive the darkness seemed even more dense and the street lamp that should have illuminated the end of the drive wasn't working. 'I won't be able to see a thing,' protested the elderly man.

Two small hands slipped into his. 'Listen, can't you hear it?' asked one of the boys.

He could certainly hear something and he peered up into the branches. After a few seconds he was able to make out a pair of smoky-blue eyes gleaming from between some of the upper branches.

'Yes, it looks like a cat,' he confirmed. 'I doubt if it's stuck though.'

The children pulled him closer to the trunk of the tree.

'It sounds very sad ...'

'... very sad indeed.'

He didn't like it when they split their sentences and his unease increased. 'I'm sure it's all right, boys. Here, kitty! Kitty, kitty!' The eyes shone more brightly, the colour changing to a dull yellow like two small foglights. 'Come on, puss! Down you come!'

The yellow orbs began to enlarge and moved forward.

'That's right, puss. Come on then! I think it's coming down, boys.'

He looked down at the children, but they'd let go of his hands and were concealed in the shadows. He felt more than a little annoyed.

'Come down, you little pest!' he muttered, wishing that there was more light. In reply the cat made a hissing sound and then seemed to lose its balance. He heard its claws scratching at the wood.

'Don't you fall on top of me!' he muttered, taking a step back and peering up into the darkness. Suddenly the eyes flared, and the top branches were illuminated by a brilliant flash of golden light.

The elderly man's eyes took a moment to adjust, but then he gasped as he found himself looking straight into the lean, feral-eyed face of a wolf. It was crouched low on the bough, its body totally concealed from view, and it glared at him malevolently, its ears flattened.

185

'No!' He took two steps back, the blood rushing in his ears. The wolf's top lip curled back and exposed the razor-sharp teeth beneath. 'Get away! Get away from me!' he shouted. The wolf's head moved, darting forward and down towards him and in the unearthly light he could have sworn that its neck was that of a man. His chest tightened as a burning pain began beneath his ribs. He looked fearfully behind him, down the drive to where his son was standing impatiently by the car while the twins played chase in front of him. He wanted to call them but the head was growing now, snaking down towards him, and the smell from its hot breath was hideous: a mixture of sweet decaying meat and rotting vegetation.

His heart thumped wildly in his chest and he heard his own noisy attempts to draw breath. He had to move, but his feet seemed rooted to the spot and it was impossible.

The wolf-creature obviously realised this because its eyes shone even more brightly and the head drew slowly back as though for a final assault. The leaves whispered among themselves and then there was an awesome tearing sound as though the earth were splitting open and the wolf-creature leapt for the old man's throat, bringing the huge horsechestnut tree down with it, throwing up huge slabs of pavement as the roots were dragged to the surface.

Howard's father knew what was happening, understood that the tree was going to crush him and that he was going to die, but he didn't understand why until the final moment. Then, as the wolf's teeth sunk deep into his throat in the final explosion of bright, white pain he saw the faces of his adopted grandsons smiling at him, and in between them was the sullen, handsome face of the man from Georgia, whose countrymen he'd insulted.

Howard watched the big old tree fall in helpless disbelief. One moment everything had been quiet, and the next there'd been a tremendous rumbling sound – like an underground train beneath his feet – and then he'd heard his father give one dreadful, strangled scream as the tree crushed him in its path.

The twins stopped their game and stood silent and still beside Howard, their outstretched hands just touching each

186

other at the fingertips. For a few seconds nothing happened, then Howard began to run down the drive and at the same time the front door opened as Sergei and Nicola rushed out.

'What happened? Is everyone all right?' asked Nicola anxiously.

'Grandpa's there,' said the twins together.

'Where?'

'Sort of under the tree.'

Sergei caught hold of her arm. 'I'll go. You take the boys inside. It won't be a pretty sight.'

She stared wild-eyed at him. 'But how did it happen? Why did the tree fall? There isn't any wind.'

The light from the porch softened his features. 'I don't know,' he said gently. 'Take the boys in now. Someone has to be with your mother-in-law.'

Nicola began to cry. 'I can't bear it. It's horrible! What's happening to everyone? Why are so many people dying suddenly?'

He put an arm round her and kissed the top of her head. 'Shh. You have to be strong for Howard and his mother.'

'I don't feel strong.'

He turned her towards the door. 'You have no choice,' he said firmly. 'Later you can cry. But not yet.'

'Don't go!' she blurted out. 'Don't leave me. I need you here.'

'I told you I'd always be here. Now go in. I have to help Howard.'

She went weeping into the house, a twin on each side of her.

Chapter Eleven

The tragedy of Howard's father's death cast a shadow over the family that lasted across Christmas and through into the New Year. January passed and his widow began to take tentative steps towards a new life but Howard remained locked in despair, mixed with baffled incomprehension.

'I just don't understand why the tree came down!' he said to Nicola after their latest visit to his mother. 'There was no wind and no sign that the tree had rotted. Scientifically it was impossible.'

Nicola sighed to herself. 'It might seem impossible but the tree did come down, and the sooner you accept it the sooner you'll come to terms with your father's death. Really, Howard, you've been worrying away at this like a dog at a bone but there's no point. It happened. Even your mother's accepted that.'

'The local council can't come up with any explanation.'

'True, but I don't suppose they're spending every spare moment worrying about it. It was an accident, an act of God. They do happen.'

Howard snorted. 'That was no act of God! An act of the devil perhaps.'

Nicola was hardly listening. They'd been through this so many times that she could hold the conversation while on automatic pilot, and she was watching the twins digging in the garden as her husband talked.

'Did you hear what I said?' he repeated irritably.

'Yes, that the council don't know why it happened.'

188

'You weren't listening, were you? I said that it was more likely to be an act of the devil.'

'I don't know what you're on about. The twins will be through to Australia soon! Perhaps we should get them to dig up some of the lawn and turn it into a vegetable patch!'

'They wouldn't go to Australia. All they're interested in is Egypt. They talk about it more now than when they arrived here.'

'That's because they aren't enjoying the winter. They'll be better once spring gets here.'

'Perhaps we should let them go home,' he said moodily.

Nicola looked at him in surprise. 'We can't do that. We're their guardians, Rose wanted us to bring them up here.'

'A dubious compliment considering what she looked like when they were with her. Seriously, Nicola, I often think they *should* go back. Nothing's been right here since they arrived.'

'You can't blame them for your father's death!'

'They were there.'

'So were you! Even supposing they had the ability to make the tree fall — which they hadn't — why should they want to hurt your father?'

'He upset their Russian friend. I saw the way they watched him after that.'

Nicola put an arm round his shoulders. 'They're just two small boys, Howard. You talk as though you think they've brought some kind of curse into the home.'

'Someone certainly has. They hadn't been here five minutes before Melanie killed herself. Now I'm plagued with nightmares all the time and my father's dead. It makes you wonder what will have happened in another six months. It wouldn't surprise me to find Guildford wiped off the map by some unexplained natural disaster from which only they escaped. Leaving them free to return to Egypt, naturally.'

'I thought your mother looked better,' said Nicola, determined to change the subject. 'She's had her hair done differently.'

'Really? That's a great relief to me. Obviously she's totally

189

recovered from Dad's death. Perhaps she's found herself another man. Wonderful!'

'There's just no talking to you these days,' said Nicola despairingly. 'Other people have tragedies in their lives too, you know, but they cope.'

'Don't quote me the famous stiff upper lip line. I didn't see you with much of a stiff upper lip when your father died. A few skeletons came rattling out of the cupboard, then your mother killed herself because she couldn't face the truth and you went totally to pieces.'

'It was a shock,' she said defensively.

'You're a psychologist. I thought you took all that sort of thing in your stride.'

'Not when it happens to me! Anyway, nothing I'd learnt had prepared me for that. It isn't exactly commonplace, you know. And I did get over it, eventually.'

'It certainly isn't commonplace! Not many people can say that ...'

'Shut up!' she said angrily. 'You're the one who's upset. Don't try and drag me into your pit of misery, because I'm not willing to join you there.'

Suddenly his shoulders slumped. 'I'm not much of a husband at the moment, am I? I'm sorry, Nikki. I know you're having a tough time with me but I'm confused. The boys don't help. I thought I'd enjoy having them around but I don't. They're not like I expected.'

'All parents make the mistake of projecting their own unfulfilled ambitions on to their children.'

'I'm not talking about wanting them to be different. I just wish they'd look at me as though I was the head of the household not some slug from under a stone. That's not a lot to ask.'

Nicola stood up. 'I'm going to make sure they've done their homework. It's school tomorrow and even if they can't do well socially they're going to shine academically.'

'Your unfulfilled ambition?'

'They're very bright. I owe it to Rose to make sure they do well.'

Howard took hold of Nicola's hand. 'I do love you, you know. I love you so much it hurts. I wish I could show you

but for some reason since Dad died I haven't been able ...
I don't know what's the matter with me. Perhaps I should
see the doctor?'

'It's not important,' she assured him.

Howard's eyes were thoughtful. 'It should be. It was once.
What's changed you, Nikki?'

She felt guilty and took refuge in temper. 'For heaven's
sake, Howard, what do you want me to say? That I'm going
mad because you can't make love to me any more? That I'm
thinking of leaving and running off with the milkman?'

'It isn't the milkman I'm worried about.'

'If you mean Sergei, I haven't heard from him since your
father died. As far as I know he's still in Egypt concentrating
on his bunsen burners.'

'You do like him though, don't you?'

'He's all right. Howard, I'm giving up my work.'

This at least distracted him. He was astonished. 'But
why?'

'The boys need more of my time. I can't concentrate on
anything as well as I should. My patients and the twins are
being short-changed. It's better that I give it a rest.'

'The boys are at school all day. How can they need you
all the time?'

'There are things to do even when they're not in the house.
The need clean clothes, cooked meals, and someone to come
home to.'

'You've always loved your work.'

'Well, I don't love it now. I'm sick and tired of listening
to neurotic, selfish parents asking me to find a solution to
their children's problems − solutions that don't require the
parents to give up anything at all, of course!'

'You'll be bored out of your mind in a month.'

'I doubt it.'

Howard looked hard at her. 'Are you sure there isn't
anything else behind this?'

Her heart raced but she kept her face blank. 'Like
what?'

'I don't know. It just seems very odd.'

'Everything seems odd to you at the moment. Call the
boys in, would you? They've been out there long enough.'

After he'd gone she felt miserable and guilty. She too was uneasy about the death of his father, and knew he was right in saying that the twins seemed to carry disaster around with them, but none of this counted when set against her terrible need to be with Sergei again.

If anyone had told her a few months earlier that she'd find herself in the grip of such a physical obsession she'd have laughed in their face. She'd never understood women who gave up everything for love, had had no time at all for friends' affairs. Now everything apart from Sergei seemed insignificant.

She knew that Howard needed help to cope with his loss, and was aware that she shouldn't really give up her work, but if she was at home all the time then she'd be free to see Sergei whenever he wanted, and that came before everything.

He wasn't in Egypt. On the night that Howard's father died he'd left Guildford and gone straight to the Egyptian Embassy in London. He'd rung her regularly, suggesting several meetings in town but she'd never been able to go. It had been his idea that she gave up work, although she wondered why she hadn't thought of the solution herself. It was so simple.

That night Howard tried unsuccessfully again to make love to her, but although she felt sorry for him she was relieved because she no longer wanted him near her. It was Sergei she wanted; her feelings for Howard were more maternal now.

It took time for her to stop working; her patients had to be found suitable alternative psychologists, and one or two of the cases she saw through to the conclusion herself, but by the first week in April she was finally free.

'Your first day as a full-time wife and mother!' said Howard.

'That's right.'

'I shall expect home-made bread on the table and flower arrangements in every room when I get back!'

'I'll be grateful if I get to the bottom of the dirty linen basket.'

He tried to kiss her on the mouth but she turned away and his lips merely brushed her cheek. 'I might be late home. There's a lot piling up on my desk.'

192

'Don't worry, I won't be looking out of the window waiting for you.'

'No,' he said sadly. 'I didn't imagine you would be.'

Nicola grinned at him. 'You'd hate me to be that kind of a wife.'

'Sometimes I wouldn't mind. Nor would most men, if they're honest.'

'Chauvinists all! Are the boys up?'

'Up and running. They were fighting with bicycle pumps when I last saw them.'

'Only another week and they'll be back at school. You'd better hurry. You're going to miss your train.'

Still Howard lingered. 'I'm beginning to wish I'd taken today off. We could all have gone out somewhere.'

'What about that work piling up on your desk?'

'One day wouldn't have made much difference. Still, it's too late now. I'll see if I can take Thursday and Friday off instead.'

'Lovely,' she murmured automatically, impatient for him to be gone.

Almost at once the boys came running down the stairs.

'We thought he was ...'

'... never going!'

Nicola felt excitement fizzing in her. 'Eat your breakfast and then get ready. We're meeting him at Victoria Station at ten o'clock.'

They nodded and smiled at each other. They were almost as excited as Nicola.

'What would you have done if Howard had stayed at home?' asked Torquil.

'I've no idea. Fortunately it didn't happen. Hurry up now!'

By the time they arrived at Victoria Station Nicola felt exhausted. Her own excitement, coupled with a guilty fear that something would stop them at the last moment, had worn her out, but when she saw him waiting under the clock she knew it had all been worthwhile.

He didn't see them immediately and she was able to study him at leisure, and to see the amount of attention he attracted from passing women, most of whom turned

193

and gave him a second glance. And he was hers, thought Nicola triumphantly; at least, he was hers for the rest of the day.

'There he is!' screamed the twins and they rushed up to him, chattering excitedly in French. He looked over their heads to where she stood waiting and gave a small smile of satisfaction.

'You're really here at last.'

'Did you think I'd cry off at the last moment?' she asked.

'I thought you might lose your nerve.'

'As you can see, I didn't.'

'I'm very glad.'

'Kiss her!' shouted the twins, much to the amusement of passers-by.

He kissed her lightly, like a friend, not a lover.

'Boring!' declared Tarquin. 'Are we going to the exhibition now?'

'We certainly are. I've got the tickets in my pocket.'

The taxi ride meant nothing to Nicola; she wasn't interested in London, she wasn't really interested in an exhibition of Egyptian artefacts, it was Sergei who interested her, and she found her obsession shaming.

'Here we are.' He touched her lightly on the elbow and her whole body seemed to jerk reflexively. She coloured and climbed out of the taxi, the boys spilling on to the pavement ahead of her.

'Come on, we'll explain everything to you,' they declared, taking hold of her hands and dragging her up the steps to the gallery.

'Steady on, you'll have me over,' she murmured, looking back to where Sergei was in deep conversation with the taxi driver. 'Trouble over the fare?' she asked when he caught up with them.

'No, I was asking him to pick us up in two hours. The boys have been invited to a children's birthday party at the Embassy.'

'They aren't dressed for a party,' she protested. 'Besides, what about me?'

'I've got other plans for you,' he whispered. She turned

quickly away from him before he could see desire flare in her eyes.

The exhibition was impressive. Ancient gods carved in stone, funeral masks and gilded funerary caskets, mummys and coffins from the twenty-first dynasty. It was all rich and splendid.

'So many gods!' exclaimed Nicola as they passed from room to room.

'They had one for everything,' agreed Sergei.

'Some of them didn't last long,' said Torquil dismissively.

'Osiris did. He keeps turning up,' said Nicola, anxious to show that she'd been paying keen attention. There was a strange silence. 'Was there something special about him?'

'*Nothing at all*!' declared the twins together. 'He wasn't even clever. His brother chopped him up into hundreds of pieces, remember?'

'Oh, yes, of course. I'd forgotten the name. What was his brother called?'

'Set,' said Sergei casually.

'Right! I'm sure it was the story of Set and Osiris that gave Howard his nightmare one night.'

'He was really scared,' said Torquil to Sergei with relish. 'We saw him. There was blood all over his face!' The Russian smiled.

Nicola shivered, suddenly cold. 'Let's move on. I'd like to see the pyramid room. I've always wanted to know how they were built.'

'Even now no one really knows,' said Sergei.

'And I'd like to see the craftwork. Is there time?'

'The boys won't be collected for another hour. Will that be time enough?'

She nodded, her imagination suddenly conjuring up images of herself and Sergei alone in some bedroom after the boys had gone. The images shocked her. She couldn't imagine where the ideas came from.

When they emerged into the spring sunshine she could heardly breathe for excitement. The taxi was waiting at the bottom of the steps. Sergei put the boys inside it and then returned to her.

'You'll all meet up at the station at four o'clock. That gives

195

us over three hours alone. What would you like to do?'

'You told me you had plans,' she reminded him.

'So I do.'

'Then lead on.'

He caught hold of her arm and hustled her down the steps and on to the crowded pavement. 'A friend of mine has a house only a short distance from here. He's given me the key.'

'There isn't any chance of anyone else coming while we're there, is there?' she asked anxiously.

'Of course not. He knows me too well to let anything like that happen.'

'Is this friend connected with the Embassy?'

'Not exactly, but he's also from Egypt. We have common interests there.'

She was hardly able to keep up with him he was walking so fast. 'What kind of interests?'

'You're far too curious for your own good, Nicola. Why not just accept that we've been lucky.'

'Sorry! I was talking for the sake of it.'

'Are you nervous?' The idea seemed to amuse him.

'What if I am?'

He didn't answer, but guided her up a small side street and into a cul-de-sac with a row of tiny terraced houses all with shining front doors.

He turned the key, looked back over his shoulder for a moment and then pushed her inside. He didn't seem to know his own strength because she staggered and almost fell.

'Careful! I don't want to break an ankle,' she cautioned.

Sergei's eyes were dark and bleak. 'Take you clothes off,' he said abruptly.

She looked about the tiny, lace-curtained front room. 'Not here, surely?'

'Yes, here. I want to see you with your clothes off.'

'I'd rather go up to the bedroom first.'

He took a step towards her and she felt almost frightened of him. 'Perhaps I didn't make myself clear.' There was no mistaking the menace in his voice and Nicola suddenly realised that, apart from the children, no one except Sergei even knew she was in London, and by coming to this tiny house with him she'd put herself entirely at his mercy. It dawned on her with dreadful clarity that she didn't know anything at all about him and that if he were a madman or murderer she had no possible chance of escape.

She tried to make her voice firm. 'I'm afraid I've changed my mind, Sergei. I'd like to go now. This was probably a bit of a mistake.'

For a moment longer he continued to stare bleakly at her, but then his eyes lightened and he smiled reassuringly. 'Don't tell me I frightened you! It was only a game! I thought you might enjoy the caveman approach.'

She felt furiously angry. 'You idiot! You terrified me.'

He looked aghast. 'I'm really sorry. It was meant to be fun; a fantasy game, that's all.'

'A bloody stupid game if you ask me.' She was shaking all over, her desire gone.

Sergei rested his hands on her shoulders and looked deeply into her eyes. 'You have to understand that we've had different childhoods, different experiences in our lives, and because of this we're both going to get things wrong from time to time. Obviously my idea was a big mistake, but I meant it to be a special surprise for you. I was trying to make our meeting memorable after our separation. You see, I thought you trusted me too much to imagine I'd ever do anything to hurt you.'

Nicola was close to tears after her fright. 'You don't understand what it's like for a woman, how vulnerable this kind of affair makes us. Terrible things happen to women these days; they even vanish from work. I felt as though I'd walked straight into a trap.'

'I'm sorry,' he whispered against her ear. She let her head rest on his shoulder. He murmured gently. His tongue shaped soft endearments and vows of love until she rested quietly against him, relaxed once more, and never once did he let her sense his anger at himself for having nearly ruined the entire, complex operation.

After such a disastrous beginning it was astonishing to her that they ever made it to the bedroom, but they did and his lovemaking was so careful and controlled, so totally selfless,

197

that all her fears were swept away and she gave herself up to pleasure.

The time flew by and she couldn't believe it when he pointed to the bedside clock. 'Three-thirty, we must hurry!'

'Ring for a taxi!' she cried as she jumped out of bed and scrambled into her clothes.

'I ordered one earlier. It should be here any minute.'

'Aren't you coming too?' she asked as he escorted her to the taxi door.

'No, I have to tidy up before I leave. I'll ring you tomorrow morning.'

'Don't forget!' she begged, despising herself even as she made the appeal.

He touched a finger to her lips. 'How could I forget after this afternoon?'

She glanced at the taxi driver and felt herself blushing. Sergei gave her one final kiss, then walked briskly back into the house.

'Where to, lady?' asked the driver.

'King's Cross. No! Victoria Station. Yes, that's right, Victoria.'

'Had a good time, lady?' he asked with a smirk.

Nicola glared than sank back into her seat and busied herself looking through her handbag for their return tickets. It was six minutes to four when she ran up to the platform and found the children waiting patiently for her.

'Quick, into this carriage. We'll move further down once it's on the move. Come on, hurry!' She hustled them through the door just as the guard blew his whistle.

'You were nearly . . .'

'. . . too late!'

She looked at their indignant faces and felt even more guilty. 'I'm sorry.'

'What were you doing?' asked Torquil as they found themselves three seats and sat down, Nicola next to an elderly lady.

'Well, we just sort of wandered around,' she said lamely.

'Did you have any lunch?' demanded Torquil.

'Yes, of course. We had a sandwich at a sandwich bar.'

Tarquin curled his top lip. 'Not very nice! What kind of a sandwich did you have?'

'Let me think. It was, er ...'

'What's an "er" sandwich? Is it tasty?'

'Egg and cress!'

They raised their eyebrows at each other. 'A salmonella sandwich. Yum, yum!'

Nicola took a deep, steadying breath. 'How about you two? Did you have a good time?'

They nodded enthusiastically.

'Oh, yes, we did ...'

'... but it was very tiring.'

'Were there many other children there?' she asked curiously.

They frowned. Torquil shook his head. 'No, of course not!'

'You mean, you were the only two at the party?'

Tarquin stared out of the window, absorbed in the passing scenery, or so it seemed. Torquil was left to keep the conversation going, and to Nicola's surprise he seemed as uncomfortable as she'd been during their interrogation about her lunch.

'There were lots of children at the party, but we were given a special welcome when we got there, because of Daddy having been a famous doctor. We were given a medal thing that belonged to him.'

'That's nice. May I see it?'

'No!' said Tarquin, suddenly entering the conversation again. 'It's private, a family heirloom.'

She tried not to smile. 'I see. So, what did you play?'

Torquil rolled his eyes at his twin. 'Lots of things. The usual sort of games, you know!'

'Well, did you play pass the parcel?'

'Yes!'

'And blind man's bluff?'

'Yes!'

'And pin the tail on the camel?'

'Yes!'

'On the camel?' she repeated in amusement. 'That was a joke. It's pin the tail on the donkey!'

'What a frigging stupid sort of joke to make,' said Tarquin angrily.

The old lady next to Nicola stiffened indignantly and Nicola shrugged a helpless apology. Tarquin looked pleased with himself and resumed his perusal of the scenery while Torquil shut his eyes and pretended to sleep.

Nicola understood that because she'd been secretive about her time, the boys had decided to pay her back and she was amused by their need to appear unchildlike even though Torquil's language upset her.

When they got home they went upstairs to change. 'I don't think we'd better mention our trip to Howard,' she called to them from her bedroom. 'He might stop us seeing Sergei another time.'

The boys poked their heads round her door.

'Of course we won't tell. We like you and Sergei . . .'

'. . . much too much to tell tales.'

'*We want you to get married and live for ever after*'

'You forgot "happily",' she laughed, fortunately not realising that her happiness wasn't part of the future as they envisaged it.

'I met David on the train,' said Howard as soon as he arrived home. 'I've invited him and Andrea round for drinks about eight.'

Nicola's heart sank. 'Tonight?'

'I thought you'd be pleased to get some adult conversation after a day at home with the boys.'

'You might have asked first. I'm exhausted.'

He grinned. 'Don't tell me it's harder work being a housewife than a child psychologist!'

'I'm just not in the mood for Andrea's brittle chatter.'

'You'll feel fine once you've had a bath and got dressed up.'

She didn't dare make too much fuss in case Howard began to question her closely about her day. 'I suppose so,' she conceded reluctantly.

'I also thought I'd take the boys ice skating on Saturday.'

'I can't skate.'

'That's all right, I thought a men only outing would suit

them down to the ground. They are Labib's sons after all!'

She felt uneasy. 'I'm not sure that's a good idea.'

'Come on, Nicola. I've decided to make a bit more of an effort where the boys are concerned. I need you to support me, not throw cold water over my ideas. You keep saying I'm not involved enough with the boys, and I agree with you.'

She wondered why he'd chosen this evening to start trying to improve the situation at home. After her day in London all she wanted was an early night and an indifferent husband, not this cheerful, eager partner full of good resolutions.

'Aren't you pleased?' he asked in surprise.

'Yes, of course I'm pleased, it's just a bit sudden.'

'I thought it was the least I could do. After all, you've given up your entire career to build us a proper home.'

Guilt rose like a physical lump in her throat and she swallowed hard. 'That's really thoughtful of you, Howard.'

'Give and take, that's what marriage is all about really. What's for supper? I'm starving.'

'The boys and I ate mid-day. I've got a lasagne for you, courtesy of Marks and Spencers.'

'No sign of the freshly baked bread yet!'

She managed a strained smile. 'Not today.'

'Right. Well, I'll go up and change.'

When he'd gone she leant against the kitchen table and put her hands to her cheeks. They felt hot and her stomach was churning. It was far easier to contemplate her affair when Howard was moody and withdrawn; his new enthusiasm for their marriage made her feel terrible.

David and Andrea arrived bearing a huge bouquet of flowers. 'For you, darling,' said Andrea, kissing her lightly on the cheek.

'What have I done to deserve these?'

Andrea looked at her and her eyes gleamed with amusement. 'How should I know?'

Nicola bent her head and sniffed at the flowers. 'Gorgeous! I'll go and put them in water. Howard, would you see to the drinks?' He and David went into the drawing room but Andrea lingered with her hostess.

'Howard told David today was your first day as a full-time wife and mother. How did it go?'

'Fine, I'm just surprised how tired I feel.'

'*I'm* not surprised,' said Andrea silkily.

Nicola glanced at her. 'What's that supposed to mean?'

'I saw you, darling.'

For a moment she couldn't breathe. 'Saw me where?'

'Coming out of an Egyptian exhibition in London.'

'Don't be ridiculous. I was here with the boys all day.'

'At first I thought I'd made a mistake, but then I saw the handsome Sergei putting the boys in a taxi — and let's face it, the twins are unmistakable.'

Nicola felt sick. 'You're talking nonsense,' she said weakly.

Andrea shook her head. 'You're the one talking nonsense. You might as well own up.'

'I was here all day,' she repeated stupidly.

Andrea took a step towards her. 'Listen, Nicola darling, I don't care if you make arrangements to meet the entire English football team in London, but don't insult my intelligence like this, it makes me feel quite angry.'

Nicola closed her eyes for a moment. She wished it had been anyone but unreliable, frustrated Andrea with her love of intrigue and mischief-making. 'All right, you've caught me out. I was there. I admit it. Now can we go and join the men? They'll wonder what we're doing.'

'Nonsense, we're arranging the flowers. Here, let me do the chrysanthemums, you're all fingers and thumbs. Was it worth it then? Did he come up to scratch?'

'It was a day out, nothing more.'

'I might have believed that if I hadn't seen him getting rid of the boys! Where did he send them? Lost baggage at Heathrow?'

'I really don't want to discuss this, Andrea,' said Nicola, pushing past her friend.

'Well, I do. What's he like?'

'You've met him, what did you think?'

'I meant in bed,' said Andrea tightly. 'Is he a good lover?'

Nicola glanced anxiously at the door. 'For heaven's sake, keep your voice down!'

'Don't worry, they're too busy talking petrol prices to eavesdrop on our boring conversation.'

'I really don't think it's any of your business what he's like,' said Nicola.

'Actually, it is my business in a way. You obviously don't realise it but your fabulous lover puts himself about quite a bit.'

'Meaning?'

'This is going to come as quite a shock to you, but for the past two weeks he's been having a passionate affair with my husband,' she said viciously.

Nicola stared stupidly at her. 'But David's married!'

'I do know that. I happen to be his wife.'

'What I mean is, David wouldn't ... I mean, David's always having affairs with other women. He's the last man who'd ...' She couldn't bring herself to say any more.

'Wake up, Nicola! There's an entirely new breed of men out there, men who like any kind of sexual partner as long as he or she's beautiful. Why do you think AIDS is spreading through the heterosexual population at such a rate?'

'I don't believe it.'

'Read any newspaper and see for yourself.'

Nicola shook her head. 'I didn't mean that! I meant I don't believe it of David. If he were a bisexual you wouldn't stay with him.'

'Nicola, David and I suit each other. We've both got our little peculiarities. It all balances out in the end. The important point is, you're the one sharing his lover this time round!'

Nicola's cheeks were scarlet. 'That's absolute rubbish! I can't believe you expect me to believe it either.'

Andrea shrugged lightly and stood back to admire her flower arrangement.

'I only wanted you to realise you weren't the love of his life or anything dramatic like that. I'd hate to see you and Howard break up because of a handsome pervert! Now I've told you, the rest's up to you.'

'You're just jealous! You wanted him yourself. You told me as much right here in the kitchen the first time you met him. I suppose it's difficult for you to see someone else taking a lover. You've always had a monopoly on infidelity before.'

'Believe me, I wouldn't touch him with gloves on after what David's told me!'

'David tells you all the details, does he? How very convenient.'

'We tell each other everything. It's part of the fun.'

'I see. And the risk of disease obviously doesn't worry you as much as you feel it should worry me!'

'We only practise protected sex, but I don't imagine that's the Russian's style.'

Nicola's mind flashed back to the bedroom that afternoon. 'I'm not listening to this filth any longer. I think you need professional help – your sexual fantasies are totally out of control.'

Andrea picked up the vase and stood it on the windowsill. 'There, they look lovely. I'm glad I did that flower arranging course. It's made such a difference.'

Nicola caught hold of her friend's arm. 'Did you hear what I said?'

'Yes, Nicola, I did, and thank you for the free advice. Unfortunately you're the one caught up in a sexual fantasy, not me. However, each to his – or in this case her – own.'

'It was a lie, wasn't it?' she demanded urgently.

'No, it was the truth, but you were right about one thing.'

'What's that?'

'I'm jealous. David said he was an incredible lover. Out of this world.'

Nicola wanted to hit Andrea, to get hold of her hair and shake her until she admitted it was all lies, but all she could do was walk away from the amused blonde and try to push the whole sordid conversation out of her mind.

She had no idea what the four of them talked about for the rest of the evening. Once or twice she caught Howard looking rather strangely at her and realised she was too quiet but she couldn't help it, because along with Andrea's words one other thought kept intruding into her mind – a picture of Sergei and David deep in conversation at the gate. She remembered seeing David's hand on Sergei's arm on the night they met and how she'd thought that she'd seen Sergei touch

David gently on one cheek. It was a memory that wouldn't go away.

Andrea and David left at twelve. Nicola went straight to bed and pretended to be asleep when Howard joined her.

Then, once he was asleep, she lay on her back staring into the darkness while her mind transposed images of herself and Sergei with Sergei and David. When she did fall asleep the images continued, but even more confused so that she found herself in bed with Sergei, David and Andrea, their limbs a tangled heap as hands and mouths went to work in previously unimagined combinations.

She awoke, sick and shaking, before dawn and made herself stay awake until the alarm rang because she was afraid of the perverted images she'd conjured up and ashamed of her own imagination. Ashamed, because her body still tingled and ached from her imaginary couplings and she knew that in the dreams there had been great pleasure.

In his room at the Egyptian Embassy, Sergei sank back on his bed totally exhausted, finally free to sleep now that dawn had come and his night's work was over.

Chapter Twelve

Howard was hot, tired and depressed. He stared uncomprehendingly at the figures on the desk in front of him and wondered — as he'd wondered a lot recently — what was happening at home.

He'd hoped that once Nicola got used to being a full-time housewife she might regain some of her former enthusiasm for their married life, but it hadn't worked out that way. Now she had even less energy in the evenings, and as she refused to leave the boys with babysitters — not that he could imagine any of their friends being willing to take on the task — they never went out and spent their time indoors in uneasy silence.

Their sex life no longer existed. His own problems in that area had grown far worse. There were times when he wondered if he had any control over his own body any more, and Nicola's interest in him had apparently disappeared. That was bad enough, but it was made worse by the fact that she had the glowing air of a woman who was well loved. He'd never seen her looking so well, and her good health and vitality seemed to mock him.

He hated the twins, and knew that they hated him. At weekends they walked around him as though he were a piece of the furniture, something to be negotiated but ignored. When he spoke to them they never answered, never pretended to pay any attention to his words. The most he ever got in response was muffled laughter. They were strange, dark, secretive children who made him feel afraid in his own home.

None of this was sudden. The situation had evolved gradually over the past few months until now, in early June, it seemed established. Yet today was different. Today he couldn't get any of it out of his mind. Several times he'd put out his hand to phone home, to find out what was going on, always assuming that Nicola bothered to answer the phone. And he kept hearing voices. Twice he'd heard the twins so clearly that he'd spun round in his chair, convinced they were in his office, and once he'd heard Nicola laughing in her old way, so that he could picture her with her head thrown back, her mouth wide and smiling. The sounds were real, close at hand, while the day itself was unreal. The silence of his office, the bright light from the sun streaming in through his window, none of that was real. It was like a dream, a dream where you know you're dreaming, yet he was awake and restless. He sensed that today was going to be special and knew equally instinctively that it wasn't going to be a day for celebration.

The phone on his desk pinged as though the line were being tested. It had done that several times already and the sound added to his unease. He tried to focus his attention on the budgets again but this time the phone rang twice and he picked up the receiver.

'Overseas Department, Howard Grainger speaking.'

There was a low hissing sound and intermittent crackling, like an electrical fault, but behind it all he thought he could hear voices. 'Is there anyone there?'

The laugh was deep; a rich, secretive sound of mirth.

'Who the hell is that?' he demanded irritably, but there was no reply and once again the hissing sound filled his ear. He banged the receiver back in place and realised that sweat was trickling down between his shoulder-blades while his forearms were covered with goosepimples.

The phone rang again. He ignored it. It stopped and he felt a brief moment of triumph, although over what he had no idea. Opening his door he asked his secretary to get him a cup of coffee. 'Strong and sweet, please, Lizzie!'

The secretary looked up. 'Of course, Mr Grainger. Do you feel quite well?' she added hesitantly.

'I'm fine.'

It seemed as though she were about to say something further but decided against it and went off. Howard shut his door again and looked nervously at the phone. Lizzie returned with his coffee and put it in front of him.

'Thanks, I'm having trouble concentrating today. Perhaps this will help.'

'You look very pale,' she said anxiously. 'Perhaps you should go home. There's a lot of summer 'flu around.'

'I'm fine, really. I didn't sleep too well, that's all.'

Alone again, he took out his calculator and started checking the columns. The mewing sound was so faint at first that it scarcely impinged on his consciousness but as the noise increased in volume it was impossible not to notice and he glanced out of his window expecting to see a cat sunning itself on the ledge. There was nothing there. Howard frowned and opened the door of his office again. 'Lizzie, have you got a cat out there?'

She looked justifiably astonished. 'A cat? Of course not, Mr Grainger.'

'I thought I could hear one around somewhere.'

Hurriedly he shut the door again, not wanting to see the anxious expression on her face. The noise was still in his room and he prowled around checking all the corners and even in the wastepaper basket.

Then, out of the corner of his eye, he saw something move on top of the tallest filing cabinet. He stood on tiptoe and saw a small blue shape huddled back against the wall. Quickly he moved the step that was used for the top files and balanced on it to get a closer look.

It was a cat crouched back in the shadows. A tiny, stunted cat, and it was bright blue with black spots.

Howard knew immediately that he had to get out of the room. This was no ordinary cat and he didn't want to be alone with it. He turned too quickly and the portable stool slipped from under him, sending him sprawling on the carpet. A sharp pain stabbed through his left ankle.

'Damn!' He rubbed it hard, hoping to disperse the pain, and at the same moment he heard the cat scrabbling on the top of the metal cabinet, its claws trying to get a foothold. Howard tried to stand but his foot couldn't take any weight

208

and he looked up apprehensively as he waited for the pain to ease.

The cat came to the front edge of the cabinet and peered down at him, still making the high-pitched mewing sound that had initially attracted his attention. It was a horrible cat. Its eyes were dark and too large for its face and the ears were totally wrong, too wide and high for a cat's ears, while it kept its tail curled flat round its hindquarters. But worst of all, as he'd originally thought its fur was a bright shining shade of blue. Not a smoky blue or a grey-blue mixture, but a clear sky blue.

He felt as though the cat were hypnotising him as it stared down, its black eyes surveying him thoughtfully as he stood clutching his throbbing ankle and glancing longingly towards his door.

'Here, kitty!' he said hesitantly. 'Nice pussy, come on down then.'

The cat smiled and Howard's blood ran cold. His foot was agony and he sat down slowly on the carpet, never taking his eyes off the cat as he started to inch his way backwards towards the door. It hissed at him and its ears flattened but its tail never moved and its front paws seemed stiff. Howard's breathing was giving him trouble as fear tightened his chest. The fear was uncontrollable, and yet it wasn't a big cat. It didn't need to be big. He could feel the malevolence pouring out from it as it watched him through its curiously large eyes.

It inched forward itself, almost copying him, until it was lying right on the front of the cabinet top. Slowly it began to move its paws. They pattered against the metal, then started to scratch, and then to pound until he could hear the echoes of the sound and the whole cabinet began to vibrate with the rhythm.

The paws moved faster and faster until they were just a blur. The cabinet creaked. Howard glanced at the heavy drawers, realised what was happening and suddenly pushed as hard as he could with his feet as the cabinet crashed down on to the floor. It missed him by a fraction of an inch, but one of the drawers flew out and the edge struck him on the cheek, splitting the skin open and as the blood began to pour down his face the blue cat leapt onto him and its tiny tongue lapped frantically as though it were dying of thirst. Howard finally lost control of himself and started to scream.

The door crashed open and Lizzie came rushing in. 'Mr Grainger, whatever's happened?'

He looked up at her. 'Get the cat off!' he cried.

Lizzie blinked in surprise. 'What cat?'

It had gone, he realised stupidly. The moment the door had opened it had vanished into thin air.

'There was a cat in here. It brought the cabinet down.'

'You've cut your face!' She took out a clean handkerchief and dabbed ineffectually at the blood. 'This is quite deep. You'd better go over to the medical room and get them to take a look at it. I'll ring for one of the maintenance men to come and pick the cabinet up. You're lucky you weren't killed,' she added. 'Those drawers weigh a ton.'

He couldn't be bothered to talk to her. All he wanted to do was get out of the room. 'I'm taking the rest of the day off,' he muttered as she helped him to his feet.

'Of course, Mr Grainger. I'll cancel your afternoon meeting.'

'Cancel anything you damned well like! I'm getting out of here before that bloody animal comes back.'

An hour later, with the cut covered by an impressive plaster, and a rapidly swelling right eye, Howard was on a train back to Guildford.

He took a taxi from the station and asked the driver to drop him off at the end of the road.

The house was suspiciously quiet when he hobbled in. Nicola had told him she would be washing most of the curtains if the weather was fine but all the curtains were in place and there was no washing on the line.

He limped through the downstairs rooms calling her name without getting any reply. The garden too was deserted. Finally, reluctantly, he decided to go up to the bedrooms.

The twins were waiting silently for him at the foot of the stairs and he realised they'd been there all the time.

'Didn't you hear me calling?' he demanded irritably.

They studied his face with interest, looking at the plaster and swelling cheekbone, but they didn't ask for any explanation.

'Where's Nicola?' he asked them.

They glanced at each other and then turned back to him, expressions blank.

'Come on, you must know where she is.'

Tarquin held out a clenched fist. 'Guess what I've got here.'

'I don't know.'

He opened his hand triumphantly and Howard stared down at a tiny blue-glazed earthenware cat. He felt sick. 'Where did that come from?'

'Sergei gave it to us.'

'When?'

'Today.'

'He's in Egypt,' said Howard automatically.

The twins shook their heads. 'No, he isn't. He's here.'

'What is that cat?' he asked, delaying the final confrontation a little longer.

'It's a good luck charm. It's Bastet, the cat goddess.'

'That cat was in my office earlier. It damned nearly killed me.'

They didn't bother to reply. Howard reached out to grab Tarquin, determined to make him speak, but immediately Tarquin thrust the cat in front of him and Howard stopped, afraid to continue.

'Where's Sergei now?' he asked angrily.

Both children lifted their hands and pointed up the stairs. Howard closed his eyes for a moment and they moved to one side, making room for him to go up.

He knew that he had to go and see for himself. That was why he'd been brought home, and it had to be done, but if it hadn't been for the presence of the twins he would probably have crept out of the house and made a far more noisy entrance. However, they were watching and he had no choice. He stopped outside the bedroom door, took a deep breath and went briskly in.

Nicola was sprawled naked on top of the bed, her arms and legs spread wide as though she were some kind of sacrifice.

211

Sergei was lying beside her, his hands roaming possessively over her body as she moved languidly under his touch, giving small sounds of pleasure.

Howard gave an exclamation of shock and Nicola's head twisted towards him. She tried to sit up, but Sergei pushed her back down and looked at Howard across her body, his hands resting possessively on her naked flesh as he gave a smile of satisfaction.

For the first time in his life Howard understood what was meant by seeing red. A mist formed in front of his eyes and he hurled himself across the carpet, his hands reaching out for the Russian.

Sergei moved fast. He jumped from the bed and kicked Howard hard between his legs. Howard screamed with pain and as he doubled up, Sergei's right hand caught him on the chin, felling him like a tree.

He lay on the bedroom carpet, gasping and retching, the ache from his cheek and eye mingling with the worse pain from Sergei's kick until to his utter humiliation he suddenly vomited on to the carpet.

He was dimly aware of Nicola and Sergei dressing, and of Nicola leaving the room, but he felt so ill he couldn't say a word to either of them.

Once they were alone, Sergei pulled him roughly to his feet and dumped him on the end of the bed.

'You should have telephoned first,' he said dryly.

'You bastard! I could kill you for this.'

'You couldn't satisfy her any more. What did you expect her to do?'

'Whose fault was it that I couldn't satisfy her? Tell me that.'

'You tell me.'

'It was yours!' said Howard furiously. 'Ever since you first came here I've been unable to function as a husband. I don't believe that's a coincidence.'

'Well, you're not stupid. I expected you to guess.'

Howard stared into the arrogant face and longed to smash his fist into it, to break the nose and shatter the cheekbone, disfigure him so that no woman would ever find him handsome again.

'Don't try it,' said Sergei softly. 'I'd only have to hurt you again.'

'Who are you?' asked Howard in confusion. 'What do you want with us?'

'I came for Nicola and the boys. As far as you're concerned, it's all over now.'

Howard grabbed hold of Sergei's arm. 'Why do you want Nicola? You're not in love with her. Men like you don't know the meaning of being in love. Take the boys. We won't fight you over them. Take them back to Egypt and leave Nicola and me alone.'

'She wouldn't want to stay with you any more,' said Sergei in amusement. 'She has more sophisticated tastes now. You're better off without her.'

'She's my wife and I love her!' shouted Howard. 'I won't let you take her away.'

'Give her up now,' said Sergei softly. 'You've caught us in a compromising position, your honour surely demands that you let her go immediately.'

'Sod my honour! I want Nicola to stay with me.'

'Let her go now or she'll come to me as a widow.'

Howard stared into the emotionless dark eyes and was reminded of a shark. He'd always been repelled by the flat bleakness in a shark's eyes and was equally repelled now. He was also afraid.

'Who are you?' he repeated.

The Russian leant down to him and put his mouth close to Howard's ear. 'I'm death,' he whispered softly. 'I'm despair, and darkness and everything that people fear. I think you already know that, Howard.'

He nodded. 'There's nothing I can do to stop you, is there?'

Sergei straightened up. 'Nothing at all.'

'What will happen to Nicola?'

'The same as happens to everyone in the end — she'll die.'

'Why her? Why not someone more suited to your kind? Why not Andrea?'

'Nicola has certain attributes that are necessary to me. You don't need to know any more. I think it will be best

213

if you pack up a few things and find yourself a hotel for a few weeks. The Shirleycroft's very good, I'm told.'

Howard felt drained of all emotion. 'I certainly don't want to spend another night in this house.'

'I'll send Nicola up to you. There are probably one or two things you want to say to each other. After that you'd better go.'

Resentment flared again. 'This is my house. I'll leave it when I choose!'

'Be careful,' cautioned the Russian, and Howard remembered the blue cat.

When Nicola came in she stood hesitantly in front of him. He looked terrible. His face was dark and swollen, his clothes dishevelled and his posture utterly defeated. She knew it was all her fault.

'I'm sorry,' she whispered. 'I can't help myself.'

Howard looked up at her. 'You do realise that he's dangerous? He isn't normal, and neither are the twins.'

'They're just different, Howard. They come from a different culture. That's why we never liked Labib, I suppose. I'm beginning to understand him a little better now.'

'No you're not,' said Howard, suddenly moved to urgency. 'You don't understand anything at all. You're infatuated with Sergei, it doesn't mean anything.'

'It means a great deal.' she said sadly. 'I know it shouldn't, but it does.'

'He's evil,' said Howard fiercely. 'He admitted as much to me. He just wants to spoil and destroy things. He doesn't love you, he doesn't know the meaning of the word.'

'He does love me.' She said it automatically, without conviction, and Howard was surprised.

'You know that isn't true, don't you? You know that and yet you still want to spend the rest of your life with him?'

'I can't live without him.'

'You can! You'd forget him after a while. Let him take the boys, Nikki. You stay with me, we'll get through this somehow.'

'You know that isn't true. How could you forget what happened here today?'

'Listen to me,' pleaded Howard. 'He and the boys have got

214

some kind of strange power. They can make things happen. That blue cat charm the twins have got — well, it came alive in my office today. That's how I cut my face. It pulled the filing cabinet down on top of me.'

She smiled sadly. 'They're just ordinary little boys who are homesick.'

'Nicola, you're not listening to me! They are not ordinary little boys, and he isn't an ordinary little Russian. Perhaps Labib wasn't ordinary either. God knows he turned Rose into some kind of zombie quickly enough. That wasn't normal. At least face the truth.'

'All right, suppose they're not normal, does it matter? I like what Sergei is, I like the things we do and the way he makes me feel. Maybe I'm not normal either, Howard. Perhaps you're better off without me. I only know that I *have* to be with him.'

'What if you change your mind later on?'

'Then I'll come home. I won't be a prisoner in Egypt, you know. We're going to live in the boys' home. We saw pictures of that years ago, it looked lovely.'

'How nice!'

'The point is, Howard, this isn't such a final step. If I've made a mistake, I'll come home and start all over again. At least I'll have lived! I'll have escaped, broken out of the rut. I want new experiences.'

'He might not let you come home.'

Her eyes gleamed. 'I'm not afraid of him, Howard. He excites me, and he makes me feel more alive than I'd have believed possible, but I'm not afraid. You've no idea what he can make me feel.'

Howard stood up and the room spun crazily round him. 'No, and I don't think I want to hear either. You're obviously quite beyond reason, so all I can do is move out and give you time to pack up and go. I think you're making a terrible mistake but since you're obviously not going to listen to anyone you'd better go ahead and taste these wonderful new experiences. Let me know when you're leaving because I'd like to move back into the house eventually. I take it we're going to wait and get a so-called civilised divorce?'

215

Nicola nodded. 'Probably. I hadn't really thought about it. You could always divorce me for adultery.'

'I don't think that counts for much these days, and I'm not in a rush. I don't intend to marry again. I'm just beginning to realise that it's possible to be married to someone you don't really know at all.'

Nicola put out a hand but he moved away from her. 'I'm truly sorry, Howard. I was happy with you before ... You know, until Sergei arrived.'

'Not happy enough, it seems.'

Briefly he thought he could see a flicker of despair behind her eyes. 'I can't do anything about it, Howard! He's like a drug. The more I'm with him, the more I need him. Sometimes, when I'm alone, I think of the things you're saying, but when I'm with him nothing else matters. I don't seem to have a mind of my own any more.'

'Then there's nothing left to say. I wish you luck, Nicola. Not happiness, because I don't honestly think I want you to be happy, but you'll certainly need the luck.'

She nodded, and started to leave but stopped by the door at the last moment. 'Howard?'

He looked up questioningly.

'Is it true that David's a bisexual?'

'Who?'

'David, Andrea's husband!'

'Why ask that now of all times?'

She shook her head. 'It doesn't matter. I just wondered.'

'Since you ask, he certainly belongs to a couple of rather strange clubs in the City.'

Nicola went out quietly. Considering she was planning a whole new life with Sergei Cheparukhin, it wasn't the answer she'd hoped to hear.

Part 2

Chapter Thirteen

Nicola glanced at her watch and saw that they were due to land at Cairo International Airport in ten minutes. The twins were chattering excitedly to each other, their voices shrill. Ever since they'd boarded the plane they'd been keyed up and impossible to control. She could understand it, but wished they could be a little quieter.

The past weeks had been hectic and unreal. Sergei had seen to their passports and visas while she'd shopped for suitable clothes and taken the children to the doctor so that they could all have their innoculations, but although busy with the practicalities she had found it difficult to believe she was actually leaving England behind, and going to make a new life in Egypt. Yet now she was nearly there, and she still felt totally unprepared.

Sergei had gone on ahead to make sure the house was ready for them and sort out the financial side of affairs. Now that the boys were returning to Egypt a trust fund set up by Labib came into operation and although he'd been hazy about the details, Nicola had the distinct impression that a lot of money was involved.

Recently, she had found that her belief in Sergei's declaration of love and his sworn desire to make a home for her and the boys faded with his absence. In fact, the previous evening she'd thought of telephoning him to say that she'd changed her mind and the boys would be travelling alone. It was such a big step to take, and she'd known Sergei such a little time. She felt a touch on her hand and opened her eyes. The twins were peering anxiously at her.

'You'll like it once we get there,' Torquil assured her. 'It might be a bit strange just at first, but not for long.'

'No horrid fog and drizzle,' said Tarquin with a smile. 'Just lots of sunshine and happy things.'

She was touched by their concern. 'I'm sure you're right, but I might be a bit homesick at first.'

They nodded. 'We were very homesick in your house. We *never* got over it.'

'Time to fasten our seatbelts,' said Nicola as the sign in front of them lit up. 'I hope Sergei's there waiting for us.'

'We know what to do if he isn't.' Torquil squeezed her hand reassuringly. 'Don't worry, we can look after you.'

When they stepped out of the plane Nicola blinked in amazement and reached for her sunglasses. The light was brilliant and the heat overwhelming.

'It's Terminal one we want,' said Torquil, walking briskly ahead of her.

'Are you sure?'

'Yes, terminal two's just for foreign airlines.'

Nicola could feel the beads of perspiration on her forehead and her feet and legs ached from the flight. She pushed back her long hair and wished fervently that she was back in England.

Inside the terminal, people thronged about her, chattering in foreign languages and waving their hands around as they shoved and pushed at each other, but all in a surprisingly good-natured fashion.

She looked around helplessly, unwilling to face customs until Sergei had joined them, but he was nowhere to be seen. 'He promised he'd be here,' she muttered to herself.

'He's busy,' said Tarquin. 'Something's gone wrong at the lab.'

'How do you know?' asked Nicola.

He smiled disarmingly. 'I just expect that's what's happened. It often happened to Daddy.'

'I shall be furious if he doesn't turn up,' she said irritably, wondering why everyone in Egypt found it necessary to talk so loudly.

'Look, there's Ayeesha!' shouted Tarquin suddenly. He began pulling on Nicola's hand.

She followed apprehensively. 'Who's Ayeesha?'

'She's the beautiful lady we told you about. I expect Sergei sent her,' explained Torquil. He dragged her across to where a tall, elegant woman with jet black hair swept up into a french pleat stood waiting. Her deep blue eyes were fringed by dark lashes, and in her red Valentino suit with its long, slimline jacket she looked like an international model.

Horribly conscious of her own crumpled linen dress, and aware that her auburn hair had gone into a frizzy mass of curls in the heat, Nicola felt at a great disadvantage and cursed Sergei for his thoughtlessness.

'Where's Sergei?' demanded Torquil, jumping up and down in front of Ayeesha.

'He's been delayed at the laboratory. Stand still, you wretched child. It makes me feel hot just looking at you.' Her voice was low and controlled with a hint of an accent that Nicola couldn't place. Much to her amazement, Torquil obeyed without demur.

The blue eyes swept over Nicola and a smile hovered round the corners of the carefully made-up mouth. 'So you're Rose's sister? I can hardly believe it. You're not at all alike. Rose was so colourless.'

'It's the hair that makes the difference, I expect.'

'No, not just the hair. You're far more vital than your poor sister.'

'I don't feel very vital at the moment. I'm exhausted.'

'You'll soon get used to the heat. Now, we'd better get on. I'm sure you're anxious to see your new home.'

'I haven't been through customs yet.'

Ayeesha held up a form. 'It's all been seen to. My chauffeur should have collected your luggage by now. There were only three leather suitcases, weren't there?'

'Yes, but how ...?'

Ayeesha turned on her heel and a path seemed to appear miraculously in front of her as she walked gracefully through the teeming mass of people and out into the blazing sunshine. Nicola struggled along behind, carrying the hand luggage and trying to keep an eye on the twins.

Ayeesha stopped beside a black limousine with smoked glass windows. Her chauffeur opened the boot and Nicola peered in at their luggage. 'That's fine,' she murmured, smiling at the small, dark-skinned man. 'Thank you so much.' His eyes registered nothing at all. She might just as well not have spoken.

'Into the car, boys,' said Ayeesha quietly. 'No fighting on the journey, please.'

Much to Nicola's relief the car was air conditioned and the contrast with the heat outside was so great that after a few minutes she felt positively chilled. She also felt like a grubby schoolgirl sitting beside a sophisticated older sister.

'Is Labib's house actually in Cairo?' she asked Ayeesha.

Ayeesha shook her head. 'No, it's in Heliopolis; that's about fourteen miles from Cairo. Quite near enough in my opinion.'

'It won't be long now,' said Torquil, hugging his knees tightly and grinning at his twin.

The limousine swerved violently and Nicola was thrown against Ayeesha, who couldn't conceal her instinctive withdrawal from the contact.

'I'm sorry,' apologised Nicola awkwardly.

'It's the taxis. The standard of driving here is unbelievable. A taxi ride is an absolute nightmare, and you wouldn't believe the traffic jams they conjure up out of thin air. Horrible!' She shivered with distaste.

'I suppose it's all part of the atmosphere,' said Nicola with a smile.

Ayeesha shrugged. 'To a tourist, I suppose it is.'

Somewhat downcast by her lack of enthusiasm, Nicola fell silent and was relieved when the car slowed and turned left off a wide boulevard, drawing up in front of a white villa that was far more spacious than Nicola had remembered from the photographs.

She climbed gratefully out of the car and looked about her appreciatively. 'This is fantastic! I had no idea it was so modern.'

'Did you think they lived in a tent?' asked Ayeesha dryly.

'Of course not, but the photos certainly didn't do it justice, and look at the flowers! I imagined it would be all cacti and palm trees.'

'How quaint!' Ayeesha glanced at her tiny gold wrist watch.

222

'Would you like me to come with you? I've got a few minutes to spare and Sergei won't be back until five o'clock.'

'That's not for three hours!' said Nicola despairingly.

'That's men for you. They're never there when you need them. No doubt he'll make up for his absence by the warmth of his welcome.'

'No doubt he will,' said Nicola briskly, not caring for the expression in the other woman's eyes.

'How clever you've been to trap him,' murmured Ayeesha, leading her in through the arched doorway. 'You'll be less than popular with the ladies, I'm afraid. A handsome, unattached man is such a blessing to a hostess.'

'I hardly trapped him,' said Nicola coldly.

'Of course not. Sometimes my choice of English words is not quite accurate. You'll have to forgive me.' Nicola was certain that Ayeesha's command of English was as perfect as her dress sense but she nodded and followed her into the cool of the villa.

It took time for her eyes to adjust after the brilliant sun outside but she was immediately aware of the sharp sound of her heels on the marble floor. One room led to the next through an archway overhung by an ornate curtain of beads. She was a little surprised by the lack of furniture. A few low tables, even lower sofas with plump cushions, and the occasional incongruously delicate high-backed chair scarcely made any impression on either room and she wondered if most of Rose and Labib's furniture had been put into storage.

Ayeesha gestured to a low divan in what appeared to be the main living room. 'Would you like to sit there a moment? I'd better see if the servants have prepared your room yet. You'll find they're difficult to motivate. Everything's *bukra* as far as the Egyptians are concerned.'

'What's *bukra*?'

'Tomorrow, although it's more likely to be next month in most cases. One just has to get used to it but it is irritating.'

'Where have the boys gone?'

'Their rooms are on the other side of the house. They have their own servants, their own tutors, in fact everything they need. Once you've settled in you won't have to see them more than once or twice a day if you don't want to.'

223

'Heavens!' said Nicola faintly. 'Guildford must have seemed positively cramped to them!'

Ayeesha disappeared through the archway and Nicola went to the nearest window and looked out. The villa had been built in a square round a small but most attractive courtyard which had a water fountain and several small palm trees. From what she could see it appeared that two sides of the villa were really nothing more than glorified passageways with the main rooms situated at the front and back of the square. She assumed that if the twins were self-contained at the back of the house then there must be bedrooms above the drawing rooms at the front.

After a few moments, Ayeesha returned. 'Amazingly enough everything's ready. Sergei must have threatened them with a fate worse than death. One of the women will show you to your room. I have to go now. I'm late as it is.'

'It was very kind of you to come and meet me,' said Nicola.

Ayeesha's eyes widened. 'How polite you are! I'm sure you'd have much preferred to see Sergei, but your meeting will be all the sweeter for the delay.' Again Nicola was disconcerted by a suggestion of some secret knowledge in the other woman's expression.

'My home is just across the road only a few minutes' walk away,' she continued. 'Sergei will bring you to see me before long, I'm sure.'

'Well, thank you again,' repeated Nicola.

'I'll show myself out,' Ayeesha assured her. 'You rest and tidy up. You look very travel-weary!'

'Thank you and good afternoon!' muttered Nicola to herself as the woman left. She didn't know what to do next. No helpful maid had arrived to take her to her bedroom, and she had no idea where to go to find her. She was also getting cold and wished she'd got her cardigan with her.

Just as she was beginning to feel extremely lonely and sorry for herself the beads over the archway began to move and the twins poked their heads through.

'Where's Ayeesha gone?' they demanded, their eyes searching the room.

'Back to her own home.'

224

'*Good*!'

'Don't you like her?'

Torquil pulled a face. 'She's all right — a bit bossy. She thinks she's in charge of everything, but she isn't. Daddy used to keep her in her place.'

'Does she work at the hospital?' she asked curiously.

Tarquin looked surprised. 'Of course not. She's a courtesan, they work at home.'

Nicola laughed. 'I'm sure she isn't a courtesan!'

'Well, a kind of courtesan. That means mistress, doesn't it?'

'Yes, in a way.'

'That's what she is then. She was ... Shall we take you up to your room now? I saw them carrying the cases up ages ago.'

Nicola wondered what he'd been going to say but decided not to press him. 'I'd like that,' she agreed. 'I was wondering what had happened to all your furniture.'

They looked about the room in some surprise. 'Nothing. It looks all right, doesn't it?'

'I just wondered where the rest of it had gone.'

'This is all there is,' said Torquil impatiently. 'The upstairs rooms have all the best things.'

'How extraordinary!'

The twins looked uneasy. 'Well, upstairs is quite important,' said Tarquin. 'It's where all the parties were held.'

'I thought it was just bedrooms upstairs; you know, like at home.'

'This is home,' said Tarquin quickly.

'I meant Guildford.'

They lost their patience with her and darted off through the beaded curtain and up the spiralling whitewashed staircase. The rooms upstairs all had heavy wooden doors and it took the combined strength of the twins to lift the latch and open the one that led into what Nicola assumed had once been her sister's bedroom.

She'd never seen such an enormous bed before, and it was piled high with pillows and gold and crimson scatter cushions. There was a scarlet and black carpet on the floor, its pile deep and luxurious, while the dressing table and built-in wardrobes were strictly western in origin. However, the brightly patterned wallhangings and ornate wooden masks above the bed reminded her that this certainly wasn't home.

'It's a lovely room,' she said faintly, amazed that Rose should have chosen such an ostentatious bedroom.

'Yep! You can see into our rooms from here.'

She joined the boys at the window, grateful not to be left staring at the enormous bed. 'We can wave to each other,' she said with a smile.

'You'll be too busy to wave to us!' said Torquil. Tarquin sniggered.

Nicola ignored them. 'I think I'll get washed and changed. Where's the bathroom?'

'Through that door over there. There's another one along the passage, but this one's just for you — and Sergei too of course.'

She had to duck her head to get through the small door but then there were two steps leading down to a glorious jade green sunken bath with shining gold taps, all surrounded by a jade and gold marbled floor.

'This is very splendid!' she exclaimed turning back to the boys, but the boys hadn't followed her. Instead it was Sergei who stood in the doorway. He blocked out all the light and before she recognised him she felt a brief moment of fear.

'You're here at last!' she said with relief.

He didn't move towards her. 'Didn't Ayeesha meet you?'

'Yes, yes she did, but I was very disappointed it wasn't you.'

'I hope you didn't show your feelings too clearly. It was kind of Ayeesha to give up her time.'

Nicola felt confused. 'Of course I know that, and I was suitably grateful. What's the matter? You sound quite cross.'

'I'm sorry. I've had a difficult day.' He didn't sound sorry. He sounded totally disinterested and she felt a chill of anxiety.

'Sergei, I've flown over two thousand miles to be with you, and you haven't even said hello properly.'

He still didn't move from the doorway. 'Hello.'

Nerves, exhaustion and homesickness combined suddenly overwhelmed her and to her acute annoyance she began to cry. This, at least, had the effect of moving him into the bathroom. 'What's the matter?'

'Everything! I get dumped in a strange house, ignored by the servants, and then when you finally arrive you seem totally disinterested. Not unreasonably I'd expected a slightly warmer welcome.'

'I suppose Howard felt obliged to apologise for hours if he was late home.'

'This has nothing to do with Howard!' she cried. 'Aren't you pleased to see me? You said you wanted us to spend our lives together and now you're bored after five minutes.'

He shook his head, apparently unable to understand what she was saying, but he put his arms round her and let her cry against his shoulder. 'You must be tired. Travelling's always tiring,' he murmured. 'I'm sorry if I didn't say the right things. I'm not used to having any obligations outside my work. I'll get used to it.'

Nicola continued to sob, unable to believe that this same man had ever made such passionate love to her or whispered such wonderful endearments in her ear.

He helped her lie down on the bed and stroked the hair off her face. 'Shall I run you a bath? Would that help?'

She stared at him through swollen eyes. 'I suppose it might, it's just that ... Well, you haven't even said you love me yet!'

'You know I love you. That's why you're here.'

'I've left my home and all my friends behind just to be with you but you're behaving like a stranger!'

'What kind of stranger offers to run you a bath?'

'You know perfectly well that isn't what I meant.'

'I'm sorry if I've disappointed you, Nicola. Obviously I've got a lot to learn about women.'

'I'm not just any woman, Sergei. I'm the woman you love — or so you said. Was that true?'

He'd been looking intently into her eyes but her words seemed to disturb him because he glanced away, unwilling to continue the intimate eye contact.

'Are you having second thoughts?' she asked anxiously. 'Is that it?'

He sighed and she had the feeling that he'd have liked to shake her. 'No, I'm not having second thoughts, and yes I do love you very much. Now, since I'm tired and you're exhausted, I suggest that you have this bath, then we'll both have a sleep and start all over again at dinner tonight. Wait there while I run the water.'

Nicola closed her eyes. Where was the ardent lover now? she wondered. What had happened to all the physical passion that had sparked between them? He was a polite stranger and she didn't know him at all, couldn't believe that they'd ever been intimate. At that moment she would have given anything to have been safely in England again.

'Bath's run,' he called. 'I'll use the one down the passage and I'll come and collect you at eight.'

'Aren't you going to be in here?' she asked incredulously.

'I think you need some privacy for a couple of hours. Try and sleep.'

She tried, but even after the bath she couldn't sleep at all. She'd started out from Gatwick airport that morning so full of excited anticipation, longing to see Sergei again, and now with his extraordinary behaviour he'd turned their meeting into the biggest anticlimax of her life.

When Sergei tapped on the bedroom door just before eight o'clock, Nicola was feeling a great deal better. After lying sleepless for nearly an hour she'd decided to get up and try and make herself feel more like a human being again. She'd washed her hair, using a wonderfully scented henna shampoo that she'd found in the bathroom cabinet, then carefully made up her face before changing into a cool blue sleeveless cotton shift that just reached the top of her knees and which she knew flattered her. A final check in the mirror reassured her that she looked a great deal better now than when Sergei saw her earlier and it was with increased confidence that she went to open the door.

His eyes lit up in appreciation and for the first time since she'd arrived in Egypt she saw him smile. 'I was right — all you needed was a good sleep. Now you look like the Nicola I remembered!'

'You don't look bad yourself,' she retorted, noticing how

228

the short-sleeved white shirt with its thin orange stripe emphasised the muscular strength of his forearms, something she'd never really noticed before.

'Labib and Rose usually ate upstairs when they were alone. I thought we might as well continue the custom.'

'The boys said their parents spent a lot of time upstairs. It seemed rather peculiar to me,' she said, following him along the passage and in through a door at the far end.

'Rose was often unwell. The stairs tired her.'

'People all talk about Rose as though she was an invalid. Was there something wrong with her that I didn't know about?'

'Mind your head, the ceiling's rather low here. From what Labib said, which wasn't a great deal, I took it that she suffered from her nerves rather than any specific physical ailment.'

'I'm surprised he didn't get her professional help. He was a doctor after all. This is a lovely room!' she added, glancing around her admiringly.

'Labib dealt with things he could see. Lumps to cut out, wounds to sew up, diseased organs to remove. He had no time for nerves.'

Nicola looked about her. The room was long and narrow and overlooked the courtyard. The walls had been whitewashed, then decorated with various paintings depicting ancient gods and goddesses.

'Who did these?' she asked, her hands tracing the outline of one particularly striking jackal god.

'The twins did most of them. That one you're looking at is Anubis, the god of embalment, and the goddess with the cow's horn is Hathor, she represents love and childbirth.'

'Who on earth's this?' She pointed to a green face suspended above what appeared to be a pair of primitive scales, on one side of which there was a rather unpleasant-looking lump of red meat dripping blood.

Sergei laughed. 'I think the boys have used their own imagination on that one. It's meant to be Osiris — he's in charge of the judgement hall — weighing up a human heart to see if it's pure. A pure heart was said to be as light as a feather. There's a very small feather the other side if you look closely.'

'And what happens if it isn't?'

'If it isn't then the owner, minus — one assumes — his heart, is condemned to eternal hunger and thirst in the darkness of the tomb. There was a picture of that but it used to upset your sister and Labib had it painted out.'

'Why a feather?'

'It was the symbol of truth.'

'The boys seem to be fascinated by ancient beliefs.'

'It's a fascinating story. Even today there are pageants telling the story of the life and death of Osiris.'

'Perhaps you could take me to one sometime?'

Sergei shrugged. 'I could, but it's pretty tame stuff for adults and the boys get upset by the ending.'

'You mean when the brother — what's his name?'

'Set.'

'That's right. You mean when Set cuts Osiris up into pieces?'

'No, they like that bit. It's when Set's nephew Horus finally defeats his uncle after a battle and the gods defend his victory that they get upset.'

'Why?'

'They prefer Set!'

'Children always like the villains. It's because they're so powerless themselves. They enjoy reading about adults who can get away with things they'd like to do.'

'I forget you're a psychologist. It must be wonderful to have a logical explanation for everything.'

Nicola laughed. 'Don't be silly; there aren't any answers in psychology, just theories. A lot of it's little more than common sense.'

'Of which you have an abundant supply?'

'I used to think so. Since I met you, I'm not so sure.'

Sergei put out a hand and caressed her cheek. 'I'm glad. I don't want you to be too practical.'

Nicola sat down on one of the cane-backed chairs. 'Are the boys eating with us?'

Sergei shook his head. 'They've got their own rooms.'

'So Ayeesha said. Does that mean they never join us?'

'You'll find we have a busy social life. The opportunities for us all to eat together will be few.'

230

'That sounds exciting.'

'I hope our life here will be very exciting.' He looked into her eyes and she shivered with anticipation.

At that moment the door opened and a man wearing wide-fitting blue cotton trousers and a loose white tunic belted with a gold sash came in. He was carrying an enormous silver tray which he set down on a table by the window. He was dark-skinned and weatherbeaten with a heavily lined face and a fierce, high-bridged nose. A bright green turban concealed most of his greying curly hair.

Sergei spoke sharply to the man who seemed apprehensive as he waved his hands around in reply and made what Nicola took to be vehement excuses which he didn't seem to expect Sergei to believe. When he'd finished he gave a small apologetic bow and backed out of the room.

'What was that all about?' she asked, eyeing the assorted dishes on the tray with some apprehension.

'Some of Labib's research work has been moved and there are one or two files missing. Sayyid is meant to be keeping an eye out for them, but as usual nothing's happened.'

'Are the files important?'

'Only to the hospital.'

'I shall have to learn some Arabic,' said Nicola.

'Most of the servants speak some English. Your sister never bothered to learn a single word of the language but she managed to cope.'

'Just the same, I'd feel less of an outsider if I learnt a few phrases.'

Sergei shrugged. 'As you like. I hope you don't mind eating some of the local dishes tonight? I was too late to ask the cook for something more European.'

'I don't mind. What's that?'

He picked up a steaming bowl and began to spoon some of the contents on to a plate for her. 'It's *fool mudhammas* — a kind of bean and tomato stew. You'll find the Egyptians eat it all the time, even at breakfast — only then they put a fried egg on top! You can have some of this rice mixture with it; it's got currants, meat and nuts in, and the green spinach thing there is called *moulukhiya*. It's nice like this, but the Egyptians do a hundred and one other things with it too.'

231

Nicola picked cautiously at the food. She enjoyed the stew but found the moulukhiya too bitter. When they'd finished, Sergei pulled on a silk bell rope and Sayyid quickly reappeared with two small bowls and a steaming pot of coffee.

'This is delicious!' she murmured, spooning a sweet white mixture into her mouth.

'Egyptian sherbet; Rose liked it too. This is American coffee, Labib prefered it to the national variety. You can try that when we're out sometime but it's terrifyingly thick and strong.'

'What I'd really like is a cup of tea,' she confessed.

'You'll have to ask them to get some in. Not that Egyptian tea bears any resemblance to the kind the English like. And if you tried to drink it without sugar, you'd probably die in the attempt!'

'Perhaps I'd better get some sent over.'

'As long as you don't mind waiting twelve months for it to get through customs. Nothing happens quickly here.'

'Ayeesha mentioned that.'

Sergei finished his coffee and moved his chair closer to Nicola's. 'What else did Ayeesha tell you?'

'She said that I'd be unpopular with other women here because they'd enjoyed having you around as a spare man.'

He smiled. 'Trust Ayeesha. What she really means is that she used to enjoy having me around as a spare man.'

'Is she married?'

'She claims to be a widow. Labib told me there's a child away at school in Europe but no one's ever seen it, and there are no pictures of the dead husband in the house.'

'How well did Labib know her?'

Sergei raised his eyebrows. 'Very well, I imagine. She was his mistress.'

Nicola stared at him in astonishment. 'His mistress! Did Rose know?'

'Of course Rose knew. It happens a lot here. She was probably grateful. Labib was a man of considerable sexual appetite.'

'You mean she actually didn't mind?'

'Ayeesha used to attend parties and dinners here, so presumably she couldn't have minded too much.'

232

'I'd mind,' said Nicola fiercely.

His eyes darkened. 'I know you would.'

Suddenly she wanted him very badly and he seemed to know because he stood up and held out a hand. 'Let's go to bed,' he said urgently.

She'd forgotten what a wonderful lover he was, and very soon her body was soaring and she heard herself crying out with pleasure. He waited a long time before he took her properly, and even then there was no sign that he was ever anything but in control of himself. Although she appreciated his selflessness she couldn't help hoping that before long he'd lose himself in their lovemaking just as much as she did.

'Happy?' she asked softly when it was over and he was lying quietly at her side.

'Of course. Do you think you'll be able to live here happily?'

'I think I could live anywhere as long as I was with you.'

He ignored the compliment. 'Is Howard living in your house again?' he asked thoughtfully.

'As far as I know he moved back today.'

'And I suppose he said that you could return there too if things didn't work out?'

She didn't want to think about Howard. 'As a matter of fact he made it quite clear that it was all over between us. I'd never go back to living with him. I couldn't. Not after nights like this.'

'But you know he's there, don't you? As a kind of safety net?'

'He's the only person in England who knows where I am. I suppose there's a kind of security in that, but I don't see why that should bother you. After all, you're not planning to make me so unhappy that I need him there, are you?'

He laughed and she saw his teeth gleam white in the darkness. 'Of course not. I intend to make you very happy indeed.'

'That's all right then.' She yawned, her eyelids heavy.

'You go to sleep,' he murmured, running a hand down over her hip. 'I'm not tired yet. I think I'll go and have one last look for those missing files.'

She was surprised, but far too sleepy to argue with him.

233

'Don't be too long,' she murmured, and was asleep before he'd left the room.

Sergei padded silently down the stairs and out into the courtyard. Keeping close to the wall he entered the boys' bedroom through the low balcony window.

'Wake up!' he ordered harshly.

They came awake instantly, sitting up in bed with their hands tightly clasped as they'd been in sleep.

'We have work to do. Come quickly.'

Still in their pyjamas they followed him into the room next door — the large, airy laboratory where they spent so much of their time. Without hesitation they moved to the bench at the far end and climbed on to the top where they sat cross-legged, waiting while Sergei opened a cupboard and took out a tall, black candle shaped like a pyramid.

Sergei lit it, placed it in front of the boys and then sat opposite them, reaching out and taking one of their hands in each of his.

'Ready?'

They nodded.

'You know what you have to do?'

They smiled.

'Begin!'

Howard was sitting in front of the television eating his supper off a tray when he heard a soft rustling sound. It was intermittent at first, like a piece of paper being moved by gusts of air, but then it became continuous and distracted him from the news programme. He got up and switched on the standard lamp. The rustling sound increased dramatically and now he could tell that it came from behind the drawn curtains. He pulled them back and realised that something was trapped in the venetian blind. Assuming it was a moth he pulled on the cord and opened the slats. With an angry buzzing sound a large fly fell on to the window ledge and spun helplessly around on its back.

Howard pulled a face. It was a very large, fat fly and he hated its clumsy movements. None the less, he didn't think he was up to squashing it so he picked up his evening paper, intending to turn it the right way up again. As he started to slide the paper beneath the squat body another fly fell on to the page and bumbled around, its heavy body seeming too large for its wing span.

He'd never seen flies like these two before. They were similar to bluebottles, except that their bodies glinted green rather than blue and they were definitely bigger. He decided to fetch the fly spray. Nicola wouldn't have approved, but Nicola was gone and he realised with a glow of satisfaction that he could now do exactly as he liked.

He knew the spray was under the kitchen sink but it took him several minutes to find it among the assorted air fresheners, oven cleaners, and furniture polishes. Finally, clutching it firmly in his right hand, he returned to the lounge, but the buzzing was much louder now and he hesitated in the doorway, wondering if there were more of the insects elsewhere in the room.

There were.

The entire wall at the far end of the lounge was black with them. They were hanging there, their wings scarcely moving, making a concerted buzzing sound of irritation as they heaved around, one or two of them losing their grip and falling to the mantelpiece with a soft, squishy plop.

He stared disbelievingly at the wall and his stomach began to heave. The spray felt ridiculously ineffectual in his hand and he began tiptoing from the room, terrified of disturbing them. Scarcely daring to breathe he made it into the hall and softly closed the door behind him. Sweating with relief he returned to the kitchen, wondering who on earth he could contact about pest control at nine o'clock at night.

Putting the spray down on the kitchen table he decided to ring his mother. She always had a long list of useful numbers pinned to her cork phone board, and even if she couldn't help it would be someone to talk to. He reached for the phone, but his hand froze in mid-air as he realised that the cream handset was covered with the same disgusting flies.

'Ugh!' He shivered and drew his hand back, but the movement of air disturbed the insects and one of them flew clumsily on to his hand. 'Get off!' He struck out at it and felt its fat body disintegrate beneath his fingers, leaving him covered in a mixture of blood and slime. His stomach heaved again and he made for the sink, but the flies were already there, creeping slowly over the whole surface.

'What the hell's going on?' he asked himself, and suddenly he had a mental picture of Sergei Cheparukhin sitting at some kind of table staring into a flame. It was then that he started to panic.

With a dreadful sense of despair he made a quick run for the kitchen door, knowing that he had to get out of the house immediately, but before he was halfway across the room the flies had risen into the air and they descended on him in a hideous black cloud of writhing bodies.

They were everywhere. He could feel them creeping into his ears and up his nose, trying to force their squat bodies under his tightly closed eyelids and into the corners of his mouth. He began to strike out with his arms, feeling himself make contact but well aware that no matter how many he struck and killed, more came to replace them.

They crawled up the inside of his trousers and made their laborious way up his legs, their wings beating against the confines of the material. He shook his legs, trying to dislodge them, but it was impossible. Soon they were creeping down the inside of his collar, wriggling and squeezing their way in. Then, once trapped inside his shirt, they became frantic and tried to force their way out, flapping their undersized wings and hurling themselves against each other.

His hair was alive with them. They moved awkwardly over his scalp, getting stuck and then buzzing angrily as other flies landed on top of them. The irritation was driving him mad but his hands were totally covered now and he had no protection at all against them.

The angry buzzing grew louder and the weight of them increased as more and more flies poured into the kitchen and joined the dark writhing mass by the kitchen door.

As his legs began to give way Howard attempted to hurl himself around the room, crashing against the furniture and walls, his arms and legs going in all directions in his frantic efforts to shake them loose. Tears ran from under his lashes and the flies dabbled in them, their legs sticking to the salty fluid.

He no longer knew what he was doing. He was nothing more

than a terror-filled creature himself as he fell to the ground, rolling about on the cushion floor and squashing dozens of the flies beneath him. But for every fly that died, six more arrived to replace it.

Driven to the edge of insanity he opened his mouth for one final, primaeval scream, but the sound was short-lived as the flies poured into the gaping hole and crawled down the back of his throat, filling his windpipe and closing the airpassage.

He choked, his body convulsing as he tried to eject them from his throat, but it was futile and he spent the last terrible seconds of his life choking and gagging on an ever-increasing horde of the fat, greeny-black flies, until finally the hideous gagging sounds died away and the flies rose in one huge column in the middle of the room before vanishing into thin air, leaving Howard's body alone amidst the upturned kitchen furniture.

Sergei released the boys' hands and extinguished the candle flame between finger and thumb. 'It's done,' he said with satisfaction.

The boys nodded, their faces pale. 'All done.'

'Now you must sleep.' They let him lift them from the bench, their bodies warm and trusting against his.

'That was good,' said Tarquin in an awed voice. 'The best thing we've ever done.'

Torquil nodded. 'Will he be pleased with us?'

Sergei nodded. 'Very pleased. Now rest.'

They went back to their room, wrapped their arms round each other and fell instantly asleep while Sergei returned to his room, woke Nicola and made love to her with an intensity of passion that had been missing from their earlier lovemaking. She smiled, then wound her arms round him as she too slept again, unaware that her final link with England had just been ruthlessly severed.

Chapter Fourteen

Nicola would never have learnt of Howard's death at all if his family hadn't thought to send a message to the British Embassy, who didn't make contact with her until five days after his funeral.

She was so stunned that she couldn't even cry. Instead she sat in her bedroom and stared dry-eyed out of the window, remembering. If she was honest she had to admit that it had once been a good marriage. They were friends as well as lovers and Howard had always encouraged her in her work and accepted her lack of maternal instinct. All that had been missing was the intense, almost unbearable passion that Sergei aroused in her. A passion she was beginning to fear would utterly consume her.

When Sergei returned home as usual in the middle of the day, he found her still clutching the letter from her mother-in-law. Taking it gently from her, his eyes scanned the page.

'Well, that's that then. We're free to get married.'

Nicola blinked and tried to focus her attention back in the present. 'Is that all you can say?'

'He's no loss to me. We were never friends.'

'He was my husband.'

'And you left him.'

'That doesn't mean I wanted him dead. Besides, it doesn't make sense. He's thought to have died of an asthma attack but he never suffered from asthma.'

'According to this letter he's already been cremated. What he died of is hardly important any more.'

'Even if you don't care, you should have the sensitivity to allow me a little time for grief.'

A look of impatience crossed his handsome face. 'You're being thoroughly self-indulgent and hypocritical. I find it rather irritating.'

'Then go away!' she shouted, guilt and sorrow combining to make her feel utterly miserable.

He turned and left the room, calling out for the twins as he went down the stairs. Nicola looked across the courtyard and saw them running from their side of the house. She was amazed that they could hear him through the thick stone walls of the villa, but they always did. He had only to raise his voice and they would come running. It didn't work for her; she could scream until she was hoarse and they claimed not to have heard.

The fan in the ceiling rotated sluggishly as she slumped back on the bed. She wasn't enjoying the heat at all. Even when she did venture out – either in the early morning or late afternoon – dust got into all her clothes and after her bath the bottom of the tub would be covered in a fine film of it. She never felt clean.

Sergei came back to their room just before he returned to work. 'We've had an invitation to a cocktail party tonight. It's being held by the English doctor who took Labib's place at the hospital. I thought you'd like to go, but after your letter perhaps I'd better refuse.'

Nicola could think of nothing more likely to cheer her up than a chance to talk about England. 'No, I'd like to go. Howard's death was a shock, that's all.'

He looked impassively at her. 'You want me to accept?'

'Yes, please.' She hesitated. 'Sergei, kiss me before you go.'

'I thought you were longing for Howard's kisses.'

'Of course not! You know perfectly well you're all I want.'

'I need to hear you say it.'

She held out her arms and he came and lay down beside her, gripping the tops of her arms with his hands as he turned her to face him. 'I don't like thinking about you with him,' he said angrily. 'You're with me now. That's what counts.'

239

She kissed him tenderly. 'He's dead. Surely you're not jealous of a dead man?'

'I'm jealous of anything that takes your attention away from me.' He bent his head and began kissing her hungrily, his lips bruising hers as his tongue flicked inside her mouth.

She felt his hand moving inside her waistband, his long fingers working their way down her flat stomach before hesitating at the top of her cotton bikini briefs.

She pressed herself against him. 'Yes,' she murmured. 'Go on. I don't want you to stop.'

With a sigh of satisfaction he rolled on top of her and within seconds she felt him enter her and then there was nothing for her to do but give herself over to the mindless pleasure of their lovemaking.

It ended more quickly than usual, but she knew that Sergei was usually back at the laboratory by two and it was already two-thirty.

'You're going to be late,' she murmured.

'It doesn't matter. I didn't want you thinking about Howard all the afternoon.'

'I won't,' she promised drowsily.

'The party begins about nine. We'll eat first. English cocktail parties are famous for their lack of food.'

'What should I wear, I wonder?'

'Something sexy,' he said firmly. 'If you haven't got anything then go into Cairo, but take Fatima with you.'

She thought of the crowded streets teeming with shouting people, and shook her head. 'I'm sure I've brought something suitable. The last time Fatima took me out I ended up paying far too much for a rug I didn't even want.'

'There are modern shopping facilities too, you know. You want Talaat Harb, off Liberation Square. That's where Rose used to buy her clothes.'

'Did she tell you that?'

He shook his head. 'Rose and I barely communicated. Probably Ayeesha mentioned it.'

'Kiss me goodbye,' she said abruptly.

Sergei looked uncomfortable. 'I've just kissed you.'

'That was sexual. I'd like an ordinary, goodbye kiss.'

240

Much to her discomfort he laughed aloud. 'Don't be ridiculous! You're not in England now.'

No, she thought to herself, she certainly wasn't. In England her life had been totally different, but there was no point in thinking about it any more because even if she wanted to go back — and she didn't — there was nothing there for her now. Howard had been her only close link with the past, and it was disturbing to realise that now no one in England knew her address. After resolving to send it to his family she dozed for most of the afternoon, only waking when someone tapped on the door.

'Master Sergei awaits you on the telephone, mistress,' murmured Sayyid deferentially from the far side of the door.

'I'll come straight down.' She swung her legs off the bed and slipped on a cotton wrapper before padding downstairs in bare feet.

'Sergei?'

'I'm sorry if I woke you but I can't get home until late tonight. You'll have to eat without me.'

'What about the party?'

'I'll be in time for that. Why not let the boys have dinner with you?'

'Yes, I think I will. So when should I expect you?'

'When you see me,' he said curtly.

Nicola replaced the receiver thoughtfully. It was becoming increasingly obvious that Sergei disliked being answerable to her for his movements. To be fair he was totally disinterested in hers. So far she'd only ventured into Cairo twice, but when she'd tried to explain how overwhelming she'd found the sights and smells he'd begun reading a newspaper in the middle of the conversation.

At least if they started going out to parties she'd meet more people, she thought gratefully. It would be nice to have a woman to talk to. Ayeesha visited several times a week, but knowing that she'd been Labib's mistress, Nicola found it difficult to feel any warmth for the woman. In any case, Ayeesha herself kept the relationship distant. Her calls usually seemed more like a duty than a pleasure.

Nicola went upstairs, put on a short-sleeved, loose-fitting dress and went in search of the twins. She found

241

them sitting quietly on their bedroom floor playing cards.

'What's that, snap?' she asked.

Torquil lowered his head to hide his smile but Tarquin looked up politely. 'Not exactly.'

'Is it pairs? I used to be quite good at pairs.'

'It's a sort of memory game,' he conceded, picking up the cards and putting them back in the box.

'I didn't mean to break up the game,' she said quickly. 'I only wondered if you'd like to have your dinner with me tonight. Sergei's working late and I haven't seen you much lately.'

They glanced at each other, then nodded.

'Thank you, we'd like that,' Torquil said graciously.

'It isn't always this hot, is it?' she asked, feeling sweat breaking out on the back of her neck as she went to leave.

'This is the hottest time. Our mother was always miserable in the summer. Well, more miserable than usual!'

'Poor Rose,' said Nicola with feeling.

'She didn't do the right things. She wore tight clothes and tried to go out in the middle of the day. She just didn't want to be Egyptian. She thought England was the best place to live.'

'It isn't easy to go and live in a foreign country, away from everyone you've known, as I'm discovering.'

'Then go home,' said Tarquin over his shoulder. 'We don't need you here.'

Nicola stared at his rigid back. 'I thought you liked being here.'

'He means that you could go home on your own,' explained Torquil.

'But I'm your guardian. If I went back you'd have to come too.'

'You won't go back, though, will you? There's no point now Howard's dead.'

She felt suddenly cold. 'How did you know that?'

Tarquin turned back to her and sighed in irritation. 'Sergei told us, of course. He was here at lunch time.'

'Oh, yes, of course. I forgot that.'

'How did you think we knew?' asked Torquil with interest.

242

'I'll see you at seven,' said Nicola quickly, unwilling to admit to her ridiculous fear that they had some kind of telepathic power.

Dinner was much the same as for the past few days. Grilled meat — in this case beef — with side dishes of blackbeans and assorted salads, followed by either a custard or a fruit ice. Nicola picked listlessly at it. The heat took all her energy and appetite away and she longed for a cool breeze. The boys ate everything in sight, including the flat bread that was served with every meal. 'You'll fade away if you don't eat,' said Torquil cheerfully.

'We're going out tonight. I might eat something there.'

'Is it a party?' they asked eagerly.

'Not exactly, but there will be some English people there.'

'Now you know why we used to long for Sergei's visits,' said Tarquin. 'He was a part of home for us.'

'I always understood that. You know I never tried to stop him coming.'

'That was because you wanted him for yourself.'

She flushed. 'It was not!'

They giggled. 'You've gone all red!'

She pushed back her chair. 'I don't think this was such a good idea. It's so hot in this room. Doesn't the air conditioning work in here?' They watched her hurry off and smiled at each other.

Once upstairs she took her third bath of the day and then stood indecisively in front of her wardrobe. It was already dark outside. Night came quickly here, and with the disappearance of the sun the temperature dropped dramatically. Later on she might even need a wrap over her shoulders.

Although Sergei had requested something sexy she'd already learnt that Egyptian men had an unnerving habit of staring, and she was anxious not to offend against the strict national demand for modesty in a woman's dress. She was still undecided when Sergei arrived back.

'I thought you'd be ready,' he said brusquely. 'It's nearly nine.'

'I don't know what to wear.'

'Did you go shopping?'

'No, it was too hot and ...'

243

'You're as bad as your sister. She never went anywhere because she was always too hot, too dusty or too tired.'

'I'm waiting for you to show me round properly,' she said indignantly. 'It isn't much fun getting your first look at Cairo through the eyes of a not-too-bright servant girl.'

'I'm busy at the moment. Wear this. Dark green suits you, and I like your hair loose on your bare shoulders. It's extremely alluring.'

'I didn't think I'd better look too sexy. Rose used to say that ...'

He pulled the dress off its hanger and threw it on the bed. 'Don't quote Rose for heaven's sake. She was the dowdiest woman at every gathering. We're not meeting a room full of Moslems tonight. It's a gathering of sophisticated Europeans. You can rely on me to warn you when you need to cover up.'

'If you're sure,' she said doubtfully.

'I'm absolutely sure. Ayeesha will be there, dressed to kill as usual. You don't want to let her have it all her own way!'

Nicola obediently pulled on the green satin sheath and smoothed the skirt down over her hips. It was cut tight at the waist and the off-the-shoulder neckline emphasised the creamy skin of her shoulders. She knew that Sergei was right. It made her look extremely sexy.

She saw him come up behind her in the mirror and he smiled over her shoulder. 'Fantastic!'

'You've cheered up suddenly.'

'There was a problem at work. I find it difficult to shake these things off. Let's go now. The car's waiting.'

Brian and Angela Hughes lived in a large, modern flat right next door to the new hospital. The rooms were packed with people and Sergei kept his hand possessively on Nicola's waist as they picked their way through the crowd. Several people greeted him effusively but he barely acknowledged them, intent on finding their host and hostess.

They found Angela, a petite, vivacious blonde, trapped in the corner of the dining room by an overweight Irishman who was trying to explain the intricacies of his country's politics. She greeted Sergei with obvious relief.

'Sergei, how lovely to see you again!'

244

'It's nice to see you too,' he said with unusual sincerity. 'As you know it take a few weeks to get used to the heat here, and poor Nicola's arrived at the worst time of year!'

Angela looked sympathetically at her. 'It must be awful for you. We came last September, just as it was beginning to cool off and I still felt dreadful. In fact I was so homesick that I seriously considered leaving Brian here on his own and running home to Mother.' She glanced quickly at Sergei. 'I'm glad I didn't now, of course!'

Nicola smiled. 'It is pretty dreadful, but I don't like to keep saying I'm homesick. After all, I chose to come here.'

'Wouldn't we all if we were going to live with Sergei! Why don't you go and find Brian?' she asked him with a smile. 'Then Nicola and I can have a good gossip without boring you.'

He looked questioningly at Nicola. 'I'll be fine,' she assured him, and much to her surprise he reached out and touched her cheek before disappearing into the crowd.

Angela looked at her thoughtfully. 'How did you do it?' she asked.

'Do what?'

'Melt all the Russian ice and find the man underneath. Many women have tried, I can tell you, but without any marked degree of success.'

'I didn't do anything,' she said awkwardly.

'Perhaps that was the secret! Let me get you something to drink. Is wine all right?'

'Perfect. Who are all the people here tonight?'

Angela placed a tall glass of white wine in her hand. 'Mostly hospital people. Doctors, nurses, radiologists, administrative personnel, they're all represented. I can't think of anyone who isn't connected with the hospital in some way. We tend to stick together for socialising.'

'Did you know my sister?' asked Nicola.

Angela's face clouded. 'I'm afraid not. Brian took over Labib's job. Until then we'd always lived in England, but it was too good a position for him to pass up. He had friends here already, which was how he came to be recommended.'

'I see.'

'I'm sure plenty of people here did know her. I could ask around for you.'

Nicola held out a hand. 'No, really, it's all right.'

'What did you do before you came here?' asked Angela, smiling brightly at a young man who was blowing her kisses from the other side of the room.

'I was a child psychologist.'

'Really? How fascinating! I'm afraid I was just an occupational therapist, but even that's better than being a full-time housewife, or flatwife, which is all I am here. I'd love to work again but Brian's hours are so ridiculous that if I did we'd probably never meet up at all. Besides, despite what they say about Egyptian women being emancipated compared to other moslem women, they don't seem very keen on letting me work.'

'Who are "they"?'

'Oh, I don't know, the hospital authorities I suppose. Brian keeps coming home and telling me jobs have been taken or that the language difficulty would spoil my chances.'

'I wouldn't have thought that mattered too much for an occupational therapist.'

'Let your fingers do the talking!'

'Something like that,' Nicola agreed with a smile.

'Well, actually, once you get caught up in the social life it doesn't matter quite so much. Some days I sleep until mid-day. I couldn't do that if I were working. Hi, Matthew! Is that box of chocolates for me? How kind! Nicola, this is Matthew Westrop. He's a research assistant under Sergei so you should have plenty to talk about!'

She drifted off towards the young man Nicola had seen earlier, leaving her with Matthew, a brown-haired earnest man in his thirties. At first she found him hard going, but gradually his initial awkwardness disappeared and she found herself intrigued by his descriptions of the lab work that Sergei always claimed she'd find boring.

'You mean you're actually doing scientific research on psychic powers?' she asked in considerable surprise.

'Of course. Didn't your husband tell you?'

'We're not married,' she said uncomfortably.

'Oh, I thought . . .'

'I'm still married to someone else, at least I was. He died the other week.'

Matthew looked understandably shocked. 'I'm not sure what to say. Under the circumstances I suppose sympathy isn't quite so much the order of the day.'

'I don't know. I don't even know what I feel myself. But do go on about your work. Where do your volunteers come from?'

'We don't really have to worry about that, not with Cheparukhin's contacts. He's been invaluable to us. Of course, everyone knew that the Russians took this kind of thing seriously but until I saw him at work I'd always dismissed it all as nonsense. Believe me, his abilities took me totally by surprise.'

'I'm sure they did,' she murmured non-committally, her mind racing.

'And the people he brought to us were nearly as good. Not quite, but certainly good enough to enable us to get further funding. And of course Labib's legacy took away all financial worries.'

'Of course.'

'Are you gifted in that way at all?' he asked with sudden interest.

'No, I'm really depressingly normal.'

She felt familiar hands on her shoulders and shivered as Sergei's fingers lingered on her exposed skin. 'You don't depress me,' he whispered, brushing her ear with his lips. She caught the expression of surprise in Matthew's eyes and tried to move away.

'Matthew's been telling me about your work.'

Sergei bent his head and kissed the nape of her neck. 'I hope you haven't forgotten the secrecy agreement you signed, Matthew?'

He turned rather red. 'Of course not.'

'That's good. Perhaps you'll excuse us now? I'd like to introduce Nicola to someone in the next room.' Matthew nodded, anxious to get away.

'He's a complete fool,' said Sergei dismissively, guiding her through the doorway. 'All his work has to be double checked. I doubt if we'll keep him on much longer.'

'Why didn't you tell me you were involved in psychic research?' she asked abruptly.

'I didn't think you'd be interested.'

'It's your life, of course I'm interested.'

'It's more mundane than you'd imagine. Come and meet Liam Kesby. He worked with Labib and knew your sister well.'

She was momentarily diverted. 'Did he really? I've been hoping all evening to meet someone who knew her.'

Liam was a small, rotund man with shrewd eyes behind tortoiseshell glasses. 'We were all so sorry about your poor sister,' he said kindly. 'She had such a difficult few years here and then to die like that — tragic!'

'In what way difficult?' asked Nicola.

'All those problems with having children! It must have been terrible, especially with a husband like Labib. He talked of nothing but children. The twins seemed like a gift from heaven, but sadly she was always too tired to enjoy them. My wife used to call on her occasionally, but she usually found Rose resting in bed.'

Nicola fiddled with the stem of her glass. 'I never realised Rose was unwell until shortly before she died. She came over for our father's funeral and she did look dreadful, but Labib claimed she was perfectly well.'

'As indeed she probably was. According to Labib she simply suffered badly from her nerves.'

'I find that very difficult to believe,' said Nicola sharply.

'Why do you say that?'

'Because she'd never had trouble of that kind. She used to catch everything that was going — 'flu, colds, gastric bugs, the lot — so possibly she wasn't physically very strong, but when she was battling to be allowed to marry Labib she didn't show any signs of nervous weakness. It was my mother who fell apart over that.'

'It may have been difficult living out here,' he said kindly. 'Labib claimed to be a cosmopolitan but he had a very Egyptian approach to women.'

'I just hate to think she was so unhappy and we didn't know!'

248

'At least you're here to look after her sons. It's what she would have wanted.'

'I'm not so sure. I got the distinct feeling Rose wanted her children brought up in England.'

Liam Kesby shook his head. 'Not at all. You're quite wrong. She understood the importance of the boys' heritage. You were right to bring them back.'

'I didn't do it just for their benefit,' she said wryly.

He glanced to where Sergei was standing talking with Ayeesha. 'Of course not! We all understand the situation between you and the Russian, but the real reason you're here is to help the boys through the final few years.'

Nicola frowned. 'What do you mean, final few years?'

'Until they become young men. After that their care and control passes into the hands of the male members of the family. That's how it's done here, you know. The women bring the children up, thoroughly spoil and indulge them, and then they go out into the world convinced – thanks to Mother's training – that they can have anything they want. It's why Egyptian men do so well on the international scene. They believe totally in their own importance!'

'I don't think that's what you mean at all,' she said slowly.

He raised his glass to her. 'You're more intelligent than your sister, my dear. Try not to let that become a disadvantage. Go with the flow, it will make life much easier. This is an old country rooted in pagan religion and superstition. We must all respect that.'

'I do respect it, but I can't see how that affects my position here, or the future of Rose's boys.'

He patted her on the arm. 'It's early days, my dear. Enjoy yourself. Sybaritic pleasure is one of the Russian's main interests in life. I envy you.'

A few minutes later, Angela arrived and led Nicola off with her. 'I hope Liam wasn't boring you? He can be a bit tedious after a few drinks.'

'I'm not quite sure what he was trying to tell me. He knew Rose, but when I asked about her he seemed to get side-tracked before he could tell me anything useful.'

'He's hooked on ancient Egypt, full of tales about pharaohs

249

and old religions. Brian says he's very intelligent but you wouldn't know. I had to sit next to him at a dinner last month and I nearly fell asleep. He talked utter rubbish!'

Sergei suddenly materialised at Nicola's elbow. 'Ayeesha's wondering why you haven't spoken to her this evening. Here's another glass of wine. Now, would you like to have a few words with her before we go?'

'We're not going yet, are we?'

'It's two o'clock. I have to be back in the lab by eight tomorrow.'

'I've lost count of the amount of wine I've drunk,' she confessed, putting her empty glass down on the window ledge. 'Honestly, I'd have thought I saw enough of Ayeesha in the week. We really don't have that much to talk about.'

Angela pulled a sympathetic face. 'She's always so depressingly cool and poised. I don't think I've ever seen her looking less than bandbox neat, and in this heat too.'

Sergei's fingers tightened on Nicola's arm. 'I'd better go,' she murmured ruefully. 'Perhaps we could have coffee together one morning?'

Angela nodded. 'I'll call you. I'd love to see your nephews too. Brian says they're gorgeous-looking children.'

'I suppose they are.'

'I can't wait to get you home,' muttered Sergei, running his hand down the inside of her arm.

'Control yourself!' she laughed, and turned smiling to greet Ayeesha.

'I'm having a few friends round for cards on Friday evening,' said Ayeesha smoothly. 'Sergei's such a wonderful bridge player it just wouldn't be the same if he wasn't there. I wondered if you could lend him to me for a few hours?'

Nicola had drunk too many glasses of wine to be inhibited. 'You mean I'm not invited too?'

'Do you play bridge?'

'No, but I could always watch!'

'You'd be very bored. Your sister came once but she left early.'

'You mean Labib was a good player as well? My goodness, Ayeesha, you've hit on a wonderful way to get the men to yourself, haven't you? Perhaps I should get Sergei to teach me a few tricks. Cardwise, that is.'

'There will be other women there,' responded Ayeesha coolly.

Nicola leant back against Sergei and was rewarded by a definite look of irritation in the other woman's eyes. 'Can I trust you, darling?' she asked him lightly.

'Of course not. Think how boring life would be if you could!'

Nicola giggled, aware that she must have drunk too much but thoroughly enjoying herself. 'Then you must promise to tell me *all* about it when you get back!'

'I promise,' he whispered, putting his hands on each side of her waist and sliding them round to the front of her stomach. She saw Ayeesha watching them and caught his hands in hers. 'Then you can go. And now I think we ought to get home. I can tell you're tired!'

His breath was warm on her bare skin and she was almost as intoxicated by his touch as by the wine. She looked triumphantly at Ayeesha and was shocked to see the hatred on the other woman's face.

'You're quite right,' agreed Sergei, gripping her painfully by the wrist and almost dragging her from the room, watched all the time by Ayeesha's dark far-seeing eyes.

The air outside sobered her a little and she felt a moment's embarrassment, but it quickly disappeared as Sergei pinned her against the car door and began to kiss her as she'd expected him to kiss her when she'd first arrived in the country.

'I want you now,' he said urgently, his hands tugging at the zip at the back of her dress.

Nicola's head was spinning and her legs felt as though they were going to give way. 'Wait until we get home!' she laughed.

'I don't want to wait.'

She half-pulled away from him. 'You'll have to!'

'I don't have to do anything at all,' he said fiercely, and before she knew what was happening she was on the hard ground as he pushed her skirt up round her waist and covered her body with his, moving roughly against her until she finally moved too and he was able to enter her.

251

Despite the discomfort of the ground and fear of being discovered, she found his obvious urgency exciting, and as his breathing quickened she found his rhythm and matched it so that they climaxed at the same moment and she turned her head to muffle her cries against his jacket.

The moment it was over he withdrew and pulled her roughly to her feet but when she swayed against him he bent down and kissed her again, his fingers lingering against her neck. She moved into his arms and rested her head on his chest and as she closed her eyes he looked up at the brightly lit windows of the flat and when he saw the people standing pressed against the glass looking down at them he smiled triumphantly to himself. Now they would know that Nicola had been a good choice for them all.

Matthew Westrop arrived at the laboratory at his usual time of six a.m. and was surprised to discover the front door unlocked. He assumed that Sergei Cheparukhin had needed to finish off some work from the previous day, and thinking of the Russian reminded him of the scene he'd witnessed through Brian's binoculars the evening before. His body stirred at the memory. He'd thought Rose's sister a highly desirable woman and hoped that now he was more advanced on the programme he'd be allowed to play an active part in the group's social activities. It was a stimulating prospect.

He passed through the two inner sets of security gates and put his identity card into the machine by the lab door. There was the usual thirty-second wait before a buzzer rang and the doors swung open. He strolled into the long, well-lit room and glanced about him.

'Sergei?' No one answered. Slightly surprised he opened his locker and took out a sheaf of cards and coloured pencils. Today was a testing day; the boys would soon arrive and he liked to be ready for them. It was only when he moved to the far end of the room that he realised they were here ahead of him, sitting at opposite ends of the long bench.

'You're very early,' he said in surprise.

'We thought we'd quite ...'

'... like to get it over.'

Matthew found their broken speech pattern disturbing,

although he always tried to conceal this because he had the nasty suspicion that they enjoyed making people uncomfortable.

'Fine. I'll go and get the screen.'

One of the twins — he never knew which was which — bent down beside his chair. 'Here it is. We're ready to start.'

'Excellent! Which one of you wants to do the drawing?'

One of the boys reached out for the crayons. 'I will.'

'And you're . . . ?'

'I'm Torquil.'

Matthew noted it down on his pad. 'OK, then, Torquil. Start when you're ready.'

Torquil hunched himself over his piece of card and began to draw while at the opposite end of the bench his twin stared aimlessly out of the window. Matthew frowned. 'Tarquin, you're not concentrating.'

Tarquin yawned and looked lazily across at the researcher. 'It doesn't matter. I know what he's drawing.'

'Without locking in?'

'I don't have to lock in — we're the same person!'

'You're a twin, that doesn't mean you're the same person at all. It's merely the probable reason for your ability to communicate without words. You have to work at this, you know. If you don't concentrate I shall have to tell Sergei.'

'He won't mind.'

'I think you'll find he does.'

Torquil put down his pencil. 'I've finished.'

Matthew was secretly looking forward to Tarquin making a mistake. 'What can you see, Tarquin?'

'A blue cat with black dots on,' he replied, still staring out of the lab window.

'Really? Well, Torquil, is he right?'

Torquil smiled brightly. 'Of course he's right, look!'

Matthew was disturbed. 'But that's impossible. You didn't even try to make contact with each other.'

'Perhaps we're getting better at this now.'

'I'd prefer you to do the whole routine properly. This is against all the rules.'

The twins glanced down the table at each other and then

swivelled round on their chairs until they were both facing Matthew.

'*You* broke the rules last night . . .'

'. . . at the party.'

Matthew frowned. 'What do you mean?'

They pulled their feet up onto their chairs and hugged their knees. 'You told Nicola about our work,' they said accusingly.

He felt slightly uneasy and tried to justify himself. 'I don't know what she's been saying, but all I did was mention psychic research. I didn't tell her about you two.'

'You shouldn't have said anything,' said Tarquin quietly.

'I thought she already knew. After all she and Cheparukhin are close enough. How was I to know she hadn't been told anything?'

'You know perfectly well . . .'

'. . . this is all secret.'

He was feeling distinctly uncomfortable now. 'Look, I only mentioned the psychic side of things. I didn't say anything about the sect.'

As soon as he'd said the word he had a sense of impending disaster and the boys' eyes glittered under the flourescent lighting.

'You never, ever . . .'

'. . . say that word.'

'*It's absolutely forbidden*!'

'I didn't say it! I keep telling you, I didn't give anything away.'

They stared hard at him and then, just as the tension grew unbearable, they dropped their eyes and lost interest in him.

'Shall I do another drawing?' asked Torquil politely.

'That's a good idea,' agreed Matthew, feeling the muscles at the back of his neck relax.

Tarquin sighed and sat back in his seat. 'I'll do it properly this time. Will you come and help me?'

'I didn't think you ever needed any help,' said Matthew in surprise.

'I'm tired; it's difficult to concentrate.'

He positioned himself behind the boy and was struck, as he had been before, by the contrast between the children's mental abilities and apparent physical frailty. They were both small-boned and immature for their age; sometimes he wondered if all their strength went into their minds leaving little behind for physical development.

Torquil was already busy drawing as Tarquin bent his head and closed his eyes. Then, quite out of the blue, his left hand reached out and grasped a green pencil. This was a departure from the normal routine and Matthew moved to the side of Tarquin's chair, waiting with interest to see what was going to happen. The tiny brown hand gripped the crayon so tightly that the knuckles turned white before the tip of the crayon was lowered to the paper and began moving smoothly across the surface.

At first he seemed to be drawing a pattern, making a long wavy line from one end of the paper to the other, but then his hand moved more slowly back up the card and Matthew realised that it was a drawing of a snake. The large cylindrical body had a long tail and the neck was stretched up in the familiar 'hood' of the powerful cobra.

Tiny beads of perspiration stood out on Tarquin's forehead and his eyes remained tightly closed even when the drawing was complete. Matthew looked up the bench and signalled for Torquil to hold up his card. As he'd anticipated the drawing was identical, except that on Torquil's picture the scales were more clearly defined.

'That's excellent!' He put his hand on Tarquin's shoulder and the boy's eyes flew open as the point of his crayon snapped.

He stared up at Matthew as though he'd forgotten who he was.

'Well done!' he enthused. 'That was tremendous. Perhaps you'd better have a rest for a few moments.'

Tarquin frowned and looked to his twin. 'Is it done?'

Torquil nodded and smiled. 'It's done.'

'Phew!' He slumped against the back of his chair. 'I'm hot. I need a drink.'

'I'll get you a can of Coke in a moment. First I'd like to compare the cards in detail.' He held out his hand and Torquil handed him his. 'Thanks, now if Tarquin will just ...' He looked down at Tarquin's piece of card in astonishment. The picture of the cobra had vanished. The card was totally blank.

'Your drawing's gone!' he blurted out.

Tarquin frowned. 'What drawing?'

'Your snake – it's vanished.'

'I didn't draw a snake. It was Torquil who was drawing.'

'You drew too! I saw you. You drew exactly the same thing as your brother. I stood there while you did it!'

'I think you're a bit mad,' said Tarquin rudely. 'We'll have to tell Sergei.'

'I am not mad. I saw you doing it. You might not have realised, you seemed to be in some kind of trance, but you certainly did it. I showed it to Torquil, isn't that right?'

Torquil shook his head. 'I didn't see anything. You showed me a bit of plain card, that's all. It's very hot in here. Can I have a drink too?'

Matthew was beginning to get annoyed. 'Not until you tell me what the pair of you are up to. Where's the drawing gone?'

'It's right behind you,' said Tarquin casually.

'Behind me?'

'Take a look.'

Matthew turned and there on the laboratory floor, not two feet away from him, he saw an enormous green cobra, at least nine feet long. As he stood frozen in shocked immobility it reared up, its tongue flicking out towards him as it hissed a warning.

He started to edge backwards towards the bench. He was sure that he'd read somewhere that cobras were only aggressive if attacked, but this one looked far from passive.

He put his hands out behind him, groping for the edge of the bench, but instead he felt his wrists being circled by small fingers and something else, something that felt suspiciously like cord. He attempted to pull free, but the children's grip was strong and within seconds his wrists were tightly bound behind him.

He moved his gaze away from the snake for an instant and looked straight into the eyes of the children, who were now sitting cross-legged on top of the bench. He stared dumbly at them.

256

'You betrayed us,' they said implacably. 'Now you have to die.'

'I didn't betray you! I never said a word about either of you, I swear it.'

The snake hissed again. It reared at least four feet off the ground and lunged at him open-mouthed, so that he could see the deadly fangs inside its gaping jaw.

'You betrayed Set. Death's the only possible punishment,' they intoned.

'I never mentioned your precious Set! Why should I? He doesn't mean anything to me.'

'Don't you believe in him?' asked a voice from the far end of the room.

Matthew half-turned, most of his attention still on the giant cobra that was now lying in a coil on the floor.

'Sergei! For God's sake, help me. There's some kind of a freak snake here.'

'I asked you a question.'

The cobra began to uncurl, slithering around on the smooth floor.

'Just help me!' shouted Matthew.

'Do you believe in Set?' repeated the Russian.

'Of course I don't bloody well believe in Set! I'm not some kind of religious freak, I'm a scientist.'

'You came to our group meetings.'

'I'm only human. What man wouldn't come to meetings like that!'

'Then you've betrayed us twice.'

'You can't possibly believe all that religious crap either. Just get me out of here, damn you!'

'You've condemned yourself,' said Sergei coolly. 'We'll enjoy watching you die.'

The boys jumped down from the bench and ran to join the Russian but the snake's attention never wavered. Its black eyes remained fixed on Matthew Westrop who – hindered by the rope on his wrists – was still trying to scramble onto the lab bench. In his terror he hit his hip bone sharply on the hard edge of the surface and gave an exclamation of pain, stumbling slightly because he couldn't use his hands to steady himself.

257

The snake sensed his vulnerability, raised itself up and struck like lightning. Matthew felt a burning sensation in his upper thigh and cursed the extreme heat that had persuaded him to wear shorts rather than trousers.

He knew what should happen. He should lie down with his leg raised and constricting bands round the wound to contain the poison until he could be given the antiserum, but unless someone helped him he had no chance at all. The snake drew back into itself and at first he thought that it had finished but before he had time to move its head shot forward again, but at ankle height this time and once more the fangs punctured his skin.

'Help me!' he screamed desperately. 'Sergei, for God's sake, do something.' But Sergei only stood impassively by the door watching the scene with detached interest while the children hopped up and down beside him, occasionally uttering small squeaks of excitement.

Realising that he had nothing more to lose, Matthew turned his back on the snake and stumbled up the laboratory to where Sergei and the children stood waiting. The Russian raised a hand and pushed hard against his frantic research assistant's chest.

Matthew staggered, hopelessly off-balance as the twins darted forward and grabbed at his ankles, pulling his feet up from under him so that he fell heavily to the ground. His bound hands took the full brunt of the fall and he heard his wrists crack under the impact.

By the time he'd got over the shock of the fall the wounds on his thigh and ankle were beginning to throb, while his mouth felt dry and there was a pounding pain in his head.

He still couldn't believe that they were going to let him die and he tried to plead with them, to ask for help or beg for a doctor, but his tongue felt huge and swollen in his mouth and his lips and throat were already turning numb. Saliva dribbled from between his paralysed lips and trickled down his chin and then his body jerked in a brief convulsion, making him bite his tongue.

Torquil and Tarqin straddled his body, the snake cradled lovingly in their hands as they let its tail brush against the dying man's face. Their fingers roamed over the

258

smooth scales of the huge reptile as they caressed it adoringly.

Matthew Westrop took several hours to die but the twins didn't miss a second of it. They and the snake remained vigilantly on watch, and every laboured breath and terrible, body-breaking convulsion was ecstacy to them. Only when his heart finally gave way did they reluctantly turn away.

They both kissed the snake carefully on the top of its head, then put it down on the floor and watched it slither swiftly away from them, until it reached the lab bench where they'd been sitting earlier. Once there it settled into a coil that grew smaller until it totally disappeared while on Tarquin's discarded drawing pad the outline of a green snake slowly resurfaced.

Chapter Fifteen

Nicola opened her eyes and flinched as a beam of sunlight hit her full in the face. She glanced at the bedside clock and saw that it was already ten o'clock. The greater part of most of her mornings was spent in bed these days. She and Sergei had such a hectic social life, frequently partying until dawn, that she wondered how he managed to keep up with his work as well. The pace was far too frantic for her to cope with unless she slept late. She rang the bell beside her bed and waited for Fatima to arrive and run her bath.

The woman was a devout moslem and her mistress's hangovers made her grateful that she would never be at the mercy of alcohol. She wondered what it was about English women that made them so vulnerable. Labib's wife had suffered in the same way, although her drinking had always had a more despairing edge to it.

Unaware of her servant's critical judgement, Nicola managed to smile at her. 'We were horribly late again last night so I didn't have time to look in on the boys. Are they well?'

'They are well, as always,' responded the woman quietly.

'I know. They never catch anything, do they? They must take after their father.' She got out of bed and caught her breath at a sudden twinge of pain in her right side.

A few weeks earlier she'd gone into the hospital for twenty-four hours for a laparoscopy to try and establish the cause of the pains, but nothing had shown up and the doctor had told her it happened to a lot of women in the middle of their monthly cycle. Mentally checking her dates in her head she realised that his diagnosis was probably right.

She'd been touched by Sergei's concern when she'd first mentioned the pains. Despite her assurances that this had happened to her intermittently ever since puberty he'd insisted on the examination, and only when it was all over and she was cleared did he finally relax.

Nicola had now been in Egypt for four months, yet her obsession with Cheparukhin had if anything increased. Even among friends and colleagues he remained essentially a private man but his feelings for Nicola were unmistakable. She often caught other, more sophisticated women looking at her with blatant envy on their faces and couldn't help the surge of triumph that she always felt at such moments, because wherever they went he was easily the most attractive man in the room.

Sometimes, in the beginning, she'd had worries about the depth of her feelings for him in other respects. He was so reserved that it was difficult to feel as close to him as she would have liked, and he was far more difficult to talk to than Howard had ever been, but this seemed to make their physical closeness even more stimulating. There was triumph in knowing that only she was able to see him truly relaxed, expressing his feelings without restraint.

The one area where she was still totally excluded, however, was his work. Shortly after her arrival, the research assistant Matthew Westrop had been found dead in the main laboratory of the hospital and if anything that had increased Sergei's secretiveness, but Nicola still hadn't given up trying to get him to talk about it to her.

She climbed into the rose-scented water and sighed with contentment. Her figure was better than when she left England. Although she drank a great deal more wine she often ate nothing except dates, figs and the delicious thick Egyptian yoghurt until early evening. That combined with the exercise class that she attended two afternoons a week with Angela seemed to suit her.

Climbing out of the tub she realised that Fatima had forgotten to leave her out a towel. She was no longer irritated by the careless mistakes all the servants made. It was part of the way of life in Egypt, and for Nicola servants – however incompetent – were still a luxury.

She opened the slatted wooden doors of the linen cupboard and tugged at a thick pink towel near the top, but when it fell to the ground it brought several fine cotton sheets with it.

The sheets were exquisitely made. Nicola ran her hands over them in admiration, only to feel something hard and rectangular beneath her touch. She carefully unfolded the material and drew out a leatherbound book with a lock on the front. Intrigued she tried to open it, but it wasn't possible without the key unless she forced it. She climbed on to a stool so that she could rummage about on the shelf again.

Just as she was about to give up, her fingers tightened round a tiny metal key. She was drenched with sweat after the effort, but to her delight the key fitted and she opened the book carefully. The pages were all covered with the cramped, unmistakable writing of her sister, Rose.

Nicola began leafing quickly through the book. It was a journal, but not a diary. Sometimes there were long gaps between the entry dates, and sometimes there was no date at all, just one or two paragraphs apparently scrawled down in considerable haste.

One entry, even more badly written than the rest, caught Nicola's eye and she sat down on the edge of the bathtub to read it.

I can't believe that these terrible things are really happening to me. When I arrived I remember Labib telling me that Cairo was the Gateway to the East. If only that were true. For me it's been a Gateway to Hell.

Nicola's hands began to tremble, but then a sound from the other room made her shut the book abruptly.

'Nicola, are you there?' called Sergei from the bedroom.

He often came home unexpectedly, and normally Nicola was delighted to see him, but not today. She knew instinctively that she had to hide the book quickly and had just managed to slide it beneath the pink towel before he was standing in the doorway.

He smiled, appreciating her nudity. 'How did you know I was coming home?'

Her answering smile felt stiff and unconvincing. 'Perhaps I'm psychic.'

'If you are we could use you in the lab. Sometimes I think we're just following a red herring.'

'Did you come back for anything special?'

'Only to make sure you were recovered after last night — local brandy can have quite a sting in its tail!'

'Is that what I drank? Well, I'm certainly not feeling at my best.'

'Are you standing there for the rest of the day, or were you planning to come back to the bedroom?'

She didn't want to leave the journal but was even less anxious for him to come into the bathroom. 'I'm just coming through to dress.'

He moved to one side, running a hand down her spine as she passed. Her skin quivered and she hoped he didn't know how much she always wanted him.

'Ayeesha isn't too well at the moment. She's had to cancel her bridge evening tonight.'

'Oh, what a shame!'

'It leaves us free to go out. I thought we might try the casino at the Ramses.'

'Are women allowed?'

'I could get you in.'

'Fine.' She was distracted by the thought of the book in the bathroom, anxious to find out why Rose had sounded so despairing.

'You don't seem very enthusiastic. Perhaps there's something else you'd rather do?'

He was watching her closely and she felt uncomfortable. 'I don't mind. How about the Son et Lumière?'

'Far too touristy.'

'Then we'll go to the casino.'

He knew that she wasn't giving him her full attention and it annoyed him. 'We could always stay at home; entertain ourselves.'

'I think we ought to go out.'

263

'Does that mean you're tiring of me?' he asked lightly, cupping her bare breasts in his hands and bending his head to lick at the nipples.

'I'll never tire of you!' she said thickly, ashamed at her body's instant response.

He straightened up and held her jaw tightly between his hands. 'I know,' he said triumphantly. 'You can't get enough of me, can you?'

'Don't say that!'

'Why not? It's true.'

'You make it sound horrible.'

'I make it sound the way it is,' he laughed, and despite her protests pushed her back on to the bed. Within minutes she was writhing beneath him again, but for the first time, after he'd finished, she felt a sense of shame at how easy she'd made it for him.

She kept her eyes closed to conceal her feelings and the moment he'd gone she sprang from the bed, rushed into the bathroom and picked up the precious journal which she then buried beneath her cotton blouses in a bottom drawer. She would wait until Fatima had tidied the bathroom before she began to read.

The maid was never quick, but this time she took longer than usual to straighten the bathroom, and Nicola felt like shouting at the woman to leave everything and get out. Even when Fatima did emerge she looked worried, and hesitated in front of her mistress.

'Is something the matter?' asked Nicola impatiently.

Fatima spread her hands palm upwards in the air and looked pleadingly at her. 'What is it? Have you broken something?'

Fatima shook her head but she still looked worried and Nicola wished Rose had taught the woman more English.

'*Kitab*,' said the Egyptian woman softly. '*Kitab*!'

Nicola shook her head. 'I don't understand any Arabic. *Ana ma bakallimsh 'arabi!*' Fatima dropped her eyes and

264

backed out of the room and if Nicola hadn't been in such a hurry to read the journal she would have gone after her and asked Sayyid to explain what Fatima wanted.

There was no lock on the bedroom door but she pushed the heavy bedside table against it before taking out the journal and beginning to read.

Some of the pages were totally illegible, the words had blotted together as though they'd got wet, while in other places several sheets had been completely torn out. Nicola flipped through the first few pages which were mainly concerned with Rose's failing relationship with Labib, but stopped when she found a reference to herself.

July 16th – *Home again, thank God. I loathe that hospital. Our poor little daughter was born on Sunday night and died at two o'clock Monday afternoon. I'm beginning to think I'll never see a child of mine grow up. Perhaps that's for the best. She was a beautiful little girl too, but so frail. Labib is furious. They probably heard him shouting at me all over the hospital, but is it really my fault? He says I want his babies to die, but they're my babies too. I wish I'd died as well, yet if Labib were free, would Nicola be safe? At least for a time he'll leave me alone now. A few weeks of peace before it begins again. I'm so lonely.*

Nicola frowned. The year wasn't mentioned but she remembered that Rose and Labib had lost a daughter about a year before the twins were born. Rose had written to their mother shortly after, saying how supportive Labib had been and talking brightly of having better luck in the future. There was no brightness in the diary. And what did she mean about Nicola not being safe?

The next few entries were mainly details concerning her failing health but a few pages later she seemed to have recovered.

265

September 5th – *Labib came back to our bed last night. It seems that I'm to have another chance. He was quite kind and came alone. I tried to tell him how much the others frighten me but he didn't listen. Could we have been happy if it weren't for the sect? How will I ever know? If it hadn't been for that he might never have made me his wife. I asked him if I could go home for a few weeks but he only laughed. I won't be able to go. He has my passport, and he knows what I did to baby Jamie. I don't want to be sent to prison. I'd go mad.*

Nicola thought hard. Jamie had been Rose and Labib's first child. She remembered how thrilled they all were in England when they heard, and how her mother had bought champagne to toast her first grandson. But six weeks later the little boy had died. It had been pneumonia as she recalled, so what did Rose mean? She turned the page, but the following entries had all been removed and it didn't resume for nearly a year.

August 14th – *Labib says that the babies are to be born by Caesaerian section at the end of December. I know why. They want to take them away from me, but I won't let it happen. I'd rather kill myself than let them take my babies again. I had a letter from Nicola today. She sounds so happy that it made me cry. Labib took the letter away and burnt it. He said I had to keep calm because of the babies but that isn't the real reason. He hates being reminded of my sister because he chose the wrong one. How could my parents have done this to us? It isn't fair.*

Nicola was jolted back to the present as the twins started making a noise in the courtyard. She opened the wooden shutters.

'I thought you two had lessons this afternoon?'

They stopped their chasing and looked up at her. 'We were going to Ayeesha for a music lesson but she isn't well.'

'Can't you play more quietly out there?'

'Why don't you come down?' called one of the twins. 'We could go round the bazzar or something. We're bored.'

Nicola knew she should spend more time with them. 'All

266

right,' she agreed reluctantly. 'I'll be ready in ten minutes. Sayyid can drive us there. Ask him to bring the car round.'

She went back to the bed and picked up the journal. So far all it had done was puzzle her. Why was Rose so unhappy? And how could she hold her parents responsible? Also, why did she talk as though Labib had wanted to marry Nicola when the two of them had rarely managed to hold a civilised conversation? She picked the journal up and slid it under her clothes again. At least she was beginning to get a better idea of what Rose's marriage had been like — or, more accurately, how Rose had seen it.

The twins were jumping around in the entrance hall, their eyes bright with excitement. She wondered what Rose would have to say about them in her journal.

As usual the drive itself was an adventure. Nicola had never imagined such appalling driving as took place every day on Egyptian roads. Once she'd seen a car knock a man down and drive on but when she'd told Sergei he'd warned her that was the only thing to do. 'You must always drive straight to the nearest police station,' he'd emphasised. 'If you stop and get out you'll be lucky to escape with your life. They're a volatile people here.'

On the outskirts of Cairo, she and the boys left Sayyid guarding the car and wandered slowly through the bazaar. The smells and colours were so acute that they almost overwhelmed her, the spices and perfumes mixing with the food and drink that Sergei had cautioned her against trying unless she wanted a nasty attack of turista, or *gyppie tummy* as the Egyptians called it. She didn't. A sharp attack soon after her arrival had been more than enough, and although she let the boys sample some of the kebabs, she didn't join them.

It was the Coppersmith's bazaar that she liked the best. She could easily have spent an hour looking at the displays of pots, vases, urns and dishes that hung outside the shopfronts, but the boys tugged at her arms.

'Not here,' said Torquil impatiently. 'This is boring.'

'It isn't boring for me!'

They moved on to the tunnel of the Khayamiyyah, the covered tentmaker's bazaar. A shop just at the entrance specialised in canvas bags in an unbelievable assortment of colours and Nicola stood hesitantly in front of them, wondering if she had the courage to start bargaining with the smiling merchant, but the boys kept pulling her on.

She made them stop in front of one alcove that was totally covered by brilliantly coloured wall hangings in beautiful geometric designs. 'I'd like one of these for the main living room,' she murmured.

'But it doesn't mean anything!' said the twins.

'What should it mean?'

'You want proper words on wall hangings, not just patterns. Proper hieroglyphics of tombs and things.'

'I like these,' she said stubbornly.

'Come on!' cried the twins. 'We want to buy some spices.'

'Spices? I'd have thought there were more than enough of those in the kitchen at home.'

'We have to find the spices,' insisted Tarquin and they led her through the maze of narrow streets, turning this way and that until she was totally confused. Finally they came to a halt in front of a large spice shop, in front of which were sacks each labelled with its Egyptian name and an additional English explanation of its medicinal powers. She was amused to see that some of the spices were sold for obesity and wondered how they worked.

'Since we've come here at such a rush I hope you know exactly what you want,' she said dryly.

They pointed at a sack near the back, in the dark part of the shop. 'Some of that.'

Nicola peered at the label. 'That's for nerves!'

'We want something for nerves.'

'Why?'

They smiled a strange, secretive smile and then began jabbering to the merchant who'd come forward. He seemed apprehensive and looked at Nicola anxiously once or twice, but she smiled and nodded to show that the boys could have what they wanted. After a moment he shrugged and began to measure out some of the spice.

It was a crowded stall and people were pressing all around them, so when a man in front of her suddenly turned and thrust his way past, Nicola wasn't surprised. Egyptian people

268

pushed as a matter of course. Then suddenly a woman at the front began screaming, and Nicola looked round for the boys. Everyone was falling back now, shouting and tripping over each other in their anxiety to get away. As Nicola watched, all the sacks suddenly began to move, heaving around and falling sideways, spilling their contents into the road. She couldn't think why everyone was panicking until to her horror she realised that it wasn't spices that she could see spilling to the ground but insects.

Hundreds and hundreds of insects were pouring out of the sacks. There were big, black, leather-winged beetles; large grasshoppers with long antennae; fat green flies that seemed half-dazed in the brilliant sun, and in the midst of the teeming insects, giant yellow and black frogs which leapt forward croaking loudly.

There was pandemonium in the bazaar. A hand caught Nicola full in the face and she half-fell, shouting for the boys as she tried to keep her balance. The shop merchant and his assistants had already fled.

The insects continued pouring out of the sacks and the grasshoppers took off clumsily into the air, forming small clouds, while the beetles too managed to get their heavy bodies airborne, but they blundered into people's faces causing more panic and Nicola heard too the sickening sound of frogs being squashed beneath the panic-stricken feet of those trying to escape.

An elbow caught her in the solar plexus and she doubled up, gasping for air. Some of the green flies landed on the sleeves of her loose cotton top and she tried to shake them off, then screamed herself as one of the frogs landed on her foot. She tried to kick it off, slipped and began to lose her balance.

She knew that if she did she stood a good chance of being trampled to death because people were milling around everywhere, screaming hysterically and rushing around in circles as they prayed aloud for divine assitance. Then two hands suddenly gripped her waist and she was half-lifted into the air and dragged unceremoniously towards the spice shop. She stiffened. 'No, not there!' she shouted.

'It's the safest place,' said a familiar voice, and she realised with indescribable relief that it was Sergei who had saved her.

He pushed her into the shadow of the deserted shop and bent down to shout in her ear: 'Where are the boys?'

'I don't know. They were at the front of the queue and ...'

He looked as though he wanted to strike her. 'If anything's happened to them, I'll never forgive you!'

She stared dumbly at him. 'But ...'

'Fancy bringing them here on your own! I told you never to go out unless you had someone with you.'

'But I had the boys,' she shouted.

'They're only seven years old! Get out of my way.' He pushed past her and out into the crowd again, while she stood trembling and shaken. Fortunately he was back within minutes, with a boy on either side of him.

'We're getting out of this place,' he said curtly. 'It's murder out there. People dead and dying on the ground and wailing relatives blocking the entire street. We can get out the back here. Come on, keep right behind me.'

She could hear the sound of people sobbing all the way back to the car, but there was no sign of any police or medical assistance.

'They won't be able to get through,' said Sergei in answer to her question. 'God knows when the traffic jam will clear. Now get in the car.'

She sat in the back seat with Sergei between her and the boys and she couldn't stop shivering, but Sergei ignored her. He spent the whole drive in a heated conversation with the children, conducted entirely in Arabic of which the only phrase she knew was *lissa bardu*, meaning 'not yet'.

The moment they arrived back at the villa the boys climbed out of the car. 'Now you know why we wanted spices for our nerves,' laughed Tarquin.

Nicola looked incredulously at him until he finally turned away and went into the house.

'Are you all right?' asked Sergei belatedly.

'No, I'm not! I only went out to please the boys, then I got caught up in some biblical plague of disgusting insects, was nearly killed by panicking Egyptians, and then when you arrived to rescue me all you did was shout abuse at me. It wasn't my fault, you know. I didn't start any of it. It was horrible! Absolutely horrible!' And she burst into tears.

Sergei propelled her into the house. 'There's no need to cry. I'm sorry if I shouted at you but I was worried. They're so small. They could have been crushed to death.'

'So could I!

'I knew you were all right.'

'I don't believe you love me at all,' she said furiously. 'I think you only brought me here to look after the boys.'

'Don't be ridiculous. Anyone could look after the boys. I didn't need to bring you all the way from England to act as a nursemaid.'

'You didn't sound as though you loved me.'

'Oh, for heaven's sake! Come here, let me look at you.'

She lifted her smudged and tearstained face to him. 'Do you love me?' she asked seriously.

He stroked her hair. 'Yes, I love you. When are you going to marry me? I've asked you often enough.'

'I'm not sure I want to get married again,' she admitted.

'Then perhaps I should be asking if you really love me.'

She rested her face in his shoulder. 'I'm sorry, I'm still shaken up. It was all so ghastly. Where did those horrible things come from? And how did the twins know what was going to happen?'

'There probably weren't as many insects as you think. Even a few scarab beetles can look pretty foul, and once people start panicking, mass hysteria takes over.'

'It looked an awful lot to me.'

'That's because you don't get many creepy-crawlies in England! You go up and get changed. I'll have a word with the boys. They should have known better than to go to the bazaar alone with you.'

'It wasn't just the insects,' she persisted. 'What about all those frogs? They were revolting. The sound of them being squashed underfoot was sickening. Surely you wouldn't expect to get that many frogs at once?'

Sergei began to look irritated. 'How the hell should I know? I'm not an expert on frogs. Perhaps they'd lost their bearings, or maybe someone let them loose deliberately to cause a panic.'

'Who'd do that kind of thing?'

271

'Anyone with a taste for the bizarre!' He laughed. Nicola looked blankly at him. 'Bizarre, bazaar − it's a joke.'

'You wouldn't make jokes if you'd been there. It was horrible. Do you know where the boys went?'

'I think they hid under a stall.'

'They didn't seem very frightened. It's almost as though they enjoyed it.'

'If they did, I'll soon change their minds.'

Still troubled, Nicola went upstairs to the bedroom and drew out Rose's diary, flicking through the pages until she found the entry she wanted.

December 15th − *My babies were delivered safely three days ago and they're still alive, but for how long? Labib told me they were joined at the hip and shoulder. I couldn't stop crying. He warned me that we must never tell anyone, he says Siamese twins are regarded as freaks and I know he's right. Why doesn't anything go right for us? Am I really cursed? Perhaps Nicola knows the truth. Is that why she says she'll never have children? I'd love to talk to her about it, but how could I begin? They're beautiful babies. I wish I dared to love them.*

Nicola gave an exclamation of annoyance as she realised that once again pages had been torn out. The next entry wasn't until the end of December.

December 31st − *It's over now. The boys have been separated and are doing well. Later a skin graft will cover the physical scars, but not their strangeness. They lie in their cot like two halves of an apple, turned towards each other their hands clasped in silent unity. Are they still innocent? Labib won't say, he just thanks me for his sons.*
January 4th − *They are not innocent. I shall have to kill them.*

From across the courtyard shouting drifted in through the open shutters and Nicola slammed the book shut. Suddenly the chest of drawers didn't seem a good enough hiding place. Still reeling from the shock of discovering that the boys were

272

Siamese twins, she went into the bathroom and replaced the journal in the top of the linen cupboard. It had been safe there for long enough. Tomorrow, as soon as Sergei had gone to work, she'd read the rest and hopefully discover why Rose had made such a terrible final statement, but now she must hurry and change so that she was ready to go to the casino with Sergei.

The casino at the Ramses was packed to overflowing and Sergei's eyes flicked over the small ante-room where they were waiting. His gaze finally came to rest on a familiar face and he took hold of Nicola's elbow. 'There's a table over there we could sit at. Liam won't mind.'

'Liam?'

They'd reached the table now and she vaguely remembered the man who rose politely to his feet, hand outstretched. 'How nice to see you again, my dear.'

She smiled awkwardly. 'I'm afraid I don't . . .'

'This is Liam Kesby,' said Sergei smoothly. 'You met him at Brian's party.'

'Yes, of course! I'm sorry, for a moment there my mind went blank.'

The small, rotund man smiled back at her. 'Why should you remember me when you're meeting so many interesting people?'

'Actually I do remember you because you knew Rose.'

Serei looked at the man over Nicola's head and a complicit glance passed between them. 'Indeed I did. Why don't you and I have a talk together while your young man wastes his worthless Russian roubles at the gaming tables?'

'I'd hoped to have a few bets myself,' she admitted.

'They don't let women in,' said Sergei in amusement. 'The country isn't that emancipated!'

Nicola wondered why he'd brought her if he'd known that, but he was already walking away leaving her with Liam, who gave a sympathetic smile. 'I'm sure he's a very maddening man at times, but exciting too, yes?'

'I suppose you could say that. He's certainly different!'

'And women are always attracted to something different. My late wife found him quite irresistible.'

273

For a moment the eyes behind the glasses ceased to twinkle.

'How long has she been dead?' asked Nicola.

'A little over two years. She killed herself.'

'I've always thought that killing yourself is a really mean thing to do. Everyone immediately blames themselves.'

'She was very religious. It became impossible for her to reconcile her lifestyle here with her duty to God. If anyone was to blame, I suppose it was God!' He smiled, called a waiter over and ordered them both drinks. 'Are *you* happy here?' he asked after a moment.

Nicola hesitated. He seemed a kind man, genuinely interested in talking to her, but his dismissal of his wife's problems made her wonder exactly how genuine the kindness was.

'I suppose I am,' she said slowly. 'I mean, it's an amazingly beautiful country, and the people are totally different from the English, but it's a big adjustment to make.'

'What kind of a man was your husband?' he asked casually as the waiter placed a brandy glass in front of her.

'Well, he was a typical Englishman really. I mean, he was hardworking and conscientious, but he knew how to enjoy himself too. Like most men over there he enjoyed football and ...'

'My dear girl, you could be describing anyone at all! What was he like as a person? As a husband?'

Nicola felt uncomfortable. 'He was a very nice man.'

Liam smiled to himself and sat back in his chair. 'As I suspected, dull.'

'That's not what I meant!' she protested.

'Worthy but dull; no wonder you fell for the handsome Russian.'

'I didn't just fall for Sergei's face, you know, he's a fascinating man.'

Liam nodded. 'Extremely fascinating, anyone with a gift like his — a gift that's been honed to perfection by the KGB — can't fail to be interesting!'

'I didn't know he had any connection with the KGB. Why were they interested in Sergei?'

'Don't be naive, my dear. Almost any secret society in the world would be interested in a man of such intense psychic power. He was born in Russia, naturally they used him. Fortunately for us the disintegration of the USSR left him free to offer his services elsewhere.'

'Why are you telling me all this?' she asked curiously.

'We feel it's time you understood things a little better.'

'We?'

'Those of us with an invested interest in your lover and your nephews.'

She blushed, aware that he was gazing intently at her. 'I can't imagine why it should matter to you what I know about Sergei.'

'He wants to marry you. That's an important step in his life as well as your own. We wouldn't like him to make the wrong choice.'

'You mean the hospital wouldn't like him to make the wrong choice?'

Liam looked intently at her. 'He isn't employed by the hospital, he's employed by the Research Foundation set up by your late brother-in-law. It's the Foundation that's concerned about you.'

'Look, all I know about Sergei's work is what he's told me, and you could write that on the back of a stamp.'

'But you do know that your nephews are special, don't you?'

She remembered Rose's terrible words. 'In what way?' she asked.

'They have great gifts, as does Cheparukhin. You must ask them to give you a demonstration some time.'

'What makes you think that I'm going to stay here?' she asked. 'How do you know I won't just tire of Sergei and go home?'

'Tire of Sergei?' This time the smile was unmistakably lascivious. 'I've yet to meet a woman who chose to walk away from his bed!'

Nicola half-rose from her chair. 'I don't think I want to hear any more of this.'

'Sit down!' It was a command, and against her will, she obeyed. All around her people were laughing and talking, and yet it was as if she and Liam Kesby were totally alone. He leant across the table to her.

275

'Your sister was a fool. You, on the other hand, are an intelligent woman. Don't make the same mistakes as she did or you might very well end up the same way. You can be a great asset to Sergei Cheparukhin. He needs a wife, someone to provide the stability he's never had. We'd all like you to stay, but you have to know the truth as well.'

'I might not like the truth,' she said nervously.

'Then you would have to ask yourself whether you could bear to live without Cheparukhin.'

'And if I could?'

He shrugged. 'Naturally if you could then you would have to walk away.'

'If Rose was so unhappy, why didn't *she* walk away? She could have taken the boys with her.'

'Rose wasn't unhappy, she just felt that she ought to be unhappy. Her puritanical upbringing – so hypocritical considering the reality of your parents' marriage – made it impossible for her to follow her true desires.'

Nicola jumped to her feet. 'I'm not going to sit here listening to you any longer. How dare you talk about my parents like that?'

'I dare because it's the truth,' he said mildly. 'You should be grateful. If you hadn't been born into original sin then you would never have been chosen. An ordinary woman would have held no interest for Cheparukhin.'

'Go to hell!' shouted Nicola, regardless of the people around them. 'I don't know who's been talking to you, but my parents were good people.'

Liam stood too, his lips pressed into a thin line. 'Your parents broke all the natural laws. You and your sister were the products of an incestuous union, and were both damned from the moment you drew breath. Normal, decent people would turn from you in disgust. It is only those of us who dare to be different who can accept such things.' He glanced over her shoulder. 'Here's your Russian lover now, ready to take you home and share your bed again. Go with him. You belong here, with the Foundation. That was your parents' legacy.'

She turned and began pushing her way through the crowded room, tears streaming down her face. Once outside, she leant against the wall and breathed in the cool evening air, closing her eyes as Liam's words resounded through her brain.

'The car's waiting,' said Sergei quietly.

'How long have you known?' she asked.

'Known what?'

'About my parents, of course!'

'I've known for years, ever since I joined Labib's household.'

She caught her breath. 'But Rose and I didn't know then. We didn't find out until my father died.'

'Labib knew before he ever met Rose. That's why he went to England — to find and marry her.'

'I don't understand!' she cried. 'How did he find out? And why did he want her?'

Sergei pushed her hurriedly into the car. 'I'll explain when we get home.'

'I don't want to go back there. I want to go home to England.'

'It's midnight, you can't jump on a plane in the middle of the night. Besides, as Liam said, your place is here with us.'

'No, it isn't. I should never have come here. I should have stayed in England with Howard and let you bring the boys back alone. That's what he wanted me to do.'

'Of course he did. He was your husband, what else would you expect him to say?'

'If I'm coming back with you then I want to know everything,' she said determinedly. 'You've got to be honest with me, Sergei.' He turned his head away and looked out of the window. 'Did you hear what I said?'

'Yes, I heard. I was just wondering if you knew what you were saying.'

'Of course I do,' she said firmly, but she wasn't really sure at all.

Chapter Sixteen

When they arrived at the villa, Sergei made straight for the stairs but Nicola sat down on one of the low couches in the living room. 'I want us to talk here, not upstairs, otherwise we'll only end up in bed.'

'That's as much your fault as mine.'

'I'm not blaming anyone, simply stating the truth.'

He leant against the pillar of the curved archway that divided the room. 'So, what do you want to talk about?'

'I want to know why Labib married Rose, why you want to marry me, and all about this Foundation that Liam belongs to, and which seems so concerned about us.'

'I work for the Foundation — it deals with psychic research. I'm quite gifted in that respect, they pay me a lot of money and naturally want me to stay on here. That's why they're concerned about you. They're afraid you'll drag me back to England to live.'

Nicola shook her head. 'I don't think that's the whole truth.'

He gave a small smile. 'I didn't realise you wanted the whole truth!'

'Why don't you ever talk to me about your work?'

'Because you wouldn't understand. It might scare you away. The power of the mind can be frightening to those who don't understand. I didn't want to lose you.'

'What kind of thing do you do, for God's sake?'

'Quite simple things, but to the uninitiated it can still be a shock.'

'Give me an example.'

'All right. Think of something I can't possibly know about. Picture it in your mind.'

'What kind of thing?'

'Anything,' he said impatiently. 'As long as it isn't something I could guess it doesn't matter.' Almost unbidden a picture of Rose's journal came into her mind.

'Have you got an image?' She nodded. 'Fine, then hold on to it.' She concentrated on the picture, remembering not just the book but also the badly scrawled pages of Rose's handwriting. Sergei had closed his eyes but continued to lean casually against the pillar and she felt faintly ridiculous, like a child being tricked by a conjuror at a party.

'Well?' she demanded. His lips moved soundlessly. 'What am I seeing?' she asked.

'*Kitab*!' he exclaimed, and she remembered Fatima saying the same thing.

'What's a kitab?' she demanded.

His eyes opened and he stared impassively at her. 'So you've found Rose's diary, have you?' he said softly. 'What a clever girl you are. We've been looking for it ever since she died, but without success. Where was it?'

Nicola's mouth opened in astonishment and she swallowed nervously. 'It's a trick, isn't it? Some kind of trick. You didn't really see into my mind, you couldn't have done.'

'The Foundation doesn't pay me to do tricks, Nicola.'

'But it's impossible. No one can do that.'

'Where was it?'he repeated.

'If you're so clever, find out for yourself. It's a private book, nothing to do with you.'

'It can wait. What else do you want to know about the Foundation?'

She was still stunned by his demonstration, horribly aware of the implications of such a gift and almost afraid to think at all in case he invaded her mind again.

'Can the twins do this too?'

'Yes, they're fairly profficient for their age.'

'How do you get this kind of ability?'

'It's present in all of us when we're born, but most people lose it — along with their innocence perhaps. It stayed with me. As a result people got to hear about things I'd done and

I was taken away from my family to a special school where they understood such matters. Later, when I'd been discarded by my own country, I was lucky enough to meet Labib at a medical conference. He told me that he'd been blessed with two similarly gifted sons and wanted someone to teach them how to use it. I agreed to take the boys on, but I wanted time to continue my own studies as well — hence the Foundation.'

It was too pat an explanation and Nicola searched for flaws. 'How did he know the twins were psychic?'

'They'd been passing on information without conversation, that kind of thing. Identical twins are often able to do this but he sensed that they were special.'

'I can't imagine why he should have assumed that. It isn't as though he or Rose were special.'

'Don't all parents imagine their children are gifted in some way?'

'That kind of thing isn't a gift, it just turns them into freaks.' She remembered Rose's journal, pictured the tiny babies joined at hip and shoulder, and shivered.

'So you know about that too?' he murmured in surprise.

'Don't do that!' she said angrily. 'It isn't fair.'

'I could teach you to do it too if you like.'

'I don't want to learn. What are the Foundation's aims?'

'Just the pursuit of knowledge.'

'Why did Labib want to marry Rose?' she asked abruptly.

'Here in Egypt some people are fascinated by anything different or bizarre. It's almost a religion with them. Labib was just such a person. He belonged to a kind of sect that was centred around moral and spiritual depravity. When they heard about your parents' secret he was fascinated; he wanted to marry into what he considered original sin. I imagine Rose disappointed him a little.'

'And is that why you wanted me?'

Sergei sighed impatiently. 'I don't belong to any religious sect. It doesn't matter to me who your parents were. It's you I want.'

'Liam said . . .'

'Liam doesn't get everything right. He was close to Labib, and imagines that because I was close to him too, I'm the same. Actually, Labib and I had little in common apart from

280

my work. I love you and I want to marry you. Does there have to be some sinister reason behind it?'

'All the women here want you,' she said fiercely. 'You could have had anyone at all. I don't understand why you should choose me.'

'Because you're beautiful, sexy and intelligent. It's a wonderful combination!'

She didn't believe him. 'I'd like to see some of your work. Will you show me your laboratory?'

'What, now?'

'Of course not now, but soon. Tomorrow?'

'If you like.'

'I have to see the kind of thing you do.'

'There's no problem there.'

'And what the boys do?'

He hesitated. 'The boys don't do a lot as yet.'

'I think they do. I think that's why they couldn't settle in school. They invaded the other children's minds. That's why their classmates had bad dreams and were afraid of them, isn't it?'

'It could be. They aren't meant to experiment but they're young and don't always do as they're told. I was a long way away. It was difficult to control them.'

A dreadful thought occurred to her. 'They didn't have anything to do with Melissa's death, did they?'

He looked annoyed. 'There, that's just the kind of thing I was trying to avoid when I didn't discuss my work with you. How could they possibly have been involved in that? They hardly knew the woman.'

'She babysat for them that night.'

'And what do you think happened?'

'I don't know. Perhaps they invaded her mind.'

'I doubt if she had a mind to be invaded. She seemed a pretty empty-headed woman to me.'

'She was my friend.'

'And the children are mine. I don't like to hear you criticise them.'

Nicola's head was aching. 'I'm tired. We'll talk about it tomorrow.'

Sergei put out a hand and pulled her to her feet. 'Nothing's changed, Nicola. I'm still the same person I was before.'

'You're not the same person I thought I knew.'

Once in the bedroom she expected him to make love to her but he only yawned and poured himself a whisky from the decanter on the bedside table. 'I'm exhausted. Do you want a nightcap? It's been a confusing day for you one way and another.'

She nodded, afraid that otherwise she might lie awake for hours with everything she'd learnt spinning round in her head. Sergei picked up his untouched glass. 'I'm going to have a bath. I'll take this through with me.'

She drained her whisky and began to undress. Her head was spinning from the alcohol, and she had difficulty unfastening her skirt. Her eyelids began to droop and she didn't even have time to take off her underwear before she'd fallen back on the bed, and within seconds she was deeply asleep.

She was woken by the touch of Sergei's hand on her hip and she struggled to regain consciousness, her head still heavy and her limbs slow to move. She was on her side, facing him, and as soon as he realised she was awake he kissed her softly on the corner of her mouth.

'You looked so beautiful lying there I couldn't resist you,' he whispered, his hand moving lower and his fingers creeping between her thighs. She gave a small sigh of contentment and began to move on to her back but he stopped her, easing the straps of her camisole top down over her arms and sucking gently on her exposed nipples.

'Wait, let me look at you,' he murmured, and with his other hand began pulling down her flimsy panties. She tried to help him, but her arms wouldn't go where she wanted, and somehow he seemed to have grown extra hands because although she could feel them both on her body she also felt him hook his fingers in the waist of the panties and peel them off her with quick expertise.

Still muzzy-headed, she giggled softly. 'You're all hands!'

'That's right! Do you like what my hands are doing to you?'

She squirmed against him, already damp between her thighs. 'Slow down,' he whispered. 'There's plenty of time.' Again his mouth returned to her breasts, and this time he

282

sucked harder on her nipples, drawing more of her breast into his mouth and setting off a chain of pleasure that ran the length of her body, terminating where his fingers were playing so skilfully between her legs. His teeth grazed the soft flesh and she moaned.

'Is that good?' he asked, his tongue flicking into her ear. She groaned, wanting his mouth on her aching breasts again, and he seemed to know instictively because almost at once she felt him suckling at her breasts again while the hand between her thighs pushed her legs apart. Wanting him inside her as soon as possible she obeyed his touch, spreading her thighs wide open.

He bit her flesh a little harder, so that it almost hurt, and she opened herself to receive him, only to gasp in shocked disbelief at the unmistakable touch of a velvet tongue darting inside her, and then soft lips touched her moistness, kissing her so knowingly that ecstasy flooded through her. She could feel lips and teeth at her breasts, lips between her thighs, hands on her hips and stomach, and then hands wandering everywhere. All the sensations surged together in one incredible burst as she climaxed violently, shouting his name aloud.

For a few minutes everything was still. Nicola's body collapsed back on to the bed and the hands and mouths were motionless, but almost before she felt ready for it, they began again, teasing and tantalising her body until she thought that it would burst with the sensations and she twisted frantically, trying to tear herself free so that she could see what was really happening to her, but the hands were unyielding and inexorably the pleasure took over until she was again wracked with spasms of pleasure. As her body quietened she thought for an instant that she could feel long, pointed nails trailing down her body but then Sergei moved his body and slid into her, and at last he began to take his own pleasure.

Her nerve ends felt frayed from too much stimulation but she couldn't find her voice to protest and anyway she doubted if he would have heard as he thrust in and out of her with a violence she'd never experienced before, a violence which frightened her at first, until her body became caught up in the rhythm and she tumbled over the edge of excitement into a savage orgasm that was almost too intense to be pleasurable.

She could feel the sweat dripping off her forehead and moaned, trying to move away from Sergei. He laughed softly and rolled off her, running a hand possessively down her flat stomach.

'I'm tired,' she mumbled, wondering why her lips and teeth were so difficult to control. 'I want to sleep.'

'Sleep then,' he soothed. 'There's always another day.'

She obeyed, but just as she was losing consciousness she thought that she heard another voice, far lighter than his, asking a question which she couldn't understand. Then, as Sergei whispered a reply, she finally drifted off into unconsciousness.

When she awoke, daylight was streaming into the room. Her heart was racing and she felt weak and unreal. Sergei was standing by the dressing table putting on his tie and he caught sight of her in the mirror.

'Awake at last?' He looked amused and she remembered the events of the night.

'I think I had the most extraordinary dream,' she said slowly. 'At least, I'm not sure if it was a dream or not.'

'About what?'

'About us, it was very erotic. We didn't really make love, did we?'

He turned round and faced her, dark eyes unfathomable. 'Actually we did. I tried to wake you but you kept falling asleep again.'

She shivered. 'I suppose that's why it seemed strange. You had too many hands.'

'I take it that's a compliment! Does a blue tie go with this suit?'

Nicola frowned. 'There wasn't anyone else here with us, was there?'

He looked astounded. 'In the middle of the night? Hardly!'

'I was sure there were two lots of hands.' Her voice tailed off.

'I have to go,' he said briskly. 'I'll see you in the lab at twelve.'

She frowned, still puzzled by the dream. 'At the lab?'

'You said you wanted to see me at work, remember?'

She nodded, and was immediately afraid her head was going to fall off her shoulders. 'Did I drink a lot last night?'

'I've no idea. Liam can knock them back a bit quickly.'

'I suppose that must be it. I can't remember anything properly any more.'

'You will come at twelve.'

'Yes, of course.'

She was surprised that he was so insistent, but relieved as well, because it must mean that he didn't feel he had anything to hide from her. She fully intended to read more of Rose's diary before getting dressed, but instead she drifted off to sleep again. When she woke she only had half an hour to bath and get dressed, so all she had time to do was check that it was still in its hiding place before setting off for the laboratory.

When Nicola arrived at the hospital laboratory the children were already sitting on stools writing. They glanced up briefly and then turned their attention back to the paper. She looked around the spartan room. Apart from a couple of small locked cages at the far end there was nothing to show it was used for research purposes. It was more like a school science lab, its gleaming uncluttered surfaces awaiting the arrival of pupils.

Sergei wandered in through a side door. 'There you are. I didn't see the car.'

'I took a taxi, I still feel a bit muzzy-headed.'

He smiled. 'I woudn't have thought a ride in a Cairo taxi would have done that much good.'

'What are you going to show me?' she asked.

'The boys will do one or two of their party tricks as soon as they've finished their work. I make them write up their own experiments, it's a good exercise in discipline.'

'Are you going to do anything?'

'Like what?'

'I don't know, anything at all.'

'I think you'll find the twins more interesting. They're such naturals it's a joy to watch them. Ready, boys?'

285

They slid off their stools, handed him their sheets of paper and then stood in front of Nicola.

'What do you want us to do?' asked Tarqin, chewing the skin round the edge of his thumb nail.

'What are my choices?'

'I'll get the cards, we'll do that.'

'You shouldn't chew your thumb,' she said gently, looking at the jagged skin round the nail.

Torquil hastily put his hands behind his back. 'Do you chew yours too?' she asked in amusement.

'No, but it's all sore.'

'Why's that then?'

'Because Tarquin won't stop!'

'He doesn't chew your thumb, you know, only his own!'

Torquil held out a very sore thumb for inspection. 'He did this.'

'I don't think so!'

A loose flap of skin suddenly appeared round the base of the nail and Torquil jumped. 'Ouch! That bloody well hurt.'

'Don't swear,' said Sergei automatically.

Nicola looked at the thumb's newly exposed raw patch, turned round and saw Tarquin chewing at his thumb ferociously. Torquil watched her carefully, waiting for the moment when she accepted what he'd told her as the truth. All at once, Tarquin pulled out the cards, slammed the cabinet drawer shut and trapped two fingers of his left hand in the process. He yelled with pain and before Tarquin thought to put his hands in his pockets, Nicola saw an ugly blue wheal appear across the knuckles of the same fingers on his right hand.

'Hurry up!' said Sergei, who'd missed what was going on.

'I hurt my finger,' said Tarquin irritably, sucking on the finger as he threw the cards on the table. 'There you are, Torquil. I'll do the looking.' He moved off to the far end of the laboratory and sat down with a theatrical sigh.

'I take it Tarquin isn't keen on giving me this demonstration,' said Nicola wryly.

'We're a bit tired,' confessed Torquil, 'and it's his turn to feel poorly.' He handed the pack of cards to Nicola. 'Here, you shuffle them.' She did as he asked and then cut the pack.

286

Torquil drew out a card and showed it to her. It was the six of diamonds.

'Six of diamonds!' called Tarquin from the other end of the lab.

Torquil chose another card at random. 'Five of hearts.'

And another. 'Ace of clubs.'

And another. 'Ten of diamonds.'

Torquil looked at his card in astonishment. 'No it isn't!'

Tarquin looked at Sergei with a grin. 'I know that really! Ten of spades.'

'Don't mess about,' said Sergei crossly.

Tarquin groaned and then whizzed through half the pack, calling out the cards almost before Nicola had time to identify them.

Suddenly Torquil threw the remaining cards into the air and watched them fall to the floor, scattering everywhere. 'Don't do that,' said Nicola, bending down to pick one up.

'No!' shouted Sergei, but he was too late to stop her and as her hand closed over the card it changed into a black widow spider, a female with the unmistakable red patch below its abdomen. Nicola screamed and drew back her hand, watching the creature scuttle across the tiled floor. As it approached Sergei he lifted his foot but before he could crush it, it disappeared into thin air.

'Where on earth did that come from?' she asked in astonishment. Sergei didn't reply and she looked at the two boys. They were watching her with interest, their eyes dancing. 'You could have killed me!' she shouted furiously.

'No we couldn't,' said Tarquin dismissively. 'It wasn't a real spider. It only existed in your mind.'

'You mean it couldn't have bitten me?'

'Only if you thought it could.'

'I *did* think it could.'

'Well then, it probably would have bitten you quite badly — in your head.'

She looked at Sergei whose face had gone white with temper. 'Can't you two give one simple demonstration without showing off? I spend hours teaching you self-restraint, but I might as well talk to the wall,' he snapped.

'Card tricks are boring,' said Tarquin. 'Can we do something else?'

'I think you've done quite enough already.' Nicola stood close to Sergei. She didn't like the look in the twins' eyes and was beginning to wish she'd never asked to see the laboratory.

'Have you see our monkeys?' asked Torquil, strolling across to one of the cages she'd noticed earlier. 'Look, its a mother and baby. They're sweet.'

'They're very small,' she said, looking at them with interest.

'They're marmosets. Mummy monkey likes bananas a lot. I give her two a day.'

'What about you, Torquil?' she asked.

'I give her two a day.'

'Four bananas a day — lucky Mummy monkey!'

Tarquin put a finger to his temple and moved it in small circles to indicate her brain wasn't working properly. 'She doesn't have four, she has two.'

'You give her two each, that's four.'

'How can we give her two *each* when we're only one person?'

'You're two people,' she said firmly. 'I thought you'd stopped all this nonsense a long time ago.'

Tarquin looked angry, but he sounded polite enough. 'You like the Mummy monkey do you?'

'Yes, she's sweet. Is she a good mother?'

'She is so far,' said Tarquin darkly.

Torquil looked at his twin and began to breathe more quickly, turning his head from Tarquin to the monkey repeatedly until Nicola felt quite dizzy. Tarquin kept his gaze on the cage and after a few seconds both the marmosets fidgeted uneasily, running along their wooden perch and chattering to each other.

The mother marmoset drew back her top lip exposing her tiny teeth as she started to tug on the bars with her front paws, then she began running round the floor of the cage in tiny circles, obviously distressed, while her baby huddled in a corner and whimpered.

'What's going on over there?' called Sergei.

288

'Come away,' said Nicola, tugging at Tarquin's arm, but he shook her off. Then his body went rigid as he exhaled slowly and a thin vapour trail appeared from his mouth and drifted into the marmoset's cage.

Immediately pandemonium broke out. Both the marmosets began shrieking in terror, dashing themselves against the bars and pulling at their fur. Alerted by the noise, Sergei left what he was doing and came across but he was too late. In front of Nicola's stunned gaze, the mother marmoset turned on her baby and wrenched off its head. Bright scarlet blood shot everywhere, splashing Nicola's clothes and flooding the floor of the cage.

There was a buzzing sound in Nicola's ears and she just managed to move away from the cage before being violently sick on the laboratory floor while behind her the twins clapped their hands and cheered in excitement.

'Poor Mummy marmoset!' crooned one of the twins. 'Now she's all alone.'

Nicola crouched on the floor, sobbing, while behind her Sergei threw a cloth over the cage and hustled the twins from the room, speaking sharply to them in Arabic as they went.

He returned alone and helped Nicola to her feet, then thrust a glass into her hand. 'It's brandy. Go on, drink it. It will help.'

'They're horrible,' she cried, shuddering as the spirit burnt its way down her throat. 'What kind of children are they to do a thing like that?'

'The boys didn't do it!' he exclaimed. 'We've been testing a new drug on the marmosets and one of the side effects is aggression. Last night they had an increased dose, and obviously it was too much.'

'They did it,' she repeated stubbornly. 'I saw Tarquin staring at them. It was his fault.'

'Nikki, it had nothing to do with Tarquin.'

'Don't call me that,' she said sharply. 'Only Howard ever called me Nikki.'

'Nicola, you've had a dreadful shock, but when you've calmed down you'll realise how ridiculous you're being. They're only children. How could they possibly have done something like that?'

'Very easily, I imagine. That little card demonstration you arranged was only the tip of the iceberg, wasn't it? They're way past that kind of thing now. Like turning cards into spiders and tearing heads off baby monkeys. They should be destr − .' She stopped, remembering Rose's journal.

'*They are not innocent. I shall have to kill them.*'

'Rose knew,' she whispered. 'That's why she said what she did.'

'Let me take you home,' said Sergei gently. 'We'll talk about this later when you've got over the shock.'

'It was all them, wasn't it?' she said wildly. 'Melissa's death, Howard's father, everything that went wrong after they arrived in England was their fault.' She began to laugh hysterically and Sergei pressed another glass into her hand. 'Drink this.'

'I don't want more brandy.'

'It isn't brandy, it's medicine. Now drink it.' He tilted her head back and poured the bitter liquid in, closing her mouth and rubbing her throat at the same time as though she were a dog. She swallowed automatically and almost at once the room began to swim and her eyelids felt heavy.

'What was it?' she asked thickly, but he was already pulling her to her feet and half-dragging her across the floor towards the door. The last thing she remembered was him picking her up in his arms and as her head fell back against his shoulder everything went dark.

Chapter Seventeen

Her eyes fluttered open and she turned her head towards the window. The shutters were closed, and the only light in the room came from an oil lamp set high on the opposite wall. For some time she lay quite still watching the strange patterns made by the flickering flame. Her head ached a little but otherwise she felt quite well, almost unnaturally well — as though compressed energy were flowing through her veins, making her limbs twitch restlessly.

The door from the bathroom opened and Sergei emerged, a towel tied round his waist. 'Awake at last? That's good.'

'I can't remember ... Did we go to a party or something?'

'Not exactly. How do you feel?'

'Marvellous, absolutely marvellous.'

He nodded to himself. 'That's good.'

'What time is it?'

'A little past midnight. You've been asleep nearly twelve hours.'

She was surprised, but for some reason it didn't seem to matter that much. What mattered was seeing Sergei standing at the foot of the bed half-naked. She wanted him, and the power of her need was overwhelming.

Their eyes met and he let the towel slip to the floor, then moved on to the bed, pulling back the cotton sheet so that he could look at her naked body.

He trailed a finger down between her breasts, his touch so light she could barely feel it. 'You want me, don't you?'

'Yes,' she said urgently.

'Let's just have a drink first.' He poured out two whiskies from the decanter and handed her a tumbler. 'To us, Nicola.'

'To us,' she echoed, draining her glass in one go. 'I don't usually like whisky but that's nice,' she murmured.

Sergei put his hands beneath her shoulders and pulled her into a sitting position, letting her head fall back so that he could nuzzle at the pulse at the base of her throat.

'You're beautiful,' he murmured, 'really beautiful, and so gloriously damned.'

His words didn't make any sense to her, but it didn't matter because his touch was perfect, his lips delicately teasing, and her body was tight with desire for him. Carefully he laid her back on top of the sheet, positioning her with great care. Then, murmuring something about a surprise, he left her for a moment. She wanted to sit up and see where he'd gone, but her body felt heavy and she gave up the attempt.

The bathroom door clicked quietly and she knew that he'd returned, but she still jumped when his fingers circled her ankles, moving her legs wider apart as she sighed in anticipation.

Then his fingers were on her wrists, moving her hands up above her head and spreading out her arms so that she was lying in the shape of an X. She wondered vaguely how he was able to hold her wrists and ankles at the same time, and giggled, feeling wonderfully light-headed.

Her eyes were closed already, but out of the blue she felt a scarf being placed over them and her head was lifted as the ends were tied tightly at the back of her head. For the first time she began to feel nervous. 'Sergei, don't! I want to be able to see you.'

'It's all right,' he soothed, his hands caressing the insides of her arms. 'It's only a game, a new game.'

'I don't want to play games.' She tried to sit up, but the hands on her ankles and wrists gripped her tightly and more hands pressed down on her shoulders.

'What's happening?' she cried anxiously. 'Sergei, who's there?'

'You have to belong to us all now,' he whispered. 'This

292

is your initiation. Relax, there's nothing to fear. It will be wonderful.'

Her brain felt like cotton wool as she struggled to make sense of what was happening. She could hear whispers around her, voices belonging to both men and women, and as the whispers increased in volume so her panic grew.

But then, gently and insiduously, people began to touch her. Fingers moved softly over her body, hands touched and explored her, lips kissed her in intimate places and soft tongues licked and caressed until her whole body sang and the voices no longer mattered because all her entire being was centred on the incredible sensations that were sweeping over her.

It seemed to go on for hours. She was turned this way and that. Her limbs were arranged and re-arranged to allow maximum access and she climaxed time and again as they found more and more sophisticated ways of exciting her.

There was nothing in her world but pleasure. It sparked through her body in shockwaves, flashing in colours behind the blindfold, white-hot flames of glorious sensation, and if occasionally there was a moment of pain or discomfort it didn't matter because her body knew that it would quickly be followed by mind-shattering pleasure that would blot out everything that had gone before.

Hours ticked by; the voices rose and fell, and Nicola's body was passed from one to another, from long-nailed women's hands to the harder, but no less knowledgeable hands of men, and still she wanted more. She was terrified that it would stop before she was ready, and groaned her need aloud, no longer caring about anything but her satisfaction.

All at once Sergei's voice was raised above the general noise. '*Bass! Imshi!*'

There were muted protests, but they were brief. Slowly, hands relinquished their hold on her. Mouths ceased to suckle and kiss, tongues flicked one last time and then withdrew, and the voices retreated until there was no one left in the room apart from Nicola and Sergei.

He rolled her on to her side and untied the blindfold then pushed her roughly on to her back and thrust into her. Her eyes were open now, but her vision was blurred from the earlier pressure and all she could make out was the general shape of him kneeling above her and to her own shame she heard herself urging him on as he took both of them higher and higher in a pinnacle of ecstasy until they climaxed together, Nicola's body arching and shuddering for an eternity before she was finally sated and still.

With a look of contempt Sergei drew the sheet over her and left the room while Nicola's exhausted body took refuge in a deep, dark sleep.

'*Saida*,' said Fatima gently, placing a tray of morning tea on her mistress's bedside table.

Nicola groaned and opened her eyes. 'Is it a good morning? I feel dreadful!'

Fatima grimaced in sympathy. There had been many mornings when her previous mistress had looked like this, but tea had always helped her and she pressed the cup into Nicola's hands.

Nicola sat up, then watched her maid's eyes fasten on her breasts. She glanced down at herself, saw the purple bruises and quickly reached for her robe. She'd hoped that the events of last night had been a dream. It appeared she was wrong and she could hardly look Fatima in the eye.

'Thank you,' she said hesitantly. Fatima smiled and glided from the room, only to return a few minutes later looking anxious. 'Madam Sharif,' she said apologetically.

Nicola's heart sank. She'd never felt less like seeing Ayeesha, but it would be too rude to send her away. 'Show her in, Fatima. It's all right.'

Before the maid had even left the room, Ayeesha pushed past her. She looked as immaculate as usual in a cream linen dress with coffee-coloured buttons and matching piping round the armholes and hem. Her face was perfectly made up, her beautiful almond-shaped eyes emphasised by black kohl, smudged to soften the effect.

Nicola, her hair still a tangled mess and without any make-up, felt a spurt of dislike which she tried to conceal. 'You're making an early call today, Ayeesha!'

The woman smiled a cool smile and sank gracefully on to

294

a chair. 'I wanted to thank you for last night. A wonderful evening.'

'Last night?'

'Of course, you couldn't see us, could you? I quite forgot, but it works much better like that the first time.'

Heat rushed to Nicola's face and her hand trembled. She replaced the tea cup on the tray before she spilt the contents. 'I'm not sure what you mean,' she said weakly.

Ayeesha smiled again, her eyes more cat-like than ever. 'Your initiation ceremony, of course. You can't have forgotten it. You were having such a marvellous time.'

'I think I'd like you to leave,' said Nicola stiffly.

'That wasn't the impression I got last night!' She bent forward and whispered in Nicola's ear, describing in graphic detail what her contribution had been. 'And you enjoyed it, didn't you?' she exclaimed as she drew away again. 'I thought you would. Rose was the same. Sensuality seems to run in your family. You're not at all like the reserved English women we hear about.'

'Get out!' said Nicola, her voice rising. 'I don't have to listen to this filth. Get out of the house.'

'Everyone feels like this after the first time, but it soon passes,' she assured her.

'Get away from me!' shouted Nicola, and then both women turned their heads as the door opened and Sergei strolled in. He didn't seem in the least surprised to find Ayeesha there.

'I thought I heard raised voices. Not quarrelling, ladies, I hope?'

'What did you do to me last night?' shouted Nicola. 'You must have put something in my drink.'

'It's easier that way.'

'What's easier?'

'The initiation.'

'Into what?'

The other two stared at her. 'Why, the cult, of course,' said Sergei with an amused smile.

Ayeesha's eyes glowed and a light flush covered her cheekbones. 'It's the only true religion,' she said fervently. 'We all belong to Set.'

'Set? I thought he was a god from the past. Didn't he kill his own brother?'

'Yes,' said Ayeesah, her voice rapt. 'But he was deprived of his kingdom and condemned to the underworld for ever. Now, through us, he will return and rule his country for ever more.'

'You must be mad,' said Nicola shortly. 'Everyone knows those stories are allegorical. He didn't really exist. In any case, what's this sect got to do with last night?'

'He wanted you,' said Sergei curtly. 'His children over-reached themselves in the laboratory, you'd seen too much. Now you belong you can't betray us.'

'I don't belong to anything, and I'm getting out of here as soon as I can book a flight.'

'You enjoyed last night,' said Sergei softly. 'You were just like your sister. You couldn't get enough. And you'll come back for more now. You wait. Come nightfall you'll be begging me to pleasure you again.'

Nicola swung her legs out of bed, regardless of the way Ayeesha's eyes fastened hungrily on to her. 'Excuse me, but I'm getting dressed now. I don't know what's going on here, but I'm sure the police would be interested in it all. And in your laboratory and what happens there.'

'If the police are interested in anyone, it will be you,' said Sergei.

'Me?'

He held a video tape out towards her. 'Look at this. You're the undoubted star of the show, and what a show it is! There were men, women and children there last night. I doubt if you'd get out of an Egyptian jail for a very long time.'

'Children?' she asked, totally stunned.

'The children of Set. They are always allowed to watch initiations.'

'What children are you talking about?'

'The twins naturally, and Ayeesha's daughter. You haven't met her yet but she's home right now so she came along last night as well.'

'The twins are Roses's children, Rose's and Labib's. You've no right to drag them into your perversions,' she shouted.

'Biologically they're certainly the children of Rose and

296

Labib, but Labib was one of us, a founder of the cult, and Rose — product of an incestuous union between brother and sister — was chosen as mother because Set can only use children whose souls are damned. Children of incestuous unions are damned from generation to generation. There is no salvation for them. They're the perfect tools for Set's reincarnation.'

'If that's true, what about your own child?' Nicola asked Ayeesha. 'How come she's in this too?'

'I was simply the incubator for Kyra. I bore her because of your sister's inability to bear healthy children. She isn't mine. She is a full blood sister to Alpha and Omega.'

'You mean Rose let them put a child of hers into your womb?'

'Rose had no choice,' said Ayeesha quietly. 'The egg was taken during a routine operation on her fallopian tubes and fertilised in the hospital by Labib himself.'

'You're sick,' whispered Nicola in horror. 'You're all sick. How can you possibly justify tampering with nature like this?'

'These children are justification enough,' said Sergei complacently. 'Their souls are damned anyway, and then within hours of their birth they're baptised into the sect. They have no existence outside of Set's plans.'

'Give me that tape,' said Nicola coldly.

'Take it, there are other copies.'

'Who filmed it? Who's sick enough to stand back and film that kind of thing?'

'It was Liam's turn to film. He's good. The colour's excellent.'

'Liam Kesby? You mean he belongs? God, how widespread is this cult of yours?'

'We have followers everywhere. Ever since the coming of Islam, people have been waiting to see the true religion restored to their country. Now the waiting's nearly over.'

'And what will happen when this Set does arrive?' she demanded.

'He will destroy all the unbelievers,' said Ayeesha simply. 'They will perish and his followers will inherit everything.'

Sergei glanced at his wristwatch. 'It's time for you to go, Ayeesha. You're needed at the clinic.'

She rose to her feet, poised, elegant and outwardly sophisticated. 'I'll see you again soon,' she said to Nicola. 'Next time you won't need the blindfold.'

'There won't be a next time!' retorted Nicola, wishing she could hurl herself at the other woman and mark the perfect beauty of her face.

Left alone, Nicola and Sergei stood on opposite sides of the bed and stared at each other. 'Why did you do that to me last night?' she asked at last. 'What was the point of it all?'

'The point was that they had to see for themselves that you were committed. That, like Rose, you couldn't endanger us because of your own involvement.'

'Why didn't you just kill me?'

'The last thing they want to do is kill you. Rose's death was a disaster. It took long enough to get you here in her place. You'll never be safer than here, in the cult.'

'I can't imagine why.'

'Because your soul is as black as the children's. Because your children will take the place of those that Rose never had, that Rose died trying to destroy.'

'I've never had any children,' she said stupidly.

'Your children will be born, Nicola, and we want you to look after them, to nurture them better than Rose nurtured hers. The twins are almost perfect, but not quite. Rose hated them, she even tried to kill them, and they've grown up without any love. You're a psychologist. You know what that means. They won't be able to love themselves. They won't form proper relationships, raise families as they should. You're different from Rose, you do care. Even now you care about the twins.'

'I shall never have any children,' she said though gritted teeth.

'The matter's been taken out of your hands, I'm afraid. When you had the laparoscopy they extracted some of your eggs. They've been fertilised in the laboratory and implanted in surrogate mothers.'

'I don't believe you.' She was white with shock.

'It was easy. Labib pioneered the work, and Brian carried

298

it on. The surrogates are all believers. They're pleased to do this for Set.'

Nicola shook her head. 'You've got me all wrong, Sergei. I wouldn't nurture any child that you'd produced in your laboratory, mine or not. I'd kill it.'

'We'll take a chance on that.'

'Do you really believe in all this?' she asked incredulously. 'Are you as fanatical as the rest of them?'

Sergei shook his head. 'I believe in myself, Nicola. I want power, and through these children I'll get power. I don't care what god they call up. I'd worship anyone they liked as long as I had ultimate control, and that's what I've got here. Labib produced these children, but he couldn't control them. I can, and that's my pathway to power.'

'But you do believe that they can call up Set — that he's really going to return?'

Sergei nodded. 'There's no question of not believing; I've seen his power for myself. Mostly it's channelled through the children, but sometimes he works alone. He caused your father-in-law's death.'

Nicola almost laughed. 'A tree falls on an old man in an English town and you claim it was because of an Egyptian god? Why would he be interested in someone like that?'

'The children summoned him. I'd been insulted and they wanted revenge. That's the trouble with using small children, they can over-react and misuse the power.'

'Suppose this Set doesn't want you controlling his children? What then?'

'He needs me too,' said Sergei confidently. 'My own abilities are useful to him as well.'

'Don't you think he might be a little annoyed that you're not a true disciple?'

'I respect him, that's enough.'

'For a man of science you're incredibly gullible,' she said shortly. 'If you ask me you're mixed up with a bunch of wealthy weirdos who use their so-called religion as a cover for sexual perversions.'

'You must think what you like. Just remember that Rose tried to escape Set, and Rose died.'

'Rose's death was an accident.'

'Of course it wasn't! Your sister tried to kill the twins. She fixed the brakes on the car that took them to the laboratory every day, and because Labib's car wouldn't start that morning, he decided to keep the boys at home and use theirs instead.'

'I don't believe you.'

'The twins told me about it themselves. Set knew what she'd done and they put sugar in Labib's petrol tank so that he'd have to change cars.'

'But didn't they realise he'd be killed as well?'

'They didn't need their parents any more. They had me, and their main aim was to protect themselves. Set knew Rose would always be a threat while she was alive.'

'I thought Rose was vital to Set's project?'

'We knew that you were alive. You were a satisfactory replacement.'

'You mean the twins are of more importance to Set than anyone else?'

'The twins are vital. As Siamese twins their own natural gifts combine well with the powers given to them at their baptism to make two very special people.'

'Well, I think you're all mad − or pretending to be mad − and I didn't come all the way from England in order to get caught up in some advanced game of wife-swapping. I'm leaving you, Sergei. I'm leaving you, the twins and this country. It drove my sister out of her mind, her journal's full of incoherent ramblings, and I'm not going to let that happen to me. Give your video to the police, if you dare. Broadcast the whole thing on television even. I don't care what you do, I'm leaving.'

Sergei leant against the door and clapped his hands. 'Bravo! A fine speech, and just what I'd have expected from you. You have so much more spirit than Rose. Labib would have had a wonderful time with you.' He turned to go.

'I was meant to be taking the boys out later,' she murmured, 'but I don't think I want to any more. Perhaps you'd tell them I've got a headache.'

'Don't you think it's rather unfair to punish them for something they can't help? Surely one small outing wouldn't hurt.'

300

Nicola had banked on this response, but she was careful to keep her triumph out of her mind. 'It's only one of their fossil hunts. I can't believe they'll be heartbroken if they miss it.'

'I think you should still go,' he said firmly.

Nicola shrugged, careful to keep her eyes averted from his. 'All right, since I'm leaving this country as soon as possible, there won't be many more opportunities.'

Sergei put a hand under her chin and tipped up her face so that she was forced to look into his eyes. 'We're not going to let you go, Nicola. You're far too important and desirable to leave us. It will be easier for you if you accept that now.'

She twisted away from his grasp, furious with herself because her flesh had responded to his touch. 'Go to hell!' she snapped.

'I probably will, but at least the company will be interesting!'

She waited until she heard him drive away from the villa, then went to the boys' room and collected the small canvas bags that held their fossil-hunting tools and one or two pieces of unsorted rock. During the drive to the lab she filled her mind with pictures of the three of them clambering over the dusty site where the boys liked to go. If, as she suspected, they could tune into her thoughts from a distance then they would learn nothing of importance. Surprise would be her greatest ally.

Rose's journal and the horror of the scene in the laboratory had combined to make it clear to Nicola that the boys had to die. The twins had been as responsible for the marmoset's death as if they'd torn its head off themselves, and they'd done it simply because she'd annoyed them. Given their powers it was only logical to assume they could inflict similar retribution on human beings who displeased.

Rose had known the danger and had been determined to kill them. Now it was Nicola's responsibility to carry out her dead sister's wishes. Set or no Set, the twins were too dangerous to be allowed to live and without them Sergei's desire for power would be thwarted too.

One apparently insignificant entry from Rose's journal had given her a clue as to how this could be accomplished.

November 12th – *Today the boys threw a terrible tantrum and Labib spanked them both. At least, he smacked Tarquin. Torquil cried at the same time and the imprint of Labib's hand appeared on his leg immediately. I've noticed before that if one of them cuts himself they both bleed. I hate them. Their strangeness terrifies me.*

The entry had given Nicola pause for thought, and it encouraged her to think that the task she'd set herself would be easier than she'd originally imagined, but she still had to be very quick, and if she failed she dreaded to think what would happen to her.

She drove to the laboratory where they'd been studying, parked in the private car park and announced herself over the intercom at the main gate. Sergei had obviously told the twins that their outing was still on because she was immediately cleared and the main gates swung open.

She walked briskly through the corridors, her footsteps echoing in the empty passageways. She hesitated for a moment at the main laboratory door, looking through the tiny glass window to try to spot the twins. They were at the far end, gazing out of the window at the teeming streets below them. Taking a deep breath she pushed at the door and walked straight in.

The twins turned to look at her, standing shoulder to shoulder as they watched her walk towards them.

'Are you ready to come yet?' she asked cheerfully. They nodded. 'I thought we'd have a picnic on the site, so I've packed some food up in a hamper.' Still they watched her and she knew that she was talking too much, but she had to fill the silence, had to keep her thoughts away from what was about to happen. 'I've brought your fossil kits,' she added.

'Well, that's good because ...'

'... we couldn't dig anything out without them.'

'Right! Shall we go then?'

Just for a second they seemed to hesitate, but then they nodded and began to move, walking past her hand in hand, on their way to the door. She concentrated very hard on images of their outing as she slid her hand into the wide pockets of her cotton skirt and wrapped her fingers round the handle of one of their geological hammers, with its potentially lethal point.

The boys were still moving, their steps slowing as they reached out to push at the heavy doors. Her heart racing, Nicola swung the hammer swiftly into the air, knowing that this was probably the only chance she would ever have to destroy them.

The twins didn't move, didn't even turn their heads, but as the sharp metal point began its downward arc it seemed to shimmer and the edges blurred. Her hand felt heavy, her arm pulled backwards, stopping the natural fall of the weapon until it came to a halt level with her eyes and she found herself staring straight into a ghastly miniature of Howard's face.

The handle of the hammer formed the neck and her lips moved in a frantic denial as his eyes stared sadly at her from this hideous replica of his features. He opened tiny lips to speak and she heard herself moan with terror as disgusting green flies crawled from the aperture, swarming over his cheeks and chin. They obliterated much of his face, but left his eyes clear to stare out at her from behind the moving mass of insects.

She stared at the grotesque puppet-like face and felt the bile rising in her throat. With an exclamation of terror she hurled the hammer away from her and it flew harmlessly through the air, landing against the filing cabinet with a dull thud, the head once again a metal point.

Only now did the boys turn. They looked gravely at her.

'That's a nasty weapon. It could ...'

'... hurt someone very badly indeed.'

Nicola was too shocked to answer them. All she could do was stare stupidly at the discarded tool. They shook their heads slowly in reproof and Tarquin stepped forward.

'You were going to kill us, weren't you?' It was a statement, not a question, and she could see no point in dissembling.

'Yes, I was.'

She was amazed when they both smiled broadly, their eyes a mixture of amusement and pity.

'*Set wouldn't allow that!*' they said together, then reached out and tugged at her cold hands.

'Come on,' said Tarquin cheerfully. 'It's party time!'

303

'Party time?' she echoed stupidly.

They nodded, prancing round her in their excitement.

'It's a special party, in your honour,' cried one.

She swallowed nervously. 'I'm not in a party mood.'

They tugged at her arms, their fingers like steel bands. 'Time to go!' said Torquil cheerfully. 'Everyone's waiting for you. Come on.'

They led her unresisting along the corridor, down a small flight of steps and in through a pair of double doors with darkened windows, doors she'd never seen before. At the last moment the twins looked up at her.

'You're the guest of honour,' said Tarquin reassuringly.

Torquil nodded. 'And later on there'll be ...'

'*A big surprise!*'

Chapter Eighteen

Nicola took two hesitant steps into the room and looked fearfully about her. The room was rather dark and packed with people, making it difficult to identify individual faces, but she saw Ayeesha standing calmly on a raised platform at the opposite end, directing her cool green gaze at Nicola. Sergei was with her, standing at her shoulder with one hand possessively on the nape of her neck.

As the twins led her further into the room the unnatural silence was broken by the sound of clapping, scattered at first but gaining momentum as more and more of the guests joined in. She tried to pull away, but the twins' hands were possessed of superhuman strength now and it was impossible. Instead they led her straight through the middle of the crowded room and people fell back to make a path for them.

At the edge of the platform the boys released her and Sergei held out a hand to help her up beside him. He was smiling warmly but she glared at him, hoping her terror wasn't too obvious.

Once up on the platform she had no choice but to look out over the sea of faces. There were over a hundred people in the room, and a lot of the women — particularly those nearest to the platform — were heavily pregnant. They watched her closely with something approaching adoration in their eyes. She shrank back a little, until Sergei put a hand reassuringly round her shoulders. She wanted to tear herself away, but in the midst of this staring, silent throng of strangers she needed even his unwelcome support.

'What's happening?' she muttered.

305

'You'll see.' He cleared his throat and began to address the gathering. 'As you all know, this is a very special day for us.' An excited whisper ran round the room, and in the far corner a projector was switched on. 'As I'm sure many of you know through personal experience, Nicola has been judged an even more worthy founder of the second dynasty of Set than her sister Rose. A child of darkness herself, she has provided him with children who will carry his name throughout the entire country, and even beyond.'

There was a burst of clapping, the lights went out and the projector whirred. Nicola watched sickened as she saw images of herself projected on to the far wall. She was lying naked and blindfolded on the bed while a group of men and women made love to her, using her body as they wished, and all the time she could hear herself gasping and moaning, begging them to go even further in their sophisticated perversions that so obviously pleased her writhing body.

As the film continued she heard Sergei's breathing quicken, and he reached round her body, cupping her breasts and pressing against her so that she could feel his body quickening. She bit her lip, helpless and shamed but determined to keep her mind alert. She couldn't afford to let the humiliation and embarrassment overwhelm her, not if she was to stand any chance of escaping from the assembled cult.

Eventually the film ended, and with Nicola's cries of passion still echoing round the room the lights came back on. Glittering eyes looked up at her from flushed faces, men and women alike staring at her hungrily. She looked away from the mass of people and saw the twins standing aloof from it all, watching not her but the way the others were watching Nicola, analysing the reactions of everyone in the room.

'Set is pleased,' said Sergei softly. 'The woman delights him, her children will be just as it was foretold. And because of this, it is now time.'

There was a soft collective sigh from the throats of the people. Sergei signalled for the twins to come to the platform and they obeyed, moving slowly, aware of the importance of the moment and their role in this ceremony. As they closed their eyes and lifted their faces, Nicola turned to Sergei.

'I don't understand why I'm so important to them.

306

Why are those pregnant women staring at me like that?'

'They're all carrying your children. The eggs we took from you have been fertilised with Labib's sperm that had been stored frozen here for this very purpose. When they're born they'll be like Alpha and Omega. Through them Set will achieve everything because they will truly be his children — children from hell.'

'Is that what this party's about? To celebrate a mass pregnancy?'

'No,' said Sergei softly. 'This party is to welcome Set.'

Nicola stared at him. 'You don't honestly believe in this god of destruction, do you? You can't think he's going to appear!'

'He will join us here,' he said unhesitatingly.

'As what?' she demanded. 'Some kind of mutation breathing fire and smoke, is that what he'll be like?'

'I doubt it,' said Sergei softly. 'I've always pictured depravity as having a far more guileless face, otherwise how could it possibly draw in the innocent?'

'I want to get out of here, I ...'

'Shut up!' Sergei twisted her arm up behind her back and she gave a moan of pain then froze in immobility as she saw twin columns of dark smoke coming out of the boys' mouths and moving over the heads of the assembled people before vanishing into the air.

For a few seconds the room was in utter silence; they were all waiting.

Finally Nicola looked about her. As nothing happened, people began to fidget and whisper to each other. Nothing had materialised. There was no god after all, no creature from hell to make them fall to the ground in worship, and they were stunned.

Nicola felt a laugh beginning inside her; a hysterical reaction to the terror that had gone before and she turned to Sergei. 'No luck! I hope they tear you limb from limb for encouraging their stupidity.'

'He's here,' said Sergei calmly.

'Really? I must have missed him among all the other princes of darkness!'

307

As the whispers of discontent began to grow, Ayeesha stepped forward, but her eyes were blank and she looked like a sleepwalker.

She moistened her lips nervously. 'I am no longer able to nurture a child, great one,' she said softly. 'I'm to have a hysterectomy and the baby I carry now will have to be aborted. If you're truly here, show me other ways in which I can help. Comfort me, Set. Help me now.'

Immediately a fearful rushing sound filled the air, the lights flickered and dimmed and suddenly people fell back from near the platform as Ayeesha turned her head sharply, trying to locate the source of the noise, but just as her frightened eyes met Nicola's there was a muffled explosion and Ayeesha was enveloped in a ball of fire that wrapped itself around her, turning her into a human torch. The beautiful features were illuminated for a moment in startling clarity before they began to disintegrate, melting into each other like wax. The elegant hands contracted into black claws, eyebrows and eyelashes burnt away and the eyeballs swelled in the blackened, blistering flesh.

People screamed hysterically as they watched the fire consume her, they turned in panic towards the doors, terrified that the flames would spread and trap them all, but even Nicola – standing only two or three feet away – was untouched by the heat, and as Ayeesha finally died both she and the fireball vanished. There was nothing to show it had ever happened.

'The doors have jammed,' called a man's voice from the back. Nicola peered out over the shocked faces and recognised Liam Kesby. There was no disguising the terror on his usually amiable features as he hammered on the doors.

'There's no need to be alarmed,' called Sergei, still keeping a tight hold of Nicola. 'You are all needed. Ayeehsa's time was over.'

'I'm not worshipping someone who kills his own followers!' shouted a man, and his view was endorsed by others whose sense of self-preservation was greater than their religious beliefs.

The twins came and stood by Sergei, their expressions contemptuous. 'They forgot he's the god of death!' they sneered.

'Why should he spare them? They're nothing special at all.'

Nicola watched in disbelief as people continued to rush for the exits in a blind panic, and when the doors still refused to open they turned on each other and began fighting, men even striking out at women in their fury.

The noise was terrible; shouts and screams of anger mingling with cries of pain as blows landed and bodies fell. The smell of fear was everywhere. Sharp and rancid, it caught in Nicola's throat and she gave a whimper of fear herself as she watched the chaos in front of her.

'You're quite safe,' the twins assured her. 'He needs you.'

'What's happening to them?' she whispered.

'It's like the monkeys,' said Sergei, clearly intrigued by what he was witnessing. 'He's just testing his strength, seeing how easy it is to fill them with aggression and fear.'

'But where is he? Why can't we see him?'

'Because he's in us!' exclaimed Sergei impatiently. 'I'm surprised you haven't realised that for yourself. He's here inside you, and me and the children.'

'That's a lie. He isn't in me. I'd know, I'd feel it. I'm the same as before.'

Sergei gripped her by the wrists and pulled her close to him. 'He's in you more than any of us, you stupid bitch! Without you he couldn't have been freed. You gave everything up for him. Your home, your husband, even your country, and then you welcomed him with your body. Rose never gave herself totally, she always held something back, but you didn't. And then you tried to murder a child. The final, necessary sin. Your soul is as dark as night. You are your parents' legacy, born into sin and unredeemed, you are the perfect mother for his children, the perfect host for his return to earth.'

'It isn't true!' She twisted against him, trying to get free. 'The children had to die. They're evil, not me.' Out of the corner of her eye she could see that a few people, mostly the pregnant women, were climbing out of a small window and down the fire escape but all around them the rest of the people were still fighting and screaming. She saw a young woman gouge out the eyes of a grey-haired old lady, laughing with delight as she trampled on her corpse.

The floor was running with blood as the carnage continued.

309

People were no longer trying to escape. They'd forgotten everything but their desire to fight and kill, and the laughter of the stronger victorious ones was as terrible as the screams of the dying.

The twins watched in silence. This was everything they had ever wanted to see. This was how their world would be, the way that Set would rule. Soon this scene would be repeated in houses and streets. The fights would turn into feuds, the feuds into private vendettas and then — most welcome of all — it would be civil war.

Brother against brother. That was the ultimate aim, the final revenge for the cult of Osiris, all the years when Set's brother had been worshipped by the ignorant, ungrateful people of Egypt.

As the rioting increased, Sergei hustled Nicola and the twins towards the window. The children concentrated their powers on clearing a path for them, filling the minds of those in their way with blood lust for whoever was nearest to them. Nicola saw a young girl in her early teens look with panic at the huge raised fist of the man next to her, and instinctively wished that the man could drop dead before the blow was struck. He was felled instantly, and the girl glanced at Nicola with gratitude, falling to her knees and closing her eyes in worship.

Sergei's lips curled. 'Now do you believe me?'

Nicola did. It was the worst moment in the entire nightmare.

As they approached the window she felt herself begin to change. Felt her compassion and sorrow shifting and altering until contempt and anger began to replace them. She knew then that she was doomed. That either because of a flaw in herself or because of her parents' unspeakable sin, Set was within her and would ultimately consume her. She would no longer be herself but a creature from this nightmare, spreading death and destruction as she made her ghastly, lust-crazed progress across the land.

'Quick, get out on the fire escape,' said Sergei urgently. 'We have to get away. No one must know we were here or our lack of injuries would arouse suspicion.'

She stepped over the sill and looked down at the women below. They stared up at her with smiling faces, pregnant

310

women, heavy with her children, and all looking to her with awe and wonder.

And she liked it.

She liked it, and she knew that she'd grow to like it more, just as she'd grown increasingly addicted to Sergei's lovemaking and the perversions of the cult. For this brief moment there was enough of the old Nicola remaining for her to see herself and her future and she knew immediately what she must do. Without giving Sergei a split second in which to react, she hurled herself head first off the fire escape. As Sergei screamed in anguish she plummeted to the path below, breaking her neck and splitting her skull wide open on impact.

Sergei and the twins stared down in total disbelief. Above them the room exploded into flames as Set's uncontrollable fury erupted in an orgy of destruction, blasting the people with a heat so intense that everyone in the room was reduced to ashes in seconds.

Sergei took one look at the primitive hatred in the boys' eyes and began to run. He dashed down the fire escape, falling the last few steps and twisting his knee savagely, but he only faltered for a second before forcing himself on. He could control his own pain, but not the fury of the demon he'd helped unleash.

The boys didn't hurry. They moved silently and implacably down, and only when he tried to turn the corner of the building to move out of their sight did they bring him down, concentrating their minds on whipping his feet from under him.

He lay helplessly on his back, his breath coming in great gasps as they stood over him.

'You let me down. You . . .'

'. . . failed me.'

'*Now you must die.*'

He didn't bother to defend himself, although when he realised what his death was to involve he began to scream protests, but they floated away on the wind as Set took his revenge in the only way he knew. The way for which all his followers honoured and remembered him. He tore the Russian's body limb from limb, scattering the pieces into the air and letting them drop in a ghastly pile of blood, bones and tissue, and it seemed as though his screams would never die away.

The twins contemplated the bloody heap for a moment, glanced back at the now silent blazing building and then walked over to where the pregnant women were huddled together in dumbstruck terror.

'Set has a place waiting for you,' said Torquil reassuringly. 'Don't worry. You'll all be quite safe.'

A police siren sounded close at hand and the group began to move away, stumbling towards an unknown future and leaving behind all the terrible sights and sounds of the past few hours.

The twins clasped hands and strode out at the head of the group. All was not lost. Their time would still come, and they were content.

Epilogue

BBC Television News Broadcast December 24th

This is Jonathan Russell reporting once again from war torn Egypt. In this country ravaged by civil strife that has brother fighting brother, something little short of a miracle has occurred here in Abydos, approximately ninety miles north of Luxor. Members of the peace force from the United Nations stumbled today on a group of tiny orphans, apparently abandoned in the ruins of the ancient temple of Seti I. The oldest of them is no more than ten years old, the youngest only eighteen months, and yet somehow they've survived here undiscovered and unharmed.

With more and more people fleeing the country every day and the economy in total ruins there's little hope of anyone here choosing to take on the responsibility of extra mouths, but at this very special moment in the Christian calendar — and remembering the international response to the plight of the Rumanian orphans a few years ago — it is to be hoped that there are loving couples elsewhere in the world who would welcome the chance to take one of these innocent victims into their home.

With a final look at their trusting, blameless faces we here in this once beautiful and now barren land of discord, wish all of you at home a very happy Christmas, and pray that these children will one day know the safety and security of a loving family, and find the peace all children crave.